PRAISE FOR ...

"The logical heir to Isaac Asim...

"'Why read Jack McDevitt?' The question should be: 'Who among us is such a slow pony that s/he *isn't* reading McDevitt?'"
—Harlan Ellison

"You should definitely read Jack McDevitt."　　—Gregory Benford

THE DEVIL'S EYE

"McDevitt fills [*The Devil's Eye*] with historical details and thrilling stunts as well as sharp political allegory ... [He] balances the two sides of his story well, never losing sight of either the fast-paced action or the message behind it."　　—*Publishers Weekly*

"McDevitt is working familiar SF territory—playing with effects of scale—but without the outsized heroic figures and shiny city-of-the-future movie sets of the pulps. There is heroic action, but it doesn't feel that way from inside the hero. The big show, Mc-Devitt seems to be saying, is Out There, and we should remember that we're just playing the lounge."　　—*Locus*

"McDevitt is one of those rare Asimovian inheritors, and he does a fine job emulating the virtues of the Good Doctor A. Just by working in this hybrid genre of SF/mystery, which Asimov practically patented, he's staked his claim to the same territory. And the latest book displays a truly Asimovian set of attractions ... The blending of supernatural motifs with the far-future technological culture is very clever ... Although not baroque at all, this book seems to belong on the shelf with recent Matthew Hughes SF/mysteries and, ultimately, with the books of that other master of SF/mysteries, Jack Vance."　　—*Sci Fi Weekly*

"The Nebula Award–winning McDevitt's gift as a raconteur and a creator of genuinely likable characters comes to the fore as Benedict and Kolpath follow the trail that leads to more than they bargained for."　　—*Library Journal*

continued ...

THE
DEVIL'S
EYE

Jack McDevitt

ACE BOOKS, NEW YORK

THE BERKLEY PUBLISHING GROUP
Published by the Penguin Group
Penguin Group (USA) Inc.
375 Hudson Street, New York, New York 10014, USA
Penguin Group (Canada), 90 Eglinton Avenue East, Suite 700, Toronto, Ontario M4P 2Y3, Canada
(a division of Pearson Penguin Canada Inc.)
Penguin Books Ltd., 80 Strand, London WC2R 0RL, England
Penguin Group Ireland, 25 St. Stephen's Green, Dublin 2, Ireland (a division of Penguin Books Ltd.)
Penguin Group (Australia), 250 Camberwell Road, Camberwell, Victoria 3124, Australia
(a division of Pearson Australia Group Pty. Ltd.)
Penguin Books India Pvt. Ltd., 11 Community Centre, Panchsheel Park, New Delhi—110 017, India
Penguin Group (NZ), 67 Apollo Drive, Rosedale, North Shore 0632, New Zealand
(a division of Pearson New Zealand Ltd.)
Penguin Books (South Africa) (Pty.) Ltd., 24 Sturdee Avenue, Rosebank, Johannesburg 2196,
South Africa

Penguin Books Ltd., Registered Offices: 80 Strand, London WC2R 0RL, England

THE DEVIL'S EYE

An Ace Book / published by arrangement with Cryptic, Inc.

PRINTING HISTORY
Ace hardcover edition / November 2008
Ace mass-market edition / November 2009

Copyright © 2008 by Cryptic, Inc.
Cover art by John Harris.
Cover design by Rita Frangie.
Interior text design by Kristin del Rosario.

ISBN: 978-0-441-01785-0

ACE
Ace Books are published by The Berkley Publishing Group,
a division of Penguin Group (USA) Inc.,
375 Hudson Street, New York, New York 10014.
ACE and the "A" design are trademarks of Penguin Group (USA) Inc.

PRINTED IN THE UNITED STATES OF AMERICA

10 9 8 7 6 5 4 3 2 1

For Mike Cabry,
the last rebel

ACKNOWLEDGMENTS

I'm indebted to David DeGraff of Alfred University, for the concept, and to Walter Cuirle, for technical guidance. To Ginjer Buchanan, for editorial assistance. To Ralph Vicinanza, for his continuing support. And, as always, to Maureen McDevitt, for major contributions.

PROLOGUE

SALUD AFAR

Edward Demery was alone the night it happened. He was sitting in his living room, half-dozing, while the HV ran images from the Sabel asteroid, which was way the hell out in the middle of nowhere.

A dozen people in pressure suits stood around a monument on an airless plain while one of them went on about God and how future generations would always come to this spot, and be dazzled by this monument, and remember what their obligations were to the Almighty. The speaker was a woman, but he couldn't tell which of the twelve was doing the oration.

"*—And maybe, when they come,*" she said, "*they will remember us, too.*"

Applause doesn't work well in pressure suits. So they all simply raised their fists over their helmets.

Demery got up and went to the window. Lightning blossomed in the distant sky. Salud Afar was on the edge of the galaxy. Was, in fact, twenty thousand light-years out from the rim. On a clear night, you could see the glow that marked the frontier of the Milky Way. At the moment, though, the glow was still below the horizon.

"*—I want to thank Vasho Colunis, for his determination to see this project through—*"

He gazed out at the only star in the sky. Callistra. Its soft azure light softened the night, inspired poets, illuminated weddings. And it sometimes appealed to those with a religious sensibility. Like the men and women mounting their monument on that distant asteroid.

It was thirty-six light-years out, part of a sea of rocks, drifting through the night, belonging to no particular system. In time, they'd drift back into the galaxy. Tonight, Callistra was performing as a religious symbol. The asteroid on which the Family of God was mounting its monument had been chosen because it lay directly between the world and the great blue star.

The monument consisted of a crystal polyhedron atop a sphere, the whole mounted on a block. The polyhedron represented the many faces of mankind; the spherical base, the unflinching support of God.

"—And Jara Capis, who conceived the motif—"

Actually there was a second light in the sky. That was the planet Naramitsu, low on the horizon. But it was easy to overlook.

"—Last but not least, Kira Macara, who designed the monument." One of the figures took a bow. The others raised fists in approval.

Demery lived in a house overlooking the sea. It was a beautiful spectacle this time of year, with summer lightning in the west and the single star overhead. The settlers who'd first come to Salud Afar, thousands of years earlier, had undoubtedly possessed a love for the outpost it had been in those days. This was where you came if you liked to be alone. It was a place that was not only remote, but which nightly reminded them how far they'd come from the crowded spaces of the Confederacy.

"—Ask the Reverend Garik to give the blessing."

He'd been born under the opulent skies of Rimway. There, inside the galaxy, the stars somehow detracted from each other. When they were, as someone once said, like the campfires of an ancient army, you didn't notice any in particular. They were simply *there*.

"In this sublime moment, let us bow our heads before the Universal God—" The voice was still feminine, but it was less

compelling. It had the ritual singsong lilt that preachers seemed always to acquire. *"—Let us acknowledge—"*

He was still looking out at the sea and the sky when the voice stopped. And he became aware that the light from the HV had changed. Had gone out. He turned and saw only a flickering gray luminescence in the center of the room. Then a man appeared, in the business dress of an anchor. *"Ladies and gentlemen,"* he said, *"we seem to have lost the signal at its source. We are trying to reacquire it now and will finish the broadcast as soon as we are able. Meantime, we will be joining a concert from the Bayliss Room in Old Marinopolis."*

Soft music filled the room. A voice told him he was listening to the "gilded strains" of the Frontrunners. He was looking across a dance floor at five musicians on a stage. They were playing something he remembered from his youth. "My Time with You." Yes, that was it.

He sat down again. The Frontrunners played through, finished, and started something else. The volume went down. Vanished. A voice informed him they were still trying to reestablish contact with the Sabel Monument ceremony. And reassured him it would be back shortly.

Eventually, he shut it down and switched to a book.

one

Civilization is about constructing and maintaining a coherent time line to the past. If we are to know who we are, and where we are going, we must remember where we have been and who took us there.

—*Etude in Black*

THIRTY-THREE YEARS LATER
THE ATLANTIC OCEAN, OFF THE AFRICAN COAST

Atlantis, despite all the hoopla, was no big deal. I mean, how could it be after twelve thousand years at the bottom of the sea? Alex and I looked out the cabin windows at the ruins, which weren't much more than mounds in the quiet, clear water. You could still pick out a wall here and there. Not much else. There'd been periodic talk of restoration over the centuries, but the prevailing opinion had always been that if you restored it, it would no longer be Atlantis.

Navigation lamps came on as we moved across the seascape. Fish and eels, drawn by the lights, peered in at us. Overhead, a tourist boat was descending.

None of us had ever been there. Alex gazed thoughtfully out at the remnants of the fabled civilization, and I knew exactly what he was thinking: how the place had looked in the sunlight, when children played in the courtyards, and trees shaded the walkways. I knew also that he'd have liked to take a few pieces of it home.

The captain's voice came over the intercom, pointing out this or that pile of rubble. *"Now passing the Temple of Akiva, ladies and gentlemen."*

"The structure just ahead is believed to have been the main library."

"On your left, just beyond that large mound—"

He wasn't happy playing escort to two Mute passengers, but I had to concede he had taken it well. His discomfort did not show in his voice.

And okay, I'll confess I wasn't exactly relaxed either. One of the Mutes was Selotta, who was the director at the Museum of Alien Life-forms on Borkarat, one of the principal Mute worlds. She was accompanied by her mate, Kassel (emphasis on the second syllable). She'd bailed me out during my trip into the Assemblage the year before. We'd promised each other we'd get together, Selotta explained she'd always wanted to visit Earth, so there we were. During the two weeks we'd been together, I'd been happy to discover I was less horrified by their appearance than had been the case when I made my first foray into Ashiyyurean society. It's going overboard to say they resemble giant mantises, but they are extremely tall, and their flesh has a husklike quality. It's leathery. Old leather. Leather that's been oiled a bit too much. Their faces are vaguely humanoid, with arched diamond eyes. They have to struggle to produce anything resembling a human smile. And, of course, a forced smile never works anyhow, especially when it's disrupted by canines.

If you've ever seen one up close, you already know that the effect they have on people, scaring the daylights out of them, isn't produced by their appearance so much as by the fact that human minds lie open to them. No secret is safe when a Mute's in the room.

I hadn't met Kassel on my journey to Borkarat. In fact, my time with Selotta had been only a few minutes. But if such a thing was possible with a Mute, it seemed we had bonded. And Alex, always anxious for a new experience, especially one that would take him to the mother world, came along.

We'd started from the Washington, D.C., site, and embarked on a round-the-world tour. We'd gone first to the world capital at Corysel. Then across the Pacific to Micronesia. It was Selotta, with her interest in archeology, who suggested Atlantis.

I'd been reluctant, at first. For one thing, they'd had to install special seats on the diver. But, Alex said, intending it as a joke, why visit Earth if you're not going to stop off at Atlantis?

Contrary to the early myths, Atlantis had possessed no advanced technology. The inhabitants had managed to install running water and central heating. But then, so had the Hellenes.

Virtually nothing was known of their history. The city had thrived for about six hundred years. It had been built on an island, of course, and not on a continent. Plato had been correct in reporting that it had engaged its continental neighbors in periodic wars. Surviving sculpture confirmed that. But who had served as their kings? What had mattered to them? We had no idea.

The city had been discovered late in the third millennium. Unfortunately, no serious effort was made to secure its archeological treasures. Consequently, during the following centuries, it had been stripped. Exploiters descended and took everything they could find. These would have been Alex's progenitors, of course, although he would never have admitted it, and I saw no reason to stir things up since I profited from the same sort of activity. In any case, by the time a security system was installed, more than a thousand years after the discovery, it was far too late.

"As far as I know," said Kassel, "there is nothing comparable to this in the Assemblage." He spoke through a voice box that also acted as a translator. It was designed to look like a silver medallion, attached to a chain around his neck. "Nothing comparable whatever." His black diamond eyes reflected his reaction. The end of a world. How must it have felt when the ocean came crashing in? Did they have any warning? Had any managed to escape? Imagine the despair of mothers burdened with young children.

"Terrible," said Selotta. "Young mothers, especially. It must have been—" She caught herself, and her eyes flicked shut in embarrassment: She'd forgotten her strategy of not reminding her hosts that everybody's mind, as she'd once commented, lay fully exposed on the table. "—Must have been painful."

"It was a long time ago," said Alex.

She pressed long, gray fingers against the viewport, as if to hold time at bay. "I have no real experience with places like this. Do they always feel this way?"

Kassel was a politician, roughly equivalent to a mayor of a medium-sized city. He had also once been a captain in the Ashiyyurean fleet. "I think it's because of the ocean," he said. "It encases everything, somehow. Preserves it. There's no sense of passing time. Everything freezes."

The other passengers had been reluctant about sharing cabin space with the aliens. In the boarding area, everyone had given us a wide berth. The place had filled with whispers, audible even above the symphonic background music. There was no hostility. But the crowd was afraid. Everybody kept their distance. *"Stay with me, Louie."*

"Keep back."

"No, they won't hurt you. But stay here."

When I tried to apologize for the attitude of the other passengers, Kassel said no harm was being done. "Selotta tells me our people were not exactly welcoming when you visited us."

"They were fine. I think I just stood out a little."

"Eventually," he said, "this will all go away, and we'll stand together as friends and allies."

That got Alex's attention. "It's hard to see that happening," he said. "At least in our lifetime."

Kassel was less pessimistic. "What we need is a common cause. Something that would inspire us to unite."

"That sounds like a common *enemy*," I said.

"That would do it, of course." He closed his eyes. "But a common enemy would solve one problem only to present us with a greater. No, we need something of a different sort."

"What did you have in mind?"

"I don't know. A joint challenge. Or a mutual project, perhaps. Like joining our resources to send a mission to Andromeda."

Selotta and Kassel were dressed in terrestrial-style clothing. They wore slacks and loose-fitting shirts. Kassel had even tried wearing an outdoorsman's hat. But it was several sizes too small. He'd taken it off and given it to me when I was unable to conceal my reaction: It looked ridiculous.

They tried smiling in an effort to calm everyone. But there was too much of the canines. Their smiles never failed to scare everybody in sight.

It was the same on the diver. The captain was supposed to come back, say hello, ask if there was anything he could do for his passengers. But the door to the bridge had stayed shut.

"And over here—" His voice came out of the address system. *"There, where the light is, was the seat of government. Nobody knows what they called it, or even what kind of government they had. But that's where they made the decisions."*

"There's a little bit of 'Ozymandias' in this place," said Selotta. "Except on a larger scale."

"You know 'Ozymandias'?" I asked.

"Of course." She showed her fangs briefly. "The theme is common at home. One of the most famous of our classical dramas, *Koros*, plays against the same idea. Vanished glory, look on my works, everything passes. In *Koros*, the overwhelming symbol is sand. Just like Shelley."

There were maybe twelve other passengers in the charter. I was in my chair while we drifted through Atlantis, down the main boulevard, still trying not to think about all that stuff that drifts around in your head that you have no control over. So I glanced at Kassel and wondered how a person would manage an affair if his mate could read his mind. It reminded me how little I really knew about the Mutes.

Had Selotta ever cheated?

I cringed as the thought intruded itself.

Kassel snorted. It was half laughter, half sneeze. "It's okay," he said. He squeezed my shoulder, and his eyes locked with Selotta's.

Selotta showed her fangs again. "You try too hard, Chase," she said. "And, if you would know the truth, we share everything."

The truth was I didn't know quite what she meant, but she picked that up, too. "Use your imagination," she added.

It wasn't a place I wanted to go.

Alex looked in my direction and delivered one of those innocent smiles to let me know he understood precisely what was going on. I swear, sometimes his ability to do that left me wondering whether he had a few Mutes in the family.

Eventually the captain showed up. He was wearing a dumb smile and went on about how he hoped we were all comfortable and enjoying the cruise. He made it a point to look everywhere except at his Ashiyyurean passengers. Don't want to stare, you know. His eyes touched mine, and he let me see how uncomfortable he was, how he wished we'd keep our friends home next time. I knew he was wondering how far the telepathic reach of the aliens extended. Was he safe on the bridge? I had no idea. But he probably wasn't.

"He is safe enough," said Selotta, "unless we extend ourselves."

"He doesn't mean anything by it," I said.

"I know. I have the same sort of reaction to him."

When he was safely away, Alex chuckled.

Kassel did that deep-throated rumble that passed for a laugh. "He's shallow water, Alex," he said. "*You*, on the other hand, are hard to read."

"Low IQ?" I asked.

"He doesn't try to empty his mind," said Selotta. "It's a bad idea to sit and try *not* to think about things."

"So Alex fills it up," added Kassel. "He concentrates on the Konish Dynasty and the kind of silverware they had, and what their plates looked like and why the latter-day glassware is worth so much more than the early stuff."

"Ah, you've found me out." There was a touch of pride in Alex's voice.

"It's rather like crowd noise," said Kassel, innocently.

Alex pretended to take offense. "Konish Dynasty antiques are *not* crowd noise."

"Point of view, my friend. Point of view."

We started for the surface. The captain's voice thanked us for using Atlantis Tours, expressed his hope that we'd enjoyed ourselves, and invited us to come back soon.

The other passengers gave us plenty of room as we filed out. The pier was big, but the deck was moving sufficiently that some people grabbed for handrails. Most looked for the taxi area; others made for one of the restaurants. We headed toward a restaurant. We were halfway there when Jay Carmody appeared. Jay was one of Alex's colleagues and a longtime friend.

It had been a marvelous two weeks, and Carmody was bringing the wrap-up, a parting gift for the Ashiyyureans. It was in a white box. And it was supposed to be a surprise. To ensure that, neither of us knew what Carmody had gotten. "Just make sure it's something to blow the roof off," Alex had said.

But as soon as Carmody started toward us, I heard somebody gasp. Selotta, I think. And she knew. They both knew.

"Jay," said Alex, "do you want to show us what's in the box?"

"Absolutely." He was glowing. We sat down on adjoining benches, and he removed the lid. The Mutes had both gone absolutely still.

It was a *brick*. Sealed in a plastene container.

At first I thought it was a joke, but I'd seen the reaction of our guests.

"Atlantis?" asked Alex.

Carmody smiled. "From the Temple of Akiva. Rear courtyard. Removed in the thirty-second century by Roger Tomas, donated originally to the London Museum, and later taken to the University of Pennsylvania in Philadelphia. Eventually it wound up in Berlin. It's been around." He reached into his jacket and removed a folded piece of paper. "Certificate of authenticity, signed on behalf of the current owner." He was facing Alex, but he was talking to Selotta and Kassel. "I've gone over the bona fides thoroughly. A complete copy of the record is in the box." He handed it to Alex. "I hope it's satisfactory."

Nobody could ever say Alex was in the antiquities business purely for the money. Well, people *had* said it. In fact, they said it all the time. But it wasn't true. I'll concede he has an affection for the bottom line, but if you show him something like a vase that had once stood in Mesmeranda's villa, or maybe the chair that Remus Alverol had tossed across the room when news arrived of the massacre at Port Walker, his eyes positively lit up. That was what I saw at that moment, watching him gaze down at that brick. Placed by human hands in the courtyard of the goddess, probably on a sunny day like this one, twelve thousand years ago, removed forty-five centuries later by an archeologist who had himself become a legend.

This was the single most valuable piece that we'd acquired in the four years we'd been in operation. And now he was about to—

—Give it away.

He handed it to me. "You were the one she took care of," he said.

And I passed it to her. "It's yours, Selotta. For you and Kassel. I hope you'll keep it for yourself."

"—Rather than give it to the museum," she said.

"Yes. It's for *you*. With our appreciation."

Carmody took pictures. Selotta, clearly flustered, shook her head in a human gesture and held up her hands to decline. "I can't accept this, Chase," she said. "Not possibly. You and Alex arranged the tour for us. That's enough."

Alex was nothing if he wasn't a charmer. He smiled and glanced at Kassel. "You're a lucky man to have so lovely a spouse," he said.

Kassel, perhaps surprised at being called a man, licked his lips with that long forked tongue in a gesture that suggested the details were wrong but it was okay.

"Please," she continued. "I can't imagine the price you must have paid. I can't let you do this."

"It's okay, Selotta," Alex said. "It's something we wanted to do for you."

The following day we caught the shuttle from Drake City and rode it up to Galileo. We had a farewell dinner in a Chinese restaurant. It was an era of occasional armed confrontations between Ashiyyurean and Confederate warships. While we dipped into the chicken and spices, an HV began to run a report of a new incident. A Mute ship had gotten too close to a Confederate world, and a destroyer had fired on it. The Mutes were saying it was an accident. The ship had gotten off course. In any case, no casualties were being reported by either side.

That got us increased attention from the other diners. Kassel ignored it. "Alex and Chase, you are welcome on Borkarat anytime. And we'd be happy to put you up at our place," he said.

We told him we'd bring some brew with us. We were leaving, too, of course. Headed back to Rimway. We paid up, this one on Kassel, who insisted. When Kassel insisted, he tended to sound as if he meant it. We took a last look at Earth. We were on the nightside, over Europe and Africa. Lights everywhere, from Moscow to the Cape. Electrical storms glimmered in the Atlantic.

Here was where it had started. The great diaspora.

They were riding a diplomatic flight. We stayed with them until they boarded. They introduced us to a few of the other passengers, who were both Mute and human, and to the captain. Then it was time to go. We retreated back down the tube, they closed the hatches, and it was over.

We made for the *Belle-Marie*, checked to make sure our luggage had arrived, and climbed on board. I went up onto the bridge, said hello to Belle, the AI, and began running my checkoff list. When I was satisfied everything was in order, I contacted the ops center and requested permission to depart. Minutes later we were on our way, gliding past the moon, adding velocity, and feeling pretty good. I could hear Alex talking in the cabin. Nothing unusual about that: He was having a conversation with Belle. We were looking at a four-hour flight, plus probably a day or two after we had made our transit out of hyperspace. It was a lot quicker than it would have been a few years back, when the Armstrong drive needed weeks to cover the same distance.

I was making final heading adjustments before initiating our jump when I heard a third voice in the cabin. A woman's. Alex was checking his mail.

I broke in. "Alex, prepare for jump."

"Okay," he said.

The last green light came on, indicating his harness was in place, and I eased us into hyperspace.

Two minutes later he asked me to join him when I was free.
I told Belle to take over, got out of my chair, and headed back.

First thing I saw when I went into the common room was a
female standing frozen, staring at Alex out of stricken eyes. It
was a hologram, of course. She was young. Good-looking.
Dark eyes and black hair cut short. She wore a white-and-gold
blouse inscribed with the name HASSAN GOLDMAN above an arc
of six stars. Something about her was familiar. "Who is she?"

"Vicki Greene."

"Vicki Greene? *The* Vicki Greene?"

"*The* Vicki Greene."

Vicki Greene, of course, was, and remains, an immensely
popular novelist, a writer who specialized in horror and the
supernatural. Voices in the night, demons in the basement:
She'd made a substantial reputation by scaring the wits out of
millions of readers across the Confederacy. "I wasn't aware you
knew her."

He lowered himself into his seat. "I don't."

"Okay. Pity. So it's a business thing. She wants us to find
something for her?"

"Listen to this," he said.

He directed Belle to run the transmission from the start. The
image blinked off, blinked back on.

Greene looked at Alex, then at me, did an appraisal, and
turned back to the boss. "*Mr. Benedict,*" she said, "*I know this
will strike you as odd, but I don't know who else can help me.*"
She was having trouble controlling her voice. "*Since you're not
here, I'm asking your AI to forward this message. I'm in over
my head, Mr. Benedict.*" She was staring at him. *Her* turn to be
terrified. "*God help me, they're all dead.*"

Alex touched a control and froze her again. "That's it," he
said.

"That's *it*?"

"That is the sum of the transmission."

"What's she talking about?"

"I don't know. I've no idea." He took a deep breath. "I'm
wondering if we're looking at a woman in the last stages of a
breakdown."

She had looked thoroughly spooked. "Maybe she's been writing too much horror," I said.

"It's possible."

"And you've never met her?"

"No."

"*Who's* all dead?"

"Don't know."

"Maybe a bunch of fictitious characters." I got coffee for both of us. "You might want to recommend she see somebody."

"It's been in the folder for several days."

"That's because we told Belle not to disturb us."

He ran the artwork from her books. *Etude in Black*, which featured a young woman playing a stringed instrument in a spotlight while glowing eyes watched her from a dark curtain. *Love You to Death*, with a vulpine creature kneeling in sorrow at a grave site. *Nightwalk*, portraying a satanic figure in the clouds over a moonlit city. And three others with similar motifs: *Wish You Were Here*, *Dying to Know You*, and *Midnight and Roses*. "What do you think?"

"Alex, she sounds like a lunatic."

"She's in trouble, Chase."

"You want my advice? Don't get involved."

We couldn't send or receive a message while we were in hyperspace. We could have interrupted the jump, but there was really no point in that. So we waited until we arrived back at Rimway. Thirty seconds after we saw the stars again, he sat down and told Belle to record. "Ms. Greene," he said. "I just received your message." He stopped and looked in my direction. "Chase, how far out are we?"

"About a day," I said. "Day and a half."

He turned back to his message. "We've been away. I'll be in my office by the weekend. Meantime, if you want to talk to me, I'm within radio range now. Skydeck can put you through."

He sat quietly for several moments, then told Belle to send it and looked up at me. "What's wrong, Chase?"

"Nothing."

"Come on. Talk to me."

"I think you should be more careful about getting involved in other people's problems. You're an antiquities dealer, not a psychologist."

"If she's in trouble, I wouldn't want to walk away from her."

"If she's in trouble, she can call the police."

TWO

We don't fear death because we lose tomorrow, but because we lose yesterday, with its sweet poignancy, its memories of growing children, of friends and lovers, of all that we have known. Nobody else has really been there in the way we have. And when the lights go out for us, for you or me, the lights go out in that world, too.

—*Wish You Were Here*

They're all dead.

We cruised toward Rimway. With its big moon, it constituted a glittering double star in the sparse sky near the galactic rim. Vicki Greene didn't respond, didn't send a message, didn't say anything. The hours dragged on, and the double star grew into a pair of spheres. But Alex couldn't put it out of his mind. When we got closer, where the delay in signal exchange wouldn't be so great, he placed a call to her but was informed the code was inoperative. Temporarily out of service. Ordinarily he'd have dismissed the whole thing at that point as the work of a crank, but since it was Greene, he couldn't let go. Maybe it was that she was an icon, the biggest name in supernatural fiction. Not that he ever read any of it, but he liked meeting celebrities as much as the next guy.

So, a day and a half after we'd tried to communicate with her, we docked at Skydeck and headed directly for Karl's Dellacondan Restaurant. It was traditionally our first stop after a flight. It doesn't matter how good the shipboard food is, and we get good stuff on board the *Belle-Marie*, it's always a pleasure to make for a real dining room, spread out, and eat from a fresh menu. We were just walking into the place when he brought her up again. "She *must* be okay," he said, "or she'd have gotten back to me right away."

He was genuinely worried. More than the meet-the-deranged-celebrity thing. I'd known him for four years by then, and I still couldn't figure out how his mind worked. I'd have been interested to know what Selotta might have been able to tell me about him. It was unsettling to realize she'd only spent a few days with the guy and knew him far better than I ever would. Maybe that's the real reason people resent the Mutes so much.

"She probably sobered up," I said.

He looked at me with an expression that told me we both knew she hadn't been drinking. So I let it go, and the host led us to a corner table. We sat down beside a window. Brilliant splotches of light were spread across the globe. In the north, lightning glimmered.

"Have you ever read any of her novels?" he asked.

"No," I said. "Never had time."

"Make time. She's good."

"When did you read them?"

"I read *Dying to Know You* on the way in." He took a moment to examine the menu. "Great stuff," he added.

"You mean the food?"

"I'm talking about Greene. I was surprised how good she is."

"I like fiction that's a little more realistic."

He went into his paternal mode. "You need to open your mind to new experiences, Chase."

"I guess. You'd really like to meet her, wouldn't you?"

"Yes," he said. "I would."

"You get in trouble," I told him, "you're on your own."

I was glad to see Ben Colbee again.

Ben had twice proposed to me. All the signs were there. I saw passion in his eyes, watched him light up whenever I walked into a room. And I think I was in love with him, too. At least, I'd never felt about anybody else the way I felt about him. Ben was a good guy, sensitive, smart, good-looking, and he knew how to make me laugh. That's the big thing. Make me laugh.

He was a musician. He played cornerstone with the Full Boat, which—he thought—was moving up and would shortly make him famous. That did eventually happen, but it's another story. Anyhow, Ben was waiting as I knew he would be when the shuttle got in. He offered to take Alex home, too, but Alex knows when he's an encumbrance, so he said no thanks, you guys go ahead, and threw his bags into a taxi and took off.

We did some smooches, and Ben asked me how the flight had been and told me about the Full Boat's latest gig at the Sundown. Then, somewhere in there, he looked at me funny. "What's wrong, Chase?"

"Nothing, Ben. Just a crank message we got on the way home." He asked me about it so I told him. I didn't mention who it was from, though.

"This guy was a complete stranger?" he asked.

"It was from a woman. And yes, she was nobody we knew."

"Not one of your customers, right? Somebody you maybe forgot about?"

"No, Ben. Not somebody we forgot about."

He rolled his eyes. "Crazy people everywhere. I wouldn't worry about it."

We left Andiquar behind and headed out over the western hills. And, to make a long story short, I wasn't very receptive to his advances, not at all what he'd expected when I'd been gone almost three weeks. Hell, not what *I'd* expected. And I don't think it had anything to do with Alex and the crazy woman. I'm not sure what it was. I had a feeling we were approaching another one of those moments when Ben was going to pour out his heart to me. I'd been gone a long time, and he'd missed me, and—well, you know. And as much as I liked him, loved him, whatever, I wanted to head it off. So I explained I wasn't much in the mood. Tired. Long trip. He deflated and said okay, he'd see me the next day. If that was all right. "You know," he added, "you're gone a lot."

"I know."

"I mean, Chase, you're gone all the time."

"I'm sorry, Ben. I can't help that. It's my job."

He took me into his arms. It was a bear hug, delicious because he meant it, disconcerting because I didn't want it to go any further. He hung on to me, squeezed tight, his cheek against mine. "It's not the only job in the world, you know. There are others."

"Ben, I like this job. I mean, I *really* like it."

"I know. But we don't get to see each other for weeks at a time. Is that really what you want?" He released me, and I stepped back and looked into those puppy-dog brown eyes. All right, I know how this sounds. But the truth is my heart picked up, and I was damned if I knew what I wanted.

When he was gone, I looked up Vicki Greene. Carmen, my AI, gave me the basic information. She was thirty-three years old, born on the other side of the continent, currently based in Andiquar. She'd written six wildly successful novels, of which three had won the coveted Tasker Award, given each year for the most outrageous horror novel. She had master's degrees in history and mathematics, which struck me as an odd combination, and had been awarded an honorary doctorate the previous year by Tai Peng University.

"What else, Carmen?"

"*Her most recent novel is* Midnight and Roses, *about a young woman who lives in a house where the attic opens out into different dimensions. But only after midnight.*"

"Okay."

"*She's prolific. Six novels in six years. Three of her novels have been converted into holocasts, and one,* Love You to Death, *into a musical.*"

"What do we have on her family?"

"*Her mother left her husband and ran off with a philosophy professor when Vicki was three. She has an older brother. The philosophy professor brought the family east to take a faculty position at Benneval College.*" Benneval was two kilometers up the coast from Andiquar. "*He died a few years ago. Apparently suffered from poor health his whole life.*"

"So does she have an avatar I could speak with?"

"*Wouldn't Alex take offense if you got involved?*"

"I'd just be another reader. Talking to her about vampires."

"I see. Well, it doesn't look as if it matters. She doesn't maintain an avatar."

"You're kidding. She's a major-league writer, and she's not in the program?

"Apparently not."

That's one of the odd things about avatars. You can go online, and you can talk to people across the ages who are effectively lost, people who were born, got married, had kids, provided a living, and did all the usual stuff. Their avatars are there, ready to talk to you about the time they cut down the elm, or the day Aunt Jenny fell into the creek. But a lot of the movers and shakers, you can't find. (I should admit here that there's a Chase Kolpath avatar. She looks pretty good, and she's ready to discuss antiquities and some of the stuff I've done with Alex. But hardly anybody ever talks to it. I stopped checking the hit count years ago.)

I also looked up *Hassan Goldman*, the name emblazoned on Greene's shirt. I'd assumed it was a corporate logo, but it matched no company anywhere on Rimway. There were some individuals with the name, but none who seemed a likely candidate for putting it on a blouse. "So," I asked, "what has she been doing recently?"

"Ah, that's what's interesting. According to information put out by her publisher, she's been on Salud Afar."

"Salud Afar?"

"Yes."

Salud Afar was appropriately named. It was easily the most remote human world, thirty-one thousand light-years beyond Rimway. Out in the galactic boondocks. People generally thought about Rimway as being far out, the place on the edge of the Milky Way. But Salud Afar was the real outpost, located in empty-skies country, out there all by itself. For most of its history it had been months away from the closest human worlds. It had never joined the Confederacy.

"Why was she on Salud Afar?" I asked.

"Gathering material for a book, according to my best information. Or possibly just vacationing. The data is contradictory."

"Her next book is set on Salud Afar?"

"The data is incomplete."

"What's it about?"

"No information there either. Only that she's off chasing werewolves."

"You're kidding."

"That's what it says. Chase, that's a phrase used by people in the horror industry. It simply means somebody's out taking time off."

Alex always insisted I take a few days to chase werewolves myself after an off-world mission. That was the official stance. In reality, when we got home after a flight, there was invariably a lot to do. So I'd show up as usual and take my vacation time at leisure.

Rainbow Enterprises, as I've mentioned elsewhere, operated out of the country house in which Alex grew up. The area had been mostly forest then, along the banks of the Melony. A cemetery lay off the western perimeter. In fact, the house had been a retreat for hunters when Alex's uncle Gabe lived there. Now, it's surrounded by private homes and parks. There's a church at the foot of Amity Avenue, two blocks away, and a sports complex a half mile east.

It snowed the first night home. I've always liked snow-storms. Don't get enough of them at our latitude, maybe one or two a year. Almost never anything heavy. This one was an exception. The neighborhood was buried. The cemetery had vanished, and the river was frozen.

Because winter storms happen so seldom, nobody here has any kind of clearing device. Including Rainbow Enterprises. So I descended into my usual parking spot and climbed out into snowbanks up to my knees. I struggled through them to the front door. It was just after nine, and I could hear Alex upstairs in his office.

Our usual routine was that Jacob, the AI, would inform him I'd arrived, and he'd say hello through the system. Then, an hour or so later, he'd wander down to greet me in person and give me the day's assignments. This time he didn't bother to call. A few minutes later, he started down the stairs. And stopped halfway. "Got a minute?" he asked.

"Sure, Alex. Anything wrong?"

"Yes."

Scary way to start a conversation. "What happened?"

He came the rest of the way down, walked slowly into the main room, where we entertain, and lowered himself into a chair. "While we were gone, Rainbow picked up an unexpected deposit."

"Somebody gave us some money?"

"Not *some*. A *lot*."

"And that's *bad*? Who did it?"

"Vicki Greene."

"What? Why?"

"The statement doesn't say. She just had it credited to our account. Four days ago."

Okay. She was going to hire us for something. "How much?"

"Two million."

That took my breath away. It would have taken Ilena Crane's Statement of Human Rights, the original document, to produce that kind of cash. "And she didn't tell us why?"

"No."

"Well, I guess we ought to call her again."

"I've tried."

"And—?"

"Her AI says she's relocated. Permanently."

"Where?"

"'That information is not presently available.'"

"So she gave us a pile of money and took a walk?"

"Apparently."

"Well, I'm sure we'll hear from her."

"No doubt."

"Alex—"

"Yes? I'm listening."

"She can't be that hard to find."

"That's what *I* thought. But you're welcome to try."

"Jacob did a general search?"

"He did."

Well, there is a privacy provision. If you don't want to be

listed in the register, you're not listed. "Look, she's certainly going to contact us. I suggest we just wait for her to make the next move."

He wasn't happy. Alex likes to make money as much as the next guy, but he doesn't like things hanging over his head.

"You know," I said, "what was that line about *they're all dead*? Maybe we should check for accidents. Maybe she was involved in something that might have produced a few casualties?"

"If that were the case, why contact us? She'd need a lawyer."

"That's the best I can do."

"Anyhow, I looked into that possibility. There's nothing, Chase. She's not linked to anything I can find."

I sat looking around at the display cases. We had Markey Close's reading lamp, and an early version of *The Moravian Chronicles*, and the gun Ivor Kaska had used to kill himself as the Kastians closed in. "She's a pretty big name," I said finally. "If she were involved in anything, she'd have had a hard time keeping it quiet."

"I agree."

"So"—I adopted my most reassuring manner—"nothing bad has happened. Except possibly in her mind."

"She has a brother in Carmahla. But he's shut down, too. Doesn't answer."

"That might mean she contacted him, and he's keeping out of sight."

"It's a possibility."

"Did you know she was on Salud Afar recently?"

"I saw that. But the message she sent us on *Belle* originated in Andiquar. So she's back home."

"Maybe the problem, whatever it is, happened on Salud Afar."

"It's possible. We don't get much news coverage from there."

"You want me to look for the brother? Or do you want to let it go until she contacts us?"

He pushed back in his chair. "Let's find the brother. Exactly what I was going to suggest."

"I'm on it," I said. "Jacob."

"Yes, Chase?"

"You heard the man. Contact every major hotel in the city. We're trying to locate—What's his name, Alex?"

"Cory Greene."

"Let me know when you have something, Jacob." I looked across at Alex. "Okay?"

"Very good."

The AI needed about three seconds. *"He's in the Townsend."*

"Ah." Alex glowed. "Give us a channel."

"Open," said Jacob.

A young woman appeared in front of the Kaska gun case. She looked artificial. A construct. But these days you can never be sure. *"How may I help you, sir?"*

"Would you put me through to Cory Greene, please? He's a guest."

"One moment." She vanished.

I pushed my chair back so I wouldn't be visible during the exchange.

The construct reappeared. *"Mr. Greene wishes to know who you are and why you wish to speak with him."*

"Alex Benedict," he said. "Please tell him it concerns his sister."

Cory Greene had the same dazed look Vicki had worn. He was a young, good-looking guy, except maybe his ears were a bit large. He wore a green pullover with a white collar. His hair was as black as hers, and he had the same intelligent deep-set eyes. Vicki gave nothing away to other women, but she looked tough-minded and not the sort of person you'd want for an enemy. The same was true of Cory.

"I got a call from Vicki a few days ago," Alex said. "I was away and couldn't respond. Is she okay?"

"Not really," he said. *"She's gone."*

"What do you mean *gone*?" Alex leaned forward. "Where is she?"

"She's had a mnemonic extraction."

A mind wipe. All conscious memory removed. Permanently. I heard the wind whispering in the trees. "When?"

"Several days ago." Cory bit his lip and looked off into the distance. *"What did she say when she called you?"*

"Just that she needed help. She said, 'They're all dead.' Do you have any idea what she might have been talking about?"

"No. None. There's nobody dead that I know of. Except her." He was right about that. A mind wipe took you away and left the body alive. *"Do you have any idea why she did it?"*

Alex frowned. "None. I was hoping you could tell me."

Cory's eyes slid shut. *"It makes no sense. She was having a wildly successful career. She had all the money she'd ever need. She had an army of guys to pick from."* His eyes opened and grew wide as if he'd just become aware of Alex. *"Who are you exactly?"* He sounded resentful.

"I'm an antiquities dealer."

"An antiquities dealer."

"I've no idea why she contacted me."

"Did she tell you anything at all? Give you any idea what the problem was?"

"No," he said.

They sat there, looking helplessly at each other. Finally, Cory threw up his hands. *"Well, Mr. Benedict, I don't know why she involved you, or what she expected you to do. And I don't guess we're going to get to ask her."*

"Mr. Greene, I take it you didn't know in advance she was going to do this?"

"Of course not. I'd never have allowed it." His voice trembled. *"I didn't even know anything was wrong."*

"Had you seen her since she got back from Salud Afar?"

"You know about that?"

"It's public knowledge."

"She called to let me know she was home. That was all."

"How'd she seem?"

"I didn't notice anything out of the ordinary."

Alex fell silent. He was staring out the window at a sky that was threatening more snow. "How did you find out?" he asked at last. "About the mind wipe?"

"I got a message from her. Recorded before—"

"What did she say? She must have offered *some* kind of explanation."

"I already told you I don't know why. She said that her situ-

ation had become intolerable. But that was all. She said she couldn't live with it."

"Was she in any kind of trouble that you know of?"

"No. Not that I know about."

I was wondering whether her publisher had been informed. They weren't going to be happy.

"Have they let you see her?" asked Alex. "Since the procedure?"

"No. They won't let anyone near her."

I was trying to remember what they did with people after a mind wipe. She'd be given a new identity and a new set of memories. And she'd be cared for until she reacquired basic skills. Learned the language. Learned to walk. Her estate would be liquidated and the funds made available to her. And when she was ready, she'd be moved to a distant location. Nobody would be told where, and she'd start a whole new life.

"She must have told *someone* why."

"If so, he hasn't come forward."

It was a radical treatment, reserved for habitual criminals, for psychopaths beyond the reach of therapy, and for those who wanted to leave their lives behind and start fresh. It was an expensive last resort, still opposed by a sizable portion of the population on moral, ethical, and religious grounds. I was inclined to agree. It's hard to see how it's any different from suicide. Vicki Greene had ceased to exist.

"Where is she now?"

"At St. Thomas Psychiatric. Why do you ask?"

"Would it be okay with you if I went over?"

"Why? What's the point? They won't let you see her."

"I'd like to talk to her doctors."

His eyes took on a hostile glint. But he nodded. *"Do as you like. I couldn't get anything out of them."*

"Thank you. By the way, is there any kind of memorial planned?"

"Yes. Day after tomorrow."

"May I come?"

"Why? What's your interest in this?"

"Mr. Greene, she called me. And I should inform you

she transferred a substantial sum of money to me. With no explanation."

"That's crazy. How much?"

"I think she wanted me to do something for her. I'd like you to help me find out what that might be."

THree

The mind is a private room, fully furnished with a brain, that may or may not be functional; with passions, ideology, superstitions, and delusions. And a given level of decency. It is a point of view, a perspective, a coming together of everything that makes us human. It is who we are. Once we let someone else in, we are never the same.

—*Love You to Death*

St. Thomas was a care center for people with psychiatric disorders. It was located twenty kilometers north of Andiquar, in a small suburb at the foot of a mountain. It consisted of a drab, square, two-story building wrapped around a domed courtyard. We arrived at midmorning. People were out on the grounds as we descended, some walking, others playing board games. One or two were reading.

We descended onto a pad, between snowbanks, and I shut off the engine. Alex sat staring out at the front entrance, at the large white sign marked ST. THOMAS PSYCHIATRIC, and sighed.

We climbed out, got onto a cleared walkway, and went inside. The interior was more like a private home than a medical facility. The reception area seemed to open out onto a tranquil ocean scene. In place of desks and counters, there were sofas and armchairs and coffee tables. Windows looked out onto the grounds and the courtyard, and lines of shelves were filled with vases and lamps and flowers and pitchers, anything that might have added to the general serenity.

A young man in light blue medical garb came out of an adjoining office. "Mr. Benedict?" he said.

"Yes."

The man said Dr. Hemsley knew we were there. "He's with a patient at the moment," he said. "Please make yourselves comfortable."

Hemsley joined us a few minutes later. He was small, overweight, and looked tired. Without waiting for introductions, he led us into another room. "Please sit," he said. He dropped into a large purple leather chair, propped his feet up on a footstool, and smiled at us. "Mr. Benedict," he said, "you understand she's not my patient."

"Oh. I'm sorry. I was directed to you."

"May I ask, what's your connection with Ms. Greene? Are you a relative?"

"No, I'm not."

He looked in my direction. "Is *she*?"

"You may talk directly *to* me, Dr. Hemsley," I said. "And no, I'm not a relative."

He looked puzzled. "A friend? Is there a legal connection here somewhere?"

"No." Alex sat back, crossed one leg over the other. "Ms. Greene contacted us for assistance. Several days ago."

"I see." He took on the demeanor of a man about to deliver bad news. "Well, in any case, she seems to have negated all that. You're aware of the procedure she's undergone?"

"Yes."

"It severs her old world. She's—" He hesitated. But I got the impression he was only pretending to search for the proper phrase. "She's no longer with us. What kind of assistance did she request?"

"She didn't specify, Doctor. She merely asked for our help."

"And what kind of help would you have been able to provide, Mr. Benedict?"

"We're fairly flexible, Doctor. Is it possible to speak to whoever was charged with her care?"

"I think there may have been a misunderstanding. Her psychiatrist is prohibited by ethical considerations from discussing her case with anyone except family members. Or her lawyer. And there are even strict prohibitions on that. It would therefore be pointless to proceed further." He got up. "I'm sorry you wasted your time."

We called Cory again. Would he be willing to see her doctor and ask some questions?

No. *"It's over,"* he said. *"She's past help now. Let's just let it go."*

"But somebody may be in danger."

"Look, Benedict," Cory said, *"if something unusual had been happening in her life, I'd have known about it. Nobody's in danger."*

"You didn't know the mind wipe was coming."

"Just go away. Please."

Naturally they wouldn't give us Greene's new name. Nobody gets that. Not even a spouse or a mother. It wouldn't have mattered, of course. There was nothing to be gained even if we could speak with her. Cory was right. She was gone.

Alex sat in the big living room at the country house, staring at logs burning in the fireplace. "After the procedure," he said, "St. Thomas provides her with a couple of people who masquerade as family. I checked before we went out there. They create the illusion of a whole new life." Alex had discovered years before that a close friend had gone through the process. Had lived an earlier life of which he was completely unaware.

"Time to walk away," I said.

"Sure." He smiled at me. "Take the money and run."

I couldn't see any point in attending the memorial service. It's basically a funeral, and I hate funerals. But Alex insisted on going, so I accompanied him.

Vicki had lived in a spacious, double-tier, early-Valaska manor, surrounded by broad lawns, clusters of trees, and a high fence. Two sculpted fountains flanked the front of the house, made to look like demons and wolves. They were shut down the day of the memorial, maybe because of the continuing cold, maybe because someone thought a functioning fountain would be improper.

I wondered who would be getting the property. "They've put it up for sale," Alex said. We were in the skimmer, beginning our descent. "The proceeds will be put into a sealed fund and made available to Vicki's new persona on a periodic basis. She won't know where it's coming from."

"Has anybody ever gone through this procedure and later recovered her memory?"

"It's happened. But not very often."

We got clearance from the AI and came down in a parking area a mile or so away. There, along with a dozen other people, all appropriately subdued, we boarded a limo, which flew us to a pad at the side of the house. We got out and were directed across the frozen ground by two valets. The front doors opened, and we climbed stone steps onto the portico and went inside. A somber young woman greeted us and thanked us for coming.

There was a substantial crowd, maybe two hundred people wandering through a cluster of sitting rooms and spilling out onto a heated side deck. Cory showed up and managed a frigid hello. We tracked down Vicki's editor, an older woman with tired eyes and a clenched jaw that never seemed to relax. Her name was Marjorie Quick.

Alex expressed his sympathy and engaged her in a few minutes of small talk, how he was an avid reader of Vicki's work, and what a loss this was. Was there by any chance another book coming?

"Not that I know of," she said. "Unfortunately, she took the last year off. Vacationed. Enjoyed herself. Just let it go."

"But she'd been producing a book every year, hadn't she?"

"Yes," she said. "But that can wear on you."

"I'm sure it would."

Quick had recognized his name. "Aren't you *the* Alex Benedict—?"

He admitted that yes, he was, and steered the conversation back to Vicki: "I read that she'd gone to Salud Afar," he said.

"Yes. She wanted to get away."

"It's a long way out. Even with the new drive, it's a month. One way."

"I know. But she wanted to go." She started looking around for a way to extricate herself from us.

"You say she wasn't working on a book? I mean, that would be the ideal place to work, on a long trip like that."

"The reality is that she was *always* working on a book. More or less."

"Did you see her after she got back?"

"No. I haven't seen her for eight or nine months."

I got the impression that she'd tried to dissuade Vicki from making the flight. "Vicki needed to fill her tank, Mr. Benedict. It's as simple as that." She adjusted her jacket. "If it weren't so far, Salud Afar would be the perfect place for a horror writer on vacation."

"Really? Why's that?"

"Read the tourist brochures. It has lost seas and beaches where monsters come ashore and God knows what else."

"You're kidding."

"Of course I am. But those are the stories. I know she'd paid a virtual visit to Salud Afar in the spring. But if you understand writers, you'll understand that's not enough. If you write horror, and you want atmosphere, Salud Afar is your world."

Somebody had put a picture of Vicki Greene in the center aisle. She looked bright and happy, holding a kitten in her lap. They could have used an avatar, of course, and a lot of people do that. You go to a funeral, and they have a replica of the deceased delivering a few final sentiments. It's always struck me as creepy.

Instead, they'd settled for a picture. Vicki had been a lovely woman. I don't think I'd realized *how* lovely.

As ten o'clock approached, the guests wandered toward the main room. It wasn't big enough to accommodate everyone. We joined the crowd, watching the proceedings from a passageway. Precisely on the hour, somebody sat down and played "Last Light," the moderator appeared, and the service began.

There was no religious element, of course. According to all

reports, Vicki and her family were believers, but she wasn't really dead. So it was a memorial, and no more. Friends and family members went forward one by one to talk about her, to remember her, and to express their regret that, for whatever reason, she had resorted to such extreme measures. "So many of us loved her," said one man, who described himself simply as a friend but could not hold back tears. "Now she's gone from us."

It was the first time I'd attended a service for someone who was still technically alive. Who could have walked through the doors at any moment.

The last of the speakers finished, and the moderator turned things over to Cory, who thanked everyone for coming and announced there'd be refreshments in the dining room. He hoped, he said, everybody would stay.

Some did. Others began to drift away. We wandered through the gathering, offering condolences, looking for someone who might know why she'd done it. I got introduced to a few other people whose names were familiar. "Horror writers," someone told us. "They're a pretty close-knit bunch." I tried to imagine what an evening at a bar would be like with a group of people who wrote about swamp monsters.

She had a lot of friends. Women talked of good times, men spoke admiringly of her abilities, which were supposed to be references to her writing, but which I came to suspect were code words for Vicki's lustrous brown eyes and her up-front equipment. But maybe I'm selling them short. She'd had a lot of boyfriends, one of whom had apparently put together an avatar of Vicki and now sat talking with it for hours at a time. I wasn't aware of that fact when I met him. Found it out later in the day. But I remember sensing that he was obsessed with the woman. Most painful for him, probably, was knowing she was still alive, her personality more or less intact. But whatever he might have meant to her was gone. He was not even a memory.

I found only one person who'd seen her since her return from Salud Afar: Cass Jurinsky, a craggy, ancient-looking female author who wrote *about* the horror genre. When she asked what I did for a living and I mentioned Alex's name, she got excited. "Vicki was a big fan of his," she said. "She used to talk about using him as a character in one of her novels."

Alex in a horror novel. I tried to imagine him playing tag with a poltergeist.

"Seriously." She looked at me with sad eyes. "I guess she never got in touch with him, did she?"

"Not exactly," I said. Maybe it explained why she'd come to us for help. "What was her state of mind when she got back from her vacation? Did you notice anything unusual, Cass?"

"She seemed depressed," Jurinsky said. "I don't know what it was. It was as if all the spirit had gone out of her."

She had white hair and a lined face. But her eyes took fire when she talked about Vicki and her diabolical creations. "Nobody was better at it. She didn't have the biggest audience because she wrote a subtler kind of horror than the rest of them. But if you were tuned in to her, nobody could scare the pants off people the way she did."

"Where did you last see her?" I asked.

"A few weeks ago. At the World Terror Convention. It's for horror fans." (I could have figured that one out.) "They hold it every year in Bentley. Vicki showed up without warning. She wasn't on the schedule, but at one point I looked up and there she was. I didn't even know she was back."

"You got to talk to her?"

"Oh, yes." She sighed. "I loved that woman. I asked her how the trip had gone, and she said it was all right but she was glad to be home. And I remember thinking she didn't *look* glad."

"How *did* she look?"

"You want the truth? Frightened. And older. She'd aged while she was away." Jurinsky stopped, and I saw her replaying the scene in her mind. "I asked if everything was okay, and she said sure. She said it was good to see me again, then somebody interrupted and I drifted away from her."

"That's it?"

"That's it." Her lips tightened. "I should have paid more attention. Maybe I could have helped."

We stood quietly for a moment. She seemed far away. Then

I brought her back. "Why do you think she went to the convention?"

"Well, she usually attended World Terror. She enjoyed spending time with her fans. Or, maybe she was looking for someone to talk to."

"You?"

"I'd guess anybody. Looking back now, I think she just wanted to be in a crowd. A crowd that knew her. But I was too busy to notice." She took a deep breath. "Too dumb."

It was on the whole a depressing hour and I was glad when it was over. Alex had found a couple more who'd seen her, and who'd thought something might be wrong. But nobody had pursued the issue with her. "I talked with Cory again," he said.

"And—?"

"She bought a new notebook after she got home from Salud Afar."

"What happened to the old one?"

"Apparently left behind."

On the way home, he mentioned that he'd gotten the name of her psychiatrist.

FOUr

Trust your instincts, Shiel. In the end, it's all you've got.

—*Nightwalk*

The painful truth about humanity is that the only people who can't be bought are the fanatics. Clement Obermaier was *not* a fanatic. He was the authorizing psychiatrist in Vicki's case. And when Alex offered to contribute substantially to a fund in which he had an interest, he discovered a way around the ethical dilemma posed by the need to talk about a patient.

Alex met him at Cokie's Place, a cabaret in the mountains north of St. Thomas. Afterward, he reconstructed the conversation for me.

Obermaier apparently thought Alex hoped there'd be a manuscript around somewhere. If there were, it would be worth a considerable sum. "At first," Alex said, "it was pretty obvious he was hoping he could talk to me, collect the contribution, but not tell me anything."

"So what did he tell you?"

"Somebody did a lineal block on her."

"A *what*?"

"It's a procedure that's used with psychotic patients. Or with those who have extreme emotional problems. It allows the doctors to isolate a memory, or a set of memories, and prevent the patient from acting on them. From even talking about them."

"Why would they want to do that?"

"It can negate a wish for vengeance, for example. Or prevent stalking. That sort of thing."

"So who used it on her? *Why* would they do it?"

"Obermaier has no idea. There's nothing in her medical record."

"Which means it was an illegal procedure."

"Yes."

"Can they estimate *when* it happened?"

"He's pretty sure it was within the last year."

"So what you're telling me is that she had some sort of specific memory that was locked away. She couldn't even tell anybody what it was."

"That sounds about right."

"But the memory was still there."

"Yes."

"Why wouldn't they—whoever did it—just do a mind wipe?"

"If we can find them, we'll ask. My guess would be that you can't hide a complete memory abstraction. I mean, the poor woman wouldn't even have been able to find her way home."

"Couldn't this guy help her? Other than by removing her memory completely?"

"He says he tried. But apparently lineal blocks tend to be permanent."

"So he did the extraction because she was having a problem with the lineal block? Do I have that right?"

"They did the extraction because she requested it."

"Couldn't he have refused?"

"He said he saw no recourse except to allow her to proceed."

"Why?"

"He said that, left to herself, she might have committed suicide."

"You think it happened on Salud Afar?"

"I don't think there's any doubt."

"Are you suggesting maybe she ran into a *real* werewolf? Something like that?"

"I think she found out something she wasn't supposed to know."

* * *

Two days later, Alex had something he wanted me to watch. "This is from the Nightline Horror Convention," he said. "It took place a few days before Vicki left for Salud Afar. She was among the guests, and this is one of her panels."

The hologram blinked on. Four people at a table. Vicki at one end. I could hear an audience behind me. A tall redheaded man sitting beside her held up his hand, and the crowd quieted. *"My name's Sax Cherkowski. And I just want to say my latest novel is* Fright Night. *I'm the moderator of the panel, and I'd like to take a moment to introduce everyone. We'll be talking about how to set mood, which is to say, how to scare the reader."*

We fast-forwarded through most of the comments until it was Vicki's turn to speak. *"It doesn't have to be dark,"* she said. She used a dazzling smile to demonstrate that all the mummies and vampires were in fun. *"It doesn't have to be gloomy. All you need is a hint that you're setting the stage. The wind suddenly becomes audible.*

"It might be two o'clock in the afternoon in an office building with a thousand people moving around. But if you know what you're doing, you can still arrange things so that every time someone opens a door, your reader will jump."

The panelists took turns responding to questions from the moderator and the audience. Vicki didn't really *talk*. She *performed*. She sparkled. The audience loved her. *"Keep in mind,"* she told them, *"that you're not telling a story. You're creating an experience. When those floorboards creak, your reader should hear it. When a log falls in the fireplace, your reader should jump. That means if you write anything that doesn't move the action forward, throw in an adjective you don't need, do anything that doesn't keep things going, you remind the reader that she's in a comfortable chair at home reading a book. When that happens, everything you've worked to accomplish goes away."*

Alex let it run for about twenty minutes. Vicki held the audience in her hand. She got laughs, collected applause, traded quips with the other guests, joked with people in their seats, and was the star of the show. Then he showed me a second panel in which she tried to explain why people love to be scared. She was, if anything, even better.

"This next," said Alex, "is a teachers' luncheon. She was the guest speaker."

A long table appeared. A tall, rangy man stood at a lectern and introduced her. While he delivered accolades and the applause heated up, she took her place beside him. She thanked everyone for coming, announced that she would be talking about the importance of literacy and the critical role teachers play in the process of enlightening the rest of us, and she proceeded to do so. In a workmanlike, methodical manner.

She was good, but the energy, the flash and dazzle, were gone. They listened, and when she'd finished, they applauded politely.

She was a different woman. Her eyes drifted around the room; her tone wasn't flat, but—

Alex shut down the sound.

"This one," I said, "was *after* she got back."

He looked into the center of the room, where the hologram had been playing. "Yes. She'd been home six days."

Every world has its uneasy places, sites where gruesome killings, real or mythical, have taken place. Where spirits are said to be in command. Where people hear things whispering in the wind. Most of these locations, of course, are the products of people with overactive imaginations. And sometimes they are enhanced by entrepreneurs, interested in attracting tourists. Oh, yes, madame, up there on the hill, when the moon is high, Miller's dead daughter can still be seen. Usually near the large tree right on the eastern edge. She always wears white.

If you run a search for such places, a substantial number of them turn up on Salud Afar: haunted buildings, haunted forests, a river with a demonic boatman, another river that is home to the spirit of a young woman drowned trying to reach her lover, a temple in which high priests (supposedly) had lopped off people's heads and where the screams could still be heard at certain times of the year. And there was even a phantom aircraft. My favorite was a laboratory, abandoned centuries ago, which locals claimed had once produced a time machine. Members of the long-dead staff, it was claimed, still showed up on occasion, their earlier selves traveling happily through the ages.

"Why?" I asked Alex. "How come there's so much nonsense on this one world? Do those people really buy into this stuff?"

Alex had been in a somber frame of mind since the memorial service. Ordinarily he'd have responded with a detailed analysis, attributing the effect perhaps to starless skies, or romantic trends in the literature. But he hadn't recovered his customary good spirits. "I've not been there," he said. "But I doubt the stories have anything to do with the credibility of the inhabitants."

"What then?"

"I don't know. Maybe we should ask a sociologist."

"You have a theory."

He nodded. "I can suggest a possibility."

"You want to share it?"

"Salud Afar, until its revolution thirty years ago, had suffered under six hundred years of authoritarian rule. Worldwide. Think about that. No place to hide. The only escape was off-world, and the government had to okay it before you could leave." His eyes narrowed. "I hate to think what life must have been like."

"Six hundred years?" I said.

"Under the same family. The Cleevs. It was a place where you had to keep your mouth shut. And you never knew when the Bandahr's thugs were coming through the door."

"That was the Cleev family?"

"Yes."

"What's your point?"

"Maybe none. But I suspect, when things get bad like that, when there really are monsters running loose, people tend to invent fantasies they can cope with. It might be an escape mechanism and maybe reassurance at the same time, because they know vampires don't exist. And they aren't nearly as terrible as what they face in real life but don't dare talk about."

Alex did a round of speaking engagements, contributed a set of Myanamar dishware—three hundred years old—to the Altreskan Centenary Museum, cut the ribbon at a cultural center at Lake Barbar, and attended the inauguration of the newly elected governor of West Sibornia. But he remained bothered by what had happened to Vicki Greene.

He began subscribing to news reports and summaries of current events from Salud Afar. Because of the distance involved, they were about ten days old when they arrived. When I asked what he was looking for, he told me he'd know it when he saw it.

He spent hours in his office, going through everything that came in. He didn't trust Jacob to do it because he couldn't spell out the specifics for the AI. He discovered that Vicki had done an interview show, conducted by a local academic, and managed to get a copy of the show. It was called, as best I remember, *Imkah* with Johansen. *Imkah* was apparently a concoction like coffee.

And there was Vicki, fresh and alert, the *real* Vicki, talking about why people love to be frightened, how glorious it feels to hide under the bed while the storm rages outside. *"Storms are what we're about,"* she told Johansen. *"Lightning bolts and other things that come out of the night. There's nothing like a good scare. It's even good for your heart."* It was the Vicki from the Nightline Horror Convention.

Alex took me to lunch once a week. Sometimes twice, if we had something to celebrate. He liked celebrations and rarely missed an opportunity. Usually we went to Debra Coyle's. It looks out over the Melony, they keep a fire going, the food is excellent, and the prices are right. Three or four weeks after the memorial, he came down the stairs and hustled me out the door. A few minutes later we were walking into Debra's. It was one of those dreary, cold, rainy days. The sky sagged down into the river, and occasional gusts shook the building. We ordered salads and talked about nothing in particular although I could see there was something on his mind. When he finally got around to it, I wasn't particularly surprised: "Chase," he said, "I'm going to Salud Afar."

"Alex, that's crazy." But I think I'd known it was coming.

He looked at me and laughed. "We both know why she paid me the money. She was asking me to find out what happened to her. And do something about it."

"You're sure you want to do this. That's a long run out there."

He was staring through the window at the soggy weather. "I've gone through everything I can find about Salud Afar. There's no indication of an incident of any kind. And certainly nothing about anybody getting killed. But Chase, *something* happened."

They brought a decanter of red wine and poured two glasses. I didn't say anything while he made some sort of nondescript toast. Then he put his glass down, folded his arms on the table, and leaned forward. "It's the least I can do."

"It's a long ride."

"I know." He stared at me, looking guilty. Actually, I knew him well enough to be sure he wasn't *feeling* guilty, but was putting on a show. He paid me generously, and I was supposed to be ready when the bugle sounded. "I know it's asking a lot, Chase. Especially on such short notice." He hesitated, and I let him hang. "I could hire a pilot, if you can't manage it."

"No," I said. "I'll take you. When are we leaving?"

"As soon as we can pack."

That left Ben to deal with.

"No," he said. "Not again. Not so soon."

"Ben, it's an emergency. And I can't let him go alone."

"That's what you always say, Chase. I've been living with this now for a long time. I think at some point you have to decide what you want."

"I know."

"So what are you going to do?"

"I can't walk away from him when he needs me."

"You know, Chase, if I thought for a minute this would be the last time, I'd say fine, go ahead, and I'll see you in, what, three months?" We were in his car, riding on River Road. I was supposed to be taking him out to dinner. *My* treat. His birthday was three days away, but I wasn't going to be there for it. "So what can you tell me? Is it going to be the last time?"

I thought about it. I was still thinking when he said, "You don't have to answer. I guess I know."

Five

The storage area occupied a cramped space above the concert hall. It didn't hold much. A few old instruments, some costumes, some electrical gear. Certainly nothing to be concerned about. Furthermore, it was securely locked and no one could have gotten into it without Janice's knowledge. Therefore, when she started hearing sounds, knockings, sighs, and heavy breathing, coming from behind that locked door, she would have been prudent to get out of the house. To call the police. But then there'd be no story.

—*Love You to Death*

I didn't usually look forward to getting back on board the *Belle-Marie*. Maybe I was getting old. But it's a bit confining, physically and otherwise. I'd become a city-lights type, I guess. I liked parties and guys. I liked the social side of my job, which kept me running around with Alex, playing Rainbow's public relations maven. I got to meet a lot of interesting people, interesting in that so many of them had serious accomplishments on the record. And also that many of them were passionate about the bits and pieces of our past that had survived, sometimes across thousands of years. Watching them walk through our traveling exhibit, pressing their fingers against a display case, holding the captain's insignia from a vessel that left Earth in the first years of the interstellar age, staring at the laser rifle that misfired while Michael Ungueth was trying to hold back the giant lizard during the evacuation of Maryblinque, listening to their voices drop to a whisper—What other line of work could have matched any of that?

Maybe too much had changed. Alex had become driven, and I knew there'd be no peace until he figured out what kind of message Vicki Greene had been trying to send. Nonetheless, this time, I was glad to see the ship again.

He was back in the passenger cabin, still making calls to clients while I got ready for departure. When he finally signed off, he buzzed my line, thanked me again, admitted we were probably on a wild-goose chase, but pointed out we were being paid very well. Twenty minutes later, we were on our way.

When the quantum drive first appeared on the scene fourteen years earlier, replacing the old Armstrong, it had seemed like near-instantaneous transportation. It could cover five light-years in a few minutes. But it was less accurate than the older system, so there was inevitably a long glide time, often a few days, into the target area. This was true regardless of the range of the hyper-space transition. If you arrived, say, twenty-five million klicks out from the space station and tried to jump closer, you might find yourself twice as far away on the other side. It was, at best, an erratic system.

I'd always thought of Rimway as being on the edge of the galaxy. But Salud Afar was thirty-one thousand light-years farther out, pretty much in intergalactic space.

As we pulled away from Skydeck and began accelerating, I tried to picture going all the way out there on Armstrongs. "I just can't imagine how they did it," I told Alex.

"Actually," he said, "they didn't have the Armstrong when people first went to Salud Afar."

"What *did* they have?"

"We're talking four thousand years ago, Chase. I'm not sure anybody knows what they had, or how long the flight took. But the Armstrong had only been around a few centuries." We talked about it in the past tense because it was now in the process of being supplanted by the technology the Dellacondans had developed during their war with the Mutes. The quantum drive, which got you around a lot faster.

Traveling all the way to Salud Afar with a primitive system

made no sense to me. "I can understand that explorers might have found the place, but the flight must have taken years. Why would anybody settle out there?"

Alex grinned. "Some people like solitude," he said.

"Back to Eden."

"Something like that. It's apparently a nice place. Oxygen content perfect. It has broad oceans, beautiful views. Gravity's light, a little more than eight-tenths of a gee. So you don't weigh so much. The only thing the place lacked was stars."

"So what's the plan when we get there?"

"Find out where Vicki Greene went and track her. It shouldn't be hard to pick up her trail."

"Alex, she was one person on a world of, what, about two billion?"

"But she's well-known. There'll be media stories. Some people will have met her. It should be easy."

Alex had been collecting the names of Salud Afar's reviewers, book dealers, other horror writers, the president of the Last Gasp Society, anybody who would have had an interest in talking to Vicki. We sent off about a hundred messages letting everybody know we were coming and inviting anyone who'd seen her or worked with her or knew about her to get back to us.

When that was done, we made our jump into hyperspace and settled in for a long ride.

Alex had always been an easy guy on this kind of mission. There aren't too many people I want to be cooped up with for a month at a crack. But Alex was okay. He could talk about almost anything, he could listen, he had an open mind, he let me pick the entertainment, and he was always good for a laugh. Once under way, he put the Vicki Greene puzzle aside. There was, he said, no point dwelling on it until we got more information.

He took to reading her novels. I tried one of them, *Etude in Black*, in which a full-throated singer could, when aroused, literally bring down the house. And I know how that sounds, but if you've ever read Vicki Greene, you know she can get away with the most outrageous stuff. She made it believable, and I sat there for most of it with my hair standing straight up. The guy didn't want to do any damage, but his voice was so magnificent he simply couldn't resist occasionally taking things to the wall.

After that, I'd had enough. But I read *The Moron's Guide to Vicki Greene*. It maintained she liked abandoned buildings, particularly crumbling churches, which inevitably produced terrible surprises for her characters, who, usually, were there because they'd been stranded in some way, a flyer had gone down, or a boat blown off course.

The danger comes not from a manic supernatural creature, as is usually the case in modern horror novels, but from a supernatural source accidentally provoked. One of the summaries argued that Greene's primary strength, the characteristic that makes her so popular, was her ability to create a sense of empathy with the person wielding the force that is scaring the wits out of everyone else. She wrote about people "getting lost in the cosmic maelstrom." I'm quoting here, and, yes, I don't know what that means any more than you do. But it gets its punch from a demonic possession, or a ghostly presence from another time, or a spirit bound to the mortal world because it can't get rid of some aspect of its physical existence. Or it's a lover who simply can't let go, or, as in *Love You to Death*, a man whose passions cause their objects to overheat. Literally.

Well, okay. Not my kind of leisure reading. I scare too easily. But I could see that for some people, that sort of thing could become addictive. In the meantime, Alex read each of the novels and expressed his admiration for Vicki's writing ability. "I know the academic world doesn't take her very seriously," he said, "but her name is going to survive."

I began devoting my attention to working on the Rainbow catalog, which had to be updated on a regular basis. I would have liked to include the Atlantean brick, which would have been a star attraction. It was a bit late for that, though. Most of the items, almost all of them, did not belong to us. Rainbow usually acted simply as a trading partner, putting buyers and sellers together.

But that wasn't enough to occupy me for more than a couple of days. So we took to attending virtual concerts and watching musicals and doing whatever we could to help time pass. Alex had a passion for ancient American music, and we spent one particularly riveting evening listening to the Bronx Strings perform a medley of tunes from that distant era, including two of the earliest pieces of music known: "All That Jazz" and "That Old Man River." It was the first time I'd heard either, and they were the high point of the flight.

A month after departure, we emerged from hyperspace. Usually, you make your jump out into normal space and the sky lights up. You get the local sun—assuming you've jumped into a planetary system, which is almost inevitably the case—and a sky full of stars. And maybe some planets and moons. Near Salud Afar, you get the sun and not much else. In our rear, a gauzy arc marked the rim of the Milky Way. Salud Afar was a small bright globe, dead ahead. Otherwise, the sky was utterly dark, save for two stars, one bright and one dim.

"It's unique among worlds with large land animals," said Belle. *"It's the only such world known that has no moon. It's believed to have had one originally, but it was probably lost during the Transit."* The Transit referred to the passage of an object, probably a black hole or a dwarf star, that had scrambled the system. *"Theory has always held that a large moon is necessary to prevent a terrestrial-sized world from developing a distinct wobble. Which would, of course, play havoc with climatic conditions."*

"Of course," I said.

"Here, for whatever reason, the wobble has not happened."

"How far are we?" I asked.

"Three days out."

One of the two stars, the dim one, was actually the planet Sophora. The other, a dazzling sapphire in the sky, was Callistra, twelve hundred light-years away. *"It's a supergiant,"* said Belle.

And that was it. Otherwise, the sky was jet-black.

"Okay. Belle, let's open a channel to their operations center."

She complied. "Samuels Ops," I said, "this is the *Belle-Marie*. Approaching from Rimway. Range 4.1 million klicks. Request log-in and instructions."

A female voice replied: *"Instructions are being forwarded to your AI in separate package,* Belle-Marie. *Welcome to Salud Afar."*

"Thank you, Ops. Estimate arrival three standard days."

"You are clear. Continue on course. By the way, Belle-Marie, *we have some mail for you."*

"Would you forward it, please?"

"Doing it now."

They were responses to our inquiries about Vicki. Most were negative. Didn't know her. Knew she was here but didn't get a chance to meet her. Got her to sign a crystal but they were moving us right along. Johansen, the guy who'd enjoyed several cups of *imkah* with Vicki, told us he hadn't actually been with her. *"She was at her hotel during the interview. I never left the studio. Didn't actually see her in person."*

Of the rest, five claimed to have spent time with her. Among them was Austin Gollancz, who represented the local firm that published her on Salud Afar. *"I hope,"* he added, *"she's okay."*

He lived in Marinopolis. It was the original name, now restored, for the capital of Komalia, which was the principal state on the world. During the height of the Directorate, it had been Cleev City, named for the family that had for so long held global sway.

We set up a conference with Gollancz. There was a time delay, but it wasn't a problem. *"She came here the day after she arrived,"* he said. He was a small, round, prosperous-looking guy. It was obvious he'd liked Vicki. *"We talked business."*

"Anything else?" Alex asked.

"Well, she was excited to be here. Talked about visiting some of our spookier places. She expected to have a great time."

"Did she have an itinerary of any kind, Austin?"

"Not that I know of."

"Anybody she planned to travel with?"

"If so, she didn't mention it to me. And look, Alex, I know I'm not being much help. But this is such a shock. I want you to know if I can do anything, anything at all, just ask. Okay?"

"Sure."

"Thanks, Alex."

six

Over the ages, it is a world whose name has become synonymous with great art. Nowhere else can we find music and sculpture and literature on their level. Whether one thinks of drama or symphonies or architecture or even botanical displays, one always has to confront their contribution. It may be related to their separation from the rest of us, or it may simply be something in the water, but we always have to make room for them. The power of their contributions, of luminous towers, concerts by the sea, brilliant comedy, tragedy on the summer stage, enriches us all.

—Dr. Blanchard, in *Midnight and Roses*, speaking of the mythical world Marityne

Salud Afar orbits Moria, a quiet, stable class-G sun. The planetary system at one time is believed to have possessed eight worlds, but the passage of an unknown dense object eleven thousand years ago scattered them. Two worlds, Varesnikov and Naramitsu, were stripped of rings and moons, but left otherwise in place. Sophora had been thrown into a wildly irregular orbit, which brought it careening in and out of the inner system at centuries-long intervals. Fortunately, it made for occasional spectacular views, but posed no threat to the human establishment on Salud Afar. Miranda, a frozen terrestrial far from the sun, had, like Salud Afar, been unaffected by the event. The remaining three had been ejected and were adrift in the void.

Early accounts suggest it was this wildness in the system

that had inspired the first settlement, which had apparently been a scientific colony. (Most historians are more inclined to attribute settlement to the years-long journey back to the Confederacy. Why go through that when you had a virtual paradise at hand?) In any case, by modern times, it was a thriving world not entirely disconnected from the Confederacy but with a history all its own.

We came in over the nightside, riding above a dark ocean. Illuminated patches were visible on the ground. Cities, glowing along a distant coastline. *"There are,"* said Belle, *"eleven substantial landmasses, ranging from continents to islands with a minimum area of ninety thousand square kilometers."* She went on in that vein, citing temperature gradients and average rainfall and dozens of other details. Meanwhile, the E. Clifford Samuels Space Station turned on its lights and took control of the *Belle-Marie*. It's a modest operation by almost anybody's standards. Only six docking areas.

"Apparently they don't have much traffic," I said.

Alex was gazing quietly at the empty sky. "Look around," he said. "Where would you go?"

Samuels was more like a government station than a commercial operation. Customs and immigration had of course scanned and interviewed us on our approach. We submitted medical histories, completed forms, and answered questions about why we were visiting Salud Afar, how long we intended to stay, and whether we'd be working. We were issued visitors' visas and warned against performing any kind of remunerative work without getting permission. Later, we heard that they were procedures left over from the days of the Bandahr.

When we'd finished, we checked in by link with Central Reserve. Because of the time required to communicate between Salud Afar and Rimway, Alex had established a local corporate account for us. We activated it and wandered out into the concourse looking for a place to eat. They had one restaurant, Sandstone's, a few offices, a lounge, a gift shop, and not much else. We got sandwiches at Sandstone's.

We knew Vicki had landed in Marinopolis, but we'd just missed a shuttle into the capital. So we rode down instead to

Karmanda, a major commercial city not far away. The weather was rough, so it was a bumpy ride. Some of the passengers, including Alex, didn't look too good by the time we reached the spaceport. The captain apologized, hoped we were all feeling okay, and came out of the cockpit to smile at his passengers as they stumbled down the ramp. A middle-aged overweight bearded guy stood off to one side, checking faces against a reader. I knew immediately what that was about. He spotted Alex and was waiting for us in the terminal.

"Mr. Benedict?" He waved a hand as if he were an old friend. "Mr. Benedict? May I have a moment of your time?"

He wore a drab gray jacket with a lapel button featuring a star and a sphere. He had a wide-brimmed hat, pushed jauntily back on his head. "My name's Rob Peifer. I'm with Global." He smiled at me, signaling he had no clue who I was but was glad to see me anyhow. "Welcome to Salud Afar."

"Thank you," said Alex. He looked my way. "Global's one of the major news agencies."

"We're the best there is, Mr. Benedict. But"—he waved it away as a matter of relative inconsequence—"I was wondering if you could take a moment to tell me what brings you all the way out here? Is there a mysterious artifact involved, maybe? Or a lost world?" He leaned forward, inviting a provocative reply.

Alex smiled politely. "We're just here on vacation, Mr. Peifer. Just want to see the sights."

"You're not on the track of anything?"

"No. We're just hoping to enjoy ourselves."

"Would you tell me if you *were*? On the track of something?"

Alex thought about it. "Sure."

"Okay."

"We're just here on vacation."

"You sent some inquiries out about Vicki Greene—?"

"We're fans."

"She just underwent a personality transplant."

"That's correct."

"It wouldn't have anything to do with your visit?"

"No. Not really."

"All right. I'll just say you had no comment."

"Mr. Peifer, do what you like." We started to move away, but Peifer stayed with us.

"You think it happened here, huh?"

"What happened here?"

"Whatever sent her over the edge."

"I told you we're here on vacation."

"Okay. Stick with your story." He paused. "You want me to say nothing about your being here?"

Alex shrugged. "It doesn't matter to us." He looked at me and I shrugged. "Mr. Peifer," he said casually, "did you by any chance meet Vicki Greene when she came here? Were you standing at the terminal for her, too?"

He nodded. "Sure. She was really something." He shook his head. "I heard what happened to her. That *is* why you're here, isn't it?"

"What can you tell us about her?"

"Mr. Benedict, I'll be happy to answer your questions. But only if we can make a deal."

"And that would be?"

"You and Vicki Greene together would make a pretty big story. If you find out anything, you give me an exclusive."

Alex blinked a couple of times.

"You promise? It doesn't cost you anything."

"Sure. I don't see a problem with that."

Peifer gave us his code so we could reach him. Then: "She told me the same story you did. Said she'd come to Salud Afar as a tourist. That she'd always wanted to see how things looked outside the galaxy. She wasn't at all what I expected."

"How do you mean?"

"Horror writer? I thought she'd be dressed in black. That she'd be, you know, depressing."

"Did she say where she was going?"

"No. She said she hadn't made up her mind yet. She was going to visit oddball places."

"Oddball?"

"Her term, not mine."

"I don't understand. What's an oddball place?"

"I'm pretty sure she was talking about something with a haunted flavor."

"But no specifics?"

"No. She didn't want to tell me where she was going because she figured I might start showing up." He looked puzzled. "She looked too innocent to be the same woman who wrote those books."

"You've read them, Rob?" I asked.

"A couple of them. They're scary."

We caught a glide train to the capital. The vegetation was striking. Usually, it is what it is. Lots of chlorophyll trying to get at the sun. But Salud Afar has giant flowers in a wide range of colors, though predominantly purple and yellow. The blossoms are bigger than I am. Gravity's light, so everything gets taller. In some areas, we could not see the sky for them.

The towns themselves were quaint. A bit old-fashioned. The architecture might almost have been out of Rimway's Kalasian era, two centuries ago. It made me feel as if we'd done some time-traveling.

It was midmorning when we arrived at the capital.

Marinopolis was a study in dazzling architecture and planning: sunlit towers and broad avenues and sculpted air bridges and wide parks. Water was everywhere: It ran through conduits, spurted from fountains, spilled from flumes. Glowing walkways were crowded. Monuments to the heroes of the revolution were still being put in place. Despite all that, or probably because of it, there was still the flavor of another time.

We checked into the Blue Gable Hotel. Alex had made appointments to talk with a few of the people who'd responded to our appeal. While he did that, I sat down with the hotel AI and started to search the archives for Vicki Greene. Mostly I was looking for general news. But I also kept an eye open for dead bodies.

Other than an announcement of her arrival in Marinopolis, there wasn't much. A few speaking engagements. Some signings. A couple of interviews that told me nothing. Alex was in his room talking over the link with one of the contacts. I decided I was hungry so I left a note and went down to the hotel restaurant for an early lunch. When I got back, he was out of the building, gone to visit a book dealer.

It was a warm day, and they had a rooftop pool. One of the nice things about pools is that, when you're trying to make a gravity adjustment, they're exactly what you need. So I changed into my swimsuit and went topside. But things were a bit more freewheeling in Marinopolis than they were at home. Topless bathing was in vogue. I drew a few disappointed stares, thought about it, and decided what the hell, a little exhibitionism can be good for the soul. I took a deep breath, and, as casually as I could, as if I did this sort of thing every day, I removed my top. Somebody applauded.

I draped it across the back of a chair and dived into the water. When I came back up, several guys were trying hard not to look directly at me. It was a little bit like hanging out with Mutes.

I didn't stay long. Exposure provides a kick, but it wears fast. As soon as I was out of sight of the pool I put my top back on. Then I rode the elevator up and checked the room again. Alex was still gone, so I went for a walk.

A pedestrian ramp, several kilometers long, skirted the edge of the ocean. This was the Seawalk. It was three blocks from the hotel and something about it rang a bell. When I asked in the hotel lobby, a young female staffer explained: "It's where Aramy Cleev was assassinated. Right down from here. Go to the Seawalk and turn right. One block. They have a marker."

Aramy Cleev had been the last in the line of dictators who'd run the Bandahriate. The assassination had happened in the early spring thirty-three years earlier. "He was shot by his own guards," she said. Her voice acquired an angry tone. "Pity it didn't happen sooner."

Like most colony worlds, Salud Afar began its calendar with the arrival of the first mission. In this case, it had been the *Aquila*, with William Corvier in charge. There was a statue of Corvier outside the hotel, although I learned later no one was certain precisely what he had looked like. Furthermore, the exact date of the initial landing was in doubt. The log had disappeared thousands of years before, and the range of estimates varied by as much as six centuries. But Salud Afar had made its best guess, and that became the year 1. It was now 4198.

The woman in the lobby was too young to have been alive at the time of the assassination, but the animosity was there all the same. That was when I started discovering that feelings about the former dictator still ran high. On both sides. There were some who would have liked to get him back.

The assassination had been followed by three years of turmoil, of revolution and counterrevolution. The Bandahriate, a worldwide polity, had split first into four states, and eventually, through evolution and a series of upheavals, into nine. Komalia emerged by 4184, a kind of corporate republic. Eventually, the states formed various cooperatives and reunited as the Coalition.

Komalia's executive authority, the Administrator, was Tau Kilgore, who also possessed some sort of senior status in the Coalition's Executive Authority. I listened to a political show while looking out at the ocean. *"He's not the brightest guy in the world,"* one panelist was saying.

"He means well," said another.

And a third: *"Everybody knows that, but he couldn't find his way out of a closet."*

"Doesn't matter, though," said the first panelist, a man with a deep voice, *"he's a vast improvement over Betsy."*

I didn't know who Betsy was.

The hotel entrance was on the third level. I was standing outside the front door, high enough off the ground to see the ocean, thinking what a lovely day it was, when I realized I couldn't *hear* the sullen roar that oceans always deliver. That struck me as odd until I remembered that Salud Afar had lost its moon.

People go on about how spooky a thousand-year-old derelict ship might be, or an ancient space station adrift in the middle of nowhere, or a city left behind by a vanished civilization. But nothing ever chilled my heart quite like standing near that beach at Salud Afar looking out at an ocean and hearing only dead silence.

I spent an hour on the Seawalk. The salt air was invigorating, and mostly I was thinking how good it was to be out in the sunlight again. People were strolling past, and kids charged up and down with balloons.

A couple of guys made passes at me, and, while I was ordering a sweet bun, a boy who was about eight whispered to his mother that I talked "funny."

Alex called and asked whether I'd eaten yet. Well, then, would I care to join him anyhow? So we met at a place called Morey's on the Seawalk, and I sat and sucked on a plate of red fruit with a lemony taste while he explained how he'd learned nothing from the people he'd talked to. They'd all seen Vicki within days of her arrival. She'd seemed fine, not especially anxious about anything. Nobody knew where she'd gone from here. There was only one person left to interview, Cirilla Kopaleski, and we'd see her tomorrow.

He was putting away a plate of bacon, eggs, fried potatoes, and toast. Something was on his mind, but I let him get to it in his own time. We talked about what a beautiful city Marinopolis was. Andiquar, by contrast, looked almost mundane.

"Dictatorships tend to do that," he said. "Strongmen always have a taste for architecture." And finally he came to what had been bothering him: "The Mutes seem to be interested in Salud Afar."

"How do you mean?"

"There've been a number of incidents out here. Intrusions. Sightings of Mute warships insystem."

"That's odd. What interest could the Mutes possibly have in *this* place?"

"That's exactly what I've been wondering, Chase."

"What kind of intrusions?"

"No shooting incidents. As far as I can tell, the Mutes have just been tracking fleet vessels."

"Why would they do that? It makes no military sense."

"Don't know. I'm not a military tactician."

"What kind of fleet does Salud Afar have?"

He scooped some jelly onto his toast. "I gather it's pretty small. A dozen or so patrol vessels. And three destroyers."

"That's it?"

He nodded.

"Well," I said, "I don't think they need to worry. An attack out here would probably provoke retaliation from the Confederacy."

He kept eating.

"The only reason I can imagine is that they're trying to intimidate the locals."

"Could be."

I slushed down a piece of my red fruit. "Okay," I said. "Why do we care?"

"We don't."

"Then why's it bothering you?"

"It's not bothering me."

"It's on your mind."

"The incidents started while Vicki Greene was here. In fact, just shortly before she left." He looked out at the crowds wandering past on the Seawalk. A dark-haired woman who could have profited from some clothes strolled past and caught his eye. He started pretending nothing unusual was going on.

"You're not suggesting there's a connection?"

"No. Of course not."

"Then why—?"

"It's just a coincidence. But I went back years and couldn't find another instance of an incursion. Not one. And suddenly we're getting all these sightings."

"How many?"

"Well, four."

"That's not exactly a rash."

"It is when there weren't any previous ones during the whole of recorded history. When you're a zillion light-years away from the Assemblage."

More half-dressed women paraded by. He gave up trying to hide his interest and laughed. "Sorry," he said. "It's hard to concentrate here."

seveN

Do not let them mislead you. Your fate is indeed written in the stars.

—*Wish You Were Here*

The Mainline Distribution Services not only saw that Vicki Greene's work was made available, but they also handled the public relations. Its headquarters operated out of a gleaming structure that soared into a steeple, located in a park complex that it shared with IQ, Inc., which sold, serviced, reprogramed, and replaced AIs. (And claimed to be run by AIs.)

Cirilla Kopaleski occupied a suite near the top. We were ushered in by an impeccably dressed young man who smiled too much. Kopaleski was seated on a long, lush sofa, looking through a folder. She glanced up as we entered, raised a hand inviting us to be patient, turned another page, made a face, and closed the folder. "Sorry," she said. "It seems as if we can never get things right the first time around."

She was a tall, stately woman with gray hair, a trim body, and the presence of a queen. She put the folder down with a resigned sigh. "Come in," she said. "Please make yourselves comfortable. You're here about Vicki Greene?" She shook her head sadly. "Can I get you something to drink?"

"Sure," Alex said.

I decided to try something called a *carolla*. She pushed a tab and relayed the request. "So tell me what happened," she said.

Alex gave what had now become our standard answer: "That's what we're trying to find out."

"We're going to miss her," she said. "And not only because it will hit us in the pocketbook, but she was genuinely likable. I can't understand it. She had everything to live for. Whatever could have possessed her?"

"Ms. Kopaleski, it might help if you tell us what you can about her visit. When did she first contact you?"

"I knew in advance she was coming."

"You mean to Salud Afar?"

"Yes." She was wearing an emerald-colored blouse and white slacks. "She let me know before she left Rimway."

"Had you met her before?"

"No." She shook her head sadly. "We connected right away. She went to dinner with us, with me and my husband. She was a good woman. Not often you meet someone that talented who hasn't let it go to her head."

The drinks arrived. We were in a place where everything was unfamiliar. I had no idea what was in the glass, so I took it cautiously. It was okay, but I decided I wouldn't have any more.

Kopaleski picked up her glass, sipped from it, studied it in the daylight that fell through a set of blinds. "It's a disaster."

Alex bowed slightly. "For everyone concerned," he said. "May I ask what services Mainline provides for its writers?"

"We handle distribution and publicity, arrange their appearances, and so on. And, if they wish, arrange quarters."

"Did you do that for Vicki?"

"Yes. I set her up at the Schuyler Inn."

"That's here in Marinopolis?"

"Yes."

"How long did she stay? In town?"

"I can check. But I think she was here only two or three days." She consulted a display and nodded. "Three days." She gave us the dates, which, since they were expressed in the local calendar, meant nothing to me.

But apparently Alex had done his homework. "That would have been immediately after her arrival from Rimway," he said.

"That's correct. I'd set everything up in advance."

"Did you see her the first night?"

"The second."

"How did she look?"

"How do you mean?"

"Did she seem upset? Depressed? Bothered by anything?"

She shook her head. "She seemed perfectly fine to me. I don't know if you've ever met her, but she's very energetic. Laughs all the time. She certainly seemed to be looking forward to her stay."

"Did she tell you why she'd come?"

"She said she'd never been to Salud Afar, and she wanted to do some touring."

"That's it? Nothing more?"

"That's all I can recall. Why? Do you think what she did to herself is connected with her visit here?"

"I don't know, Ms. Kopaleski. Did you have any contact with her after she'd left?"

"I got a posting from her several days later. She said she was enjoying herself and wished I were there." She smiled. "You know the routine. But that was all."

"Do you still have the posting?"

"Yes, I'm sure we do."

"Might it be possible for us to take a look?

"Of course," she said. "Mr. Benedict—"

"*Alex* is good."

"Alex, I know who you are. Your reputation has preceded you even out here. Marvelous work with that Margolia business last year."

"Thank you."

"I'm glad you're looking into this. It's just a terrible loss. Where will we ever find another like her?"

She gave instructions to her AI, and Vicki Greene appeared in the center of the room. She looked the way Molly Black had looked in those jungle adventures we'd all grown up with: intense eyes, sharp features, a scrambler strapped to her hip, and a devil-be-damned attitude. She wore khaki shorts with enormous cargo pockets and a gray pullover top. She had a billed sun cap, with an "M" mounted prominently on it. A red scarf was slung casually around her neck, and sunglasses shaded her eyes.

"Hello, Cirilla," she said. *"Greetings from Boldinai Point, Home of the Undead. I got here yesterday and went to see Barryman's Tomb last night. I'm sorry to report that local myth to the contrary, everything was quiet. Here's a look at it."* She vanished and was replaced by a stone block. A grave marker. But a big one. Someone had inscribed on its side the legend LIE STILL. The imager moved back to give us a wider view. The block lay in the middle of a cemetery. *"This is it. The locals insist this is all that keeps him in his grave. Anyhow, having a great time. See you when I get back."*

She gave us a wide, self-satisfied smile. The world in her lap.

"But you never heard from her again?"

"No. Of course, there was really no business reason for her to contact me. And I assumed she was otherwise occupied."

"What's Barryman's Tomb?" I asked.

Kopaleski was delighted to tell us the story: "Forrest Barryman lived four centuries ago. He died in an experiment gone wrong, Chase. A treatment that was supposed to make him a supercop or something. But according to local tradition, he wouldn't *stay* dead. Eventually they put that rock over his grave to keep him in it."

I looked at Alex.

Alex smiled. "Okay."

She maintained a neutral expression. "Don't be too sure. Boldinai Point is a strange place. Over the years, there've been other odd claims."

"Like what?" I asked.

"They have a beach that seems to encourage suicide. People with no reason to kill themselves go down there and walk into the water. It happened again just last year. The locals stay away from it. And then there's a patch of forest—"

"Hold on," said Alex. "Let's stay with Vicki. She said she'd see you when she got back. But she left without getting in touch."

"That's correct. Next I heard she was back on Rimway."

We sat looking at one another. "You didn't make any effort

to contact her after the message from Boldinai Point? Do I have that right?"

"Yes, that's correct. Alex, she's an important client. I didn't want to seem intrusive."

"Of course. Did you try to get in touch with her after she'd left?"

"No. I had no reason to. I knew if she needed me, she'd contact me."

Alex got up. "Thanks, Cirilla. We appreciate your time."

"I hope I've been some help."

"Where's Boldinai Point?"

She had the AI show us. "If there's anything else I can do, please don't hesitate to contact me." She gave us her private code. "By the way," she added, "if you find out what this is all about, I'd appreciate it if you let me know."

I set up our trip to Boldinai Point. That evening, while Alex buried himself in a book, I went back to the ocean. When I was a kid, the big thrill in my life came every summer when we took the train to Seaside. We built sand castles and played in the surf with a beach ball. But I especially loved going out in the evening and seeing the ocean at night. I can still remember standing on a place they called Gorgon's Pier and looking at the stars.

So that night, in that very distant place, I did it again. It was a way to feel at home, I suppose. But the sky above that ocean was different. There was only a single star.

Callistra.

I wondered what might have happened had a sentient race developed on that world. How they would have perceived that single bright light peering down at them. It was a beautiful star, its azure glow amplified by the dark night surrounding it.

The eye of a compassionate deity, perhaps.

I wondered whether Vicki Greene had stood out there, perhaps in the same place. What would she have thought? She with her vampires and demons, under so striking a sky?

eiGHT

Yes, Colton. It is quite true that we enjoy the sun, that it illumi-
nates our lives, and serves as a metaphor for all that is good. But
the reality is that we *love* the night. It is where all women are
beautiful, where the imagination has free rein, where plots are
hatched and terrible things happen. And we would have it no
other way.

—*Love You to Death*

Boldinai Point was best known for its cemetery. Maybe it was
the only claim to fame the place had.

It was located in an area called the Outland, on a large island
a quarter of the way around the globe. We caught a morning
flight and landed three hours later in a coastal city. From there
we rode a gravity train inland to Boraka. We stayed there overnight, and in the morning rented a skimmer, sat back, and let
the AI take us the rest of the way to Boldinai Point.

It was rough country. Dry, flat, sandy, with lots of rock. To
the west, a chain of mountains cut across the horizon. The Point
itself is a town of about four thousand. I couldn't imagine how
the term *Point* had gotten into the name. It was located in the
middle of nowhere.

It had a distinction, though. It was one of the few places
where people had been relatively free under the Bandahriate.
Though it had been part of Cleev's domain, it was a long way
from the center of power, and so small as to be apparently not

worth worrying about. So it was the place where, for three centuries, rebels and malcontents and renegade scientists had retreated. It looked remote enough that they wouldn't have been able to cause any trouble, so the dictator might have been just as happy.

Salud Afar did not have—and still does not have, so far as I know—the minimum payout system that allows a citizen to loaf for a lifetime if he so desires. No one in power on that world had thought it was a good idea, so they never incorporated it. There, you worked or you became dependent on the charity of others. Or worse. As Alex and I descended into that lonely place, I wondered how the inhabitants made their living.

The Point was a collection of weatherworn buildings erected along a small series of cross streets. Its celebrated cemetery was located north of town. From the air, it had looked like every other cemetery I'd seen, just a collection of markers inside an iron fence. Outside the fence, the land was flat and gray and ran unimpeded to the horizon.

The hotel and the restaurant were crowded. "I guess it's a fairly prosperous tourist spot," said Alex.

"Is there something I'm missing?" I asked. "Or is it just the cemetery?"

"I think it's just the cemetery," he said. "And don't get that look on your face. It's not every town that has an unquiet grave."

The elderly owner of a souvenir store told us the story: "Peter Cleev started it."

"Cleev?" Alex said. "One of the dictators?"

"Four centuries ago. He got upset because some of his enforcers were being killed by rebels. So he launched a program to develop a better enforcer. Somebody you couldn't take down with just a shot or two from a scrambler. He wanted something that wouldn't feel pain."

"Are you serious?" asked Alex.

"Do I look as if I'd lie to you?" The shopkeeper laughed and showed us a print of Peter Cleev. Long, thin guy with a pointed beard and satanic eyes. The evil emperor right out of an over-the-top HV. "He didn't want anybody to know about it because it would undermine his image. The Cleevs thought the rest of

us were damn fools. Thought we believed they were compassionate, easygoing types who only had the welfare of their
people at heart.

"It's why they always had to have people around them who
smiled a lot. The world, under the Bandahr, was relentlessly
happy. Or else.

"So he sent a team out here to produce his—" He tried to
think of the term.

"—Android," said Alex.

"Android, yes. And the townspeople watched as a lab and
support facility were set up on Route One."

"Route One?" I said.

"That's it running through the center of town."

"It's the only road you have."

"That's right. Route One. You know, if you're going to keep
interrupting—"

"No. Please. Go on."

"Okay. Anyhow, when they got everything built, the lights
burned all night, and they started burying stuff in unmarked
graves at the back of the cemetery."

"Experiments gone wrong?" asked Alex.

The shopkeeper nodded solemnly, as if the truth was to go
no further than the three of us. As if it were something for
which the world was not yet ready. "Yes," he said. "That's exactly what they were burying. They brought prisoners in at
night and did their goddam experiments. And they stayed at it
until they succeeded. Or thought they had.

"Forrest Barryman was a high-school history teacher when
they grabbed him and brought him here. He'd said something
in one of his classes. Or somebody thought he did, and that was
enough. They made him proof against most small weapons.
Made him so he didn't feel pain. But Forrest, he didn't like
what they'd done to him, so he got loose one night and tore up
the lab. And tore up some of his tormentors, too.

"Then he took out the security people and disappeared into
the woods. By then he'd gone crazy. One night he came into
town and went on a rampage, strangling and beating everybody
he saw. They couldn't stop him. Eventually, an enraged mob
was able to drive him out. They tracked him into the nearby

hills, took a few more casualties, and finally brought him down with a plasma shell.

"They buried him in the cemetery, along with their own dead. Members of his family were notified, and several came for the service. They were horrified to hear what had happened. Forrest had simply vanished. Nobody had known what had happened to him. When it got out that *he* was behind it, Cleev had been so worried he went public and denied the story. Claimed it was renegade scientists. Within a week of the burial, somebody descended on the ruined lab and removed everything that could connect it with the government."

"My God," I said. "Is that really true? Did that actually happen?"

The shopkeeper's eyes were gray. His hair was also gray, and his skin was sallow. I remember thinking that he needed to get away from the souvenir shop. Get away from the cemetery.

"It gets worse," he said.

"What else happened?" asked Alex.

"Several weeks after they took down the lab, something attacked the town again. They didn't know what it was. But they started finding bodies. Beaten to death. Clubbed. Strangled. Witnesses swore it was Barryman. A reporter went out to the cemetery."

"The grave was empty," said Alex.

"Yes."

That part of the story I'd heard before we left Marinopolis.

"They asked for help from the authorities. But they just laughed. And so did the media, which, in those days, wasn't worth a damn anyhow. So the town got up an action committee. They went out after him, tracked him down a second time, and killed him again. Everybody agreed it was the same person. This time, they encased the body in concrete before putting it in the ground. They brought in a priest to perform an exorcism ceremony, and they put a stone block on top of the burial site to keep him in his grave."

Had the shopkeeper by any chance seen Vicki Greene? Had she actually come to town?

"Who?" he asked.

So we moved on. To one of the town's two restaurants. The

hostess was tall and looked a bit too sensible to be living in a place like Boldinai Point. I doubted the town had much in the way of prospects. As we were getting seated, I asked whether there was anything to the Barryman story, no kidding, and she said sure, where had I been all my life? "I'll tell you something else," she added. "There's a connection of some sort with Callistra."

"With Callistra?"

"Most times you go out there, everything's quiet. But do it at night, when the star's directly overhead, and you can *feel* that thing trying to break out of its tomb."

Welcome to Boldinai Point.

We picked a hotel, but it was full. *"Try the Hamel,"* they said.

The Hamel was okay, but it wasn't the luxurious kind of place Alex liked. They didn't have suites available, so we checked into separate rooms. During the process, Alex asked the AI whether she knew who Vicki Greene was.

"Oh, yes, sir," she said. *"She's very popular at the Point."*

"Can you tell me whether she showed up here during the past year?"

"That's private information, sir," she said. *"I'm sorry, but I'm not permitted to speak of such matters. I can check to see whether she's staying at this hotel now, if you like."*

We tried calling the *Point Man*, which was the local journal. She *had* been here, had in fact stayed at the Hamel, had "starred at a special event for delighted visitors," during which she'd spoken about why people want to believe in the supernatural. She'd signed books, including some bound collector's editions, and had "joined a number of her readers at a raucous party."

She'd also submitted to an interview, which the *Point Man* made available. As before, she looked fine.

Q: *Ms. Greene, why have you come to the Point?*
A: *It's a special place, Henry. I've always wanted to come here.*
Q: *Are you working on your next book?*
A: *I'm always working on my next book.* (Laughs.)
Q: *Would you want to tell us what it's about?*

A: *It's still in its early stages.*
Q: *Can you give us the title?*
A: *The working title is* The Devil's Eye.
Q: *You're visiting the Point?*
A: *Yes. That seems to be true.*
Q: *Can I guess that means you're writing about Forrest Barryman?*
A: *You can certainly guess.*
Q: *Would I be right?*
A: (Smiles.) *Honestly, Henry, it's in the air. I'm still making up my mind.*

"She seems upbeat," I said. This Vicki bore little resemblance to the woman who'd sent that original transmission to us.

"Whatever the problem is," Alex said, "it hasn't happened yet."

We watched the rest of the interview. When asked what she planned to do while she was in town, Vicki said she just intended to look around. *"This is a nice place. I'd like to just take it easy."*

"Will you be visiting the Tomb?"

"Oh, I don't think so, Henry. It's a bit scary out there."

There was a Barryman Museum. And Graveyard Books. And the Occult Transit Company, which provided virtual trips into the hereafter. You could get shirts with a picture of the monster on them. A sim that dramatized the event. A hologram of the monster itself stood in front of the gift shop. A family were getting their pictures taken beside it when we arrived. Everybody seemed to be doing a thriving business.

We went looking for people who might have seen Vicki Greene. Everybody at the Point seemed to be a fan of horror fiction. Most of the locals we talked to said yes, they'd heard she'd been in town. Most said they'd seen her, and several even claimed to have talked with her. But nobody was particularly helpful. Several told us she'd been writing about the Barryman Monster. "Why else would she have come here?" one demanded. The word that she'd been lost hadn't gotten around, and her fans were reluctant to believe the news.

On the whole, we had trouble finding reliable sources. The details didn't match. Vicki was described as wearing different clothes. Her hair was a different color. Sometimes she spoke with an accent, sometimes she didn't.

We asked whether they believed that the Barryman story had any basis in fact. I thought we'd find some skepticism there, especially among the kids. But no. Of course it had happened. Ask anybody. Or go out to the cemetery when Callistra's in the sky.

They ran tours out to Barryman's grave during the daylight hours, using a light-grav bus marked ANDROID LOCAL. When I asked the hotel host whether there was a night tour, he looked startled. "Absolutely not, young lady. Nobody goes out there at night. It's not allowed."

He couldn't quite resist a smile.

They picked us up at the hotel, made one more stop, and headed north to the cemetery. About fifteen of us were on board, half of whom were kids. It was a holiday crowd, full of laughter, and I could hear a little girl saying, "Is it really true, Mommy?"

"No, darling," Mommy said. "There are no such things as ghosts."

Alex looked for his chance to show the tour guide a picture of Vicki. "Do you recall whether she ever rode with you?"

"Mister," he said, "do you have any idea how many people go out there?"

We passed through the town and drove about three kilometers on a flat straight road. Turned right onto a cutoff. And approached a pair of iron gates. They swung open for us. (As a security measure, they were of doubtful use because the fence was broken in any number of places.)

The cemetery was old. Markers dated back more than six hundred years, to the beginning of the Bandahriate. The tour guide, a middle-aged guy who was trying his best to look nervous, told us the town advisory committee was talking about putting the cemetery off-limits to visitors, because everybody knew it was just a matter of time before Forrest Barryman broke loose from his grave and nobody knew what he might do then.

He looked around at the children, some of whom giggled while others nestled closer to their mothers. "Of course, most of us at the Point think they're worried over nothing," he said with a straight face. "But you know how people are. One restless grave's enough to give the entire town a bad name."

Alex leaned my way. "You look a little nervous, Chase."

Anything to put me on the defensive. I smiled at him and let it go.

The cemetery was a dusty, dry place, not at all like the green, almost lush graveyard near the Country House back on Rimway. Signs reading DO NOT APPROACH AFTER DARK were posted throughout the area.

"I don't think I'd want to bury anybody here that I cared about," I said.

Alex looked past me, and I could have predicted his response: "At the end, I can't imagine it matters much."

A burst of wind rocked the bus. "Forrest is quiet in the daytime," said our tour guide. "Nothing to worry about." The bus made its way among the headstones. Eventually we topped a low hill, and the block came into view. It was higher than I could have reached and half as long as the bus.

We swung into a parking area, and the doors opened. The tour guide was first off the bus. He helped the ladies navigate down, lent a hand to the kids, all the while explaining that we were perfectly safe, that there was nothing to worry about in the daytime. "It's only active when Callistra is in the sky." He drew the word *Callistra* out, rolling the consonants and savoring the vowels. The guy really enjoyed his work.

"They're putting on a nice show," whispered Alex.

The LIE STILL inscription was, of course, the first thing that caught my eye. There was another inscription, on the far side, consisting of three rows of unfamiliar symbols. "They're Arrakesh," the tour guide explained. "They're from the *Enkomia*, which is an ancient text that some people think is sacred. The first line translates to his name, Forrest Barryman. The second is the date of his first burial. And the bottom says *Gone to Glory*." He touched the rock cautiously. "We certainly hope so," he added.

"Why the strange language?" I asked.

"It's supposed to help keep him in the ground," he said. "Most of the people who lived here at the time were Travelers. They were the faithful. Their name came out of their emphasis on the notion of life as a journey from a wicked world to salvation. If you look around, you'll notice quite a few of the graves have a star emblem. Those are the Travelers."

"Callistra," said a woman behind me.

"That's correct," said the guide. "Travelers believed Callistra was God's star, placed in the heavens as a sign of His presence."

The star, of course, was central to a number of that world's religions although I didn't know that at the time.

The site seemed peaceful enough. The block would have required a good-sized antigrav engine to move it. "He's not really at rest," said the guide, who was obviously not one to let go of a good thing. "If you come out here on a windy night, which is strictly prohibited, by the way, but come out here anyway, when Callistra is directly overhead, you can hear him down there, trying to get free."

There was a big bald-headed guy who asked him to stop. "You're scaring the kids," he said.

When we'd finished at the cemetery, the tour bus took us out to look at the android laboratory. It was a cluster of small buildings with specimen tables and tubs and exotic-looking equipment. It was, the driver explained, not the real lab, which had gone away centuries ago. But it *was* an "accurate replica." "Furthermore," he said, "this *is* the ground on which it stood."

He continued as if everything were still standing. Here and over there were the quarters of the scientists, directly to your right the dining room. The main laboratory itself was the one-story white building on your right. He stopped in front of it. "Some of the damage was done by the government when it came to recover whatever might connect it with the monster. We think it was the creature itself, though, that really leveled the place."

"They must think we're all idiots," I told Alex.

"No, no. It's all showbiz. They know no one buys it, but what they want is a momentary suspension of disbelief. Like in a sim. Kick back and enjoy yourself, Chase."

"Okay."

"Of course, who really knows?"

"About things like this? Would you please stop? You've been reading Greene's books again, haven't you?" He smiled, and we both had a good laugh. "Seriously, though, I wonder whether the story has any basis in fact? Whether they might have tried to build androids out here?"

He shrugged. "Sure. They might have tried to put together a better cop. In a dictatorship, you'd pretty much expect it. It's what makes technology so scary, Chase. Sometimes, the wrong people get to make use of it."

"You think Vicki took this tour?"

"You think there's any chance in the world she came all the way out here and *didn't* take the tour?"

For a long minute I kept my peace. Then: "How about we come back out tonight?"

"Where? *Here?*"

"Yes. *Here.*"

"Why?"

"Because that's what Vicki would have done. She would have wanted to *feel* the emotional impact of the android story. And the grave at night was part of that impact. I doubt she could have resisted it."

"You're probably right, Chase. But I don't see any point in pushing this any further. What we need to do is find out where she went from here."

"That seems like cheating. I think we should repeat the experience."

"You really want to do this, don't you?"

"Yes," I said. "I'd like to be here when the star gets overhead. That's the way she'd have done it."

"Chase—"

"We came to repeat the experience. To do what *she* did. It seems to me, this might be at the center of things."

"Okay." His voice was resigned. "If you insist."

I shook my head. "No."

"No what?"

"I'll go alone."

"Why?"

"Because she did."

"Chase, you're not fooling anybody."

"What do you mean, Alex?"

"You're still a little kid."

He didn't like the idea. It's dangerous, he said. No place for a woman. Who knows who's hanging around out there at that time of night? There might even be predators in the area. I told him not to worry, that I'd call him if anything out of the ordinary happened. Anyhow, I was armed. I'd bought a 21k scrambler, which I would have with me. "But," I told him, "you might want to keep a plasma gun handy in case there really is a monster running loose."

He said something along the lines of how I needed to work on my sense of humor.

When Callistra had risen prominently into the center of the sky, I fought my way through another series of cautionary admonitions from Alex, went up to the roof, and took the skimmer back to the cemetery.

It's an even drearier place at night. There was no light, save the soft blue evanescence cast over the headstones and monuments by the lone star. I landed in the parking area, about thirty meters from the grave site. A strong wind was blowing out of the west and carrying a lot of dust with it. I climbed out, turned on my lamp, and walked over to the grave. Something moved off to my right, on the edge of vision. A couple of teens, trying to walk and make out at the same time. They disappeared behind a mausoleum.

I shut off the lamp and stood in the silence, broken only by the drone of insects. The block gleamed in the starlight. I'd expected to be able to see the town lights, but there was only a soft glow in the trees to the south. A warm breeze kicked up.

I pictured Vicki standing at that identical spot, listening to the darkness. And she had to be thinking how she might recreate that place, how she could use it. In her *Point Man* interview, she'd mentioned *The Devil's Eye* as a working title. I looked up at the blue star. It was the wrong color. But that night, in the presence of the oversized marker, color didn't matter.

I wondered whether she'd been at all nervous. Or whether

she delighted in an experience like that. Was that maybe why she'd come? Maybe it had nothing to do with planning a novel. Maybe she just liked the inner creep, the chill, that came with standing near a grave that people insisted was unquiet.

A set of lights appeared in the northwest, passed overhead, and descended toward the glow that marked the town.

I turned my lamp back on and looked at the symbols on the marker. *Forrest Barryman.*

Gone to Glory.

The rock and the Arrakesh characters had to be pure showbiz. Who knew what they really said? Whether they said anything at all? The whole town was an enterprise based on a fantasy. Like West Kobal on—where was it?—Black Adrian, where a sea monster with enormous tentacles was periodically reported. Or Bizmuth in the Spinners, where visitors from another galaxy were supposed to have crashed. (They and the wreckage had been spirited off by the government, which denied everything.)

There's even a place that claims to have a doorway into another dimension. They'll show you the doorway, it's in the side of a mountain, cut into solid rock, but conditions have to be exactly right to get through it, which, of course, they never are. Just as well: The locals claim no one has ever come back. But townspeople swear you can get a magnificent view of this other-dimensional place.

It was easy to imagine Vicki Greene standing there, thinking the same thoughts, wondering the same things. Possibly concluding that the answers didn't matter. That it was the uncertainty that counted.

I began, that night, to feel close to her. Until then, she'd struck me as a kind of opportunist, making money by writing about things that could never be. That I personally didn't care about. But it struck me that the vampires and Forrest Barryman and all the rest of it weren't imaginative creatures dreamed up to separate idiots from their money. That they reflected light into the darkest corners of what makes us human. There was, after all, a time when we did not comprehend the natural world, did not see the order. There was only a vast darkness, a world for which no one really knew the rules. Filled with phantoms snatching unwary travelers, perhaps. With angels moving stars, and gods riding the sun across the sky.

The ground moved.

It wasn't a tremor, exactly. More like a flutter, a barely noticeable palpitation.

My imagination, probably.

It came again.

I could see nothing, but I eased the scrambler out of my pocket and took a long look around.

I was alone. The teenagers seemed to have gone.

The block moved. Began to rise.

I shook my head. Stared as one end, the forward end, the end closer to me, lifted.

I'd like to say I stood my ground. I understood immediately it was an elaborate illusion for tourists brave enough to go out there at night. To feed the legend. But it didn't matter. My hair rose, and my heart started to pound. The bottom of the rock cleared the ground, and I could see something holding it, lifting it from beneath. An oversized blue-tinted hand appeared, pushing down on the ground while the slab kept going up.

I turned and ran. All the way back to the skimmer. I ordered the AI to open the hatch while I was still running. "Start the engine," I told it. My heart was coming out of my chest. The skimmer was already off the ground when I jumped on board.

NiNe

Reality is what hits you in the head when you don't watch where you're walking.

—*Wish You Were Here*

All right. I wouldn't have you think I'm a complete coward.

I went back a few minutes later, stayed in the skimmer, and looked down at the place from a safe altitude. The grave was quiet, and the block was flat on the ground again.

I set back down in the parking area, opened up, and got out. I checked the time and stood where I'd stood before. And waited. Until it started again.

I retreated to the lander and watched the routine play itself out. The hand, blue in the starlight, raising the slab, was as far as it went. Then it shut down.

I returned again to my chosen spot. And stood there. After about two minutes, it happened a third time.

I was on my way back to the Point when Alex called. *"Are you okay?"* he asked.

"Ummm. Yes. I'm fine."

"See any monsters?"

"Just the usual ones."

"Good. When will you be back?"

"Why?"

"So I know when to start worrying."

"I'll be there in a few minutes."
"Okay. Let me know when you get in."
"Alex?"
"Yes?"
"The people in this town can't be trusted."
"I'm shocked to hear it."

In the morning, I couldn't resist going down to the city hall. Alex tried to talk me out of it, but I was annoyed that they were playing tricks on their visitors. It was a run-down building, situated next to the courthouse and across the street from the police station. They had a human receptionist who looked as if she had more important things to do than talk to strangers. "Who did you want to see, ma'am?"

"The supervisor, please."

"Do you have an appointment?"

"No."

"I'm sorry. He's not available at the moment. How can we help you?"

"You know," I said, "somebody's going to have a heart attack out there."

"Out where?"

It went on like that for a while, but I finally managed to get past her to a staff assistant. He was no help either, and relayed me to an overfed guy in a large office that needed sweeping and dusting. He looked as if he'd been there forever. He had a bristling white mustache and an enormous bald skull. He smiled in a grandfatherly way, told me he was glad I'd come by, and pulled over a chair for me. His nameplate identified him as a Mr. Collander. "Ms. Kolpath," he said, "I'll put your comments on the record, and we'll look into it."

We sat there a moment, watching each other. He was giving me a chance to say thank you very much, shake his hand, and leave. "Mr. Collander," I said, "this doesn't bother you at all, does it?"

The smile stayed in place, but it acquired a regretful aspect. "I wish I could say I'm disturbed." He pressed his fingertips against his forehead. "But I won't lie to you. No, we've known about it for a while."

"In fact you put it there."

I looked up at a framed picture of him, two young girls, and a puppy. He was presenting them with an award. His eyes followed mine. "It's our annual Pet Appreciation Day," he said. "Look, Ms. Kolpath—May I call you *Chase*?"

"*Ms. Kolpath* will do fine."

"Ms. Kolpath, may I ask what you intend to do when you leave here?"

"I haven't decided yet."

"I can understand you were frightened."

"I wasn't frightened." Terrified would be closer to the truth. "So what happens now? That thing turns on every time someone goes out there?"

I'd gotten up, and he asked me to sit again. "I won't take much of your time," he said. "I'm sorry for your inconvenience. I truly am." He nodded toward the window. "Look around you. Boldinai Point is a small town. It has no major industry. We're isolated, and the only reason we exist at all is our tourist trade. If that were to go away, this town would dry up."

The guy was good. In retrospect, thinking about it, I wonder that I could have been put off so easily. But at the time, it was hard to argue with. "There's no harm done," he said. "We have monitors. If someone in ill health were to go out there, we'd intervene. But for most people who come here, Ms. Kolpath, it's just part of the show. It's what they expect. Look, I'm sorry you took any of it seriously. But nobody really believes there's an android up there being held in its grave by a rock. We *pretend* it's so, for our tourists." He took a deep breath. "Let me ask you a question: What would you have thought if you'd gone up there and nothing had happened?"

I was starting to feel like an idiot.

He smiled and told me I should come back and see him if I had any other problems. Then he was escorting me toward the door. "I hope you'll try to see our side of things, Ms. Kolpath. And while you're here at the Point, just relax and enjoy the ride." He offered me a gift certificate for the souvenir shops. And as I was going out, he smiled. "We've been in operation for sixty years. Never lost a tourist."

* * *

When I got back to the hotel, Alex looked up from a cup of the local brew and, with one of those complacent expressions, asked where I'd been.

"Just out walking."

He examined his cup and studied the notebook that lay on his lap. "Did they agree to dismantle the gear at the grave site?"

While I was considering my answer, he said I was just in time to go with him to meet with the organizer of a local reading club. His name was Dolf, and he was waiting for us at the Boldinai Point Library.

It was next door to the city hall. We went in and found him talking with one of the librarians. We did a round of introductions, then he led us to a room that served as a small auditorium.

He was a former police officer, and he admitted to having served during Bandahriate days. "But we weren't doing any of the stuff here that was going on in other places," he said. "We wouldn't have allowed it."

He was one of the tallest people I've ever seen, his height accentuated by a pronounced lankiness. He'd been blond at one time, but his hair was going gray. He wore a thick, unkempt mustache, and his eyes possessed the shrewdness of a professional cardplayer. He was well along in years and told us that horror fiction was one of those forbidden delights that made his life a pure pleasure.

"Did you know in advance Vicki Greene was coming?" Alex asked.

He was obviously not sure why we were asking the questions. I thought he'd mistaken us for a couple of fans. "No. Not really. We only found out a couple of days before she got here. We were notified, I think, by one of the book dealers in Korimba. He called the Graveyard—"

"The graveyard?" I asked.

"Graveyard Books. Our own shop."

"Oh."

"My understanding," he continued, "is that Korimba heard it from somebody at Spirit."

"The distributor," said Alex.

"Yes."

"How did you actually connect with her? With Ms. Greene?"

"We had no code and couldn't find a listing for her. But we knew when she was coming so we staked out the hotels. And Amelia, Louie Black's wife, spotted her walking into the lobby of the Hamel." He sat back and looked immensely pleased with himself. "She let us take her to lunch. Right over there." He pointed across the street to a modest café. The Tomb. "They put a couple of tables together." He corrected himself. "I don't mean she let us buy."

"Of course."

"We wanted to. But she insisted on paying her own."

"How'd she seem?"

"She's a funny lady. Doesn't take herself seriously. And, man, she sure likes her dessert." He apparently hadn't heard the news yet.

"Dolf, do you know how long she stayed at the Point?"

"Three or four days. Why do you ask?"

Alex hesitated, then told him what had happened. He listened, shook his head, seemed genuinely saddened.

"Did she tell you where she intended to go when she left here?"

He shook his head. "No. I can check with the others. See if she might have mentioned it to any of them."

"Okay. Yes, I'd appreciate it if you did that. Did you see her at all after the lunch?"

"No." He didn't need to think about it. "No. Next we heard, she was gone."

"Did she tell you why she'd come here?"

"Sure." The smile came back. "She said she wanted to meet Barryman."

Dolf called back that night. He'd talked with the others. "When she left here," he said, "she told a couple of our people she was going to Bessarlik."

"Bessarlik? What's that?"

He laughed. We didn't know? "It's the Haunted Forest."

TEN

My advice to you, Grimly, is to do the sensible thing: Hide.

—*Etude in Black*

Living in a different world always takes some adjustment. Your weight is usually different. Not by a lot, but it's amazing what the sudden acquisition or loss of a few pounds can do. Time is inevitably a problem. It's never been possible, despite some effort, to standardize the measurements. Hours on Salud Afar are longer than at home, and minutes are shorter. I won't try to explain that. Suffice it to say that a day in Boldinai Point, defined as a complete turn on the planetary axis, is almost two standard hours longer than the one we were accustomed to. The result was that our sleeping patterns quickly went berserk.

The biggest adjustment, though, was the food. Most of it was unfamiliar and tended to be flat. We stuck as closely as we could to items that were at least reasonable facsimiles of what we got on Rimway. Nobody cares about the details of any of this, but the reader should be aware that when I refer, say, to bacon or eggs, I'm not really talking about the homegrown stuff so much as an approximation. And the coffee, by the way, never really got close.

We were finishing a pseudobreakfast next morning when Alex got a call. *"Mr. Benedict?"*

"Yes."

"Mr. Benedict, I'm calling for Dr. Wexler."

"Who?"

"Dr. Mikel Wexler. He's with the history department at Marikoba University. He'd like very much to have a few moments of your time. Will you be available later this morning?"

"What does Dr. Wexler want to talk about?"

"I believe it has to do with Vicki Greene."

"I'm available now."

"He's in conference at the moment, sir. Would ten o'clock be satisfactory?"

We did a quick search on Wexler.

He was one of the heroes of the Resistance, the underground movement that had fought Cleev's government for years. He'd been captured, tortured, and eventually broken out by his comrades in a celebrated escape. When the Coalition came to power, he took up a teaching career, and was now chairman of the history department at Marikoba.

He was the author of *Rebel on the Shore*, an account of those turbulent years. And served as an occasional advisor to Administrator Kilgore. Alex took an hour to read sections of the book. "I'll say one thing for him," he said. "He gives most of the credit to other people."

We took the call in one of the hotel's conference rooms. Alex introduced me as his associate, and Wexler commented gallantly that he wished he had so lovely a partner. Usually that kind of comment puts me on guard, but he seemed sincere.

He was a congenial guy, almost leisurely, but there was something in his eyes that suggested you wouldn't want him angry. And his manner implied that he understood his likeness would one day join the statues of the heroes in Marinopolis. He spoke with the assurance of someone accustomed to making decisions. And I could see that he worked out. He had thick gray hair and the kind of chiseled features that suggest an inner strength. He was, I thought, the kind of guy I'd want at my back if I got in trouble. *"If you don't mind my saying so,"* he continued, *"I think this young lady has played a major part in your success."*

I probably blushed.

"You're absolutely correct," said Alex. "Don't know what I'd do without her."

There was another minute or so of social fencing. Then Wexler came to the point: *"I just found out the other day about Vicki Greene. It's a pity. What on earth would possess her to do such a thing?"*

Alex gave the standard reply: "It was what we hoped to find out."

"Yes. I wish you luck." His brow furrowed. *"Did you expect to find the answer on Salud Afar?"*

"Don't know."

"If you don't mind my asking—"

"Go right ahead, Dr. Wexler."

"Mikel, if you please. You might consider me something of a fan. I'm curious how this became of interest to you."

Alex told him about the message.

They're all dead.

"Who's all dead?"

"We have no idea."

"What a strange, cryptic business. So how do you plan to proceed, if you don't mind my asking?"

"We thought we'd begin by following in her footsteps."

"I suppose that's as good a course as any."

I noticed a cane propped against the side of Wexler's chair. A souvenir, perhaps, of Cleev's dungeons.

"Mikel," said Alex, "what's *your* connection with her?"

"I met her at Samuels. When she was leaving."

"You knew her, then?"

"I knew her from her pictures. I've been one of her readers since she started her career. I don't usually admit that, but— Well, anyhow, I knew she was in the area and that she was about to leave." He was seated in a dark blue fabric chair. Behind him, two windows opened out onto what was probably the university campus. *"I arranged to be on the station."*

"Did you get a chance to talk with her?"

"Yes. For a few minutes."

"How did she seem?"

"How do you mean?"

"Did she seem upset? Depressed?"

"Not at all. She wasn't what I expected. I thought someone who wrote horror books would be—Well, you know. But she wasn't like that. Not at all." He smiled. *"She was a witty woman. I pretended I just happened to be there, of course, and asked if she was really Vicki Greene. You know how that goes. So we got talking, and she let me buy her a drink."*

"May I ask what you talked about, Mikel?"

The smile widened. *"How much she enjoys writing sequences that'll scare the daylights out of the reader. She actually giggled when she described how she sits there and reads the really inflammatory passages to herself. Out loud."* He shook his head. *"What a loss."* They were both silent for a minute. Then he continued: *"I'm glad you're looking into it. I think there are a lot of us who would like to know why she would do such a thing. But I must admit to being curious. You've come so far. Did the family engage you to pursue this?"*

"No," said Alex. "She asked for help. I felt an obligation."

"Of course. Well, I certainly hope you can come up with an answer."

Alex leaned forward. "Mikel, are you aware of anything unusual that might have happened to her while she was here?"

"No," he said. *"Of course we didn't talk long."* He picked up his cane. Held it across his knees. *"Had anything happened while she was here, the media would certainly have picked it up."*

"We checked the archives. There was nothing."

"Then I would say nothing happened. She's a major celebrity, Alex. Even out here. Her books sell on every continent. People love her. I'm reluctant to say this because you've come so far, but I'd be very surprised if, whatever drove her to do what she did, won't eventually be traced to some family or personal problem back home. A love affair gone wrong, possibly. Something along those lines."

"You're probably right, Mikel." Alex looked my way. "Did you have anything, Chase?"

"Yes," I said. "Mikel, may I ask why you contacted us?"

"I heard from several sources that you were inquiring about Ms. Greene. I was interested in why she might have done what

she did." He smiled. *"Besides, it was an opportunity to meet you and Alex. I enjoy meeting celebrities."*

"Before we leave for the Haunted Forest"—Alex could not suppress a grin—"I've something to show you."

"And what's that?"

"Take a look."

He darkened the room, and we were gliding toward a mountain range. It was the middle of the evening, the sun below the horizon, lights just coming on.

"Towns," I said. "Is there something special about them?"

"It's the Homeworld Security Project," said Alex.

"Which is what?"

"I told you about the Mute incidents."

"Yes."

"They're taking it pretty seriously."

We pulled in closer to some of the lights. Near the base of a mountain, I saw digging equipment. And temporary dwellings.

"What are they doing?" I asked

"Digging shelters."

"What? You're kidding."

"Not at all. It's described as a purely precautionary measure."

"Things haven't deteriorated that much, I hope."

"I don't know. It's hard to be sure what's really going on."

It looked like a major project. Cutters and extractors were out in force. Lots of lights, robots everywhere, even a few humans. And, of course, they were working at night.

"This is only one site. Apparently, this is going on around the world."

"I wasn't aware of it."

"We haven't been paying attention. They're digging into mountains. Or, more precisely, getting ready to."

"They really expect an attack from the Mutes?"

"Apparently. They're not making a lot of noise about it. The Administrator was on earlier this morning, talking about how they don't ever expect to have to use the shelters, but it's better to be prepared."

"If the Mutes were to attack in force, I don't think a few holes in the ground would be much help."

"I agree."

"So what's really going on?"

"It might be politics."

"How do you mean, Alex?"

"We're into an election cycle. Administrator Kilgore is running for reelection."

"He might want to look as if he's protecting everybody."

"That's a possibility." He looked worried.

"There's something you're not telling me," I said.

"The activity started within the last five months. The incursions. The Homeworld Security Project."

I knew where he was going. "It all started right after Vicki left."

eLeVeN

We're adrift in an ocean of the mind. Our lives consist primarily of navigating through shoals and storms, enjoying the experiences of a thousand ports, putting landing parties ashore on strange islands, taking visitors aboard, and dropping anchor occasionally to bask in the sunlight. The destination is of no consequence.

—*Love You to Death*

A funny thing happened on the way to the Haunted Forest. Getting there involved a flight across the Crystal Sea. We leased a skimmer from Reliable Transport and headed out. It was one of those brilliant, pleasant summer days, with the sting of salt in the air and a sense of approaching fall. Armies of white clouds drifted through the morning sky. A few fishermen were out. I watched one who'd netted something and was about to shoot it with a long-barreled scrambler.

We sat back, enjoying the ride. The AI kept us steady at about a thousand meters. Alex was in the midst of wishing he'd left me behind because somebody should be running the business. It was a mistake just to close up for three months and invite our clients to go elsewhere.

I was half-listening, wondering what Ben was up to, thinking what an idiot's chase we were involved in, when the AI lit up. *"Chase,"* she asked, *"do you have a minute?"* It's never good news when an AI in a taxi or a leased vehicle starts a conversation with you in the middle of a flight. It's usually to inform you that the main axle has fallen off, that rough weather lies ahead, or that you're over the storied volcano, Mt. Boombashi, at a bad time.

"Yes, Lyra, what is it?"

"I seem to have lost control of the vehicle."

"That can't be right," I told Alex. We were still moving steadily ahead. I adjusted my seat, sliding it closer to the instrument panel, and released the yoke. "Okay, Lyra," I said, "can you turn over control to me?"

"Negative, Chase. I am disconnected. I do not understand it."

"What's going on?" asked Alex.

"Don't know. *Something's* flying—Whoop!" We started to accelerate, then to drop. And I don't mean *descend*. The antigravs shut off, and the only thing keeping us aloft was the stubby wings, which provided *some* lift but not nearly enough. We were sliding down that pleasant summer sky.

I pulled the yoke back, but nothing happened. "You still have control," I told Lyra. "Turn loose."

"I do not have control."

The ocean was coming up fast. If I'd had time, I'd have ripped the AI out by the roots and tossed her over the side, but it probably wouldn't have helped anyhow. There was nothing at that point except to hang on to the stick.

Then, without warning, the engines went to neutral, the antigravs cut back in, and we leveled off. We rolled in over the surface. It was smooth as glass. We were maybe ten meters off the water. I could see waves, not much more than ripples. They drifted past.

The yoke moved around as if it weren't connected to anything. *"I'm declaring an emergency,"* Lyra said.

"Send the call."

"I will if I can."

We started to climb.

"Thank God," said Alex. "You've got it now?"

"No," I growled. And to demonstrate the point I banged the yoke with an open hand.

"Unable to transmit, Chase."

"Can you turn the radio over to me?"

"Negative. I get no reaction from it."

I tried to switch it on. Nothing happened. We were still going up. Accelerating again.

"Chase." Alex was hanging on to his chair. "Do something."

I was pressing pads and hitting switches. When none of that worked, I went looking under the panel for something that might allow me to gain control of the aircraft, some sort of emergency board or cutoff switch. I wasn't familiar with that type vehicle, had in fact never seen the make before.

At three thousand meters, we leveled off. But we were moving like a bandit.

And while I played around in the cabin, the thing began to shake. Violently.

"It's coming apart," Alex said. He was speaking through clenched teeth. "What's happening?"

"Going through the sound barrier." I couldn't get any kind of response out of the damned thing.

"I didn't think these things could go that fast."

I was waiting for the wings to come off. "Apparently some makes can."

Then we were through it. The rattling and banging stopped, and we were flying free again.

"Good, Chase," he said. "Now can you slow it down? And get us to land?"

As if some unseen force had answered, the drive shut off. We began to lose acceleration. The antigravs kept us aloft as we bounced and clattered back through the sound barrier. I was still strangling the yoke, trying to pull the nose of the skimmer up by sheer physical force.

"I am still off-line," said Lyra.

Me, too, kid.

I didn't bother with the skimmer's radio. I had taken two links on that trip. One was a necklace, the other a bracelet. I was wearing the bracelet that day. I called on the distress frequency. A woman responded: *"Shore Watch. Go ahead."*

"Shore Watch, we are going down. Need immediate assistance."

"Please keep calm and describe your emergency."

"We've lost control of our aircraft." We were losing altitude again. This time, though, it wasn't a free fall. Still, we were going down at a good clip.

"Your location, please?"

"Lyra, where are we?"

Lyra provided a set of coordinates, and the Shore Watch said they'd be right there.

"Better make it quick," I said.

We continued to brake. Suddenly, my weight came back. "Alex," I said, "the antigravs are off again."

"Have you resolved your problem?" asked the voice from the Shore Watch.

"Negative," I said. And, to Alex: "Hang on."

No need to worry about that.

We plowed into the top of a wave, bounced, and came down hard. The impact threw me against the harness. I heard Alex saying, "Come on, Chase," as if it were my fault. Then the cabin was filling with water, and he was trying to get me out of my seat. He'd come to my rescue like this once before, so I thought it was a good sign.

But everything was getting dark and starting to spin.

"—with me, Chase," he was saying. "Stay with me. I can't do this alone."

But he did. When I saw daylight again, we were in the water, hanging on to something, riding down the side of a wave. It was one of the chairs. "You okay?" he asked.

I looked around. Ocean in all directions. No sign of the skimmer. I needed a minute before I could speak. "I've been better," I said at last.

"Nothing broken?"

Everything seemed okay. "I don't think so."

"All right. I think if there were, you'd know it."

"I guess. Where's the skimmer?"

"Down like a rock." He watched me get hold of the chair. "Don't put too much weight on it."

"Okay."

He let me go. I kicked a little bit to stay up. "They should be here soon," he said.

"I hope. How long's it been?"

"Just a few minutes."

"Have *you* called the Shore Watch?"

"Since we came down? No."

"Why not?"

"I was too busy trying to keep your head out of the water."

"Okay. Let's try it again." I got the same operator.

"They're on the way," she said. *"Should be about fifteen minutes."*

"Good. Thanks."

"Keep transmitting."

I left it on. "Alex, thanks for getting me out of there."

"It's okay. Keep it in mind next time you want a raise."

Two people hanging on to one chair doesn't work well. Whenever either of us put a little weight on it, it went under. "Chase," he said, "you ever hear of a malfunction like this?"

"It was deliberate," I said. "Somebody had to go in and either jerry the AI or attach a parasite system."

"You're sure?"

"Absolutely. Even if the AI had simply failed, the skimmer wouldn't have behaved the way it did. What I can't figure is why the power came back at the end."

"That's because they didn't want us dead."

"Really?" I looked around at the empty sky.

"If we got killed, it would attract a lot of attention. And it would connect with Vicki. Somebody wants us to go away but doesn't want to deal with publicity."

"It's a warning?"

"Yes. I'd say so."

Another wave came by. We rode over it. "What the hell did she get into?"

We were drifting, looking at each other, watching for the rescue vehicle, when Alex's eyes widened. He was staring past my shoulder.

I turned.

Forty or fifty meters away, a long black tail had risen out of the water. There was a fork at the end. It stood erect for a few seconds, then splashed down. "Better hurry," I told the Shore Watch.

Whatever was in the water didn't seem to be going any-where. The tail lifted and fell again.

"Not good," said Alex.

I was grateful to discover I hadn't lost my scrambler. There was no way to be sure it could screw up the nervous system of a fish in an ocean on another world, but they're supposed to work on just about anything. I held it out of the water and tried to shake it dry.

"Will it work after getting dunked?" Alex asked.

"It's supposed to work underwater."

"Then why are you trying to dry it off?"

"Feels like the right thing to do." I set it for *lethal*. "Are you trying to start an argument with me?"

"No."

"I mean, that's probably not a good idea. I'm the only one here with a gun."

"I know."

"You should think about carrying one."

"Chase, normally I have no need for one. I'm an anti-quarian."

"It's the one time you *do* need one that makes it worth-while."

The tail vanished, leaving behind swirling water. Then it reappeared, closer to us, stood erect, and slapped down again. I watched it slide beneath the surface.

The water grew quiet.

"Can you see anything?" asked Alex.

"No." I handed him my bracelet. "Keep it out of the water so they don't lose the signal."

"Okay. What are you going to do?"

"Take a look."

"Not a good idea, Chase."

"Neither is staying here. I'll be back in a minute."

The water was clear, and I saw the creature off to one side. It was flat and long, shaped like a spade, maybe three or four times as big as I was. Two eyes centered close together on the snout watched Alex. Rotated to me. Went back to Alex.

Alex's legs hung down. He couldn't keep them still without sinking. They must have looked like a tasty morsel.

The mouth opened to reveal several rows of teeth.

I figured the underwater range of the scrambler was about half the distance to the creature. It was going to have to get closer. I didn't think there'd be any problem arranging that. I went back up. "It's interested in us," I said.

Alex took a deep breath. No joking around this time. "What *is* it?"

"It looks a little like a ray. It's a big fish with a lot of teeth."

"We're not its natural prey," he said.

"By the time it figures that out, you and I will be hamburger."

"There's another one."

"Where?"

He pointed. Another tail hoisted well out of the water. On the opposite side of us. It curled and straightened and curled again, then splashed down. "You think they hunt in tandem?"

"Maybe. We'd better assume they do."

We were both thinking how it would've been a good time for a second weapon. "Try not to move," I told him. I went down again. They were both watching us. They were spaced exactly opposite each other, although the newcomer was farther away. But it was approaching. I suspected that when both were at the same range, they'd attack. If that happened, and they were as quick as they looked, I thought I'd be able to take out one, but not both. I surfaced again.

"How's it look?" he said.

"Okay. Leave it to me."

"What are you going to do?"

"Explain later." At least I hoped I would. "Just keep still. Don't move." I took a deep breath and went back down. The creatures were lining up on us, getting ready. I had to take the initiative away from them. I kicked off in the direction of the first one. It started toward me. That long mouth opened again, and I looked past those incisors and saw a serpentine tongue. It charged head-on, no sign of caution, no indication it saw any reason to fear me. I was easy pickings. When it got within range, I fired a full charge past the teeth and down its throat.

The mouth gaped wide. The tongue snaked out and whipped through the water. Then the creature spasmed. It thrashed and rolled over and, trailing black blood, dived into the depths.

I spun away, looking for the other one. But we got lucky: Instead of coming after Alex or me, the creature went after its partner. Maybe it was trying to help. More likely, it was the promise of extra meat.

I went back up, and the water stayed quiet.

It's fair to say we were relieved to see the Patrol appear in the eastern sky. We were floating, hanging on to the chair, scanning the ocean for more tails. The aircraft grew larger, and they asked whether we were okay and explained how they'd have us out of the water in a minute.

It was a black-and-white skimmer, with SHORE WATCH imprinted on its hull. A door opened, and two uniformed crewmen appeared and waved. They tossed down a rope ladder, and the skimmer maneuvered until it was directly overhead. Then I climbed up, and they hauled me in. Somebody handed me a cup with a hot brew.

They pulled Alex in moments later. When they had us safely on board, they asked what had happened to our skimmer. "Don't know," I said. "It just went out of control."

One of the crew was a tall, athletic woman with red hair. "You guys were pretty lucky," she said.

"Why's that?" Alex asked.

"You don't want to go swimming in these waters."

"They dangerous?"

She heaved a sigh of relief. "You have no idea, champ."

TWELVE

There's something in the woods, Becky. We don't know what it is. No one has ever seen it. But on cold nights, when the wind turns around and comes in from the east, you can feel it. And that's when you want to stay inside and keep the door locked.

—*Etude in Black*

They took us back to where we'd started. We spent two days filling out forms for both the Shore Watch and Reliable Transport. Then we booked our crossing with a commercial carrier. We were waiting next morning for our flight to leave when Rob Peifer called. *"I heard you guys were in an accident."*

"Skimmer went down," said Alex.

"You okay?"

"We're fine. Got a little wet."

"I don't guess you got any pictures?"

"No, Rob. Sorry. I never thought about it."

"Okay. We have some file shots we can use."

Alex's eyes rolled skyward. "Why not just let it go, Rob? It's not worth reporting."

"Are you kidding me? 'Alex Benedict Down at Sea.' 'Benedict Rides Skimmer into Ocean near Maillot.'"

"Where's Maillot?" Alex asked.

"I'd like to do an interview, Alex. But the setting's not right. I wonder if you and what's-her-name, Chase, would want to go

*somewhere where we could get the ocean in the background?
One of the hotels, maybe?"*

"Rob, we're on the run at the moment. We have a flight to
catch."

*"Okay. Sure. We can fill in the background later. Listen,
Alex, why don't you tell me how you were feeling as you hit the
water?"*

Alex took a deep breath. "Scared, Rob."

We made it safely across the Crystal Sea on our second try, and
landed at Port Arbor. From there we boarded a train to Packwood, which was a coastal town whose principal claim to fame
was Packwood University. It was one of the sites where Vicki
had spoken.

According to one of the history teachers, she'd spent a day
there, won over the crowds, and even some skeptical literature
teachers with her wit and charm.

They ran the presentation for us, and she was as energetic as
ever.

Vicki had traveled to the Haunted Forest by canoe, so of course
we did the same. We set off downriver at dawn. The countryside
was wide-open, mostly plains with periodic patches of forest, a
few scattered houses, and an occasional town. The river was
narrow for the most part, and generally calm, with almost no
rough water. Neither of us was in shape to do nonstop paddling,
so for long periods of time we simply allowed the current to
carry us.

Eventually it carried us to the edge of the Haunted Forest.
We plunged ahead. The birds in the area were deafening. They
screamed and squawked, and something threw nuts and dead-
wood down at us. There was also a creature with the biggest
wingspan I've ever seen. Mostly it simply glided back and forth
overhead, watching something we couldn't see. I thought for a
while it was going to target us, so despite local assurances that
there were no predators, I sat for long periods with the scrambler handy. It never bothered us though.

There was also something that looked like a flying beanbag.

It drifted just above the treetops, sometimes touching down and apparently feeding on dead leaves, then casting loose again.

When the sun went down, we got off the river, broke out our sleeping bags, and built a fire. We spent the night in a clearing. Alex tried reading, but he drew too many bugs.

With not much else to do, we simply sat and talked and watched Callistra climb the sky. A cool breeze showed up after a while and drove off the insects.

Sophora was also in the sky. Its paleness underscored the brilliance of the star. "You know," I said, "if I were a writer and I wanted to come here to get my creative juices flowing, the major reason would be *that* sky."

He looked up at it. "Especially if you wrote horror."

"I wonder what kind of star it is?"

"I don't know."

I consulted my link. *"It's a giant blue variable,"* it said, *"approximately 1.2 million times as bright as Salud Afar's sun. It's farther out from the galactic rim than Salud Afar. Range from Salud Afar—"*

I heard thunder in the west.

"—twelve hundred light-years."

"How much brighter?" he asked.

"One point two million."

"Oh," he said. "That's different. I thought you said one point *three*."

We'd heard several different opinions about what haunted the forest. There were claims for animated vegetation, mists that moved of their own accord, voices in the trees. I lay there thinking how easily people can be persuaded to believe such things. And I won't deny it was an opportunity to relish my own superiority. I knew better.

The fire had died out, and Callistra was about to sink into the trees. The temperature was dropping, so I didn't want to get out of my sleeping bag and play with the logs. But my imagination took hold. Branches creaked a bit too much; occasionally I could hear a squishy sort of sound, like something walking through a marsh. Except that the ground was solid. And, yes, I know ordinarily that's no big deal, but it was an utterly still night. There was zero wind, and aside from the vegetative slooshing and cracking, and the squishes, the only sounds came from insects and the river.

It didn't really scare me. But I've slept better.

Neither of us was very big on food rations, the kind they pack in containers and that cook themselves. Alex had lived on the things in the old days when he'd gone to excavations with Gabe, but he'd since become accustomed to life's more ample luxuries. Moreover, he was having second thoughts about the wisdom of traveling by canoe. But it was too late to think about that.

Anyhow, we skipped breakfast, packed everything up, and headed downriver, looking for a place where we could get the local equivalent of ham and eggs. The first town we came to—I don't recall its name—had a café just off the pier. We beached the canoe, went inside, and got a table by the window where we could keep an eye on our means of transport.

It was a small place, maybe eight tables and booths, but the bacon and fries smelled good. We ordered the coffee-equivalent and sat back to relax.

There were maybe five other people in the place. The mood was subdued, as if someone had died. The waiters were all bots. Alex got up and walked over to one of the other tables. There were two men, guys who worked on the river probably. One was massive enough to sink our canoe. The other wasn't much more than a kid. He asked them if something was wrong.

"Goddam Mutes again," the big one said.

"What happened?"

"They're shooting at us."

"At Kumpallah," added the kid.

Kumpallah was a Confederate world, thirty thousand light-years away. "Well," he said, "at least you don't have to worry about them out here."

They looked at one another. "Where you been, bud?" said the big one. "They've *been* here."

Alex angled himself so he could face away from the sun. "I've heard about that."

"It's just a matter of time before we'll have to take the sons of bitches on. Isn't it, Par?"

"Looks like," Par said. "They keep coming. Starting trouble."

"Kilgore keeps telling us," said the big one, "we shouldn't get excited. That they won't bother us. But who's dumb enough to believe that? I'll tell ya, they ain't diggin' those shelters for their health."

Eventually we pulled up in front of a marker:

BESSARLIK
Oldest Settlement on Salud Afar
Believed to Be Nonhuman
2,000 B.A.

The place was fenced off. There were more signs: ABSOLUTELY NO CAMPING. And OPEN DAWN TO DUSK. And CAMPING PROHIBITED EXCEPT IN DESIGNATED AREAS.

The date, of course, referred to two thousand years before the arrival of the *Aquila*. The trees were thick, and if there'd ever been a city there, no part of it remained. "We should have brought a scanner," I said.

Alex shook his head. "It's another scam."

"How do you know?"

"I've done the research. This place was pulled together three centuries ago to make money for the locals."

I was getting annoyed. "Then why'd we bother coming?"

"Because Vicki came. And I'd be surprised if she didn't know the history of the place, too. Chase, it's entertainment. You come and let your imagination take over. That's what it's all about. Nobody's serious about any of this stuff."

We'd arrived in the early evening. There was a boat-rental operation at the end of a pier, and a campground. Along the riverbank were a sandwich shop, a souvenir store, and an inn. This, collectively, was the Hub. A few visitors were walking around, taking pictures. A tourist boat pulled up while we were there. Everybody got off and piled into the inn. We followed and found a young lady watering plants.

I got the assignment to ask the questions, since Alex thought my chemistry with her would be better. Had she ever heard of Vicki Greene?

"Who?"

"The horror writer."

She shook her head. "If you ask at the desk, they can tell you whether she's here."

"She wouldn't be here now." I showed her a hologram. Vicki dressed for a day in the woods—baggy white slacks, gray pull-over reading UNIVERSITY OF KHARMAIN, and a green cap like the one Downhome Smith wears in the sims.

She took a long look and shook her head. "Sorry," she said.

We'd made a mistake allowing the people from the tour boat to get in first. So we waited awhile, and finally I got to the service desk. The clerk was a middle-aged woman with a distinct sense that the hotel's visitors were people with too much leisure time on their hands. Unlike her, a busy workingwoman. "We have a friend who may have stayed here," I said. "About five or six months ago. Vicki Greene? Could you look her up and tell me whether she was ever at the inn?"

She gave me a polite smile. "I'm sorry. It's against the privacy laws. We're not permitted to reveal that kind of information without the consent of the subject." She talked as if that should have been obvious.

"It's important that we find her," I said.

"I'm sorry. I can't help you."

I showed her some money. "I'd make it worth your while."

"If something happened, I'd get in trouble. Now, if you decide you want a room, let me know. Excuse me." And she turned away.

Alex had been listening, and I saw disapproval in his eyes. "You sounded like a politician."

"You do it next time."

He looked across the lobby. "We shouldn't have bothered with this place," he said. "Let's go."

"What's the plan?"

"It's a safe assumption that she wouldn't come all the way out here and stay at an inn."

"Why?"

THirTeeN

The media show us that supernatural creatures, when they come onstage, are uniformly disquieting, twisted, terrifying. One has only to see them to back away. To be repulsed. The truth is quite the opposite, child. These apparitions that come out of the night, that come seeking body and soul, are in their own way extremely attractive. One might say, ravishing. They are in fact quite irresistible. And that is why they are dangerous.

—*Wish You Were Here*

As I watched, it floated away from the trees and started across the river.

I got up and went to the bank, as close as I could get, and took some pictures. It was a patch of luminescence, a radiant mist. A candle adrift in the night. I activated my link. "Identify," I said.

"Range, please?"

"Fifty meters."

I watched its reflection in the water.

"Object unknown."

"It does not match with any life-form on Salud Afar?"

"Negative. There are various microscopic—"

"Any natural phenomenon?"

"None known."

It was almost across. I hurried forward, but it was drifting downstream, away from me. It floated over the riverbank and merged with the forest.

I watched for a while, until long after it was gone. It was, I decided, a reflection. Or possibly some local machination, another unquiet grave, to entertain tourists.

Well, they had me hooked.

I went back and put another log on the fire. The river was dark and quiet. I climbed into my blanket, closed my eyes, and tried to laugh at myself. The insects got a bit louder, and somewhere a branch creaked.

Go to sleep, Kolpath.

The fire cracked and popped. I liked the smell of the burning logs. There was something reassuring about it.

I opened my eyes and looked again. Still nothing out there.

But I couldn't get back to sleep. I lay several minutes, listening to the forest and the river, and finally I got up, pulled my jacket around my shoulders, switched on my lamp, and walked back to the edge of the river. There was nothing. I wondered if someone in a control room somewhere was having a good laugh at my expense.

Callistra had set. The area where the apparition had entered the trees was dark. The only light anywhere, other than that I was providing, came from the misty edge of the galaxy, now rising in the east.

It was getting cold. I started back to the campfire. And saw a glimmer in the forest.

It was back.

I turned off the lamp.

It appeared to be just at the edge of the forest, not quite at treetop level, drifting quietly with the wind while it rose and sank.

I thought about waking Alex, but he'd have complained again. He was probably right. Undoubtedly right. Still—

When I was a little girl, I had a kitten named Ceily. I used to amuse myself with Ceily by pointing a laser light at the floor in front of her. She loved to chase it, and I used to run the laser around the room and up the walls. Whenever I got it down within her reach, she'd go into her crouch and sneak up on it and try to grab it.

I felt a little bit like Ceily that night. I walked toward the light, taking my time, as if I might scare the thing off. The ground was uneven, and I wasn't paying attention, so I almost fell on my face. The apparition retreated. Moved deeper into the trees. I followed.

The grass was stiffer than anything we had at home, and it crackled underfoot. There was no clear track; I had to blunder forward as best I could through bushes filled with thorns and vines that, somehow, when they touched my skin, excited a tingling reaction. I pulled my hands up into my jacket sleeves.

Then it disappeared again.

I aimed the lamp at the trees, saw nothing, and decided to hell with it. Enough was enough.

I turned to start back. And saw it behind me.

About ten or twelve paces away. A gust of wind rattled the branches but had no effect on it. I wasn't sure if I'd simply not noticed before, but the apparition was pulsing, alternately brightening and dimming. In sync with my heart.

I was the woman in the haunted-house story who sees strange lights upstairs and goes in to see what's happening. Even at that moment I wasn't really afraid of it, so strong was my assumption that it was a hoax. I knew, absolutely *knew*, that someone, nearby, was controlling it. But I put my hand on the barrel of the scrambler.

Somewhere a bell sounded. Twice. Three times. Probably from the Hub. Maybe from a passing boat.

The apparition didn't waver. Didn't move. It simply floated in front of me. And I found myself thinking of Ceily.

Of her last day.

I'd been directed not to let her out of the house. Kittens weren't safe outside, my father had warned me. We lived on the edge of a forest, and the woods were filled with predators. But she always wanted out, always tried to get through the door when I opened it, and I felt mean and contemptible keeping her inside. So one day I held the door open for her.

She followed me onto the front lawn and we had such a good time together that I did it again the next day. I don't know why, but I've always remembered it was the second day and not the first. And I was standing there minutes later watching her crouch as if she were going after one of the birds in the feeder when a yakim came out of nowhere and seized her in its claws, scooped her up, and soared into the sky with her. The last I saw of Ceily was her big eyes fastened on me, pleading with me to help. Within seconds the yakim and the kitten were gone, into the trees, and I went screaming after them.

I never found her, of course. But I kept running and crying until I was exhausted. Then I realized I didn't know the way home. And it got dark.

It was a couple of hours before I heard distant voices calling my name. It was the only time in my life I wanted to die.

And that night, in the forest on Salud Afar, it all came rushing back, as if everything had happened at once: Ceily rolled into the yakim's claws, her eyes round and desperate, my heart pounding so loudly I couldn't breathe, the dark woods stretching for miles in all directions, the dull dead sounds of the forest, the voices behind me somewhere.

I fought back tears and thought how the world must have seemed to Ceily in those last moments, how alone she must have felt. And I traded places with her and rode with the yakim, while the ground fell away, knowing the claws would tear me apart within the next moments. Knowing I was alone.

Then Alex was there, holding me upright, asking in a scared voice what had happened?

I'm not sure what I said, but he responded by asking me about Ceily. "Say again: Who is she?"

He looked out of focus. "Where is it?" I asked.

"Where's *what*?"

"The light."

He thought I was talking about my lamp, which was lying on the ground, its beam playing across a tangle of thorns and berries.

"No," I said. "In the trees."

He looked around. "I don't see anything. Who's Ceily?"

In the morning, it only seemed like a bad dream. Alex thought it was another warning that we should back off. But it wasn't like that at all. Something out there had gotten at me and triggered a response that no simple gimmick could have managed.

I was still shaky when we called the people at Marquesi's to inquire about Vicki. She'd left her canoe in the hands of the boat-rental outfit until Marquesi's could fly someone out to ride it back. The store manager's lips tightened. *"You're not planning to do the same thing, are you?"* he asked. His voice had turned hostile.

"I'll make it worth your while," Alex said.

"Damn worth my while. You told me this wouldn't happen."

Alex made the arrangements, and we gave the canoe over to Bessarlik Boating. By the way, did the owner remember somebody else doing this? Her name was Vicki Greene.

"The horror lady," she said. "Sure. I'd never forget her."

"Why? Did she say anything out of the way?"

"Oh, no. Simply that I've read all her books. I loved meeting her."

"How'd she seem?"

"How do you mean?"

"Was she all right? Did she seem upset, or anything like that?"

"No. She was really nice. Why? She's okay, isn't she?"

Vicki had mentioned she was headed for Morningdale. It was a town with a history of werewolves. Sounded like Vicki's kind of place. Alex and I arranged transportation, and an hour later we'd leased a skimmer and were on our way again. Below, I noticed one of the beanbags drifting near the edge of the river. And suddenly, while I watched, a long green tentacle whipped out of the trees. A moment later both the tentacle and the beanbag were gone.

"Your imagination," said Alex.

Maybe. By then, as far as I was concerned, tentacles were minor stuff.

FOUrTeeN

A person must have time to grow accustomed to the idea that he will die soon. When it happens violently, suddenly, unexpectedly, he is simply not ready to leave. He will cling to a favorite chair, or retreat inside an AI. He will hang on to the things that are familiar and resist all effort at removal. In the end, you must throw out the furniture. If that doesn't work, sell the house.

—*Midnight and Roses*

The werewolf was a bust. Something howled in the woods around Morningdale, but there was no reason to believe it was anything other than a maharé, the local wolf-equivalent. Besides, I asked the lady at the hotel where we stayed, how could you have a werewolf when you don't get a full moon? Don't have a moon at all?

"When Callistra is directly overhead," she said solemnly, "it happens."

I laughed.

She got annoyed. "It's true," she said. "That star is the Devil's Eye."

"Oh," I said.

"Stay close to the hotel, and you should be okay."

The Devil's Eye. There it was again. The title for Vicki's next novel.

The archives revealed there'd been a series of gruesome killings in the Morningdale area forty years earlier. But those had been attributed to an unusually malevolent maharé. The werewolf legend had started because a young man with mental problems had claimed to be the killer. When the authorities decided he needed psychiatric help, he'd resisted. Police had been summoned; the man had fled into the forest. Next day his body was found in the river that runs past the town.

The killings stopped.

But there were two similar incidents later. Each was accompanied by a string of murders, of people apparently torn apart by a wild animal. Each time, someone came forward, claiming guilt, claiming to be a werewolf. One of the nutcases was a woman.

The killings were never resolved. And the confessions were attributed to a psychiatric disorder and the simple need to draw attention to oneself. In each case, according to one psychiatrist described as prominent, the victim had developed a morbid interest in the original werewolf story. "Ordinarily," he said, "maharés will not attack a human, but there are exceptions. What clearly happened in Morningdale is that there was a string of killings, and an unbalanced person attributed the actions to himself. Or, in this case, three unbalanced people. And I suspect, in future years, the pattern will repeat."

It had been eleven years since the last outbreak. But the town kept the story alive with the usual gift shop and several books purporting to reveal "the truth" about the killings, and an HV presentation put together by a group of true believers. I'd have thought that the possibility of running into a werewolf would keep people *out*, but it apparently didn't work that way.

In any case, I was relieved to learn that Vicki hadn't spent a night in the woods. She'd rented a room in a house at the edge of the forest and simply made herself comfortable on the porch during the hours when Callistra was overhead.

The Devil's Eye.

So we followed suit. We sat out there and listened to the sound of the woods. Occasionally, something howled. Presumably a maharé. The owner of the house, who stayed with us for a while, assured us that the creatures rarely came near the town. "They're scared of people," he said.

The psychiatrist seemed to me to have a handle on things.

Nevertheless, I had my scrambler with me. Alex smiled at that. "It's a good move," he said. "You never know. But—"

"But what, Alex?"

"We'd probably be safer if you had something that shoots silver bullets."

We followed Vicki around the world. We spent a quiet night in a church supposedly infected by demonic forces. We visited an office building that claimed to have a haunted storage room on the eighth floor. We spent three nights on Fermo Beach, where the only thing that came ashore was a harmless creature with an oversized shell.

We visited an archeological site where, seven hundred years earlier, the inhabitants had sacrificed children and virgins. (It was hard to believe that was still going on nine thousand years after the Enlightenment.) We dropped in on several haunted houses. We watched in vain for the appearance of a phantom aircraft that was said to be a relic of an accident that had occurred three thousand years ago. The vehicle developed engine trouble over a populated area, and rather than attempt a landing that endangered people on the ground, the pilot turned out to sea. The plane went down, and the pilot was lost before rescuers could reach him.

According to local legend, the plane reappeared each year on the anniversary of the event. Vicki had planned her trip well, and arranged to be present on the correct night. We couldn't duplicate the date without waiting the better part of a year.

Was there anything to the story?

There had been sightings of the ghostly aircraft, but it was easy enough to put a plane in the air and do a flyby. One year, as a stunt, the locals were able to persuade the airfields in the area to watch the traffic on that night "to prevent hoaxes." They got a lot of publicity out of it, and of course the plane was sighted anyhow. Some years there have been two or three ghost planes. "The kids," one shopkeeper told us in a moment of unbridled rectitude, "love it."

The most interesting site, for me, was the Time Lab at Jesperson. It's out in the woods, not much more than a ruin now. It was originally built and operated eight centuries ago. The government funded it for a while, but there was no success, and eventually, according to the story, they gave up and abandoned the place.

The townspeople insist that there was a breakthrough, though, but that the program directors, confronted with the ability to move through the ages, decided it was too dangerous. So they hid the truth. The lab was officially abandoned. Some of the researchers, however, had disappeared into the past and the future. People there claimed they still showed up on occasion. It's been eight hundred years, and, if you believe the story, they're still young.

"Why," a waitress at the Copper Club told us, "Gene Korashevski was here just last week."

"Who's Gene Korashevski?"

"One of the researchers. He lives in the Carassa Age."

"Lives? You mean he's still alive? After eight hundred years?"

"In the Carassa Age, he is."

Alex couldn't resist himself. "Never heard of the Carassa Age," he said. "When was that?"

"It hasn't happened yet." She was good. She was talking as if this was matter-of-fact stuff. The way you might tell somebody you collect cats.

Later, when we were alone at the table eating lunch, Alex speculated on how nice it would be to have the capability to travel in time.

"What would you do with it?" I asked him. "Where would you go?"

He loved the idea. "Imagine what we could do. How about going back and securing the cup that held Socrates' poison? Can you even begin to imagine what that would be worth?"

"Alex, is that really the best thing you can think of to do with a time machine? How about going back a few years earlier and actually *talking* to Socrates? Maybe take him to lunch?"

"I don't speak classical Greek."

"Well," I said, "I guess you have a point."

"And it would be nice to get an early draft of *First Light*."

First Light. The masterpiece by Saija Brant, the greatest dramatist of all time.

"I think I'd still settle," I said, "for a chance to say hello to Saija Brant."

Our salads came. He studied his for a moment, then looked up. "Chase, you have no imagination."

FiFTeeN

There's no such thing as the supernatural. Everything, by defini-
tion, is *natural*. But you have to find out what the rules are.

—*Love You to Death*

Eventually, we tracked her to Livingstone, the two-hundred-
year-old estate of Borgas Cleev, where the dictator had delighted in personally running drills and lasers into anyone who
displeased him, and where, according to legend, the cries of his
victims could still be heard on windswept nights, when Callistra commanded the heavens. But the trail went cold there. Vicki
had arranged to spend a night *inside* the mansion, talked the
next day with a few of the townspeople, then gone away.

We could find no sign of her after that. We roamed the area,
questioning book dealers, librarians, police officers, journalists,
anyone we found in the streets. Several reported having seen
her, and a few said they'd talked with her. She'd seemed in good
spirits, they'd said. But there was no indication of her destination after she'd left Livingstone.

So we sat frustrated in a hotel suite. Alex had been tracking
the time line, and Vicki's appearance in Livingstone had come
near the end of her stay on Salud Afar. Ten days after she'd left
here, she would board the *Arbison* and return to Rimway.

"I wonder," Alex said, "when she decided to leave." He
made a couple of calls, got the StarFlight ticket office, and

identified himself. He asked for the *Arbison*'s departure date. It was ten days after she'd left Livingstone.

"I'm trying to find an old friend," he said. "She was on that flight. I wonder if you could tell me when she bought her ticket?"

"I'm sorry, sir. We don't give out that kind of information."

Alex ran the original transmission, Vicki Greene with fear in her eyes and her hands rolled into fists.

"I know this will strike you as odd, but I don't know who else can help me." The white-and-gold blouse lifted and fell. HASSAN GOLDMAN, the blouse read. Who the hell was Hassan Goldman? *"Since you're not here, I'm asking your AI to forward this message. I'm assuming the cost."* And the arc of six stars. *"I'm in over my head, Mr. Benedict. God help me, they're all dead."*

He ran it again.

"I'm in over my head."

"Chase," he said, "who or what is Hassan Goldman?"

He ran a search. Hassan Goldmans were more numerous on Salud Afar than they had been on Rimway. One did medical enhancements. Another Hassan Goldman was a noted law firm in the capital. Hassan Goldman specialized in caring for pets. He was an actor, dead these twenty years, who'd performed comedy, and was still beloved by a substantial portion of the population. Another Goldman did landscaping in a place neither of us had ever heard of. He had been the captain years ago of the tour ship *Leesa*, who'd sacrificed himself, after his engines had blown, in a largely successful effort to save his passengers. Three Hassan Goldmans had lived in various places and apparently never done anything except reproduce. He'd been a major sports figure. He'd been one of seven people killed in an avalanche while skiing in a cordoned-off area that skiers weren't supposed to use. He prepared special lotions to help aching backs.

There were more.

Was there any connection between any of these Hassan Goldmans and Vicki Greene?

None that we could find.

Were any of the Hassan Goldmans connected with claims of paranormal events?

"None known."

Alex kept the image of Vicki frozen over a coffee table while we looked. The name on the blouse was inscribed in black above an arc of six black stars.

Six stars.

"Six people," said Alex, "died on the *Leesa*. Five other than himself." The heroic captain had saved seventeen. "Coincidence?"

"So where," I asked, "does that leave us?"

Alex sank into his chair.

I asked the AI if any of the five passengers had been connected with claims of paranormal events.

"None known."

"We're asking the wrong questions," said Alex.

"What's the right one?"

"The obvious one. Who sells shirts with Hassan Goldman imprints?"

"There is no sales source on record."

"Somebody's making his own," I said. "Probably a church, a charity, some sort of special event."

He asked the AI to connect him with the space station. "The general information desk," he added.

A young woman in a dark green uniform appeared. *"Orbital Center,"* she said. *"How may I assist you?"*

"Can you tell me," said Alex, "if the name Hassan Goldman is used by any of the businesses on the station?"

"No, sir," she said. *"However, there* is *a tour ship here by that name."*

"Do they give out shirts to passengers?"

"Not that I know of."

"Okay. What can you tell me about it?"

"How about if I switch you over to the tour company?"

"Okay. Please."

There was a pause. Then a male voice: *"Starlight Tours."*

"My name is Benedict. One of your ships is the *Hassan Goldman*?"

"Yes. That's correct."

"I'm trying to locate a friend. Her name is Vicki Greene. I think she took a tour on the *Goldman* several months ago. I was wondering if you could verify that?"

"I'm sorry. But we don't give out that kind of information."

Alex looked in my direction. Worth a try. "I wonder if it would be possible to speak to the captain of the *Goldman*."

"He's off duty," came the response. *"He'll be in tomorrow morning."*

Alex said thanks, switched off, and looked up the specifications for the *Goldman*. Among them he found the captain's name. Ivan Sloan.

"Ivan?" I said.

"Yes. Do you know him?"

"He was one of my trainers at StarFlight."

"Good," said Alex. "Marvelous." He asked the AI to find the number for Ivan Sloan. "You'll probably find him at Samuels."

"That is correct, sir. Do you wish to be connected?"

"Please." Alex got up, signaled for me to do the call, and left the room.

Ivan was one of those people who strikes you as being a bit slow until you get to know him. He was always there when I needed him and, when I was having some doubts about whether I'd ever graduate, he took me aside and asked how serious I was about piloting interstellars.

I told him I was serious. That there was nothing in my life I wanted more than that.

"Then get your act together," he'd told me. "You'll be okay. You've got all the talent you need. Hell, it doesn't take that much talent. All you have to do is be smart enough to tell the AI what to do." He said that as if he meant it. "What you don't have," he added, "is confidence in yourself. Probably from too many people over a lifetime telling you what you've gotten wrong." There was truth to that. My dad was forever warning me not to touch stuff, so I wouldn't break it.

When he saw me he knew me at once, and broke into a big smile. *"Chase,"* he said, *"what are you doing out here?"* He was seated at a table, with a cup in one hand, a dinner plate and silver-ware in front of him. Behind him I could see a mural. A sailboat.

"Came out to see *you*, Ivan. How are you?"

"I'm serious. You're the last person I expected to see in this corner of the cosmos."

"I'm on vacation," I said. "How about you? How do you come to be here?"

"I'm from here."

"You're kidding. You're from Salud Afar? I never knew that."

He shrugged. *"I might not have mentioned it."*

"Running tours?"

He looked embarrassed. *"That's pretty much what it's come down to."*

Tours from Salud Afar? I looked through a viewport at the black sky. "So where do people go? What's to see?"

"Varesnikov," he said. "It has a magnificent set of rings and moons. And people like Sophora, too. It's a crystal world. Looks great when you get the right angle on the sunlight."

"I guess." I saw something in his eyes. Pain, maybe. Or em-barrassment. As if his life hadn't turned out the way he'd ex-pected. "So how'd you turn up on Rimway?"

"I cleared out of here when I was twenty-two, Chase. Those were bad times. I didn't much like living under the Bandahr." He turned away for a moment. Spoke to someone else, then angled the link so I could see the people with him: a man and two women. We did a quick round of introductions. One of the women was his wife Mira. She was attractive, congenial, prob-ably twenty years younger than he was. The other couple were friends.

"Let me ask a quick question, Ivan," I said, "and I'll get out of your way. A couple of months ago, you had a passenger named Vicki Greene. Do you remember her?"

"The company did," he said. *"I didn't."*

"I assumed she'd gone out on the *Goldman*."

"As a matter of fact, she did. But it wasn't my ship then. Haley Khan was running her at the time."

"Would it be possible for me to talk to Haley? Can you give me his code?"

"He's gone, Chase. Disappeared."

"How do you mean?"

"He vanished. Right off the station."

"How could that happen?"

"Don't know. It happened several months ago. Right after Vicki Greene had been here. There's no record he took the shuttle down. But he didn't show up for work one day and we've never been able to find him."

"You called the police?"

"The CSS. Yes. They couldn't find him either." He paused. Said something to the others at the table. Came back to me: *"What's your connection with him, Chase?"*

I told him about Vicki. "Do you know where she went? On the *Goldman?*"

"Probably the standard tour route. I never got a chance to talk to him after the flight."

"Did anybody else?"

"I don't think so, Chase. That was the same question the Coalition guys were asking. Haley came off the flight and went back to the hotel. He usually did that. He wasn't much for hanging around. Anyway he had a couple days off coming to him, and we just never saw him again. Ride with Vicki Greene and walk out of the world. It's like one of her books."

"What about the AI?"

"The CSS took it. Part of their investigation." He paused, lost in thought. *"There was something else odd, too."*

"What's that, Ivan?"

"She bought out the ship. Wanted to travel alone. No other passengers."

"Would you guys take her someplace special if she asked?"

"Oh, sure. We'll take you sightseeing anywhere you wanted to go. If nobody objects."

"Like if there's nobody else on board."

"Yes."

"Okay. So she wanted to go off the usual tour destinations. Where else might she have wanted to go?"

"Chase, you got me. There is nowhere else. There's nothing out here for hundreds of light-years in all directions."

"Do you know where she was coming *from*?"
"No. I can check the logs."
"Would you do that for me? And get back to me?"
"That kind of information's supposed to be private."
"I'd appreciate it, Ivan."

He called the next morning. *"There's no record,"* he said.
"What happened to it?"
"Officially, the flight never happened. That tells me the CSS took it."

sixteen

Barry would have been all right if he hadn't become a physicist.
But all that nonsense about mass and energy got him believing
he really knew how the world worked. And he didn't. He never
did. And that's what got him killed.

—*Midnight and Roses*

Vicki, Ivan said, had signed on for the flight from a hotel in
Moreska. Moreska was a small town in the middle of nowhere.
It had no spectral claims, no demons, creatures from another
age still haunting the roads. But it had once been home to Demery Manor, which, for reasons unknown, had been blown
apart during the final year of the Bandahr's rule, just months
before his assassination. Nobody knew why the incident had
occurred, although everyone assumed Nicorps was involved.
The manor's owner, Edward Demery, was not an enemy of the
regime, as far as was known.

I didn't think blowing up a house was enough to have interested Vicki Greene. Until I heard that seventeen other homes,
throughout the region, had been destroyed the same night.

The Demery Manor site consisted of a few burned timbers and
a couple of stone walls jutting out of the earth. The common
wisdom held that Edward Demery had incurred the wrath of

Aramy Cleev and paid the price. According to the flyers we'd gotten at the hotel in Moreska, "most experts" believed the Bandahr had been personally offended when Demery, during an interview, had described the compassion and basic decency of Dakar Cleev, Aramy's grandfather, without mentioning Aramy's own matchless compassion. The dictator had said nothing publicly, of course, and had in fact even praised Demery's perspicacity. But anyone who knew Aramy Cleev understood the failure to note his kindness would not have gone down well.

The general destruction had come six days after those unfortunate remarks and had been spread over several hundred kilometers in all directions. Houses, villas, and manors had been leveled. There'd been no survivors anywhere.

Nicorps, it was assumed by many, was closing its books on people who had incurred the Bandahr's displeasure.

We were looking at the ruins, on a cold afternoon, while a wet wind blew in off the sea. We had an autoguide with us. *"They killed him and his wife,"* said the autoguide.

"Eighteen houses in one night?" said Alex. "That seems a bit extreme."

"There are always rumors when terrible things happen," the tour guide said. *"If you want my personal opinion, I think Nicorps simply went rogue and decided to kill everybody they didn't like. But who really knows?"*

"What did he do for a living?" I asked. "Demery?"

"He was born into wealth, ma'am. But he thought of himself as a mathematician though he never had any formal training."

"Was he a native of this area?"

"Oh, no. No. He wasn't even from this world. *Demery was born on Rimway."*

"Are there any theories about why all these people were killed the same night?" asked Alex. "Other than Nicorps running wild?"

"What other explanation could there be? I think they'd probably gotten backlogged. Decided to catch up on old work. Did it all the same night. It wouldn't be the first time they'd done something like that."

Alex stared at the ruins. "Did Demery leave an avatar?"

"It was purged. On the day of the explosions."

"By whose authority?"

"Nobody knows."

"It would," I said, "have had to come from high up."

Alex nodded. Of course it would.

Edward Demery had not only lost his life. He had undergone an electronic subtraction as well. And not only the avatar. You went looking for data on him, and there was enough to prove he existed. You could find a birth certificate, you could find brief accounts of his impending wedding, and there was real-estate information. Demery buys office building in New Samarkand. You could find an account of his acquiring controlling interest in Blackmoor Financial, and his contributions to the Aquarius Fund, which was striving to rejuvenate oceans hampered by the absence of a moon. There was an award from the Ballinger Historical Society. But of his personal life, what he thought, what he believed in, what he cared about, that was all gone.

Orrin Batavian was a banker who liked to be thought of as an historian. We sought him out because he'd organized a speaking engagement for Vicki and because he'd been a close friend of Demery's. We found him at his home, a large, landscaped property on the edge of town.

"Ed and I shared a fascination for ancient history," he told us. "For the early years." Because of that friendship, he said, he'd held his breath for several days after the explosion, wondering whether they'd come after him, too. "You never knew what might irritate Nicorps," he said. "It was the way they operated." We were seated in his office in downtown Moreska. "Somebody got in trouble, everybody he knew got swept up with him. I had my fingers crossed."

The walls were filled with framed certificates of outstanding accomplishments by Batavian's bank and pictures of the man himself with various people whose postures suggested they were VIPs.

"Why did he get in trouble?" Alex asked. "Do you have any idea?"

Batavian shook his head. "I honestly don't know. He didn't like the regime. But nobody did." His chair squeaked. "Almost nobody. Some people saw no problem with Cleev. You did what you were told and didn't make trouble, then you had nothing to worry about."

"But you do think Cleev was behind the attack."

"Well, Nicorps was. I doubt it was anything big enough to draw the Bandahr's attention. You have to understand that it was the guys further down the food chain who caused most of the trouble. They had thugs and psychopaths running everything. And the way they looked good to their bosses was to be able to show a body count every month.

"Those were bad times. So people didn't make an electronic record of themselves. Ed was an exception. People still don't do it, for that matter. Not the older ones. Call it force of habit, but there's always a sense that the Bandahr might come back. So you don't put anything up. Especially not an avatar who's going to tell the government what you really think." Batavian had an aristocratic demeanor. His family had prospered under the dictatorship, and the word around town was that he'd survived when Demery went down because he had connections. "It might be true," he admitted. "I was never a collaborator, but my father was. And my sister."

Alex's eyes narrowed. "Do you have any idea why they would have purged the Demery record?"

"They did that routinely. They didn't have to have a reason. You got in trouble, you became invisible. Look, I don't know whether he just said the wrong thing to the wrong person. Or whether there was something they were actually afraid of. Demery didn't like the Bandahriate. But he never did anything more than talk. And he tried to be circumspect about the people he spoke to. He was like me. We both had a decent life under the sons of bitches, if you played by the rules and didn't mind keeping your mouth shut. So we played by the rules. Lived with it as best we could. I don't know. Maybe they took him out because somebody just wanted to run up the numbers. Maybe it was a mistake. Maybe he had some old fertilizer in the basement. I just don't know."

"All right," said Alex, "let's try a different subject: Vicki Greene."

"Ah, yes. I knew that was coming."

"She did a program here. With you as moderator."

He smiled. "She spoke to the Martian Society. By closed circuit. It was members only. And a few guests."

"The Martian Society is—?"

"—A group of people who pretend we've been taken over by aliens. Who keep out of sight."

"The original aliens, apparently."

He laughed. "We have a pretty good time. It's strictly a social operation. Nobody takes it seriously."

"What did she talk about?"

"Her books, of course."

"That's all? Anything else come up?"

"Well, it was a fairly wide-ranging conversation."

"Did she mention the explosions?"

He stuck his tongue in his cheek while he thought about it. "No," he said finally. "Not that I can recall."

"How about Demery?"

"No. There was no reason to. But she *was* interested in him. She was excited to hear we'd been friends."

"Why was she interested in him?"

"Because of the *Lantner* world ULY447."

"Which is what?"

"Well, it's not really a world. It's an asteroid—a long way out. Light-years, in fact."

"And?"

"Two ships disappeared out there. During a religious ceremony. Ed was always intrigued by it. Always coming up with explanations."

Alex glanced my way. That sounded like another reason for Vicki's interest. "Tell us about it. About the disappearance."

"Not much to tell, Alex. We had a corporation, Starloft, that used to sell people asteroids. The inner-system asteroids, of course."

"Starloft *sold* asteroids?" I asked.

"Yes."

"Why? What can you do with an asteroid?"

Batavian put on a beatific smile. "Immortality, young lady. They name it for you. Then they take you and your family and friends out to the thing, charging everybody for the transportation, of course. They hold a ceremony and install a monument with your name on it. People bought them to honor deceased relatives. Some people provided for it in their wills. It was a pretty lucrative business at one time."

"But they don't do it anymore?"

"No. The Bandahr claimed ownership of the asteroids, and Cleev took a cut of the proceeds. The current government probably wouldn't have changed things, but we went through a Save-the-Asteroids period. People didn't think markers should be put on them. Or that the government or anyone else *owned* them. It became a political issue."

"So it got stopped?"

"The politicians saw a good thing and got on board. They eventually taxed it out of existence."

"So what about the *Lantner* mission?"

"That was a big deal for Starloft. For a long time, the business was strictly local. Then the Family of God, a religious group led by Calius Sabel, decided to go deep. Go for the outer asteroids. Out to the Swarm."

"The Swarm?"

"It's a sea of asteroids. Some of them line up pretty closely with Callistra. They picked the biggest one they could find and decided to build a monument on it. They thought it would provide religious significance."

"In what way?"

"The Family of God associated Callistra with the eye of the Deity. So the placement of a monument on that asteroid was to assure the faithful that they walked always in His light. Or some such thing.

"Starloft sent a team out and did the installation. It's still there if you want to take a look at it. When it was completed, the Sabels went out in two ships to conduct a ceremony. There were a couple of Starloft executives with them. The two ships were the *Lantner*, which the Sabels leased, and the *Origon*, which was provided by Starloft. They got out there okay. They set up imagers, spent two days in prayer and thanksgiving, and on the third day they went down to do the ceremony."

"And this was thirty years ago?" I asked.

He had to count. "Thirty-three, Chase."

"How far is it?"

He checked with his AI. *"Thirty-six light-years."*

"They'd have been using the old drive," I said. "Just getting there would have taken a week."

"Please continue," said Alex. "On the third day, they went down onto the asteroid?"

"Yes. There were two landers. They put on pressure suits and got out and assembled in front of the monument. The ceremony was transmitted back here on HV. I didn't see it live. But I've seen it since. Everybody has.

"Anyhow, they did some praying. Then they started making speeches. One of the Sabels was talking when the transmission suddenly stopped. Just blanked out. Dead at the source. It was the last anybody ever heard of any of them."

"When the rescue units got out there—?" said Alex.

"—They were gone. Ships, landers, people. Everything. Except the monument."

I was trying to imagine any sequence of events that would account for it. "It doesn't sound possible," I said.

Batavian got up, walked over to the window, and looked out. In the distance, a train moved across the countryside.

"There was a search. But they never found anything. Some people blamed the Mutes. There were all kinds of stories. Mostly that other aliens were loose out there somewhere. And there was something else."

"What's that?"

"The patrol boat that originally went to the scene, the *Valiant*, never made it home. It was the first rescue vehicle."

"What happened to it?" I asked. "Are you going to tell us *it* disappeared, too?"

"No. It filed its report, and another Bandahriate vehicle, a specialized one, I think they said at the time, went out to look around. The patrol boat returned to its usual assignment. And a day or so later it exploded."

"Sounds like a pattern," said Alex.

"They said it was an engine problem."

"Any survivors?"

"None." For several moments, no one spoke. Then he continued: "Ed loved mysteries. So naturally the *Lantner* incident caught his attention. I don't know how many times I heard him tell people how he'd watched the night it happened." He sighed. Shook his head. "Shortly after that, the government issued a warning about the area, that they thought Mutes might have established a base in the region. Everybody was told to stay clear."

"So nobody went out there after that?"

"Nobody went out there anyhow. Except on that one occasion."

We sat. We could hear a couple of people arguing outside.

"I wonder," said Alex, "if you have a record of Vicki's performance for the Martians?"

While I watched her, I was thinking how much more difficult it is to be entertaining when you don't have the audience physically in front of you, when they're spread out across an electronic hookup and you can't feed off their reactions. Or even get a read on them. I've done a few appearances with Alex, and I want them sitting out there where I can see them to get my adrenaline flowing. But it didn't seem to bother her.

Batavian had been the emcee. He introduced her from the same room we were sitting in. She came in and sat down in the chair that Alex was using and said she was glad to be there, and what a privilege it was, and so on. Most people do that and you know they're kidding. But she meant it. And it was easy to see right from the start that she was enjoying herself.

Batavian got out of the way, and Vicki took the helm. She told the audience how much she loved what she did, that the old stories about writers working out of attics while they slugged down whiskey, that their lives were solitary and dreary, that it was hard, painstaking work, was all a lie. *"We say that stuff to discourage other people from getting into the business. To keep the competition down. There's nothing as exhilarating as writing a good line or watching a plot come together."* Images of her listeners appeared. The audience was composed of young and old, equal numbers of both sexes, people with money and people who were managing. The one characteristic they all shared was enthusiasm. When she'd finished, they applauded for a full minute. Not bad for an audience scattered around the globe.

They went to questions.

We listened while they asked why she'd decided to write horror, what she did in her spare time, and whether there'd be a sequel to this or that book.

When it was done, we sat quietly listening to the wind play against the side of the building. Batavian was still staring at the spot where Vicki's image had been. "She was interested in Aramy Cleev, Alex," he said. "Did you know that? It's true. She was annoyed because Cleev's avatar is restricted."

Alex leaned forward. "Really?" That was a surprise. The guy was, after all, a major historical figure.

"Yes. You have to have special authorization to talk to it." Alex's eyes, which had been distant, came into sharp focus. "I think," said Batavian, "they just don't trust Cleev. Not even dead. And they don't entirely trust the general population. A lot of people here would love to go back to the Bandahr years."

seventeen

"It's true, Lia. People walk out of their homes and are never heard from again."

"Why, Dr. Stratford? What happens to them?"

"Bad spirits get them. It happens every day. It's why you must never wander off into the woods alone."

—Dying to Know You

I spent the next morning strolling around town while Alex stayed in the hotel looking through old newscasts and reading about ULY447 and the *Lantner* incident. The weather was cold in Moreska, so I treated myself to a new sweater and a matching cap. I put them on and went back out to where the manor had been and stood on the cliff's edge thinking the kind of thoughts you do when the wind is blowing hard at your back and it's a hundred meters straight down to some water and a lot of rocks. When I got back to the hotel in midafternoon, Alex was waiting for me. "I've been looking at the other houses that were blown up that night," he said.

"Did you find a connection to Demery?"

"Nothing on the net. But I made some calls. One of the houses belonged to William Kelton. The mayor of Mancuso, which is just down the road a few klicks. His wife and daughter died in the blast. And a visitor. Apparently the daughter's fiancé.

"The wife might be of interest."

"Why?"

"She was retired. Taught at Travis University for a while. Wrote popular science articles for a number of publications. Did some sort of extradimensional research at Quantum Labs, which is a pretty good haul from where she lived."

"She had a link with Demery?"

"Yes. Her name was Jennifer. She and Demery were at one time members of the Archimedes Club."

"For people interested in math?"

"Very good, Chase. They used to compete in problem-solving exercises. Among themselves, and with other groups. A couple of the members I talked to said that Demery and Jennifer were close friends."

"Okay. So where does that lead us?"

"Let's try to find out. Kelton wasn't home when the explosion happened. But Jennifer was."

"What happened to the husband? Kelton?"

"He was on a hunting trip. From which he never returned. Disappeared in the woods. No one ever found the body."

"Was he hunting alone?"

"No. There were five or six of them. The others said he wandered off from the campsite and didn't come back."

"Either of them have an avatar?"

"Jennifer did. But it's gone now. Incidentally, of the people who lived in the eighteen homes destroyed that night, eleven or twelve had avatars, including some kids. They were all removed. Nobody seems to know who took them down.

"Family members who weren't home when their houses were hit either dropped out of sight, or turned up dead. Including some children."

"Incredible," I said.

"I didn't realize Nicorps was so ruthless."

He'd drawn the curtains across the windows, blocking off all but a slash of sunlight. I put my new cap back on. "So, Alex, do we pay a visit to City Hall?"

Only a few remembered Mayor Kelton. It had been, after all, thirty-three years since he'd disappeared during that ill-fated hunting trip. There were two or three around town who'd been staff people at that time. They couldn't find a kind word to say for him. The mayor had been affable and easygoing in public, and a tyrant behind the scenes. He had a short temper, grabbed the credit for everything, never talked to his people except to criticize. "I hated working for him," one of the former staffers told us. "But I wanted a political career, and he was the only set of coattails in the area." Another admitted to having experienced a sense of relief when he'd disappeared. "I felt guilty about it," she said. "But I can't say I was sorry he was gone."

Never heard from again. It was the hallmark of people who'd gotten in trouble with the authorities. They went for a walk and didn't come home.

In fact, though, blowing up houses was not an aberration. We combed through twenty-seven years of Aramy Cleev rule and found that the tactic was used on a regular basis. In several of the other instances, it seemed clear that the houses had been taken out to ensure that potentially embarrassing information hadn't gone public. Occasionally, the method had been employed simply to send a message.

One older woman, who had served as a consultant, still seemed frightened when discussing the event. "My generation," she said, "will never feel completely comfortable talking politics. You just can't be sure he won't come back."

"Kelton?"

"Aramy Cleev. Some of the family is still around, and there are a lot of people who'd like to see them return to power." She lowered her voice. "There's talk they have a clone stashed away somewhere. Waiting." She looked past me into that long-gone world.

"Why do you think it happened?" Alex asked her. "What possible reason could Nicorps have had?"

"I don't know, Mr. Benedict." We were in a modest restaurant across the street from City Hall. It was the middle of the afternoon, so there weren't many customers. In fact, other than us, only two. "In those days there didn't necessarily have to be a reason. People just went away."

"Did the mayor ever seem fearful? Did he ever talk about the possibility that something like this might happen?"

"Not that I knew about, no." She stirred her tea and looked pained. Frightened.

"It strikes me," I said, "that going into politics in that kind of system was dangerous."

Across the street a skimmer was landing on the City Hall pad. She watched it set down, and a young couple climbed out. "Probably going to get a marriage license," she said. Then: "No. It wasn't really dangerous. There was a lot of corruption. But as long as you played along, didn't make any noise, you were fine. I didn't have any power, so Nicorps didn't even notice I was there."

"Did Cleev himself run for office?"

"Oh, sure. Every five years. Like clockwork. The Cleevs always pretended we were a republic. They held elections. And they always won big. Like ninety-nine percent of the vote. But nobody ever said anything about it." She grew thoughtful. "Except Katy Doyle."

"What happened to her?"

"She was running for mayor. This was before Bill's time. Anyhow, she lost. Almost unanimously. A short time later, she issued a statement about how she'd been wrong about Cleev, and what a great leader he was. Then she left town. We never knew what happened to her. I'm pretty sure she was trying to get clear, but I don't know whether she succeeded."

The young couple bounced up the walkway and into the building. I remember thinking they didn't look old enough to be getting married. "One more question," said Alex.

"Okay."

"It'll seem like a strange one."

"That's all right."

"His wife. Did you know her?"

"Oh, yes. We all knew Jennifer."

"Did either of them, Jennifer or Bill, ever talk about far-out stuff? Like aliens? Or the *Lantner* asteroid? Anything at all like that?"

"I'm not sure what the *Lantner* asteroid is. But, no. The mayor spent his time hunting, playing cards, and socializing. Other than politics, that was all he cared about. And Jenny? I didn't really know her that well, but she seemed to have both feet on the ground."

Quantum Labs had gone out of business years before, but there were still a couple of people on the faculty at Travis who remembered Jennifer.

"She was okay," one of them told us. "She was quiet. Reserved. I don't think she ever felt comfortable in a classroom. But she had a pretty good reputation as a physicist." He looked hard at us, wondering whether to say more. Then, what the hell, he plowed ahead: "Bill didn't like her much. He was always running around. Cheated on her. Not that it matters now, I guess. But you never saw them together. Except at weddings or funerals." He looked uncomfortable. "I'm sorry. Speaking ill of the dead and all that. But you asked."

"Any idea what happened that night? At their house?"

"You mean the explosion?"

"Yes."

"We always assumed her husband had gotten in over his head somewhere, and Nicorps simply took him out." He shrugged. "Unfortunately for Jenny, she got caught in the blast. Although when Nicorps got involved, *everybody* got caught in the blast."

"Did you ever hear any kind of explanation? What he might have done to get in trouble?"

"No. Nothing. Alex, the mayor took care of number one. It always surprised me, what happened, because I would have thought he'd have been the last to run afoul of the security people. But he must have offended *somebody*."

We were in his office, which he shared with two other instructors. One, a young woman, picked that moment to come in. We did a round of introductions, then she excused herself, glad to meet you, sorry to run off. She picked up a set of notes and was gone. Alex was leaning against a windowsill. "Did either of them have any connection to Edward Demery?" he asked.

"Aha. I should have guessed that was coming. And the answer is no. None that I know of."

"Not Jennifer either?"

"They knew each other. Beyond that, I'm not aware of anything."

"Did she have any connection with the *Lantner*?"

He had to think about it. "The ship that disappeared, right? No. What does that have to do with anything?"

"Probably nothing."

"Yes. I just don't know of a reason. Both houses were hit the same night. Nicorps probably just had its assassination squads out. Take care of everybody at once. You know they weren't the only people hit? There were fifteen or sixteen other places they got. All around the region."

"We know."

He shook his head. "It was probably more economical to blow them all up at the same time."

The young man who'd died that night visiting the Keltons was Jaris Cole. All these years later, his mother still carried the pain in her eyes. "You don't get past something like that," she told me. "It's the one thing in my life that I'd change if I could. And the only thing that really mattered."

She was an ordinary-looking woman, quiet, introverted, with a resigned smile. Her husband had died a few years after the incident, and there'd been no other children.

"At the time," she said, "Jaris was about to marry Marinda. The mayor's daughter. She was a pretty little thing. Would have made a perfect—" She stopped, bit her lip, and waved it away. "The date was set." We were seated in an overlook, protected from the weather, watching the forest absorb a light rain. Alex had stayed away, assuming she'd be more open with me. "You'd have liked her, Chase."

"I'm sure I would."

"Not at all like her mother."

"You didn't like Jennifer?"

"Jennifer was all right, I suppose. Not the kind of woman you could get close to, though. But as the wedding date approached, we got to working together, planning things. It was a good time."

"I'm sure it was."

"We actually became friends." The wind blew some rain in on us, but she didn't seem to mind. "One day we met in the Sunlight Diner, over near the park. You could see it from here if the trees didn't get in the way. We wanted to talk about the details of the ceremony. There'd been a problem about that. The Keltons weren't very religious. The mayor pretended to be, because people wouldn't have voted for him if they knew what he really thought. But Jennifer was the decision-maker in the family, and she was dead set against a religious ceremony. I'd asked Jaris about that, and he said it was okay, they'd get somebody to bless the marriage later.

"Tank wasn't happy with it. My husband. But we decided we'd just let it go. We didn't want to create a problem. So I was going to tell her we'd thought about it and agreed it was okay to go with a civil ceremony. I saved it for last. We finished eating and came here, right where we're sitting now. And I had just raised the subject, when she held up both hands asking me not to go any further. Her face crinkled up like she was about to start crying. She had to take a minute to get her voice under control. Then she said don't worry about it, she really didn't give a damn, do the religious ceremony if we wanted. It would be okay."

"Did she say why she'd changed her mind?"

"No. Just that it didn't matter."

"You didn't *ask* her why?"

"Chase, I quit while I was ahead." Her brow furrowed.

There was something else, and I waited for her to tell me.

Finally, it came: "What she really said, as best I can remember, was: 'Goddam Calienté.' Then, 'Elda, it just doesn't matter anymore.'"

"*Calienté*. What's that?"

"It's an island."

"Where?"

"I don't know. On the other side of the world somewhere."

"Elda," I said, "I can imagine how difficult this must be for you."

"No. That's all right." She managed a smile. "It helps to talk about it."

"Just one more question: You've told this story to other people?"

"Yes."

"To Vicki Greene?"

"Yes," she said. "I did. Do you know Vicki Greene?"

That night, I relayed everything to Alex. Then, while I got a sandwich out of the kitchen, he consulted the AI. When I sat down with him again a few minutes later he wanted to know whether Elda had specified that *Caliente* meant the island.

"She said she really didn't know *what* Jennifer was referring to. That she *assumed* she meant the island. But she doesn't think she asked."

"It's a tourist spot," said Alex. "One of the Golden Isles."

"You checked?"

"It gets tens of thousands of visitors every year."

"Okay."

"There are a lot of other Calientés around. There is a sub-stantial number of people with that name living within a thou-sand kilometers of Mancuso. There's a physicist, a mathematician, two dentists, lots of persons of leisure, retired people, screwups, you name it." He shrugged. "We could hunt forever and not come up with the correct reference.

"There was also, thirty years ago, a touring musical with the name. And a Calienté hotel chain, and a novel titled *Mission to Calienté.*"

"Did you read it?"

"Are you serious?"

"Sure."

"It's about a survey group to a planet that, as far as I can tell, is purely fictional. The mission, however, disappears, and a team is sent to find out what happened."

"And—?

"I didn't get any further. If you can find the time, you might take a look at it tonight. But I don't think it's going to help us. Despite the missing mission."

"Okay."

"There's an aircraft design called the Calienté. The thing

isn't manufactured anymore. But it was at the time the houses
were blown up."

"There's more?"

"There's a *Calienté* that makes the run between Salud Afar
and Rimway. It's named for a crewman who fought off a bunch
of lunatics who tried to take over a ship. They were going to
crash it into Marinopolis in an effort to kill Cleev. That was
forty years ago."

"You think that might be it?"

"Hard to see how." He checked his notebook. "And in geo-
graphical sites, aside from the island group, there was also at
one time, before the rise of the Bandahrs, a Calienté state. There
is currently a Calienté mountain range and a Calienté River. All
on another continent, by the way. Calientés helped lead governments and revolutions, two made literary reputations for themselves, one wrote a symphony, sixteen (that I've been able to
find) founded or led major corporations, several became well-
known entertainers, one accidentally burned down a house with
six people in it, three became judges with prominent reputations. One was a serial killer. Another gave his life to rescue a
stranger during a flood.

"There was another starship with the name, by the way, but
it goes way back. It was a second-millennium warship. There
was also a Calienté mission. That was a long time ago, too.
More than seven centuries. It was sent out by the"—he checked
the notebook—"Beila Ti civilization. That's the one the Cleevs
overthrew." He shook his head. "Did you know there's another
star out in the general direction of Callistra?"

"I didn't know. Does it matter?"

"It's Seepah. A class-G dwarf. It's a long way from here.
Over a thousand light-years. When Callistra's directly overhead, Seepah would be about halfway down the western sky."

"I've never noticed it."

"It isn't visible to the naked eye."

"And that's where the Calienté mission went?"

"Yes."

"And they found what—?"

"Not much. Eight worlds, one in an early bio state. Single-celled stuff only. They left a series of hyperlight monitors in orbit. One or two at each world."

"Okay. Why do we care?"

"After about a half century, one shut down."

"A half century? You'd expect that."

"Right. Thirty or so years later, two more shut down."

"Really?"

"Simultaneously."

"That doesn't seem likely. Unless—Maybe there was a solar flare."

Alex shrugged. "Don't know."

"What did they find out when they went back to take a look?"

"They didn't."

"They didn't go back?"

"No."

"Why not?"

"By the time it happened, Beila Ti didn't exist anymore. It had been taken over by the Bandahr. The Cleevs apparently weren't very interested in astronomy."

"Well," I said, "I can't see how it connects with anything."

"A simultaneous shutdown seems odd."

"I'll grant that. Is this place anywhere close to 447, the asteroid with the monument?"

"No. It's a couple of thousand light-years away."

"Okay. I think we should dismiss it and stick to the problem at hand."

"It *is* suggestive, Chase."

"Of what?"

He changed the subject: "Actually there *are* other Calientés. A number of schools have the name, some parks, at least one zoo, and two social clubs. There was even, at the time the monitors shut down, a comedian."

"Have you tried asking the AI to sort through it?"

"We need Jacob," he said. "This one's okay, but he has a hard time if I can't give him exact parameters. But the answer is *yes*. Nobody, and nothing, as far as the AI can see, has a direct connection with any of the Keltons, with Edward Demery, or with the prospective groom. Well, that's not entirely true. One of them was a service technician who worked on the power at the groom's home three years before he met Jennifer's daughter."

We sat looking at each other. "Maybe it's time for us to go home," I said. "We've made a reasonable effort."

Those brown eyes brightened. "I'm surprised that you'd give up so easily, Chase."

"So easily? We've come a zillion light-years. We've traveled all over the world. Talked to half the people on the planet. Lost a skimmer. Damn near got eaten. And I know you don't believe me, but I ran into a ghost. I say we take the hint."

We had the HV on, sound down. A journalist was seated at a desk marked GLOBAL NEWS. He looked excited. Alex increased the volume.

"*—Another incursion. Apparently, a Mute warship and a pair of Coalition destroyers traded shots out near Naramitsu. Preliminary reports indicate the Mute was driven off. No casualties reported. Global News will keep you updated as this story comes in.*"

"Alex, what's really going on?"

"I wish I knew," he said.

"So what's next?"

"Mikel Wexler owns an extensive estate."

"Really?"

"And he's accumulated over the last few years a substantial interest in two major corporations."

"So why do we care?"

"Maybe we don't. But the estate is up for sale."

"Okay."

"And he's recently sold off his other holdings."

"That's strange. Is he expecting an economic downturn?"

"I don't know. You may be right. Maybe we *do* deserve some time off. A few days of vacation."

"Don't tell me. We're talking about the Golden Isles."

eiGHTeeN

Ultimately everything is math. The number of protons in a given element, the gravitational force that binds Rimway to the sun, the number of heartbeats you get. Learn to count, my boy. Therein lies wisdom.

—*Wish You Were Here*

Calienté was the principal island in a group of four in the middle of the Balin Sea. These were the Golden Isles. All had beautiful beaches, and the nightclubs and restaurants were spread equitably among the four. None of the islands measured as much as seven kilometers at its widest.

They would have been an ideal location for Vicki. Two of the islands had occult connections. On Khyber Island, something spoke in the winds. And Calienté claimed a ghostly yacht.

The weather was warm when we arrived. Alex went to work with the house AI while I sat out by the pool. Topless again. I told myself a little exhibitionism was good for the soul, but I don't think I could ever get used to it.

The yacht legend had it that two lovers, one on Calienté and the other on Khyber (though sometimes he was from Sanikaw) had been kept apart by feuding families. It was the classic situation. The boy eventually made off with the family's yacht, determined to collect his lover and head for a more rational place. But a storm blew up during the crossing.

The family discovered he was missing, and the boat as well. They called him, pleaded with him to return. The boy refused, and the storm overwhelmed him. Wreckage washed ashore a day or two later. The lover was never found.

According to the story, on dark nights, when neither Callistra nor the galactic rim is visible, the yacht can be seen, still trying to get across the narrow strip of water to Khyber Island. People on Khyber claim the girl's spirit roams the beaches at such times, waiting for him.

It's an intriguing tale, and I don't think I've ever been to a remote place that doesn't have one like it. It was the sort of story that would have enchanted Vicki.

That said, we found no indication she'd ever visited the Golden Isles. There was no mention of her in the news archives. Nobody remembered her. One of the bookstores had a mystery club, and the coordinator was shocked to learn that Vicki Greene might have been in the Isles and she hadn't been aware of it.

Alex came out after a while. I picked up the notebook I'd brought out and laid it on my chest. Casually, of course. He sat down in the beach chair beside me and pretended nothing unusual was going on.

I let it go for a while. Then: "Any luck?"

"Maybe." He glanced at the notebook. "Enjoying yourself?"

"As a matter of fact, yes."

"Good," he said. "I think we wasted our time coming out here."

"I like islands."

"That's the right spirit."

I met a couple of the local guys, one of whom was maybe the funniest character I've ever seen. I remember regretting that he lived so far away. When he asked about my accent—"You're not from around here, are you?"—we both had a good laugh.

"Not exactly," I said. His name was Charjek. A strange name. He called himself *Charger*, and it fit.

We had a good time. Next day we hit the beach. That night we went to dinner and a show. He asked whether I'd be staying on Calienté and looked genuinely unhappy when I told him we'd be going home shortly. We traded contact information, assured each other we'd get together again, and even sent each other occasional messages later. I never saw him again, though, after those few days.

I can't recapture it now, but nobody has ever made me laugh so much.

Two days later I said good-bye to Charger and we returned to Moreska. We arrived on a cold, rainy morning, got off the plane, and started over to Sunlight Travel to pick up a shuttle we'd booked. Instead we picked up something else.

A man and a woman were waiting for us. They showed us credentials identifying them as agents of the Coalition Security Service. CSS. "We have a skimmer topside," the woman said without inflection. Her name was Krestoff. "We'd appreciate it if you'd come with us." She was attractive, in a cold, hard way. Blond hair, brown eyes, all business.

Alex stood his ground. "Why?"

Her partner was big and might have been a professional bong thrower. He smiled down at Alex.

Krestoff shook her head. "You've an appointment."

"With whom? You mind telling us what this is about?"

"I don't know the details, Mr. Benedict. We are here simply to provide escort. Now, I'll need your comm links." Alex's notebook was clipped to a pocket. "And that, too, please."

"Are we under arrest?"

"Not yet," she said.

NiNeTeeN

The ideal death, the death to be hoped for, is one that comes
swiftly, out of the night, that takes you while you're enjoying the
strawberries, and sweeps you away before you've had time even
to know that the lights have gone out.

—*Midnight and Roses*

"Either of you have a weapon?" asked Krestoff.

It was in my bag. She led us out onto the airfield. A white
skimmer was waiting, with Coalition markings on its hull.

Our bags appeared. They opened them, did a quick search,
confiscated my scrambler, and gave me a receipt for it. Then
they directed us to get on board.

They climbed in behind us. The pilot was in a separate compartment behind a closed door. Bong pulled the hatch shut, and
Krestoff told the pilot to go. He said something about overtime,
and we lifted off in the twilight and turned south.

"Where are we going?" Alex asked.

"To a location where you'll be quite safe, Mr. Benedict."

"I'm safe here."

"You've no reason to be worried," she said. That of course
is exactly the kind of remark that scares the hell out of me.

"Where are we going?" asked Alex again.

"Special place," said Krestoff. "You'll like it."

"Is it a detention center?" I asked.

"I'd think of it more as a vacation spot." Her tone was dismissive.

We traveled over a wide stretch of ocean and then inland. Alex looked at me and shook his head. *Sorry I got you into this.*

It got dark quickly. After a while there was nothing to see except moving lights in the sky and on the ground, and occasional clusters of illuminated buildings. After about an hour we passed over a city.

"What's it about?" I asked him, not bothering to keep my voice down.

"Later," he said.

After a while, the occasional lights revealed that we were into a mountain range. We were gaining altitude, and snow showed up on the ground. The wind picked up, and the skimmer bucked and swayed.

"Almost there," said the pilot.

The descent was, well, exciting. We got tossed around pretty good, and the pilot said that he thought we should give it up and come back later.

"Land the goddam thing," said Krestoff.

"Look, Maria, don't give me trouble."

"Can you take us down?"

"Yes. If you insist."

"Then please do it."

I looked at Alex. Alex cleared his throat and took a deep breath. In the hands of idiots.

Krestoff caught his reaction. "Don't worry, Mr. Benedict. Squeej will manage."

Squeej? What kind of name was that for a pilot? But I thought it prudent not to provide another distraction.

The wind blew us all over the sky. But we kept going down. By then it was dark, black, stygian the way no other place aboveground ever is. Our navigation lamps threw beams all around us, but the only thing I could make out was snow. Closer to the mountain peaks, O Lord. I hoped Squeej knew what he was doing, and I wished he might have been more inclined to stand up to Maria. Bong said nothing. *Whatever comes will come.*

Then, with no warning, we banged down. "On the ground," said Squeej, as if it might have been possible not to notice.

Krestoff and Bong dragged heavy jackets out of stowage and pulled them on.

"How about us?" said Alex.

"You won't need them."

That sounded ominous.

The pilot came back into the cabin, opened the hatch, and the wind grabbed it and almost yanked it out of his hand. Cold air invaded the cabin. "Okay, you two," said Krestoff. "Let's move."

You betcha.

They herded us outside into minus-zero temperatures and a snow cover. I was chattering already. And I thought: They were going to kill us, after all. Just leave us to the storm. Bong opened the cargo compartment and took out our bags. Krestoff turned on a flashlight, pointed it at the luggage, and looked at Alex. "Get them," she said.

We did. Then we waited while she got her bearings. She flashed the light around until it hit the corner of a building. "This way." I thought briefly about trying to jump them. There'd never be a better chance. But Bong stayed off to one side, and Krestoff, with the lamp in one hand and the scrambler in the other, kept behind us. The door in the skimmer closed, and the pilot, who was no dummy, stayed inside. Ahead, lights appeared in the storm. A postlight. And windows.

It was a two-story house. With a deck. We climbed the steps, and Krestoff waved me off to one side. "Mr. Benedict, stand in front, please. This will be your home for the immediate future, so it needs to get to know you."

"I'm cold," I said. "Can't we do this later?"

She ignored me. "Let's get it done, please."

Alex gave the sensors a look, then stepped aside, and I took his place. When I'd finished, the front door opened. We hurried in and dropped our bags on a carpeted floor.

I'm not sure what I expected. But there was nobody home. The temperatures were just a notch higher than outside. Krestoff looked around. Given some heat, it might have been a comfortable little place. The furniture was by no means lush, but it looked okay: a sofa, three chairs, and some tables, one with a chess set. Dark drapes, frozen at the moment, but they'd thaw. A fireplace with a stack of logs. Pictures of mountain views and seascapes on the walls. Bookshelves with four or five books, and some plastic flowers in a vase. A staircase rose to the second floor. "It'll warm up in a little while," said Krestoff.

I started over to get a fire going, but she waved me away. "When we're out of here, there'll be plenty of time to do that. You've a working AI. Her name is Kellie." She checked the time. Apparently late for an appointment. "Say hello, Kellie."

A female voice responded: *"I am at your service, Alexander."*

"You've enough supplies to last two weeks. Someone will be back before then to refurbish things. You have a refrigerator, and there's a storage compartment in back.

"There's also a utility shed on the west side of the building.

"You can't communicate with anyone except us. If you want to talk to us, tell Kellie to put you through. If you try to manipulate the AI, or break into the comm system, it will shut down. Self-destruct, actually. And maybe take you with it. I'm not sure about that detail. So it's probably best to stay away from it." Another smile.

"Do we have any jackets here?" asked Alex.

"No. You've no need for them. You won't be going anywhere. There are blankets. The temperature tonight is forty below. The wind is thirty, out of the south, so you'll want to stay inside. You're a long way from anybody who can help you."

I could feel warm air coming through the vents.

"You have a complete range of HV reception. You can watch anything you want. You can't interact, of course. Sorry about that."

"Where are we?" asked Alex.

"You're on the Valeria Reservation. It's government property. No one will bother you here. But you are at a substantial altitude. Be careful if you go outside.

"You're probably wondering whether we have the place

wired. We see no need to intrude on your privacy. You'll probably not want to believe that, but—" She shrugged. "Do you have any questions?"

"Yes," said Alex. "What happens now?"

"Someone will be here shortly to see you. Beyond that, I have no information."

I was still cold. "Where are the blankets?"

"Upstairs in the master bedroom." She graced me with a lascivious smile. Knew exactly what I wanted. "There's a closet." She glanced over at her partner. "Are we forgetting anything, Corel?"

"I think that covers it." His pronunciation was perfect. The guy looked like a thug, but I decided he was smarter than he looked.

"When can we expect our visitor?" asked Alex.

Krestoff did a casual shrug. "Don't know."

She and Bong exchanged looks. And left. Kellie closed the door behind them. I went over to the window and watched them climb back into the skimmer. Moments later the vehicle rose into the falling snow and was quickly swallowed by the storm.

"What's it about?" I asked Alex.

"Hold on a second. Let's get warm first." He went upstairs and, moments later, came down with an armful of blankets.

I threw some logs and a starter into the fireplace and pushed the button. A jet ignited the starter and, moments later, the logs began to burn. We dragged two chairs close in. Alex handed me a blanket. They were cold, but that wouldn't last long. I pulled mine over my shoulders and sank onto one of the chairs. It was hard as rock.

"So," I said, as we started to get comfortable, "what's it about?"

"They think we found out what Vicki Greene knew."

"Did we?"

"No."

"Maybe we should tell them we don't know."

"It wouldn't matter, Chase. We now know beyond a doubt she found out *something*. It's beyond simple inference at this stage."

"You think they're going to kill us?"

"If they wanted to do that, they'd have done it already."
He adjusted his blanket. "I don't think the heating unit's working. Anyhow, they can't have us turning up dead. Or even disap-
pearing."

"Too much publicity?"

"Right. The last thing they want is to attract attention."

"So what's the secret?"

"I'm not sure yet."

"Ummm. I hate to mention this, Alex—"

"Yeah?"

"But if they can't kill us, and they can't have us disappear—"

"You're probably right, Chase."

"They're going to do a lineal block."

"That would be my guess."

"It's what happened to Vicki."

Alex stared into the fire, and his eyes hardened.

TWENTY

"Dr. Ventnor, every door opens into another room, or another corridor. There are no windows. No exit. How do we get out?"

"You're wrong, Howie. There is a way out. McComber made that quite clear."

"But McComber's body is in the dining room. He never got out himself."

"Yes. I know. I wish I had an easy explanation for that."

—*Love You to Death*

I fell asleep in the chair while the storm howled at the windows. There were two bedrooms upstairs, but I was happy near the fire. Occasionally I heard Alex moving around the room.

Toward dawn, the storm stopped, or at least it lost its energy. Alex had apparently drawn the curtains. I padded across the floor and peeked out through them. The snow, illuminated by the light from the window, stretched away into a gray haze.

I thought about Vicki, who'd gone through something like this, too. Except that she'd been alone with whatever it was she'd found out. And Jennifer Kelton, thirty years ago, apparently driven to tears by the same secret.

Calienté.

It doesn't matter anymore, she'd said about the religious ceremony at her daughter's wedding.

It doesn't matter anymore.

Alex was breathing softly in his chair. The fire was dying, so I got up and tossed in another log. The supply was getting low. We'd probably have to cut more. That would be fun.

I woke again to the smell of bacon. Alex was in the kitchen. I got up, kept the blanket wrapped around me, and wandered in. He was seated at the table watching a newscast. "What's happening?" I asked.

"Actually, something *has* happened."

"They didn't come back, did they?"

"No. Nothing that pedestrian." He got up and headed for the living room. I followed.

He looked up at the shelf, with the half dozen or so books lying on their sides. "They're all cheap novels," he said.

"Okay."

"Except that one." He pointed at the coffee table, where a large book lay open. I looked at him. "Not just *any* book," he added.

We sat down on the sofa, and he opened it to the title page. It was Churchill's *Their Finest Hour.*"

"Alex," I said, "at the moment I think we have bigger problems."

"This is one of the volumes of his *History of the Second World War.* It's priceless."

"Good. If we get out of here, we can make a killing."

"Chase, the *History* is supposed to be lost. Except for a few fragments. Now we have an entire volume. Not only that, it's the Keifer translation. And let me show you something else."

I was thinking how his breakfast was getting cold, but I knew better than to bring up trivia when he was on a roll.

"Look at this." He opened it to the inside cover. It was stamped. ADMINISTRATOR'S LIBRARY. "The bureaucrats owned it and they didn't even know what it was worth."

"Maybe Kilgore himself had it."

"I'd hate to think he's that dumb."

*   *   *

The rest of the morning's news was routine. A tax revolt in a place called Champika, and a triple murder in Marinopolis. There'd been an accident at one of the shelters they were building against the Mute invasion. Two dead.

Along with the bacon, he was eating eggs and home fries. I leered at it, and he smiled. "Sorry," he said. "This was the last of it. But they have a grain dish. Something like oatmeal. You could try that. Looks good."

"You're kidding," I said.

"Well, yes. Actually, the larder's full."

I decided cinnamon toast, orange juice, eggs, and coffee were just what I wanted, and passed the order to Kellie. I can't really say I enjoyed it all that much, though. It's hard to concentrate on food when you keep waiting for the skimmer to land and bring somebody who's going to insert mental blocks of some sort.

It was hard to believe such a thing could really work. That they could induce an inhibition so strong that it would prevent me from acting on whatever I wanted to act on. But I didn't want to give them a shot at it.

The cliff edge ran right by the window. I got up, went over, and stood on my toes to get a better look down. I couldn't see much other than a tree that was growing almost horizontally out of the cliff edge.

"It's a long drop," said Alex.

"We need to go out and look around."

"Too cold. We have no coats."

"We could wrap up in blankets."

"You'd need boots, too." He scooped up some of the bacon, put it in his mouth, and took a bite out of a roll. "There's no place to go anyway. We're on a plateau."

"No way to get off?"

"Can't be sure, but it's a safe assumption."

"If we wait for it to get warm—"

"It won't help if we go out and freeze." He finished with the roll and indulged himself with more eggs. "I don't suppose you could rig a transmitter of some sort?"

"From the HV? No. I doubt *anybody* could do it. Certainly not me."

"I didn't think so."

"How long do you figure we've got? Before they come back?"

"Don't know. Not long. I think they'll want to get it done as quickly as they can."

Jackets were packed in our luggage, but they weren't worth much in those temperatures. Still, I put mine on and went outside. The air had a knife-edge to it. The plateau was small. If I'd been dressed for it, and the snow wasn't up to my ankles, I could have walked across it in five minutes.

Without getting too close, I looked over the edge. There were a few patches of forest down there, a lot of ridges and gullies. And a river. A large mountain lay to the south. (At least I thought it was the south.) And immediately below us, I could see something moving, an animal of some kind. And that was it. No human habitation was visible anywhere.

Alex came up behind me. "Careful," he said.

Something with wings showed up and took an interest in us. I found a dead branch and picked it up. Just in case.

I decided I'd go out every day and look over the edge. It didn't take long. The following afternoon, I saw five people in the valley. It looked like a hunting party. They were directly below me. I called out and waved, but they never turned around. Another one, trailing the rest, emerged from a patch of forest. I wasn't sure, but I thought he looked up and saw me. I waved again. Yelled. He kept going. They passed below where I was standing, so I found a dead branch and threw it over the side.

I tossed it well away from them, so there'd be no danger. It landed silently in the trees, but it must have caught their attention. They stopped, and I followed up with a rock. Which was all I could find on short notice. It landed in much the same place, while I jumped up and down and waved and yelled. One of them raised his weapon, and I realized he was going to take a shot at me. I ducked.

They use disrupters for hunting on Salud Afar. So I had no way to know whether he'd actually fired or not. But it was clear they weren't friendly, and as they walked away, I was tempted to lob a few more stones down on them.

But it gave me an idea. I had a paper notebook in one of my bags. I dug it out, and began writing a message on each page: HELP. WE'RE PRISONERS ATOP THE PLATEAU. NEED RESCUE. And, as an afterthought: CONTACT ROB PEIFER. REWARD. I signed it with Alex's name.

"What are you doing?" he asked.

"Giving us another shot. I wish we had some plastic bags around here." I did a search but found nothing. No bags. Also no rubber bands. No plastic containers. No paper clips.

In the end I simply crumpled the notes up, sixty-two individual pages, went back out, and walked around the rim, giving them to the wind.

"Well," Alex said, when I got back, "who knows?"

The house was comfortable enough. It had an old-world feel, with its fabric chairs and wooden walls. We kept the fireplace going, even though we no longer needed it. The living room had a wall-length set of windows and a mahogany-colored domed ceiling. The kitchen boasted a magnificent view, which included the valley and the mountain. It must have been the tallest mountain on the planet.

The furniture was all hand-carved. The chairs and sofa used gold fabric. Metal lamps stood on the tables. Under other circumstances, it would have been a lovely retreat. Except, of course, that you wouldn't want to try skiing, or any other outdoor sport. But for a place to sit by the windows with a good book, it was hard to beat.

When I got back from throwing paper off the cliff, I kicked off my shoes and socks and settled down in front of the fireplace again. "Well," I said, "it doesn't look very encouraging out there."

Alex gazed up at the domed ceiling. "You don't suppose they have any gravity belts here anywhere?"

Ah yes. It was probably a good thing that old staple of fantasy epics had never proven feasible. Drunks at six thousand meters. Not a happy prospect. Although we could have used a couple at the time.

"As soon as I get warm," he said, "I want to take a look at the utility shed. Maybe there'll be something useful in there."

The shed was sparse. We found a few spare lighting fixtures, two shovels, some nuts and bolts and nails, a backup calibrator for Kellie, a broken HV, a drill, an ax, thirty or forty meters of cable, two ladders, a box of ceiling hooks, a few flowerpots, two cans of paint, three pristine brushes, and some fishing gear.

Fishing gear.

We went back inside and debated whether we should disable Kellie. "She's probably reporting back," said Alex.

"Disable her, and we still have no guarantee we aren't being watched."

Nevertheless, we both felt it would be a good idea to put her out of action. So we asked her whether she could be safely disabled.

"Yes," she said. *"Is that what you wish to do?"*

"Yes."

"You are certain?"

"Yes. Nothing personal."

"As you wish." Her lights went out. I disconnected her power source just to be safe.

"Okay," said Alex. "We'll have to assume they're still watching us. You have anything to say you don't want them to hear, we go outside."

I looked out at the snow. Somebody was going to pay.

That afternoon, a skimmer came in from the east. It threw a scare into me. I hurried outside. It was a big white vehicle with THE DOWNTOWNERS stenciled across its hull, along with a G clef and a few musical notes. I waved and shouted.

It kept going. Then it arced around and started back. I could see the pilot, a male, with a woman beside him. And it looked like two kids in back.

I waved some more. "Help!" Alex ran outside and jumped up and down.

One of the kids saw me. I watched him push the other one and point in my direction. They laughed. "Yes!" I said. "Alex, we might get a break here."

Alex kept waving.

I cheered.

The pilot was looking at us now.

"Help!"

The pilot waved back. Hi.

You idiot. Can't you see we're out here without any jackets? Freezing?

I squeezed my neck and tried to look in distress.

The kids laughed again, and the pilot waved a final time and began to climb. We watched them dwindle and finally vanish.

That night, while Alex paged through Churchill, I sat by the window and looked out at Callistra.

Vicki's star.

Bright and solid. The anchor of the heavens. It was the kind of star people write fairy tales about. That they take their kids into the backyard to see. Blue and beautiful. A beacon of assurance that all's right with the world.

TWENTY-ONE

When you see the horseman in your rearview mirror, it's time to throttle up.

—*Etude in Black*

In the morning, I told Alex I was going out to the utility shed.

"Why?"

"I want to get a shovel. In case somebody else flies over today, I'd like to be able to make it clear we need rescuing."

"How are you going to do that?"

"You can help, if you want."

"Sure," he said. "We can use an idea or two."

We went out to the shed. "I can't just sit around here," I told him, "knowing we don't have any way to defend ourselves, and Agent Krestoff might be back anytime. With Corel. And somebody to stick pins in our heads."

"They don't do it that way."

"Good. I'm much relieved."

We got the shovels and picked a spot in front of the villa. It was still cold, but not as brutal as it had been. We began moving snow. Alex admitted it was a good idea, and within a few minutes we'd spelled *help*. In very large letters. But it didn't look as if they'd be very visible from the air, so we tore up some bushes and branches and laid them in the letters.

When we'd finished, half-frozen, we went back inside. We took the shovels with us. They'd be the weapons of last resort.

I hobbled into the washroom, filled the tub with hot water, climbed in, and sat there until I got some feeling back.

That night I made us a hot supper. First cooking I'd done in a long time. We had meat loaf with a garlic flavor, a green vegetable, and mashed potatoes. Potatoes had originated on Earth, had spread across the worlds of the Confederacy, and had even made it to that far-off place. It was a good meal.

That night we settled in again to watch news accounts from around the world. People in places we'd never heard of were arguing about the cost of education. Others were angry that their neighbors were buying things like skimmers in other areas instead of shopping locally. Townspeople in a place named Shay Gaionne objected to ordinances requiring better maintenance of houses. Juvenile delinquents were a problem in some areas. And gangs. A large city on a coast somewhere was trying to decide whether gambling should be allowed near churches. Still others complained about the quality of entertainment. There were reports of another incursion by the Mutes. *"They fired on a Coalition patrol boat,"* said the reporter. *"Fortunately, there appear to have been no injuries."*

"What do you think, Alex?"

"About the attack? I don't believe it. The Mutes are nowhere near here."

The Coalition government was entering its political season, and there was an ongoing debate about banning involuntary mind wipes. Some candidates called it murder; others insisted it constituted a fresh start for people they referred to as psychologically disabled.

Alex fell asleep during an interview of a long-winded legislative candidate. I watched for a few minutes. Then I shut it down, turned off some of the lamps, and took a seat by the windows.

The world beyond the pale illumination cast by our lights was utterly dark. Callistra must have been in a different part of the sky. Or maybe it was cloudy. At night, you never could tell.

There was nothing out there, no sign of an aircraft. No artificial lights anywhere. I rearranged the cushions and decided they smelled vaguely of pine.

I wondered about Ben and asked myself what he might be doing at that moment and whether he ever thought about me. He'd always maintained that Alex was deranged and that I shouldn't be working for him. Sitting in the villa on that night, wondering when the bad guys would come to get us, I suspected he might be right.

A lineal block.

The prospect of losing part of myself, of going back to Rimway after they'd taken my freedom of action from me, drove me into a rage. I promised myself I wasn't going down without a fight. I would at the very least take out that nitwit female agent.

I couldn't imagine what it would be like to have an idea locked away, a memory that was still there but that I could not act on. They had done it to Vicki, and she'd become so desperate that she'd gone on to a complete mind wipe. Get rid of it. Get rid of everything she remembered about her life. What a price to pay.

What was it about?

ULY447? The Calienté mission? And a religious service that just didn't matter anymore?

Alex woke me early next morning. "Got work to do."

"What?" I said. "What is it?" I remembered the sign in the snow. "Did somebody come?"

"No. The wind filled it in during the night."

"Oh."

"I don't think it had much of a chance anyhow. We don't get a lot of traffic here."

"It was worth a try. So what's the work we have to do?"

"Get dressed," he said. "I'll show you." He leaned back and smiled. "Agent Krestoff and the mad doctor could come at any time. We want to be ready."

Twenty minutes later I went downstairs into the living room and found the extension ladder leaning against one wall. Snow had been tracked through the doorway when he brought it in from the shed.

"Problem?" I asked.

"No. Why?"

"The ladder."

"No. No problem." He was standing by one of the windows. The sun was just climbing into the sky.

"This place makes me dizzy," I said.

"Of course." He pointed at the tree that hung out over the edge of the precipice. "Look," he said.

"Yeah. It's hanging on for its life."

"Doesn't it give you any ideas?"

We plowed back out into the snow. "I don't think there's an imager anywhere inside," he said. "I've gone over the first floor pretty thoroughly. They might be able to hear us, but I doubt they're getting a picture."

"Okay."

He opened the door to the utility shed and picked up the ax. I laughed. "They're going to have guns," I said. "I doubt we'd have much chance with that."

"That's true, Chase. But we're low on firewood."

"Ah."

"I'm going to get some."

"Good idea."

"Meantime, I want you to paint the living room."

"Paint the living room?"

"Yes. I'll explain later."

"Alex—"

"Trust me."

"This is why the extension ladder's in there."

"Of course."

"You want me to paint the ceiling, too?"

"No. You won't have to do that."

"Then we've got the wrong ladder." I indicated the step ladder. "This is the one we want."

"We might need both."

I picked up one of the paint cans. "It's frozen."

"It'll thaw."

"You know, working with you can be frustrating at times."

"You've said that before."

"Okay. What color did you want me to use?" There were two cans. The labels described them as forest green and sunrise gold.

"Gold," he said. "Do the gold."

"Okay."

"I'll be in to help in a few minutes."

"All right."

"I put some cable inside, too. By the fireplace. We'll want to paint them also."

"We want to paint the *cables*?"

"Of course."

"They get the *green* paint, right?"

"Nope. Same color. Gold."

TWeNTY-TWO

"You're bluffing, Carla.".

"Well, Fallow, it's all you have left, isn't it? Here's your chance to go home early."

—*Etude in Black*

By the end of the day, the living room looked resplendent in its new coat of gold paint, as did the cables. We spent the evening and most of the night getting set up. At one point, we heard a skimmer pass overhead, and our hearts sank. I ran outside and, when I saw it wasn't the government vehicle, I waved like a crazy person. But I don't think they saw me at all.

We were up early next morning to begin working on the overhead. I began to think we might actually have a chance to pull it off. But the final preparations were difficult, and I spent a lot of time on the extension ladder, inserting ceiling hooks into the overhead dome, stringing cable, attaching and finally loading the blankets.

When I'd finished, I climbed down and put the ladder back in the shed. Then I went back inside, glad to feel the warmth again. Alex walked me right back outside. "We need to get them in the middle of the living room," he said.

"That shouldn't be hard."

We went back onto the deck and looked inside through an

open door. Speaking barely above a whisper, he said, "They'll need a table to do the procedure."

"The lineal block?"

"Yes."

There were two side tables, a coffee table, and a dining table. "We don't want them using the dining table," he said. Absolutely. It was out of the target area. "When we go back in, we'll pile dishes on it. Glasses. The toaster. Laundry. Hardware. And anything else we can find."

"Okay."

He looked around the living room. "Let's give them the coffee table."

"It's not exactly in the target area."

"I know. And you're right." He thought about it. "Okay, we can load that up, too. That leaves one of the side tables."

"Isn't it going to be a little obvious if you pull one of them out into the center of the room?"

"Get the chess set," he said. He removed a lamp from the side table and pulled the table into the target area. Then he put the chessboard on it and set up the pieces to create a game in progress. We took the two chairs from the dining table and put them on either side.

When it was finished, he looked around the room. He didn't say anything, but he looked happy.

We went back outside. "Anything else, Alex?" I asked.

He studied me and bit his lower lip. "Can you cut your hair a little shorter? To look like Krestoff's?"

It would take more than cutting it shorter. Krestoff was sporting a local style that apparently emphasized taking advantage of wind resistance. "Sure," I said.

"Do it." He sighed. "Pity we don't have some dye."

"So I could go blond?"

"Yes."

"I don't think I have the right complexion for it."

"In the dark, nobody's going to notice."

After that, it became just a matter of waiting. That, of course, is when you start worrying. "You know," I said, "maybe they're just going to leave us here. Or maybe they're hoping we'll try to climb down and get ourselves killed."

"No," said Alex. "If they'd wanted anything like that, they'd have pushed us off themselves. They would not be happy trying to explain how we turned up dead. Or missing. And for another thing, they don't know whether other people are aware why we came here." He kicked off his shoes and propped his feet on a stool. "The last thing they need is for something to happen to us."

We'd expected Krestoff to return within a day or two. But the days passed, and the skies remained empty. We saw a few aircraft, though they were too far or too high after that first time for us to have any realistic chance to signal for help.

It presented a problem. We couldn't risk having them arrive, say, in the middle of the night. Or slip in when we were watching the HV and not paying attention. If they took us by surprise, our escape plan would evaporate. So we set up a system. Twelve-hour watches during which one or the other of us was constantly on the lookout.

We rearranged the furniture and relaxed as best we could, with one of us always posted by the window or the front door.

What do you do with your time when you know somebody's coming to pick apart your brain? For me, it was mostly watching stuff that didn't require my paying attention. Comedies where people fell down a lot and thrillers that were mostly chases. And light reading. Material that didn't require emotional input. I had no emotions left.

We took our meals together, and in the early evenings we sat around the living room with the lights about halfway down. Alex was reading *Their Finest Hour*. He had the book on the coffee table and turned each page cautiously. He'd stop occasionally to read me a passage. He especially enjoyed doing Churchill's lines for me: *Never before in the history of human conflict . . .* And, *Victory at all costs, victory in spite of all terror, victory however long and hard the road may be . . .* "I wish we had him here," he said.

"Which side was he on?"

Alex rolled his eyes. "The civilized side." He grew thoughtful. "It's a pity they didn't have avatars. He was too early."

On the ninth day, a monster storm hit and left us buried in

snow. We opened the door when it was over and had to climb a snowbank just to get outside.

I hoped that maybe Peifer would discover we'd gone missing and would be hot on the trail. But that was a long shot. When I mentioned it to Alex, he asked how Peifer could possibly track us to that lonely outpost.

Since it was election season, we got to watch the various candidates going on about how they'd make life better for the world. Everybody made it a point to take a stand against the Mutes. They differed, of course, on the details. Some wanted to bring in the Confederacy. But the Confederacy wasn't all that popular on Salud Afar, where it was seen as a distant power that, given the chance, would happily make off with the world's resources. I got the impression politicians on Salud Afar made it a habit to run against the Confederacy, to paint it as a threat.

Other news was generally inconsequential: the unexpected death of a well-known one-time beauty queen, the scandal caused by the discovery that a former world-class athlete was a bigamist, a show-business celebrity arrested for obscene behavior. Another entertainment icon was being accused of having thrown his wife down a staircase. He claimed someone had broken into the house and done the deed.

There were reports of still another brush with Mute ships. *"No shooting this time,"* said a young, enthusiastic male journalist, *"but these incidents are becoming increasingly numerous. It looks as if we'd better prepare for the worst."*

That evening, we picked up an interview with an economist who claimed that something unusual was happening. *"A lot of the major corporations,"* he said, *"especially the places heavily invested in real estate, are divesting themselves. Downsizing in an extraordinary way."*

I looked at Alex. "That's what you were saying, except it sounds a bit bigger than you thought."

"Why?" asked the interviewer.

"Don't know," the economist said. *"It could be coincidental, but I doubt it. I suspect a downturn is coming."*

"But the economy's strong, isn't it, Cary?"

"It was a few weeks ago, Karm. But it's become pretty wobbly suddenly."

"Why?"

"I have no idea. The long-term trends are all up. The only thing I can think of, and I want to emphasize this is only a wild guess—"

"Go ahead, Cary. Let's have it."

"It may be that war is coming. War with the Mutes."

"But wouldn't that be a spur to production? Wars historically are good for business."

Cary nodded. "That's right, Karm. If you win them."

I must have been getting morose. Alex told me to cheer up, hang in, that we'd be all right. "We'll get out of here," he said. "And we'll get *Belle* and go out to the *Lantner* world and find out what's going on."

In the evenings, sometimes, I wrapped up in a blanket, turned off the outside lights, and went out on the deck to look at the sky. At the haze that was the rim of the Milky Way. Or in the opposite direction at Callistra. On the evening that we heard the economist, Alex joined me. We stood for a while, standing in the darkness. "They should be here soon," he said.

TWENTY-THREE

Watch your head.

—Dying to Know You

The day after we'd watched the interview with the economist, they came. Alex was spread out on the sofa, reading a political history of the Koranté Domain. He'd just finished commenting on what he would give to obtain something, *anything*, from that era. A Brokasian vase from the courtroom where they'd tried the whole family. What would *that* be worth?

It was evening. We both heard the approaching skimmer long before we saw it. (It was my turn on watch.) We did a quick inspection of our setup to make sure everything was ready. Then we saw the lights overhead, and the vehicle began to descend. "Showtime," said Alex.

A cable, painted gold, ran down the matching gold wall opposite the front door until it reached the floor behind the sofa. There it passed through a ceiling hook that we'd hammered into the floor. It then ran up the arm of the sofa and was secured so that anyone sitting on the sofa could reach it and release it. The arrangement was not particularly noticeable to visitors coming in the front door.

We waited for the skimmer to set down. As it did, Alex sat up, released the end of the cable from the sofa arm, and tugged on it once or twice to make sure it wasn't stuck anywhere. He held it out of sight, gripped in his right hand, which dangled casually over the sofa arm.

I'd put a smooth gray rock on a side table about eight strides from the door. The table had an artificial plant on it. I'd made no effort to hide the rock. It was right out there where anyone could see it, like an innocent decoration.

The engines shut off, and we heard the hatch open. Then voices. I took station by the window. "Three of them," I said.

"Which ones?"

"Krestoff and the bong thrower. Corel. And somebody else. Little, dumpy guy."

"You don't mean the pilot?"

"No. The pilot's still in the aircraft."

"Okay. The dumpy guy will be the tech."

"They've closed the hatch." We'd been pretty sure that would happen. The pilot had closed it when he'd delivered us. It was too cold out there to sit with it open. "Here they come."

"Okay. We ready?"

"Yes, sir. Krestoff will be first in the door. Bong is bringing up the rear."

"Okay. The tech shouldn't be dangerous."

"Let's hope."

"Whoever can get to him first—"

The voices had gotten louder. "Here they come."

I waited by the door. Krestoff asked Kellie to open up.

She waited a few seconds and tried again.

I went over and opened the door for them. "We didn't trust Kellie," I said.

Krestoff stood in the entrance, amused. But she had her scrambler in her hand. "She wasn't spying on you. Nobody's that interested. But it doesn't matter." She indicated I should back off a few steps, and came inside. She looked over at Alex, sitting lazily on the sofa.

She was wrapped in a heavy jacket. A thick woolen hat was pulled down over her ears.

I allowed myself to look scared. It didn't take much acting. "Hello," Alex said. "We were beginning to think you'd forgotten us."

She signaled the others to come in. The dumpy little guy carried a black box. He had a straggly beard, just beginning to gray. Bong came in behind him, hauling a larger black box. He set it down on a chair and closed the door. He'd never looked bigger. Didn't even bother showing us a weapon.

"We want to run an exam," Krestoff said. "Make sure you're okay. After we've done that, you'll be released."

"Look," Alex said. "We know what this is about. Don't try to hide it from us."

"What *what* is about?"

"You're going to do a lineal block. On each of us."

She hesitated. "Okay. I don't suppose there's any point hiding the truth. But you won't be harmed."

"You're going to lock away what? Everything having to do with Vicki Greene?"

Another pause. "Yes."

"Before you do that, answer a question for me."

"If I can?"

"Who are you working for?"

"The CSS."

"I hope you're a rogue unit. That the entire organization hasn't been corrupted."

She turned to the dumpy guy. "Doctor, do him first."

"It's Wexler, isn't it?"

That stopped her in her tracks. "No," she said finally. But her eyes delivered a different message. "And that's enough nonsense." She walked over to the table with the chess set and swept the pieces onto the floor. "Use this."

I doubted the guy was a doctor. He did not look especially bright.

Bong picked up the larger box, brought it over to the table, and set it down.

"Please," said Alex. His voice quivered. "I'll give you all I have."

All I have was the operative phrase. I started a four count.

The tech set his own box down, and opened it. He signaled Alex to come over and sit down at the table.

Alex started to get to his feet, keeping the cable out of sight.

I'd gotten to three. I checked the exact position of the rock on the table with the plant.

The tech was about to say something to Bong as I reached four.

Alex let go of the cable. The far end was outside the house, looped over a branch of the tree that jutted from the cliff edge. It was attached to a heavier rock than the one I had available. *That* rock, of course, plunged downward, yanking the cable with it.

Inside, the cable jumped up the wall with a sudden slithering sound, raced across the overhead through the series of ceiling hooks and the corners of two blankets, which were held together by nails.

Their corners released, the blankets opened and dropped their loads on our startled visitors. Rocks and firewood, loose earth, paint cans, wrenches, dishware, glasses, lamps, and a glass bottle we'd found in one of the bathrooms rained down on them. I stepped in while the stuff was still falling and nailed Bong on the jaw with my rock. I'd planned to get him between the eyes, but he'd gone into reflex protective mode, and I had to settle for whatever target presented itself. He went down like a small rhino. Seconds later, Alex had the scrambler from a startled Krestoff. I went digging in Bong's pockets, found another weapon, a blaster, and aimed it at the tech.

He threw up his hands and squealed. "Don't shoot. Please. I didn't mean any harm to anyone."

"Okay," I said. "Don't—"

"I'm only here because they called me." He was bleeding from a cut on his forehead. "I'm not part of this."

I took a quick look out the window. "He's still in the vehicle."

Krestoff was getting to her feet. Alex leveled the weapon at her. She flicked on her comm link.

"Don't," he said. "Not a sound."

She hesitated. The link was on a bracelet. She gazed at it.

"Take it off," he said. "Don't say a word. Just toss it over here."

She removed the bracelet and dropped it at her feet.

"Back away from it," I said.

She did, while Bong started to growl and began struggling to his feet. He turned a look of pure hatred in my direction.

I picked up the rock and hit the bracelet with it.

Krestoff looked up at the overhead, where the two blankets dangled. She began to laugh. "Not bad," she said. "I wouldn't have thought you two had it in you."

"Just don't make any sudden moves," he said. "Corel."

Bong reacted to his name.

"Let me have your link."

He shook his head. No.

Alex sighed. He aimed Krestoff's scrambler at him and pulled the trigger.

Bong started to cry out, but the scream ended in a whimper, and he collapsed. Krestoff's eyes came up to meet Alex's. "I'll kill you," she said quietly.

The link was clipped to his collar. Alex removed it, inspected it, dropped it on the floor, and stepped on it.

I used a piece of cable to secure Krestoff's hands. Alex got the technician. I checked Bong. He was breathing.

"He'll be out for a while," I said.

The pilot was sitting out there reading.

"Don't hurt him," said Krestoff.

We gagged her and the tech.

Krestoff's eyes found me. She would have loved to get me alone in an alley.

The hatch was shut. I wondered if it was locked. If we went out through the back door, sneaked up on him, and ran into a lock, it would probably blow the entire operation. Best was to give him the opportunity to open it.

We put on their jackets. Alex and I could both have fit in Bong's. I also removed Krestoff's boots and pulled them on. They weren't a bad fit. Bong's boots, on the other hand, would have swallowed Alex, so he stayed with his own shoes. Krestoff smirked behind her gag. She didn't think we were going to make it. Her partner mostly made growling noises.

We had a brief debate over who was going to go say hello to the pilot. Alex, of course, thought it was his responsibility as the guy in the operation. But I had a better chance of getting away with impersonating Krestoff than he did playing Bong. The last thing we wanted was for the pilot to see who was knocking at the door of the skimmer and take off.

I picked up the smaller black box that they'd brought. It might provide a distraction. Any distraction would be good. I closed it, gave Alex a moment to exit by the back, then I opened the door and stepped out into the night.

It was good to be in a real jacket.

The house was illuminated behind me, but there was no easy help for that. The skimmer's lights were out, save for a convenience lamp at the hatch and the faint glow of the pilot's reading light.

I walked toward the skimmer. He saw me and looked my way. I raised one hand to say hello, but otherwise I kept walking, gazing down at the black box as if something had gone wrong with it. The less time he had to think about things, the better.

The hatch opened as I reached it. I put the box inside, on the deck, and took out the gun. His eyes went wide when he saw it. "You're not Maria," he said.

"Just sit," I said. "What's the AI's name?"

"Doc. Hey, you're not going to use that on me?"

"My name's Chase. Tell Doc to add me to the log." He hesitated, and I pointed the weapon at his head. "Do it."

"Doc," he said, "this is Chase. Take direction from her."

"Yes, Karfa. Hello, Chase."

"Hello, Doc." I turned back to the pilot. "Okay, Karfa, please get out of the vehicle. Step down slowly. Give me your link. Don't make any unexpected moves."

"Okay." He released his harness and got up. As he did I backed off a couple of paces. Alex came up from behind. He was carrying something wrapped in plastene.

Karfa was a young guy. Not much more than a kid. Not the same pilot who'd brought us out there. He shivered in the cold, and he looked stunned. He couldn't keep his eyes off the scrambler. "What did you do with Maria and Shelby?"

"Shelby's the tech?"

"No. The agent. Shelby Corel."

Shelby? Bong's given name was *Shelby*? "Go find out for yourself," I said. "You can get in the back door. We left it open."

I signaled for him to get started. He climbed down and headed for the rear of the house. "Be careful," I told him. "Don't go walking around back there." Alex got into the aircraft. I followed him and closed the hatch. As we lifted off, I saw Karfa disappear through the rear doorway.

"Congratulations," said Alex.

"Thanks." I was feeling pretty good. "Doc, take us to the nearest spaceport."

"Very good, Chase," said the AI. *"Rendel is about an hour away."*

Alex nodded. "Yes," he said. "Good. We should be able to get clear before anybody notices Krestoff's missing."

"What do you have?" I said, looking at the package.

"This? It's the Churchill."

"I should have realized."

"Absolutely correct," said Alex. "You should."

Fortunately, Miranda was in the sky that night. Over Rimway it would have been scarcely visible. But in the wide-open spaces above Salud Afar, the planet glittered and sparkled. When we settled on course for Rendel I couldn't help noticing that Miranda could have performed the function of a guide. It lay almost dead ahead.

In the cabin, I have to admit we were gloating. Well, actually, *I* did most of the gloating. I'd laid out Krestoff's muscle with one swing, and Alex was talking with Samuels. Yes, they told us, they'd have the *Belle-Marie* ready to go when we got there.

So we sat and talked and felt good about ourselves. "First thing we're going to do," said Alex, "is go out to the asteroid."

"Why?" I said.

"You'll see."

I hated it when he got like that. "It's really Wexler, isn't it?" I said.

"Sure. You saw the way she reacted."

I was sitting with my head resting on the back of the seat, thinking how glad I'd be to get on board the *Belle-Marie*, where I'd be safely out of the reach of the CSS and of Mikel Wexler, hero of the Revolution. While I was sitting wrapped up in my happy thoughts, I noticed that Miranda had vanished from the sky.

That didn't alarm me, because it probably meant only that there were some clouds ahead. One of the complications that ensues from a starless sky is that you can never tell whether it's a clear night or not. Unless they were accompanied by lightning, storms after dark had a tendency to sneak up on you.

It had been about a half hour since we'd left the plateau. Below us there were only occasional lights, a cluster of street-lamps, now and then a ground vehicle.

I don't know why I twisted around in my seat, but I did. And I saw Miranda. Behind us.

We were headed back the way we'd come.

I caught Alex's eye, let him know something was wrong, and put my finger to my lips. I wasn't familiar with the vehicle we were riding, but these things all have an AI shutoff.

"It's to your left," said Doc. *"Open the green panel."*

That shook me. But he was right. I opened it and there was the disconnect. "How'd you know?"

"It's all in the body language, Chase. How did you know?"

"Miranda."

"Oh. Well, there was nothing I could do about that."

I touched the toggle. "I'm going to shut you down, Doc."

"It won't work."

I tried it, pulled it into the position marked DISCONNECT AI.

"Chase, this is what is known as a special situation."

"You're taking us back?" asked Alex.

"Of course. I suggest you sit back and allow this special situation to run its course. It will be best for everyone."

TWENTY-FOUR

The notion that earth and sea are solid is an illusion. It is a trick
played upon us by our monkey brains. In reality it's not like that
at all. This sofa here, for example, is mostly empty space. Ninety-
nine percent empty space. So I say to you now and forever, we
are fortunate that we do not know the real world. Were we to
confront the world as it actually is, we would have nowhere
to sit.

—*Nightwalk*

"We've got the guns," I said.

Alex was looking out the window, trying to see what the
ground looked like. "No. We don't know that we have them all.
Anyhow, once we land on the plateau, we'll be stuck there
again."

"What do you suggest?"

"Can we disable it?"

"I've already tried."

"I mean the skimmer."

"You want me to crash it?"

"I'm open to a better idea."

There was storage space behind the backseat. I opened it,
but it was empty. "Have to use the scrambler," I said.

"That is not a good idea," said Doc.

"Then turn control over to me."

"I'm not able to do that."

I took out the weapon, went digging through the cockpit until I found the hardware that housed Doc. I checked to be sure the scrambler was on paralysis mode, aimed it at the hardware, and pulled the trigger.

"Doc?"

"I'm still here."

"I'm not surprised." I found a lightning icon that provided a setting to shut off the aircraft's power. "What do you think?" I asked.

Alex looked down at the ground. "Leave it on."

"Unless you want to go back, or jump, it's all we have."

"We'd lose antigrav, too, right?"

"We've got wings. We might be able to glide in."

He thought about it for a long minute.

"Doc," I said, "can you take us lower?"

"Negative, Chase. My instructions will not allow me to do that."

"I assume these instructions take effect if you are hijacked?"

"That is correct."

"You can't pretend otherwise, I guess?"

"No. I would do it if I could."

"Okay," said Alex. "Kill the power."

"Doc," I said, "if I shut down the power, will I still be able to control the flaps and rudder?"

"I can arrange that."

"Do it. Let me know when it's done."

"It's done, Chase."

"Okay." I pushed a finger against the pad below the lightning icon. "Doc, are you sure you can't help us?"

"Chase, I would if I could."

"Okay."

"I'd really prefer you not do this."

"Me, too."

"Before you act, be aware that we are in rugged country. Chances of survival are not good even if you don't die in the crash."

"I know, Doc. Thanks." I pressed. The lights in the cabin flicked off. Doc's lamps went out. The engine died. And I had my weight back. We began slicing down.

Antigrav generators are usually equipped with an auxiliary power source. I tried to restart it. Unfortunately, somebody hadn't maintained it. I got a few burps out of it, enough to slow our descent. Then it died again.

The real problem wasn't even the lack of power so much as the fact I couldn't see the ground. Couldn't see anything. We could have been about to touch down, or about to fly into a mountain. We could have been in somebody's basement.

I wrestled with the yoke, fought the wind, started doing profanities, looked for lights somewhere. *Anywhere*. Where was Callistra now that I needed her?

The problem with antigrav vehicles is that they don't carry enough wing and tail to allow you to glide properly if the engines fail. I had wings, but they weren't very good at keeping us aloft.

"Chase—" said Alex.

"Doing the best I can."

"I see lights."

"Where?"

"Over to the left."

They were not moving. Houses, probably. I started to turn. Started breathing again. They were important because they let me know more or less where the ground was.

We swung to port in a long, slow curve. My angle on the lights was changing, of course. They were rising as we went down. Then they vanished.

Alex grunted. "What happened?"

"Mountain." I pushed the yoke right and held my breath until they reappeared.

Coming fast.

I wanted to bank toward them, to keep them in sight, but I was afraid of the mountain. Had no idea where the damned thing was. So I kept straight on. They passed off the port side, and I was headed back into the night. "I'd guess we'll be down in about two minutes," I said.

"Okay."

It was a long, quiet run, with only the sound of the wind against the wings. Then we blasted into something. I was thrown hard against my harness. There was a rush of fresh air. Then darkness took me.

When I came out of it, I was hanging upside down.

"You okay, Chase?" Alex's voice startled me. I'd felt alone. "Chase?"

"I'm here," I said. "You?"

"I'm here, too. Nice landing."

"That's right." I'd forgotten. "We're down."

I heard him struggling to release his harness.

"Are you all right, Alex?"

Lights were approaching. A truck, kicking up a cloud of snow, was visible through a wall of trees.

"I think so."

"Okay. Stay put for a minute. Help's on the way."

The front of the aircraft was gone. A cold wind was blowing snow and debris in on top of us. Alex released himself and climbed down as the truck stopped. I heard a door slam. And voices.

The truck lights revealed broad, flat ground beyond the trees. "Not bad," said Alex. "Looks as if you hit the only patch of forest in the neighborhood."

I was hurting in a few places, but nothing seemed to be broken, so I released my harness and lowered myself to the ground. Our rescuers were bundled up in jackets. There were two of them, and they both wore hats pulled down over their ears. A man and a woman. The man called out: "You people okay in there?"

I guess I was staggering around. Alex was on the ground. They got me out to the truck. Then they went back in for Alex. It took a while. When they finally came out they were holding him up. "He's all right," said the woman. "But we wanted to be sure before we moved him."

Their names were Shiala and Orman Inkama. Orman was the operational director for the otherwise-automated energy-distribution site whose lights had shown us where the ground was.

They took us back to their quarters, which were located in a flat gray building perched beside a field of collectors. They applied medications to cuts and bruises and told us how lucky we were. Orman wanted to take us to Barikaida, where there was a medical facility. But it was a long ride, and since neither of us was seriously damaged, we settled for showers and robes.

We had no clothes, of course. We explained how we were sightseeing in the area, and Orman said he'd drive back to the scene of the crash to try to recover our bags. But there'd been no easy way to bring our gear from the plateau. "We didn't have anything with us," Alex explained. "But if you could take us into Barikaida tomorrow, that would help."

So we slept in the robes, me in the guest room, Alex on the sofa. In the morning, everything I owned hurt.

Shiala cooked a big breakfast, commenting on how few visitors they got in that part of the country. Then they gave us some clothes. Orman's were a bit big for Alex, but I fit reasonably well into a blouse and slacks. Shiala's shoes were too big, though, and Krestoff's boots were a mess. Nevertheless I had to stay with them.

Orman took us out to the pad, and we all climbed into his skimmer. There was a party atmosphere running by then. Orman explained how many times he'd had rough landings himself. "Though nothing like what you folks did last night." Shiala laughed and insisted it was true, that Orman was the worst pilot in the world. He didn't trust AIs, though the truth was he just loved to fly himself.

"By the way," he said, "we reported the crash for you."

Uh-oh.

"Thanks," said Alex.

"They said they'll be out this afternoon to take a look and do the paperwork."

We lifted into the air while Alex and I pretended that nothing had changed. We laughed and joked, and I wondered how long it would take the authorities to figure out who had been in the crash.

We crossed a river with a waterfall. The Turbulence. The land was broken at that point into a vast cleft, and the river fell almost a kilometer into lower country. "It is," said Orman, "the highest known waterfall. Anywhere."

Well, Alex and I both knew of a few bigger ones, but we kept our peace. They were surprised that tourists, as we claimed to be, knew nothing of the Turbulence. (The name applied both to the river and to the waterfall.)

"Well," I said, "we were just drifting through. We're from Rimway."

And that seemed to settle it. They both said "Oh," as if Rimway tourists came through all the time and they routinely knew nothing about the place they were visiting.

They dropped us off at a clothing store. We all went inside, and Alex reminded me to switch over to the corporate account we'd opened when we first came to Salud Afar. "That was farsighted," I told him.

"We didn't know what we were getting into," he said. He had a hard time not looking pleased with himself.

But we developed a quick problem: We couldn't get clear of our benefactors. Shiala wanted to follow me around and help me shop. "We shouldn't take too long," she said, "if we're going to get back before Wash comes."

"Wash is the guy doing the investigation of the crash?"

"Yes, Sara," she said. (We'd given them false names.) "He's very good."

Alex, left alone by Orman, found out that trains left regularly. "Another due out in two hours," he whispered to me when he was able to get me alone.

Meanwhile, I'd gotten some clothes and two pairs of shoes.

"Lose her," said Alex.

"How?"

"Go to the washroom or something."

"That won't work. Take my word for it."

"What do you suggest?" Shiala was standing a counter away, looking at hats.

"Tell them the truth."

"I don't think that's a good idea."

"Alex, if we take off, they'll think we're in trouble and call the police. They'll have us before we can get to the train station."

So we took them to lunch. While we ate, we told them what had happened. We didn't tell them everything. Just that we had uncovered some corruption in high places. We told them about the plateau and why we had crashed. We told them we needed for them to say nothing until we got clear. Would they be willing to trust us? And do that for us?

They listened. Surprisingly, Shiala was the more resistant. "They're wanted by the law," she told Orman. "We could get into a lot of trouble."

"All you have to do," said Alex, "is explain that you didn't know. That we came into town, and we separated to do some shopping, and you didn't see us again."

"I just don't know," Shiala said.

Orman took a long look at both of us. "Sure we'll help," he said. "You folks get as far away from here as you can. Shiala and I will stay in town for the rest of the day. Make it harder for them to find us."

We took time to go to Korvik's CommCenter, where we bought new links and opened accounts under bogus names. Then we said good-bye to Shiala and Orman and caught a train headed north. Away from Rendel. By then, Krestoff and her people would have been rescued, and there was a good chance that Wexler would expect us to try to make the flight to the *Lantner* world. That would mean they'd be looking for us at the spaceports. And they'd probably have people alerted at Samuels as well.

So we took a week and disappeared. We settled in at a northern seaside resort, played the gaming tables, hung out on the beaches, and generally had a good time. If there was a search on for us, we saw no sign of it.

Eventually, Alex called Peifer. *"Where the hell you guys been?"* Peifer demanded. *"I've been trying to reach you."*

"Why? What's going on, Rob?"

"I have somebody I want you to meet."

"Okay. Best not to mention any names at the moment." The new links should have been safe, but you never knew.

"I understand. Sounds as if you've been making some progress."

"You remember where you met us?"

"Of course."

"There's a business with the same name."

"You're kidding."

"Check the listings."

He needed a minute or two. *"Okay. I see it."*

"Meet me inside the front door at noon tomorrow."

"Okay."

"And Rob?"

"Yes."

"We're in a little trouble."

"You? How the hell is that *possible? But okay. I never got this call. Have no idea where you are."*

"Thanks."

"In fact I don't *know where you are."*

"We met him in the spaceport terminal," I said.

"Right." Alex was enjoying himself.

"What business incorporates 'terminal' in its name?"

"They sell women's lingerie. It's called Terminal Attraction."

"Ah. You did your homework."

"I always do my homework, love."

Next morning we took the train back to Marinopolis, and at a quarter to twelve we were posted in the Caribu Restaurant across the walkway from the lingerie store. The store advertised itself as THE HAPPY PLACE.

At noon sharp Peifer showed up. He was in a white jacket with a broad-brimmed matching hat. We waited until he entered the store. No one else seemed to be watching, so I crossed the walkway and went in behind him. He was standing checking out the latest in casual underwear.

There were a couple of customers. Both women. Neither looked like CSS. Of course, they weren't supposed to.

"Chase," he said. "It's good to see you." It was an atmospheric place. Soft blue lights, diaphanous blue curtains twisting in a nonexistent breeze. Misty music.

"And yourself, Rob. You want to follow me?"

He looked around at the slips and panties. "I thought we were going to meet here."

A clerk appeared on the scene and glanced from one of us to the other. "May I help you?"

Peifer pointed toward a sheer nightie. "You'd look great in that, Chase."

"Thanks," I told the clerk. "We'll pass for the moment."

Neither of the customers showed any interest in us, and I saw no one outside. We left, but to be safe we circled the block. Still nobody.

"You guys must really be scared," said Peifer.

"Call it cautious."

We went into the Caribu. He broke into a big smile when he saw Alex. They sat down together while I stayed near the window. They talked for a few minutes. When I was satisfied nobody was out there, I joined them.

"I want you to meet Ecco Saberna," said Peifer. "He thinks he knows what got to Vicki Greene."

"And what was that?"

"I'll let him tell you. Why are you on the run?"

"The CSS thinks *we* figured out what happened to Greene." Alex had suggested we not reveal Wexler's complicity until we had more information. Until we could prove it.

"The CSS? They're the good guys."

"It's news to me."

Peifer leaned across the table and lowered his voice. "So *did* you?"

"Figure it out?

"Yes. What's going on? Why's the CSS involved?"

We ordered. When the AI asked what I wanted, I asked for a beef sandwich. "And a boltslinger."

"What's a boltslinger?" asked Alex.

"Don't know," I said. I'd seen it on the menu.

Peifer assured me I'd like it.

Peifer was about average size, and he needed to get a work-out program going. His beard was unkempt. Maybe it was that beards weren't fashionable back home. In any case, he came off like a guy who was pretending to be an intellectual. That characteristic gave him an air of vulnerability, though, and made him easier to trust.

"Rob," Alex said, "we still don't know what's happening. Give me a few days, and I think I'll be able to tell you."

"Why would the CSS think you know?"

"We were looking into the Edward Demery business."

He looked surprised. "That's a coincidence."

"In what way?"

"You're going to be interested in what Ecco has to say."

Peifer knew a hotel in Sikora, a town about forty kilometers west of Marinopolis. It was a cheap place with low visibility. For a small additional remuneration, the owner would neglect to enter guest information online for CSS, as hotels on Salud Afar routinely did. (Some absolutist tendencies from the Bandahriate remained in place.)

He gave us directions, and an hour later we checked into the Starlight Suites. That evening, Peifer showed up with Ecco Saberna. He was another bearded guy, built low to the ground. Hard dark eyes like marbles. "The truth of the matter, Alex," Saberna said in a tone that suggested dark times were coming, "is that there's a rift out there. It's located somewhere near the *Lantner* asteroid."

"A rift?"

"A break in the time-space continuum."

Alex frowned. I looked at Peifer. Was this guy crazy?

"If I'm correct, and I think I am, it's moving at a substantial velocity. In this direction." He took a deep breath. "We're lucky it's as far away as it is."

"A distortion?" Alex asked. He was having trouble grasping the concept.

It was my turn: "They're supposed to be theoretically possible. But nobody's ever seen one."

"Of course nobody's ever seen one, child," Saberna said. "If you get close enough to make the observation, you'll have a great deal of trouble talking about it later." He seemed to think that was funny, and he chuckled. It was an abrasive sound.

Peifer had been standing quietly with his arms folded. "I

know it sounds wild," he said, "but Ecco's a prizewinning physicist. He knows what he's talking about. And it would explain
a lot."

Alex took a moment to appraise Saberna. "You think," he
said, "that the two ships that went out to the *Lantner* rock got
swept up by this thing?"

"Yes. That's exactly what I think happened."

"And the people who were outside on the surface of the
asteroid?"

"They would have been caught as well. In the gravity field
created by the passing rift."

"So they'd have been dragged off?"

"Yes."

"Why wasn't the asteroid also sucked in?"

He shrugged. The answer was obvious. "It was too massive.
And the effect was only momentary."

We were chewing on pastries that Peifer had brought with him.
Alex took a bite out of a cinnamon roll. "What makes you think
it's a rift?" he asked.

"We're in a highly problematic field, Alex. There's no hard
data. But let me show you what we *do* have." He proceeded to
do so. In detail. He put up a display that tracked how a deformity in the continuum might occur, resulting from too much
stress, how it might even be caused by the new star drive, the
one that had been developed by the Dellacondans during their
war with the Mutes and was just now coming into wide use. He
apparently had no conception of Alex's role in those events.

I understood none of it, and I was pretty sure Alex had gotten lost, too.

"So where is it now?" he asked. "This deformity?"

"There's no way to know without going out to find it. But
the government won't do that. They don't want to admit it's out
there. I know. I've talked to them. But it *is* there, Alex. And I'd
be willing to bet it's coming this way. That's why they're keeping it quiet. They want to avoid panic. They keep talking about
Mutes to distract people."

"How fast would it be traveling?"

"Best guess for a fracture of this nature: about ten percent of cee."

"Then it would be here in about—" He scribbled some numbers on a pad. Made a face.

Saberna grinned. It wasn't easy to be in the presence of ordinary people. "Three hundred years."

"That doesn't sound like crisis proportions."

"We think they're worried about the economics," said Peifer. "It would scare the hell out of people. The economy would collapse. It might be hard to hold society together if you have to take a short-range view."

"Short-range?" I said. "Three centuries?"

"They're probably right," said Alex. "It wouldn't be the short-range view. It would be that there's no future."

I thought about Wexler selling his property. Cashing out while he could.

"What would happen," Alex asked, "if it arrived in this area? How big is the damned thing?"

"That's anybody's guess."

"Why do you think it's coming here?"

Saberna crossed his arms. "I think the government went out and looked. And they didn't like what they found. Vicki Greene found out about it somehow, and they had to keep her quiet. Why else would they have done the lineal block?"

Alex was rubbing his eyebrows, staring down at the floor. "How would they even have known where to look?"

Saberna was having trouble keeping the exasperation out of his voice. "It would be a very easy threat to check. You would only have to be concerned if it were coming in this direction, is that not right? Yes. They could have found out its theoretical velocity. And they knew it was out near the *Lantner* world thirty-three years ago. After that it would simply have been a matter of doing the math."

Alex shook his head. "That can't be right," he said.

"Why not?"

"If you're correct, what's the point of building the shelters?"

Saberna held out his hands, palms up. Wasn't it obvious?

"It's a distraction. They know rumors about the distortion have gotten out. They're trying to sell the Mute story."

I hadn't heard any of the rumors.

"The mainline media stay away from them," said Peifer. "But we've been hearing them for the last two months. I think this is exactly what's happening. Global has been reporting that some people near the top of the government have been divesting themselves of holdings and converting their wealth into Confederate currencies. The sort of thing you might do if a major catastrophe was on the way. But on the other hand, economists are talking about a downturn, and they say divestment routinely happens at such times."

"You think it gives credence to Ecco's ideas?"

"I don't know. Maybe it just means stormy weather ahead, and they're putting their holdings in the vault. But hell, if the end of the world is coming, then yes, I'd expect the people who know about it to be trying to get clear. And take their money with them." His eyes grew hard. "And they'd have every incentive to keep it quiet."

Despite their name, the Starlight Suites had no suite. The proprietor seemed to think that a suite was a room with an elegant name. So we had separate quarters. I retired to mine, got ready for bed, killed the lights, and took a minute to look down at the street. We were on the top floor, the fourth. There were shops across the way, a legal office, a landing pad. I half expected to see someone watching us. But it was quiet.

Maybe we were safe. Nevertheless, I didn't unpack my bag, other than to hang up the new clothes I'd bought. This was my first experience being on the run, and I can't say I cared for it much. I was still pumping too much adrenaline, I guess, to sleep well. I watched the HV for a while. Finally, toward dawn, I drifted off.

We went to breakfast at a place called Bandy's, where we both grumbled about inedible food and avoided talking about interspatial rifts.

"We'll keep the hotel room here," Alex said. "But I think it's time to head for the asteroid."

I thought so, too. But on the way back to the Starlight Suites we saw a guy coming out of the building. He paused on the front steps, gazed across the street, and walked away. There was something of Agents Krestoff and Bong in the way he carried himself. I steered Alex into a turn. "Stay away from the building," I said.

"I think so, too."

"Give me your key."

He produced it. "What are you going to do?"

"Make sure we don't get picked up again. You go back to Bandy's and have some coffee. I'll come get you when I'm sure it's safe."

The Starlight Suites lacked a rooftop parking area, but there was a connecting walkway with the Weidner Building, which housed several business offices. I left Alex and walked into the Weidner Building. Rode the elevator up to the fourth floor and climbed a set of stairs to the roof. The door was locked. But my room key opened it.

I let myself out onto the roof, and crossed to the Suites in the connector. It was cold.

I hurried down to ground level, keeping to the staircases. I took a good look around the lobby before I showed myself. When I was satisfied no one was there except the bot at the desk, I walked over to her.

"Hello, Dale," she said pleasantly, using the alias we'd given the hotel. "What can I do for you?"

"Has anyone been asking for us? Either me or Henry?"

The bot nodded. "Um, yes. A police officer was in here a few minutes ago. He showed us pictures of you and the gentleman."

"What did you tell him?"

"That I'd never seen you. But I don't think he believed me."

I gave her some money for the owner. "Thanks, Hass."

I went back up to the rooms, grabbed my bags and Alex's, and dragged them up onto the roof, across the walkway, and down through the Weidner Building. I hauled the two bags out onto the sidewalk, flagged down a land cab, went to the restaurant, and picked up Alex.

Twenty minutes later we were at the train station.

TWENTY-FIVE

"It is not true, Mirra, that anyone who walks through that door simply vanishes. Walks out of the world and is never heard from again. It's true of some. I, however, would be perfectly safe. In fact, virtually anyone you brought in from the street would be perfectly safe."

"Who then, Professor?"

"Only those you love, Mirra. Only they are threatened."

—*Midnight and Roses*

We rode the train into Marinopolis. On the way, Alex asked me to make a shuttle reservation. For one. *Uno*.

"How come?" I said.

We were seated in a compartment, just back from the dining car with sandwiches. He looked out at a large patch of farmland. "Chase, we both know they'll probably be waiting for us at either the terminal or at Samuels. Probably both places."

"I know."

"We can't afford to have them take both of us."

"So what are you suggesting?"

"I'm going up alone. If I make it okay, I'll look up your friend Ivan and see if he can be persuaded to take me out to the asteroid. I won't try to get *Belle* because I'm pretty sure Wexler'll be watching it." He took a deep breath. "You think Ivan would go along?"

"Maybe," I said.

"Well, we'll have to give it a try."

"Alex, I don't like this."

"Neither do I. But we have to play our best shot." I did what he asked. But I also went into a sulk.

"I know how you feel," he said. "But we're going to do it this way. Now, before we get to the station, I have something to show you." He drew the blinds, took out a notebook, and killed the lights. "I don't think we need be concerned about a rift."

"Good," I said. "Why?"

He activated the notebook. It gave us a soft glow. "I think Saberna's a guy on a mission. I checked him out. He's been trying to make the case for spatial rifts for years. It's his pet project. If he finds one, maybe they'll name it for him."

"So we're, what, back to the Mutes again?"

"I don't think so. We talked about the Calienté mission."

"Yes."

"Watch." He primed the notebook. A yellow globe appeared in the center of the room. "Seepah," he said. Eight smaller lights, representing planets, were circling it. "Okay, let's look at the position of everything when the transmissions stopped."

The orbiting lights glided to a halt.

"The monitors that shut down were on the third and seventh worlds."

"Okay."

He paused. "Notice anything?"

"Just lights."

"The third and seventh worlds are on the same side of the sun."

"So's the fifth world. And for that matter the outermost."

"The fifth world was already shut down. That's the one with the failed transmitter."

"But the signal from the eighth was still coming in, right?"

"Yes. Maybe it was too far out."

"Too far out for what?"

Alex is a decent-looking guy. Especially when he gives you the big smile that always indicates he's figured out where the Ibritic tomb is, or some such thing. I got that smile then, underscored by the half-light. "I don't know yet."

I took a bite out of my sandwich and chewed slowly. It was good. "Alex, what are you trying to tell me?"

"The transmissions stopped six centuries ago. Six hundred fourteen years, to be exact."

"Standard years?"

"Yes."

"Okay. So what's the point?" I took another bite. Chewed some more.

"Let me show you." Seepah's system blinked off. Callistra appeared. A bright azure light near the window. Then a dim yellow star near the door. Seepah. And, finally, off to one side and still farther away, almost flat against the door, a tiny red light. The asteroid.

"I'm going to draw an arc around Callistra, at Seepah's range," Alex said. He pressed a pad on his notebook and the arc appeared, to the extent the dimensions of the room would permit it. It passed through the dwarf star.

Next, we got a second arc, drawn through the asteroid. "The distance from Seepah," he said, "to the asteroid is more than two thousand light-years."

"Okay."

"But the distance between the arcs is only five hundred eighty-one light-years."

"Alex, you say that as if it has some significance."

"The *Lantner* incident occurred thirty-three years ago. The loss of the Seepah signal happened six hundred fourteen years ago. As the good Professor Saberna would put it, do the math."

It didn't take a genius. "But it can't be the same thing happening in both places," I said. "They're too far apart."

"I'll tell you something else: The *Lantner* and the *Origon* didn't disappear. At least not in the way we've been led to believe."

"Explain."

"The ship that was sent to look around found something other than what was reported. That's why it blew up a couple of days later. So nobody would be in a position to contradict the official story. It's why the captain who carried Vicki out there disappeared."

"They saw something?"

"Yes. The second vehicle would have been manned by Nicorps people. It was a cleanup operation. They got rid of whatever was left."

"So what actually happened? Was it the Mutes?"

"I doubt it. But the answer is out at the asteroid."

The train pulled into Marinopolis. We grabbed our luggage and headed for the doors. I was still not happy as we climbed down onto the platform. "Don't be angry," he said. "You know we have to do it this way."

I noticed a uniformed police officer watching us. Looking down at a notebook. He started in our direction.

Alex saw him, too. "Split," he said.

He grabbed his bag, gave me a shove, and hurried off in the opposite direction. The officer began talking into his link and took after Alex.

I waved down a taxi and went for a ride. I didn't have a destination. "Just take me to the spaceport," I told it. Then I tried to reach Alex on his link.

An unfamiliar voice answered: *"Ms. Kolpath, is that you?"*
Damn. They had him.

"Please answer. We're not trying to hurt anybody. This is the police."

I broke the circuit and called Peifer. "Rob, they took Alex."
"Damn."

"Can you do a story? Put some pressure on Wexler?"

"Sure. Give me the details. What's going on?"

"I don't know."

"That's not easy to write."

"I know."

"Okay. Look, I'll check the police reports. We should be able to find out what's happening with him, anyhow."

"Maybe." I didn't know where to go from there. "Rob, I need to get out to the asteroid. Can you make me part of a news team or something? And we both go? If we did that, I could probably get through. And you might get your story."

"But why, Chase? We keep going around in a circle. Did you guys find evidence of the rift?"

"There's no rift, Rob. At least, I don't think there is."

"*What, then?*"

"I don't know. Alex thought we'd find out if we could get to the asteroid."

"*Great.*"

"So can you help, Rob?"

"*Let me see what I can do. I'll get back to you.*"

I moved into a hotel in the center of the city. And I sat in it, watching newscasts, watching talk shows, and I saw nothing about Alex. Heard no mention of him. There were reports, though, of another encounter with the Mutes. The administration announced that plans were going ahead to increase "substantially" the size of the fleet. And work had begun on another group of shelters. Administration officials appeared everywhere and were reassuring. "*We're protected by a cosmic ocean,*" one of them said. "*The Mutes are coming out here because they think we're an easy target. We're going to fix that.*"

"*Then why,*" asked an interviewer, "*do we need all those shelters?*"

"*We're sending a message,*" he said. "*If they come here, we'll stand our ground and go to all-out war if need be. Once they see that, once they see we aren't going to just sit here and let them run us off, we're confident they'll understand that this Administrator is not going to tolerate recurring attacks.*"

I don't usually drink alone, but I had a couple that night, in my room, while I wondered what was happening to Alex, where he was, whether they were trying to press him to find out where *I* was.

Eventually Peifer called. "*Sorry, kid,*" he said. "*But it's no go.*"

"Which part of it?"

"*All of it. When I told Howie—my editor—he ran it past the fifth floor. That's our senior people. I'm not sure what's going on, but somebody up there vetoed it. They told Howie we weren't to touch any part of the story. The official line is that it's pointless, that nobody knows anything, and to just let it go away.*"

"Rob—"

"*Chase, if you can come up with something solid, I'll do*

something with it. But I can't hang everything out there when we don't even know what it's about."

"Okay."

"Also, I checked on Alex."

"And—?"

"The police claim they released him an hour after they picked him up. They're saying it was a case of mistaken identity."

"Rob, he'd have called me."

"And he hasn't?"

"Not a peep."

"Well, maybe he—"

"What?"

"All right, look: I'll keep checking. If you hear from him, let me know." He looked tired. *"Do you need a place to stay? We've got a spare room."*

"No. Thanks."

"What are you going to do?"

"I don't know. Get your story, I guess."

"What do you mean? How are you going to do that?"

"I'm going to the asteroid. And find out what this is about."

"Yeah, good. How are you going to manage it? Grab a taxi?"

TWENTY-SIX

There are times when you must stand in the night with no place
to put your feet.

—*Love You to Death*

Maybe Peifer had something. My father always said, if you're
serious about getting somewhere, take a taxi. There was, of
course, no way I could ride a taxi to a destination thirty-six
light-years out. But I might be able to use one to get to the
space station.

Okay. Cabs will take you up to a couple of kilometers, but
they aren't designed for high-altitude flights, let alone one that
that would run out of the atmosphere altogether. But it was an
option.

I'd have to wait until the sun went down. Most people would
think that, if you went up in the daytime, up to orbital altitudes,
you'd freeze. But in fact, the sun would turn the taxi into an
oven. So I waited until late afternoon. Then I went over to Central Mall and grabbed a sandwich and a fruit drink. And some
dessert. Wasn't sure when I'd eat again. Afterward, I stopped by
a general supply shop and got some tape. I went shopping for a
plastene jacket and settled on one that looked almost airtight. It
wasn't something I'd want to wear in public, particularly, gar-
ish green with a salacious dragon on the back. But it was exactly what I needed.

Next stop was home furnishings. I browsed among the window curtains and bought a tieback, a soft strip of blue-green fabric that would have been perfect for my living room.

I carried the jacket and the tape and the tieback to the roof and picked out my cab, a late-model Karaka that looked sturdy and well maintained. It waited patiently for me, and I climbed in. "Taxi," I said, "let's go fill up. I'm going to ask you to take me to Quahalla. And bring me back."

Quahalla was halfway across the continent.

"I have adequate fuel, ma'am," she said.

"I get nervous about long trips. Humor me. Let's fill up anyhow. I'll be much more comfortable."

"As you wish, ma'am."

It takes next to no fuel to keep the antigrav unit running. The jets, of course, were another matter. So the plan was to leave them off. What I needed was to get to the right altitude and stay there. I wouldn't be able to go anywhere once I'd arrived. But that was okay.

"Where in Quahalla do you want to go?"

"I'm still deciding. I have several errands to run."

"Very good." We pulled into a depot and filled the tank. The antigrav unit and the jets used the same fuel. I'd have liked to fill two or three extra tanks and put them in the cab, but I'd have no way of getting the fuel into the system.

When we'd finished, we rode over to Kreitzel's Sea Sports and picked up an oxygen tank and a mask. Next I needed two blankets.

When everything was on board, I asked the AI whether the taxi was safe at higher altitudes.

"Absolutely," she answered.

"No leaks?"

"None."

There are rules everywhere about how high skimmers can go. In most places the limit's about three klicks. Although they are by law restricted to low altitudes, they're nevertheless equipped with a life-support system. Any piece of equipment with an antigrav unit can go pretty high if something unforeseen happens, like a drunk, so an air supply was standard. It, plus the tank, would give me roughly six hours, but if I didn't get rescued long before that, I would be in deep trouble.

I connected the mask to the oxygen tank and tied everything down so it wouldn't float around in the cabin when we lost gravity. I put one of the blankets on top of the tank and tucked it in so the tank wasn't visible. Then I put tape around doors and windows and anywhere else I could find where air might escape. When I'd finished, I told the AI to take us up.

We lifted off, but the taxi immediately started asking questions. It was designed to refuse foolish instructions in any case, so I disconnected the AI and took over manual control. That's illegal, too, of course, barring an emergency.

I suspected it had automatically sent out a signal to law enforcement, but I didn't see anybody in the area. We rose gradually out of the traffic streams and headed for the clouds. I took it easy, in order to conserve fuel. I was going up to thirty-one thousand kilometers, the altitude of the space station. Once I reached it, I would need as much as was left to keep me up there.

The sun was beginning to sink below the horizon when a red light began blinking. The radio burped and came to life. *"You in the taxi: Please answer up. Push the black button to the right of the meter to reply."*

"Hello," I said. I tried to sound panicky. "It keeps going up."

"This is Sky Traffic Fourteen. What's happening? You're too high."

"Don't know. It won't talk to me. It just keeps going up."

"All right. Keep calm, ma'am. Let me talk with the AI, please."

"That's what I'm trying to tell you. The AI isn't saying anything."

"All right. Apparently you must have done something to shut it off. You need to reactivate. In order to do that, you need first to get into the front right-hand seat. Are you alone in the vehicle?"

"Yes."

"All right. Now let's start by opening the main function panel. It's to your left. Are you in the front right-hand seat yet?"

He gave me detailed instructions. I reported back, step by step, that I was following everything he told me to do. "It still won't work."

"Okay. Keep calm, ma'am. There's no reason to worry. We'll get you down. Do you know how to operate the vehicle?"

"No," I said.

"All right." The voice was male. It was calm. Reassuring. Everything would be okay. *"Please take control of the taxi in the following manner—"* I could have shut the radio down, but that might have given the game away. So I listened while he gave instructions, warned me against the hazards of high altitudes, and assured me that Sky Traffic Operations knew of the problem and was doing everything necessary to return me safely to the ground.

"I can't hear you," I said. "The radio's shut off."

"Taxi, can you hear me now?"

I almost said *Negative*. Instead: "Are you still there? I can't hear a thing."

I was passing through white cumulus clouds.

Minutes later I got another call: *"You in the taxi, this is Traffic Control. Do you need assistance? What is happening?"*

"I don't know. It just keeps going up." I wanted to sound scared, and I guess the truth is that it didn't take much effort.

"All right." It was a male voice again. *"Don't be frightened. We'll get you down."*

"This is the first time anything like this has happened to me."

"It's okay. It happens all the time. Is the taxi responding?"

He was talking about the AI. "No, sir," I said. "She just stopped talking. I don't know what happened."

"Okay. Help is on the way. Meantime, let's try something." He gave me instructions on how to maneuver the taxi, how to get it under control.

"No," I said. "I've never operated one of these things. I'm afraid I'll kill myself."

"All right. Just relax, Miss. Everything's going to be all right."

I could see them coming. Lots of blinking lights a few klicks behind me. The operator kept talking to me, trying to reassure me. I was above the clouds by then, picking up speed as antigrav units tend to do when they get higher and the air gets thinner. It was all I could do not to pour the juice to it, to get out of there before they arrived. But I didn't dare. I couldn't afford to use the extra fuel.

I sat tight and eventually the patrol vehicle pulled alongside. There were two officers in it. One waved. Relax. Take it easy. Then her voice came over the radio: *"Miss? Are you okay?"*

"So far."

"All right. Good. Listen, we want to get you out of there before it goes any higher."

"How do you mean?"

"Let's try the controls first. Have you popped the panel?" She was talking about the controls, which rotate out when you go to manual.

"What do you mean by 'popped'?"

"Let it go. Look, here's what I want you to do."

She gave me the same instructions the earlier guy had. One step at a time. *"Withdraw the yoke."*

"I can't," I said.

"Just take it easy."

I was thinking if they told me one more time to relax, I would scream. "It won't come loose. It's stuck."

We continued like that for another minute or so. Then she sighed. *"Okay. Look, I want to get you out of there before we get any higher."*

"Good. I'm for—"

"—We're going to get above you. I'll come down and help. But I need you to open the door. Hang on to something when you do because the air pressure in your cabin will try to drag you outside."

"Outside the door?"

"Yes. So hold on."

"Listen, I'm not going to open anything up here. That's crazy."

"Miss, we're running out of options fast."

That was good news. "I'm not opening up. Please find another way."

"There is no other way."

"No. I'm sorry." I found it easy to show them some hysteria. "I can't do it."

They tried anyhow. The woman was gutsy. They got above me and matched my rate of ascent. They dropped a cable, and she climbed down on it. Right from the start she was getting blown all over the sky. Then she was outside, pounding on the door. I put on my best look of sheer terror and sat frozen in my seat. Her partner, a guy with a voice like a tractor engine, told me how I should grab hold of the chair arm. Hang on to the chair arm and don't let go, and simultaneously hit the pad and open the door. Jara would take care of the rest.

Right.

I didn't answer. I sat there and shook my head violently no, not on your life, while the wind bumped her around on the hull of the taxi. She looked through the window at me, and I had to give her credit: She kept the contempt she must have been feeling out of her eyes. She continued to beat on the door, while I felt about as guilty as I ever have in my life. But I stayed put. Pushed back down into my seat, frozen with terror. Finally, she gave up.

"She won't let me in, Kav."

"Try it one more time."

"Miss, please. The higher you get, the more difficult this will become. You'll be perfectly safe." Her eyes were a luminous blue, and they pleaded with me. Open up. Get up off your sorry ass and let me in.

If this ended happily, I decided, I would find Jara, apologize to her, and buy her a drink.

Finally, they gave up. We were piling on too much altitude. Kav assured me they'd be back for me, and they pulled away as an airliner passed in the distance. Now all I needed was to get to thirty-one thousand kilometers and get rescued. I was hoping that Sky Traffic Operations was notifying Samuels that a vehicle with a hysterical woman on board was heading up out of control and would need help.

I checked the doors and listened for the sound of escaping air. I didn't hear any. The taxi seemed as secure as the AI had promised. I checked the altitude gauge. It was marked up to three klicks, which wasn't much use in determining how high I'd gone. But I could estimate my rate of ascent, so it wasn't hard to calculate.

I was maybe halfway to my target altitude when Traffic Control started talking to me again: *"Miss, are you okay?"*

"Yes," I said.

"We've alerted the Patrol and they'll be on the lookout for you."

"Okay. Thanks."

"Try to keep calm. Everything's going to be okay."

So far, so good. I rode patiently up into black skies. The heating system couldn't keep up, so I wrapped myself in one of the blankets. The galactic haze was rising in the east. And we were burning fuel at a steady rate.

When I thought I'd reached more or less the space-station altitude, I burned some more to level off. And I began looking for lights.

The messages from groundside went on without a break. Lady in the taxi, it's okay. We're watching you. Samuels has been notified. Help is on the way. Please remain calm.

Despite all that, the sky remained empty.

My air had been leaking out, and I was beginning to feel it. I reached back for the mask and put it on. The flow of oxygen felt good. I don't think I'd been aware how foul the air had gotten. I began breathing regularly and sat back to await rescue.

The ride up from the surface had consumed more fuel than I'd hoped, and I had maybe fifty minutes before the spike would shut down. I couldn't come close to accelerating to orbital speed, so once that happened I'd simply fall back to the ground. Well, as close to the ground as I would get before burning up.

It was time to take matters into my own hands. I got on the radio. "Samuels Ops," I said, "this is Janey Armitage." I made up the name. "I'm in a runaway taxi. Something went wrong with the spike, and it's taken me God knows where. Please help. I'll leave the transmit on so you can track me. Please hurry." I looked out at the empty skies. "The fuel gauge is near empty, and I don't know what will happen after that."

They would know, of course. And they answered immediately: *"Ms. Armitage, we heard you were coming. Patrol vehicle is already on its way. Should be there anytime."* Then, a gag: *"What kind of taxi are you riding anyhow?"*

"Don't know," I said. "But I'll be glad to get out of here."

"Just sit tight, ma'am. They'll be right there."

Moments later I saw lights. Coming from ahead. And another voice on the radio: *"Ms. Armitage, this is Orbital Delta. We see you, but we may have a problem."*

Chilling words, those. The guy wasn't even close to me yet. "What's the problem?" I said.

"We're prepping a second vehicle to do the actual rescue. The taxi's too big for our cargo area. We can't fit it on board."

I'd debated picking up a pressure suit in case we had to do a space walk, but I hadn't been able to see any way to explain its presence to the rescuers. Hiding the oxygen tank would be tough enough. If they figured out that I'd engineered the whole thing, they'd waste no time turning me over to the authorities. So I'd had to take my chances. "How long before it gets here?"

"It won't be long."

"*How* long?"

"Probably within the hour."

"That's not going to work."

"What's your situation?"

"Air's okay, but fuel looks like about forty-five minutes."

"Okay. We'll have to do something else. You don't by any chance have a pressure suit over there, do you?"

"No." I held back on the wisecrack.

"Okay. Sit tight for a minute while we figure it out."

While they were figuring, a cluster of lights came out of the night behind me. The lights were higher than I was, and off to port. While I watched they grew brighter and blurred past. "That Samuels?" I asked.

"Yes, ma'am."

Only one course of action was possible, they explained. I would have to cross from the taxi to the rescue vessel more or less dressed for dinner. *"It sounds unnerving, ma'am. We know that. But we've done it before, and we've never lost anybody."*

I had my doubts. "Okay," I said. "What's your name?"

"Lance Depardeau."

"Okay, Lance. Come to the lady's rescue."

They needed a few minutes to get ready. I assume they were talking to the station, trying to make sure the other vehicle, the one with the big cargo doors, could not make it in time. Finally, they were back. *"Sorry about the delay, Janey. Okay, here's how we're going to do it. The only thing you need to do is keep cool, follow directions, and leave everything to us."*

Minutes later, the Patrol vehicle maneuvered close in, almost close enough to bump the cab. *"It's okay,"* Lance said. *"If you have any warm clothing with you, put it on."*

I wrapped myself in one of the blankets. I was starting to get used to wearing blankets. Latest fashion item.

Their air lock opened, revealing a figure in a pressure suit.

They had to stay close, not only because getting me from one vehicle to the other had to be done quickly, but also because the antigravity field extended only a hand's length beyond the wingtips. We weren't in orbit. So anyone who got outside the field was going to fall.

"Do you have something you can put over your head, Janey?"

That's why I'd bought my nearly airtight dragon jacket. I'd secured it to a seat support to prevent its floating around the inside of the taxi. Now I released it and told him *yes.*

The person in the pressure suit—I didn't know whether it was Lance or not—jumped across, and I heard the thump as he landed on the side of the cab. Just before he reached the door, I took a deep breath, shed the mask, and pushed it under the seat. The air in the cab was fouler than I'd realized.

"All right, Janey," he said. *"You're doing fine. Keep calm."*

I pulled the jacket over my head and secured it at my throat with the tieback.

"Okay. That's good. Breathe normally. And hang on to the handle so you don't get sucked out."

I couldn't really answer him anymore. But I grabbed hold of the door release and the chair.

"I'll pull you out. As soon as I get your arm, let go. You might want to hold on. But don't do it, okay. Let go as soon as I touch you."

I nodded okay. Inside the jacket, of course, I couldn't see anything.

I knew others had made this kind of crossing and that there was no real danger unless I lost my head. So now I'll confess something. I was almost enjoying playing the damsel in distress.

"Open the door."

I pulled the release and opened up.

The air exploded out. Then the world turned frigid. It was like being held naked against an iceberg. I started shivering.

He took my arm and pulled me through the door. I could see nothing; I was just trying to breathe normally when we pushed off hard away from the taxi.

Hard because for a moment we went outside the antigrav field. My weight returned and, for a terrifying moment, we fell. But our momentum carried us across.

The weight went away again, as quickly as it had come. We touched metal. Secure in my jacket, I closed my eyes. Air pressure began to push against me, and gradually, the world got warm again.

TWENTY-SEVEN

This is my promise to you, Beth. As long as there is a star in the sky, no evil will come upon you.

—Midnight and Roses

Lance insisted I check in with Medical, and there was no way I could refuse without arousing suspicion. Anyway, I was bleeding from every orifice I had. So he escorted me down. On the way, he said he knew this wasn't a particularly good time, but he wondered if he could see me again.

Considering the shape I was in, it came as a surprise. "That would be nice, Lance," I said.

"I'm on duty through tomorrow. But—" He hesitated. "Will you be staying on station? I think they're going to want to talk to you."

He didn't specify who "they" were. "I have to be getting back to my job," I said. "Can't really stay here."

He smiled. He was a big, good-looking guy. There was an innocence about him that was appealing, and we all know how women love uniforms. Not to mention guys who save their behinds.

But there was too much risk in letting him know how he could reach me, so I gave him a bogus code to go with the bogus name, and we separated, he promising to get in touch, while I batted my eyes, said thanks, gave him a hug, and thought *good-bye*.

Medical checked me out, said I was fine, but suggested I stay under observation for a day. I thanked them, but passed, and headed for the Ops desk.

I was approaching another bad moment. To get the *Belle-Marie*, I had to use my real name, which was likely to bring the gendarmes crashing down on me before I could get launched. Ivan was my best bet. But I wanted very much to get on board *Belle* and clear out.

The watch officer came out of a back room and assumed his place behind the counter. "Yes, ma'am," he said. "What can I do for you?" He was tall, thick gray mustache, speckled gray hair. Serious-looking and well along in years. He'd obviously been passed over several times, a guy who was still manning the counter.

"My name's Kolpath," I said. "I'd like to clear my ship. The *Belle-Marie*."

He wasn't good enough to hide his reaction. His jaw tightened; his eyelids flickered and came alive. "Very good," he said, trying to pretend everything was okay. "Can you hold on a second?"

"Sure."

He went back into the office, and I took off. Down the gravity shaft and out onto the main concourse. Picked out a ladies' room and hustled inside. There was one occupant, and I washed my hands until she left. Then I called Ivan.

"Captain Sloan is not available," said his AI. *"Do you wish to leave a message?"*

He was probably out on the *Goldman*. "Yes, I would."

"Anytime you're ready."

"Ivan, this is Chase. I'm in trouble. Need to talk to you as soon as possible." I added my code as the door opened, and somebody came in.

I checked the schedules. The *Hassan Goldman*, Ivan's ship, was en route to Varesnikov. It was due back in two days. See the biggest planet in the system. Cruise through the moons and rings. Gourmet meals served on board.

Not good. If I simply wandered around the concourse for two days, I was going to become extremely visible. Then, as I was trying to decide what to do, I spotted Krestoff. She was looking around and talking into her sleeve.

I had to get clear of the station. The only way I could think of to do that was to *steal Belle*. On the assumption they wouldn't expect me to go back to Ops, I did just that, slipped past the service desk, and saw a couple of serious-looking women talking with the watch officer. I kept going, and got as far as the maintenance piers. But the entrance is always locked. I stood there waiting for someone who'd open the door and allow me to follow him through. While I was considering my chances of doing that and making a run for *Belle*, getting on board, and getting under way before they closed the launch doors, a nasal voice broke in: "Who are you and what are you doing here?"

It was a technician. He was big, kind of old, and didn't look particularly kindly. "I'm lost," I said. "Can you tell me how to get to the main concourse?"

I went back and thought about booking a room. But the hotel would be the first place Krestoff would look. I could hunt Lance down. And I had no doubt he'd be happy to provide bed and board for two days. But I'd have to persuade him to keep quiet in the meantime.

The schedule showed two more tour flights that day: one to Miranda, and one that would chase down a comet. Miranda would be gone almost a week, so I signed on for the comet, which would be back in three days.

I left another message for Ivan, asking him not to leave when he got back. "Going to see the comet," I said. "I'll be in touch." It was taking a chance, letting him know where I'd be. But I doubted Wexler had made a connection between us. I spent the next few hours shopping once again for fresh clothes and staying out of Krestoff's way. When time came to board, I waited until the very last minute, then rolled through the boarding area, gave them my pass, and hurried down the tube. A flight attendant welcomed me, showed me to my cabin, and wished me a good flight.

There *was* a brief delay, apparently having to do with one more late arrival. I held my breath, but finally hatches closed, and the captain's voice came over the comm system, warning the passengers that we were getting ready to leave.

Then we were under way, and I sat back and relaxed.

The ship was the *Excelsior*. It was a far bigger and more elaborate vessel than the *Goldman*. It accommodated four times as many passengers. It was more comfortable. It had a much better menu. And the common room was transparent in all directions save along the spine of the ship. The comet, when we got to it, was spectacular. It was easy to imagine you were not even *in* a ship, but that you were out riding alongside the thing in your chair. With a glass of wine and a few hors d'oeuvres.

Despite all that, I was in no mood for sightseeing. And I wasn't thinking straight. I sat there in the resplendent glow of the comet and wondered whether, when we got back, I could hide in the washroom until everyone had left, then make off with the *Excelsior* and take it out to the asteroid. There would probably not be a refueling problem. But I'd draw every Patrol ship in the area. Ivan was a better bet.

Cavarotti's Comet had been looping around the sun and lighting the skies over Salud Afar for more than three thousand years. It had originally been reported by John Cavarotti, of whom nothing more was known. The pilot explained it was beginning to come apart, and scientists thought it would make only a few more passes before disintegrating. "There are a lot of people," he said, "who'd like to see it saved for future generations. So there's an effort under way."

The comet was close enough to the sun to light up, and it was a spectacular sight. We got in front of it and looked back at the head. We sank below it and braked, allowing it to pass above us. The tail was endless. "More than a million kilometers long," said the pilot. "As comets go, it's pretty ordinary."

During the second day, while we still watched the fireworks, the pilot came back and asked whether I was, by any chance, Chase Kolpath. I hesitated. "Yes."

"Your boarding pass says you're Jane Armitage."

"I'm a writer. *Kolpath* is my pseudonym."

He frowned, then smiled. "Okay. I have a message for you. From Ivan."

"Oh," I said. "Good."

"I told him there was nobody on board with that name. But he described you. Including the accent."

"All right. Thanks. I was hoping I'd get to see him."

He handed me the message. *Chase,* it said, *hope everything's okay. I'll be waiting when you get back. Ivan.*

I disembarked without incident and found him at the off-ramp. He handed me a box of mints. "What's going on?" he asked. He watched me checking out the crowd. "Are you looking for somebody?"

"Let's go where we can talk."

"The club?"

"First place they'd look for me."

"*Who'd* look?"

"CSS."

He made a face. "What the hell are you into, Chase?"

I shushed him. "I need to talk to you."

His features scrunched up, and he made an unhappy noise deep in his throat. "My place won't work. Kara's got her tikondo group tonight." Cardplayers.

We eventually decided on the Samuels Lounge. It was big and crowded, and when we scouted it, I saw no sign of trouble. "Okay," he said. "Tell me what's going on."

We settled into a booth with a magnificent view: Callistra, blue and brilliant above the rim of the world, and the sky dark and empty behind it. Somewhere out there other galaxies existed. But you couldn't see any of them.

I leaned across the table and lowered my voice.

In the middle of it, our drinks came, something unpronounceable for him, dark wine for me. I opened the mints and pushed them toward him. He took one, listened, stared at the table, stared at me, looked around the restaurant.

When I'd finished, he sat like a man who'd just been hit with a brick. "And you think they're holding Benedict?"

"There's no question they're holding him. Or worse."

Ivan was considerably grayer than he'd been during my flight-training days. That had only been about eight years earlier, but he looked much older. More sedate. I thought that the earlier model would have been more likely to take a chance with me. "Let me guess: You want me to take you to the asteroid."

"Yes."

"All right." He meant *All right, I understand what you want,* not *All right, I'll do it.* "What do you expect to find?"

"*Something's* there."

"It's a waste of time. It's also a violation of the guidelines. The company doesn't like us going out there."

"Since when?"

"The last two or three months. They're worried about the Mutes."

"Ivan—"

"If I got caught, Chase, I'd lose my license."

"You're all I've got right now, Ivan. Please. I'll pay you for a full load of passengers. Plus another thousand for yourself."

"You're insulting me, Chase. Look, I'd do it in a minute if I thought there was a point to it."

"Do it for me. Humor me. Do it because it may be the only chance I have to save Alex." I finished my wine. I literally gulped it down. And waited for an answer.

He cleared his throat. "Schedule's open for the next two days. Kara was expecting me to be home for a bit. I've been out a lot lately."

"Bring her along."

"I'll ask. But I doubt she'll come. She doesn't react well to trans-dimensional jumps."

"So you'll do it?"

"Damn, Chase. Kara's going to start talking to a lawyer."

We waited out the tikondo game. Then we trooped up to his apartment and said hello to Kara. He explained it was an emergency, that it was connected with Alex Benedict, who'd gone missing, and we told her everything we knew. I was reluctant about that, but we had to. We were asking her to trust her husband on an overnight alone with a woman he'd known in another life.

"You can come," he said.

She hesitated. She didn't like any part of the deal, and she probably didn't like me either. But she didn't want to send the message that she didn't trust him.

"Kara, please come with us," I said. "We're not sure what we're looking for, and we can use the extra pair of eyes."

Kara was a beauty. One of those women who couldn't help turning heads. Dark hair, bedroom eyes, pouty lips. She probably had a great smile, too, but I hadn't seen it yet.

I waited while they packed. Then they were back. Both looked uncomfortable. "I hope," Kara told me, "that there's really a point to this." There was a touch of coldness in her voice.

Ivan checked with Operations. He told them he was going to Tannemann's Dwarf. Four passengers. Husband, wife, two kids. We made up names. Mr. and Mrs. Inasha of Mt. Tabor. And his own wife would also be on board. "Taking a break from the routine," he explained.

"Okay, Captain Sloan," said the watch officer. *"You're cleared to go. You'll have to use the* Borden.*"*

"*Goldman*'s not serviced yet?"

"That's correct."

"Okay. That's fine."

"You'll be leaving out of A4."

He explained about Tanneman's Dwarf on the way to the boarding area. It was a dead star. "It's a popular destination," he said, "because it's sucking in a cloud of hydrogen and assorted gases, and that produces some spectacular fireworks. Kids especially love it. If you haven't seen anything like it before, it can be a pretty wild display. Kara's been out there a couple of times, haven't you, Kara?"

"It's lovely," she said. She still hadn't decided what was really going on.

The *Borden* was waiting at the dock. We got on board. Kara and I settled into the common room, while Ivan took his seat on the bridge.

"How long has your friend been missing?" she asked me. While I began to explain it again, the magnetic clamps let go and we started to ease away from the dock. Once outside the station, we took aim at Tanneman's Dwarf and began to accelerate.

Tannemann's was everything Mr. and Mrs. Inasha and their kids could have hoped for. Even at a range of sixty million kilometers, which was as close as we wanted to get, we could see a vivid corona brightening and dimming and exploding. "You know," I said, "something like this gives me the feeling that, despite all the light-years I've logged, I really don't get around very much."

"When this business is over," Ivan said, "provided we're not all in prison, you should spend some leisure time in the area. Take the tours."

"I've done that," I said. "I've been to Boldinai Point, the Haunted Forest, the Crystal Sea, the Golden Isles—"

"You're kidding, right?" The AI was turning us around. Lining up on the asteroid.

"No, I'm not kidding."

"That's ground-floor stuff, Chase. Couple of those I've never even heard of. Where is Boldinai Point?"

Kara was loosening up a bit. She smiled at the question. "Ivan thinks anything that's on the ground isn't worth your time. It's gotta be out orbiting some gasbag before he's able to pay attention."

"That's not true," he said.

"Right. Ivan, when's the last time we've even been groundside? Other than to visit your folks?"

He sighed. "I work hard, Chase, and that's the thanks I get." I smiled politely.

"By the way," he continued, "your friend Benedict is an antiquities guy, right?"

"Yes," I said.

He and Kara exchanged glances. "That's a clever way to change the subject, Ivan." She turned to me. "But Ivan's right. We have a lost world out here somewhere that he'd be interested in."

"A lost world?"

"Complete with ruins. Used to be somebody there, millions of years ago."

"That's the first I've heard that. You're right. Alex would want to take a look. Where is it?"

"Don't know. We lost it." She laughed at her own joke. We were beginning to accelerate. "They found it a couple of centuries ago. But they didn't keep good records, and next time they went out, they couldn't find it. It had reasonably intact cities. Everything frozen."

"Sounds like another hoax."

"Sounds like one," said Ivan. "But the original mission brought back some artifacts. And the experts say the artifacts are legitimate." We sank back into our seats. "Apparently the world got blown or dragged out of its home system. And the lights went out."

"And they lost the thing."

"It's out there somewhere. Cities. Roadways. Even a few ships frozen in harbors."

"Does the place have a name?"

"Malaki. It's named for the captain who found it."

During the short run out, Ivan tried to talk sense into me. "Don't go back to Samuels. When we're done out here, I can take you someplace where you'll be safe."

"What did you have in mind?"

"Well, I can't take you all the way to Rimway. For one thing, we don't have enough fuel."

"It doesn't matter. I can't leave Alex."

"Chase, if the CSS really have him, there's not much you can do. Except get a good lawyer."

"Maybe."

"Look, I don't know this guy Benedict. But I'll bet he'd want you to get clear. Especially when there's no point—"

"Let it go, Ivan. I've been through too much to walk out on him."

He shrugged. "Okay. You do what you think is right."

We were lucky. We came out of hyperspace almost on top of our target. Not that it was visible to the naked eye, of course. The asteroids—there were thousands of them—drifted through a dark sky. But Ivan didn't have much trouble picking out the one with the monument. Within a few hours we moved in close.

It was an ordinary asteroid, surface smooth in some areas, cratered in others. About three hundred kilometers in diameter. Even when we were on top of it, and I mean *literally* on top, just a few klicks away, we couldn't see it visually. The sky behind it was unbroken darkness.

Ivan didn't take his eyes off the monitors.

Moria, Salud Afar's sun, was behind us. But at that range it was invisible.

The three of us were on the bridge, looking down into the darkness, when Ivan said something I couldn't make out.

"What?" said Kara.

"I was just thinking how we'd react if a light suddenly went on."

A few minutes later, a soft glow *did* appear in the sky, outlining the rim of the asteroid. We'd gone halfway around it and were looking back at the haze along the edge of the Milky Way.

"Okay," he said. "We're here. What's next?"

I was wishing Alex were with us. "I'm not sure."

"Surely, madame, you jest."

"Great place for a monument," I said.

Kara smiled. "The original plan was that the monument would light up when anybody approached. You'd have come rolling in and the lights'd go on and you'd be looking at the thing. Actually, it could have been pretty striking stuff. But after what happened, they decided to leave it dark."

"I'm not surprised."

"There are a bunch of monuments on other asteroids that *do* light up. But not out here, of course."

"This is the only monument in the Swarm?"

"Yes." Ivan aimed one of the navigation lamps at the ground. But we still couldn't see anything. The light faded away.

Rachel, the AI, asked for instructions.

Ivan held out his hands. "What do we want to do, Chase? You want to go down and see what's there?"

We climbed into the lander and rode it toward the surface. "The monument?" he asked.

"Yes. That seems like the logical place."

As we descended, I asked whether either of them had ever been there before. "Nobody ever comes out here," said Ivan.

"What about the Family of God?"

"I think they had enough of the place. Something out here was dangerous, and they aren't dummies."

"What did *they* think it was?"

"I don't know. You'd have to ask them."

It was located on a bare plain.

I knew right away it was something apart from the rock-scape, even before I had a good look at it. It was tall and narrow and obviously artificial, a lost piece of a well-lit, warm world abandoned in a place where time had stopped.

We only had two pressure suits. Kara said it was okay. "You go ahead. I'll wait here."

We got dressed and went out through the air lock. Ivan had left the navigation lights on, but the ground was rougher than it looked from inside.

"This way," he said. He turned on a helmet lamp and plunged ahead. *"Watch your step."*

It was rough going. And the fact that I weighed next to nothing made it even more dangerous.

The lights played against a wall. It served as a base for a sphere. A set of steps mounted to the sphere, and a silver door stood partly open in its side.

Above, a diamond-shaped crystal pointed at the sky.

When the beam from my lamp touched the crystal, the door-way caught the reflection. "Is that what they intended?" I asked.

"I guess," he said. *"I don't really know anything about this place."*

Names were engraved on the wall. Thousands of them.

"Supporters, I guess," Ivan said.

And a legend: THEY HAVE PASSED TO A BETTER WORLD.

KYLE ROJEAU

IRA AND HARM KAMALANDA

CELIA TI

"How were they going to power it?"

"I don't know. Probably a grid installed somewhere. I'm not much of an electrician."

I climbed the stairs and studied the partially open door. And the corridor behind it, which went completely through the sphere. Into the night on the other side. The walls and overhead were rough-hewn; the floor was smooth. And I wondered if, sometimes, the asteroid turned and lined up with Callistra so its light appeared in the passageway, illuminated that smooth gray corridor.

They have passed to a better world.

The sensors had been installed, of course. It only required someone to throw the switch. But the switch had been removed, to ensure that no one circumvented the will of the survivors. The monument would stay dark.

And so it had.

I was just talking, trying to hold up my end of the conversation, while I looked for something that would tell me what Alex had expected to see out there. There was nothing. No fractured space, no alien ships, no Coalition vehicles engaged in a conspiracy.

The place, the tower, the rockscape, the sky, was simply quiet.

And dark.

"Ivan?"

"Yes, Chase."

"Where's Callistra?"

He looked up. *"Must be on the other side."*

"It wasn't. It was just as dark over there."

He grunted. *"Well, that doesn't make sense. It has to be here somewhere."*

What had Orrin Batavian told us in what now seemed that long-ago afternoon in downtown Moreska?

They'd picked one asteroid for a very special reason.

And suddenly, in that moment, in the permanent midnight of that place, it all came together.

TWeNTY-EiGHT

Whatever it is that hides in Uncle Lester's garden, it comes quickly and silently. Six have died, but no sound has been heard.

—*Midnight and Roses*

We climbed back into the air lock. "What's going on?" Ivan demanded. He was out of patience.

When we got back into the cabin, Kara was staring at us. "You mean it's missing? It *has* to be somewhere."

I couldn't stop trembling. It was cold inside the lander. I hadn't noticed it before. "No, Kara," I said. "I don't think it's anywhere."

We were getting out of our suits. "What's *that* mean?" asked Kara.

"I'm still working on it. Ivan, we need a chart."

"Why?" he asked.

"Please just do it." I'm pretty sure my voice had gone shrill. He backed off. "Rachel, give us the chart, please."

The lights dimmed, and, over the navigation display, Callistra blinked on. Its soft blue glow touched everything, softened Ivan's intense eyes, coated the chairs and the control panel. "Where's Moria?" I asked.

Salud Afar's sun. Ivan pointed toward the hatch. It was a dim yellow light. A white light, off to one side, marked SEEPAH.

"Okay. Can we see *our* position? The asteroid?"

A red light, a hand's width away from Moria.

"Good. Draw a straight line from Callistra through the asteroid and extend it as far as you can." A blue cursor left the star, crossed the cabin, touched the asteroid, passed off to one side of Salud Afar, and struck the bulkhead.

"I know what you were thinking," said Ivan, "but I could see right from the start they weren't going to line up."

"That's because we have an adjustment to make. The asteroid is, what, thirty-six light-years from Salud Afar?"

"Right."

Kara's eyes found me. They were afraid.

"Okay. Let me think about it for a minute." Math wasn't my strong suit. "Ask Rachel to move us, the asteroid, to where its position would have been thirty-three years ago, when they were putting the monument down. And move Moria to where it will be in another three years."

"How'd you get that?"

"Thirty-three from thirty-six. Okay? Now draw the line again from Callistra."

"Done."

The line from Callistra went directly through the asteroid and touched Moria.

Touched Salud Afar.

Ivan's mouth opened, and his head fell back against his seat. Kara took a deep breath. "My God," she said.

Ivan shook his head. "I don't believe it. I can't believe they'd know about something like this and keep it quiet."

"Alex thinks they knew as far back as Aramy Cleev."

"So what's next?"

"Let's go take a look."

We knew it would be somewhere along the vector, approximately three light-years out from Salud Afar. That was a pretty big target area. The problem was we didn't really know precisely when the *Lantner* encountered its problem. So we were guessing.

We jumped to within two light-years of Salud Afar but kept well off the vector. We were dealing with a thunderbolt, and we didn't want to come out directly in front of it.

Callistra was back in the sky. Brilliant and beautiful. Queen of the Night. Or a satanic spectacle. Take your choice.

We burned a ton of fuel turning around. Then we started back, jumping out every few seconds, well wide of the vector. At each stop we looked for Callistra, and each time were relieved to find it still floating serenely ahead.

Then, finally, it was gone.

Ivan delivered a string of profanities, starting under his breath and ending in a scream. Other than that, we were quiet a long time. Finally, he turned to his wife. "Start packing, babe," he said. "We'll be leaving as soon as we get home."

"A nova," Kara said. "But it's too far. It can't affect us."

I could feel my heart beating while I sat there, listening to a conversation that was going to play out on a global scale. What would happen when two billion people found out what was coming?

We jumped again. Back toward Salud Afar. Only a few light-weeks. Callistra reappeared.

Then back toward the star. And forward again.

We finally found it. The bright blue star beginning to look a bit *too* bright. Beginning to expand. To swell like a poisoned fruit.

"You sure we're out of the way?" asked Kara. "We don't want to go like the *Lantner.*"

Ivan relayed the question to me. "How big is it?" he asked.

I had no idea.

So we stayed in place, cruising through the void, watching while Callistra got brighter. And bigger. It took over the sky. Ivan switched to manual. If we had to leave in a hurry, it would be quicker just to do it rather than instruct Rachel to do it.

It would have been smarter to make one more jump back toward the star, to get behind what was coming. But the thing was mesmerizing.

Ivan began reading off Callistra's statistics. Its mass, surface temperature, diameter. It was 120 times the mass of Moria, their sun. Normally 1.2 million times as bright. God knew what it was at that moment. No. Not at that moment. Twelve hundred years ago, when this had actually happened. When it had blown apart and flung jets of radiation and God knew what else into the night.

"Its stability index was always low," said Ivan. "At least that's what it says here. If they didn't know already, they should have seen it coming."

The star grew blindingly bright.

"Uh-oh," said Ivan. "We'd better get out of here."

"I think we're okay," I said. "If we'd been in its path, we'd be dead already."

It took a while to find what we were looking for. When we did, it appeared harmless enough: a splash of gauzy light against the empty sky. "Part of the explosion?" Ivan asked.

"A gamma-ray burst, I think."

"Does it blow everything away?"

"No. But it irradiates everything."

"That can't be right."

"Why?"

"It wouldn't explain why the two ships disappeared at the asteroid. Or the people at the ceremony. Unless it just blew them away."

I told them what Alex had told me. How Cleev probably fabricated everything to maintain his hold on power.

"What a son of a bitch."

"It also explains why they had to kill off Jennifer Kelton and Edward Demery."

"Why *did* they have to do that?"

"Because Demery figured it out. He figured it out the way Vicki did, and the way Alex did. Except Alex couldn't bring himself to believe what he was seeing." I was trying to visualize the sequence of events. Demery suspected that the star might have blown. That part of it had taken out the monitors at Seepah. That another part, centuries later, destroyed the monument celebration at the asteroid. It had taken several hundred years because Seepah was that much closer to Callistra.

Demery would have gone to Jennifer for confirmation. She agreed, and made the mistake—or possibly *he* did—of showing it to someone in authority. That got them killed.

"I know about that," said Kara. "But as I understand it, seventeen or eighteen families were killed that night. They couldn't all have been in on it."

Think like Alex. "They'd have killed the others to cover what they were doing. To prevent attention from being drawn to Demery."

"It makes sense," she said.

The burst was small in the viewports. It looked like a distant comet.

"When Vicki went out to the asteroid," he said, "she just wanted to see whether the star was there. Right?"

"Sure."

"I guess," said Ivan, "it also explains why Haley Khan disappeared."

"Yes," I said. "He would have known, too."

"But," Kara said, "Cleev's long gone."

"I know. But there are still people in power."

Kara's eyes had closed. "How much damage do you think this thing will do?"

"Rachel?"

"If my measurements are correct, the burst will strike Salud Afar in exactly three years and six days. The event will last three days, four hours, and six minutes. Error ratio of four percent. They will get substantial protection from the atmosphere. Unlike those caught at the asteroid. However, the event will be lethal for unprotected higher life-forms."

He opened a channel to Samuels.

"What are you going to do?" I asked.

"Start warning people."

"No, Ivan."

"No?" His face contorted into a snarl. "Hell, Chase, why not?"

"Ivan, if you start making noise, you're going to create a stampede."

"What do you suggest? We just keep quiet so we can save our own damned skins?"

"No. Look: I'm not sure yet. I'm like you. I'm just a pilot. I don't have any experience with stuff like this. But I'm pretty sure that just getting out there and screaming about it isn't the right way to go."

"What is?"

"Somebody that people respect is going to need to step up and take charge."

He rolled his eyes. "You've lost your mind, Chase. Who's going to do anything like that? Your buddy the antique dealer? Assuming you could get him loose?"

How the hell would I know? "Look, I don't have any better ideas than you do right now. But let's just keep calm and try to figure it out. Okay?"

TWENTY-NINE

For each of us, my dear, there comes a time when one must go into the haunted house.

—*Nightwalk*

We made the jump back to Salud Afar and emerged about thirty hours from Samuels. We looked out at the calm sky, at the galactic rim, at Callistra, bright and benevolent over the edge of the world.

We were in the common room. We were all talking too much, and all talking about the same thing. There was nothing else. How did you evacuate two billion people in three years?

And what were we going to do?

"You know," Ivan said, "they may pick all three of us up as we come off the ship."

"You think they'd do that?" asked Kara. The question was directed at me.

"Yes," I said. "I've no doubt."

"We should program Rachel," Kara said. "Have her break the news unless we tell her not to."

"If they're onto us," I said, "it's already too late to do that. They wouldn't have a problem blocking a transmission from a single ship whose location is known."

Ivan nodded. "That's right." He looked at Kara. "I'm sorry I got you into this, love."

"We need to split up," Kara said.

"That's exactly what I've been thinking. Look: I'm the one they'll be looking for. How about we use the lander? To drop me off somewhere?"

"Absolutely," said Ivan. "Exactly what I was going to suggest."

"And when you guys get back to your quarters, call me."

I'd have liked to launch the lander from far out. Maybe a couple of million klicks. But we couldn't because it didn't have the braking power. And had we begun braking the *Borden* too soon, it would have attracted attention. So I launched close in, hoping no one would notice.

On the theory that we should try every channel open to us, I prepared a transmission to Rob Peifer, laying out everything we'd found. I recorded it in my link, and on the lander's commsystem. It would go out at my direction, or automatically from both sources in thirty hours unless I specified otherwise.

I rode the lander down into the atmosphere and made directly for the plateau, hoping that Wexler would have put Alex there again. But it was empty.

Landers are easy to find. Especially when they're operating without clearance in crowded skies. I left the plateau and set down in a wooded area.

Before leaving the lander, I tried to call Ivan. He would have been docked by then. But an unfamiliar male voice answered. *"Sloan,"* it said. I broke off.

I walked seven kilometers to a small train station, waited about an hour, and caught a local toward Marinopolis. During the trip, I read everything I could find about Administrator Kilgore. I listened to his speeches and press conferences. He *looked* like a chief executive. He was tall and deliberate, with silver hair and gray eyes that were at once intelligent and sensitive. He was relaxed, casual, the guy in charge. When he was there, you knew everything was under control. It was hard to believe he could be part of a conspiracy to maintain secrecy while a radiation bolt was coming this way.

He did a live broadcast while I was on a train soaring through a mountain range. It originated from his office at Number 17 Parkway, which was the seat of the executive wing of the government. He was at his desk, a fireplace flickering and crackling in the background.

He talked about general matters, about his concern that relations with the Mutes had deteriorated so severely, about a recent scandal involving one of his aides, and about several new programs he was instituting, the primary one being a response to a series of skimmer crashes. *"It's not supposed to happen, and I promise you we will do what's necessary to stop it."*

He spoke for about thirty-five minutes, and I found myself hard-pressed not to like him. I resisted the impulse to conclude he was involved.

The train wasn't going all the way into the capital, so I got off in a midsized city and decided I'd complete the journey the next day.

I checked into a hotel, showered and changed, and went across the street to the Paranova, which had a small band and good drinks. I'm not usually much of a drinker, but it had been a rugged few days, and I only had to pay for the first one. After that there was always somebody anxious to pick up the tab. I spent a couple of hours in the place, declined an invitation to join a party, met two or three guys who would have made interesting companions for the evening. But I kept thinking I needed a heroic type. Somebody who could break down doors and take out the bong thrower.

The band had two people on stringed instruments, a third on a horn, and a female singer. They called themselves The Big Five. And I know, there were only four. Don't ask me to explain it.

The music was moody. The sort of stuff they were doing during the last century on Rimway. But it was effective nonetheless, or maybe it was just my state of mind. The songs were about lost lovers, roads not taken, and being away from home. A blond guy with great looks but no sense of humor was at my table going on about something, while I sipped a drink that tasted of lemon and rum, and The Big Five played on. Suddenly I became aware of the lyrics:

> *. . . End of the world*
> *When you walked away . . .*

Drinking too much usually gives me a false sense of bravado. I always come out of those evenings with the notion I can take on anybody. But I think that had dissipated by the time I got off the train in Marinopolis and caught a taxi out to the Marikoba University campus.

The register told me that Professor Mikel Wexler specialized in Bandahriate history and that his office was located on the second floor of the Fletcher Building. But it was locked, and the people up there said he "did not come in at this time of the week."

I tried his home code and got an AI. *"Professor Wexler's residence. Please leave a message."*

I recalled that he was an "occasional advisor to Administrator Kilgore." I called the executive branch information board. They were sorry, but they had no way to reach him, nor could they advise me where he was.

So I wandered into the faculty room in the Fletcher Building and started a conversation with anyone who came in. Nobody questioned my right to be there, and I decided this was the time to take a chance and mention my affiliation with Alex.

"Marvelous," they said. "The man who got the truth about Christopher Sim."

And "the guy who found Margolia."

The *Polaris* story never surfaced, but it didn't need to. As people went out to take care of classes, others came in, asking what I was doing there, could I be persuaded to talk to this or that class, what was Benedict working on now? I was pleasantly surprised to discover that most of them knew *me*.

What was I doing there?

Every time the question was asked, I replied that I'd been hoping to locate Mikel Wexler. "I'm sorry to have missed him."

"Ah," said one portly woman dressed entirely in black, "I might have known Mikel would know Alex Benedict."

"Do you have any idea where I might find him?"

There were two or three others in the room. We were all seated around a table. "I suppose it would be all right," she said. She lowered her voice even though it didn't matter. Everyone could hear what she said. "He's at the Cobblemere Building. He has an office over there. He claims they do historical research for the government, but I think they just screw around. Did you want me to call him?"

The others looked disapprovingly at her. One shrugged.

"No," I said. "I'd like to surprise him if I can."

The Cobblemere was a nondescript, gray, three-story structure set on a tree-lined avenue about two kilometers from the university. Corporate offices lined both sides of the street, along with the National Biolab Foundation. A small metal plate identified it as the COALITION RESEARCH AGENCY.

I walked in the front door, strolled through an empty lobby, entered a corridor, and stopped outside an open office door. A desk lamp was on, but nobody was home. A tall, thin kid came out of an adjoining room, carrying a piece of electronic equipment. He stopped when he saw me. "Can I help you, ma'am?"

"I'd like to see Dr. Wexler, please."

"I'm sorry. He's not here at the moment. Would you care to leave a message?"

"Sure," I said. "Tell him Kolpath is here. He has"—I glanced at the time—"an hour and fifty-seven minutes to get to me, or the gamma-ray story will go to every major media outlet on the planet."

He looked puzzled.

"Do you want me to write it down for you?"

"Ma'am," he said, "you seem upset. May I suggest—?"

"I suggest you get that message to him." I gave him my code. "Tell him to call."

He stood with his mouth open, not sure what to do. I let the moment drag on and looked at the time again. "An hour and fifty-*six* minutes," I said. "What's your name?"

"Eiglitz."

"Mr. Eiglitz, I can assure you that Dr. Wexler will be extremely unhappy if he doesn't get that message promptly."

He managed a rattled smile. "Yes, of course. I'll see what I can do." Another grin. "Why don't you wait here? Let me see what I can do. Please make yourself comfortable." He left the office, but moments later he was back. "I'm sorry," he said, "but you *did* say the name is—?"

"Kolpath." I spelled it for him.

"Of course." He hurried out. A few minutes later, an older man showed up. Tall, wide shoulders just starting to slump with age. Congenial features. Let's just take it easy attitude.

"Ms. Kolpath," he said, "my name is Mark Hollinger. Can I help you?" His tone suggested he was speaking to a child. "Dr. Wexler is not here."

"Thanks, Mr. Hollinger. You can see that Wexler gets my message. I think I'm done here." I turned around and started for the front door.

Hollinger stayed with me. "I'm sorry. But he's really not available today. You're going to have to work through me."

"Okay," I said. "Produce Alex."

"Alex?" He tried to look puzzled. "Alex who?"

Hollinger asked me to be patient for a minute and went away. Eiglitz came back and tried to engage me in conversation. Nice weather. He was sorry there was so much trouble. Could he get anything for me? Finally, a Wexler hologram appeared. *"Chase,"* he said, mustering all his considerable charm. *"I'm glad you came by. We've been looking all over for you."*

"I know. Where's Alex?"

Wexler glanced over at Eiglitz, who got up, left the room, and pulled the office door shut behind him. *"He's all right. He's been visiting with us."*

"Let me see him."

"I can't at the moment. But I assure you he's fine. Listen, I understand—"

"This conversation goes no further until I see him. Where is he?"

"Chase, be reasonable. I'm not really in a position—"

"The Callistra story is an hour and a half from going to the world. Show me Alex."

"Chase—"

I stared back at him.

"We're trying to get to him now. But you have to give us some time. I don't know that I can manage it within the time frame."

I shrugged. "Then we don't have anything to talk about, I guess."

"No, wait. Listen, I'm telling you the truth."

"Wexler, why would I believe anything you have to say?"

"All right. I know none of this looks good from your perspective. I understand that. But you weren't hurt. And Alex hasn't been hurt. We were afraid you'd do exactly what you're about to do. I had no choice."

"I guess not. Can't sell off property if people know the world's coming to an end."

"Look, Chase, I hate doing this over an open circuit—"

"Sorry. It's all we've got."

"All right. Yes, I'll admit I moved some holdings. So did some others. I mean, who wouldn't? But that's not why we kept it quiet."

"Okay. I'll bite. Why'd you keep it quiet?"

"Because there are two billion people on this world. And there's no way we can save more than a handful."

"And not even those if you don't try."

"We're digging shelters for them."

"That's why you lied about the Mutes. And probably even put out the rumor about the rift."

"The rift?"

"Forget it. You're not that good an actor."

"Look. Chase. For God's sake. We were trying to save as many people as we could, and we needed a cover story. Something that wouldn't cause a worldwide panic." He stood for a long moment, facing me. He looked hesitant, but I watched him come to a decision. *"Look, I know we could have handled this better. But the honest truth is, when Carpenter came to us with this story, and we checked it out and found it was true, we didn't know what to do."*

"Who's Carpenter?"

"Rasul Carpenter. He's a physicist. Greene figured out what

was happening. I assume you know that. She went to him for confirmation. He came to us."

"You mean *you.*"

"Yes. Me. Within a day we knew it was true. End of the world. How the hell was I supposed to deal with that? Sure we kept it quiet. And a few of us took advantage of the knowledge. Sell off and get your family out of town. What would you do differently?"

"And you screwed up Vicki's head."

"We didn't know it would turn out the way it did. The doctors said it was just a matter of her getting past a bad memory."

"Did they know what the bad memory was?"

"One of them did. No way we could avoid that."

"So you set things up so you could dispose of your property, and take your family out, while everybody else got left."

"Chase, it would have been different had there been something we could do. But it's not like that. This thing is still three years away. But we're helpless. You go ahead and tell the media, and all you'll do is create worldwide panic. Salud Afar will become a living hell." He looked tired. Scared. *"These people still have three years of their lives left. I don't know how much longer we can keep this quiet, but once it gets out, it's over. We'll have taken those years away. And we have nothing to offer in return. No vast fleet to take them somewhere else. No way to hide more than a handful of them."*

"Where's Alex?"

"I've sent an agent to hook him up. But it'll take a while."

"Where is he?"

"In a place similar to Corvex. The place you managed to escape from. You were very clever about that, by the way." He paused, expecting a response. When he didn't get one, he continued: *"He's on an island."*

"How long's it going to take you to produce him?"

"An hour or so."

"I'll wait."

"Will you cancel the transmission?"

"When I'm able to talk to him. And if I'm satisfied with what I hear."

"Surely you understand that conditions here will become chaotic if the information gets out."

"I want Alex back."

"All right. Stay where you are. I'll get back to you as soon as I can."

He needed about forty minutes. Then he reappeared in the office. *"I believe we have him now."* He bent his head and listened to someone I couldn't see. Nodded. And returned his attention to me. *"Stand by, Chase,"* he said.

Then Alex was in front of me. He was on a beach, a placid sea at his back. *"Chase."* His eyes widened. *"What's going on?"*

Technology is what it is. I was looking at a hologram, but I didn't know if it was actually Alex, or something generated by a software system. "Alex," I said, "we visited Atlantis recently."

He saw what was coming. *"Yes. Excellent trip."*

"Who was with us?"

"Selotta and Kassel."

"What's your favorite joke, Alex?"

"I don't do jokes."

"Okay," I said. "Wexler, are you there?"

Wexler reappeared. *"Satisfied?"*

"Get him back here."

"Not yet."

Alex glanced off to one side. He wasn't alone.

Krestoff casually walked up behind him. She was carrying a scrambler. And she allowed me to watch as she reset the weapon. To *lethal.*

Wexler sighed. *"Chase, I don't like having to resort to this. But the stakes are too high, and you're not leaving me any choice."*

A door opened behind me. Bong came into the room. He looked at me with relish. I saw no weapon. He obviously didn't think he'd need one. I suspected he was right.

"Now, let me tell you how you may save Alex's life and your own. I want to know where we can locate the transmission you spoke of. And you will delete it." He paused to make sure I understood what would happen if I declined. *"When that is done, you will, I'm sorry to say, have to remain under our jurisdiction for the time being. I'll add that, should a duplicate transmission*

turn up, some fallback precaution you might have taken, that I'll feel obliged to kill you both." Bong closed the door, and I was alone with him.

Alex looked uncertain. Finally, he shook his head. *"They'll kill us anyhow, Chase. Don't cooperate."*

Krestoff must have gotten a signal from Wexler. She raised the weapon and pointed it at the back of Alex's head.

"Forget it," I said.

Wexler studied me for a long moment. *"You're sure?"*

"I can offer a compromise."

She did not lower the weapon.

"I'm listening."

"Release us both. Then I'll rewrite the message. And remove everything from it that points to you. And I'll hold it until tomorrow. That'll give you and your thugs time to get out of town."

Thugs. Krestoff's eyes locked on me. She didn't say anything but I got the message. It was the same as before: *I'd like to meet you alone somewhere.*

Wexler sucked on his lower lip. *"I'm sorry. That's not acceptable."*

My heart was pounding so hard I thought it was going to break loose. But I kept my voice calm. "Then do what you have to."

He nodded. *"All right. If that's your last word."* He gave me a few moments to change my mind. Then he turned to Krestoff. *"Kill him."*

"If you do," I said, "you'll get nothing from me. And the media will have the truth about Callistra within the hour. I wonder if the voters will be upset with you?"

He raised a palm to stop Krestoff. And stared at me.

I smiled at him. I've never in my life done anything harder than getting that smile up and running. "Pack your bags, Wexler. She pulls that trigger, we're all dead."

Krestoff waited. Alex stood motionless. Bong circled around to get a better angle on me. And Wexler stood in his faraway location and just sucked in air.

I picked up a lamp with a weighted base. It wouldn't have been much of a weapon against Bong, but it sent the right signal.

Wexler sighed. *"How do I know you'll pull my name out of the story?"*

"You'll have to trust me."

Another long pause. Somebody tried to get into the office. Then I heard raised voices in the corridor, and the noise went away. *"Okay."* Bong growled his disappointment. Alex took a deep breath. *"You can use the AI in the office. Please cancel your report."*

"I'll use my own AI. And I'm not canceling anything. I'll move it back. In case you change your mind. How long do you need to bring Alex here?"

"I don't like the arrangement."

"I really care about that."

"You said you'd hold off until tomorrow."

"I'll do that."

"Give me seventy-two hours."

"You have until midnight tomorrow. Local time."

"You're a bitch, Chase."

"Alex, how far are you?"

"I'm about three hours away."

"Get him here by three."

"Impossible."

"Well, I can be reasonable. I'll give you an extra two hours. Have him here by close of business." I was still watching Bong. "Would you get that creep out of here?"

Bong's disappointment morphed into anger. *"Shelby,"* said Wexler. *"Wait outside. And see that Ms. Kolpath gets transportation to wherever she intends to go."*

Bong delivered one more frustrated stare. Then he left.

"There's something else I want."

Wexler looked trapped. *"What?"*

"Mr. and Mrs. Ivan Sloan. He's the pilot who took me out to the asteroid."

"What about him?"

"You have him, too. I want him turned loose also."

He shrugged. *"Okay. Sure, we've no reason to hold him."*

"And there's somebody else."

"For God's sake, Chase—"

"Haley Khan."

"Who the hell is that?"

"Vicki's pilot. I want them all back."

"Okay. I'll arrange it."

"Not that I don't trust you, but I'll be in touch with them within the hour. If they're not free, all four of them, the deal's off."

"I wish," he said, *"you had some notion of the damage you're going to cause."*

"Whoever's in this with you, Doctor," I said, "will probably throw you to the wolves. You and the administration have wasted several months. That thing's a lot closer now than it was when you first found out about it. And you've done *nothing*. Except move money and real estate around."

"That's not so, damn you. We've been creating shelters. Storing supplies. Getting ready as best we can under extremely difficult circumstances."

"Circumstances, hell. Look, Wexler, I'd be willing to bet Aramy Cleev learned about this thirty years ago."

"Yes," he said. *"That's probably true."*

"He's the guy you led a revolution against."

"He was a monster. And if you're trying to compare him to me—" He stopped, his jaws clamped.

"It's hard to see a difference," I said.

They delivered Alex to me in the middle of a public park. Kids rode swings, birds chirped, a cluster of guys were playing the local version of chess. Alex took me into his arms. "You were beautiful," he said.

"You okay?"

"Yes. Still a little rattled, but I'm all right. How about you?"

"I'm good."

"They won't tell me anything. I take it the big light was missing."

"Callistra? Yes."

"I'm sorry to hear it."

"They've got three years." We sat down on a bench. "You knew all along, didn't you?"

"I suspected it from the time we heard about Jennifer's comment."

"That it didn't matter whether the wedding had a religious element?"

"Yes. That and the Caliente business and the math."

"Ah, yes," I said. "The math."

THirTY

"Parker did what he thought best. Star was tired so he took the short route home. I mean, what were the chances, really?"

"But it cut through the darkest part of the forest."

"I know. But the point is, he meant well."

—*Etude in Black*

We were sitting on top of a tidal wave, but at least we saw no reason to hide any longer. We checked back into the Blue Gable, where we'd stayed when we first arrived in Marinopolis, and took over the penthouse suite. It had a broad balcony and a magnificent view across the top of the city.

Ivan called. *"They let us go."*

"Good. You guys are okay, right?"

"Yes. We're fine."

"Glad to hear it. You hear anything from Khan?"

"No. Why? Is he in on this deal, too?"

"Supposed to be. Anyhow, I guess I'll be seeing you back on Rimway."

"I don't know," he said.

"Are you going somewhere else?"

"We talked it over."

"And—?"

"I don't know. She doesn't want to leave. We have friends and family here."

"Oh."

"We've talked to a few of them. They don't believe us."

"I'm not surprised."

"Even if they did, I'm not sure they'd go. This is their home."

"So what are *you* going to do?"

"I'll let you know."

Twenty minutes later I got a call from Khan. He said thanks.

I rewrote the report I'd stored online, eliminating everything that implicated Wexler and his stooges and also anything that I thought would tend to spread panic. That latter part wasn't easy. But I'd used the term *Thunderbolt* to refer to the gamma-ray burst, and I got rid of that. I also tried to make the account a little less breathless.

When I'd finished I directed the AI to deliver it to Peifer at one minute past midnight. Then to follow up and give it to the rest of the world three hours later. As I had earlier, I took precautions to ensure it couldn't be blocked.

Then, for the first time in a while, I collapsed and slept through the afternoon.

That evening we ate in the hotel dining room, which was filled with well-dressed patrons. They had candlelight and soft music, and it felt good to be together again. "I thought I'd lost you," I told him after the host had seated us by a corner window. We were on the ground floor. Outside, shoppers moved beneath glowing lamps, their arms filled with packages. We were approaching a local holiday in which it was customary to give gifts. There was a theater across the street, doing a musical, *Late Night Out*, which had been imported from Khaja Luan. I'd seen it two years before, enjoyed it thoroughly, and still remembered the showstopper, "Go for Broke," at the end of the first act.

A family trailing a boy and girl passed outside. The parents carried bags of packages, while the kids giggled and ran along beside them. The boy stopped and looked through the window. At us. Our eyes connected, and he waved. I waved back.

He'd be about ten when the gamma rays came. The Thunderbolt. "I feel guilty sitting here," I said. "I'm anxious to hand it over to Rob. Get it over with."

"I know."

"We're talking twelve hundred light-years, Alex. I didn't think novas could do any damage this far away."

We both had a soup appetizer. He tried his, but didn't react to it. "It's a *hyper*nova."

"The worst kind."

"Yes." Alex cupped his chin in his hands and closed his eyes. "Callistra is—*was*—a hypergiant. It's been on the verge of collapse for thousands of years. The people here knew that. *Everybody* knew it. There was a time, a couple of thousand years ago, when they kept instruments out there. Monitors. But the instruments had to be maintained, nothing ever happened, and eventually people got used to it. And forgot about it.

"I found some reports that the current administration was going to restart the program. But they had other priorities. So it never happened."

"Other priorities."

"Yes. No wonder Vicki did the mind wipe. She knew, and she couldn't warn anybody. She did it because it looked like the only chance she had to get a warning back to Salud Afar. She sacrificed herself."

"Gutsy woman. Alex, I hate seeing Wexler walk away from this."

He looked ambivalent. "You know, he's not entirely wrong about the worldwide reaction. I'd just as soon not be here when the news gets out."

"I hate this, Alex."

"Me, too, babe."

Peifer found us first. We'd just gotten back to our suite. *"Chase?"* His hologram barged into the room. *"You got Alex back?"*

"Yes, he's here."

"Thanks." His voice rasped. *"I really appreciate your letting me know."*

"I was going to call."

"What happened?"

I glanced over at Alex, who was out of Peifer's field of vision. Reading a book about the missing civilization that Ivan had described. He shook his head no. *I don't want to talk to him.* "I got lucky," I said.

"Yeah. Good. How about some details?"

"Umm—"

"Forget it. Let me talk to Alex."

"He's not here."

"Come on, Chase, you just said he was there."

"I was speaking metaphorically. I meant here as in *out. Free.*"

"Who was holding him? Was it Wexler?"

"Rob, I'm not able to talk about it now, okay? You'll have the entire story later tonight."

"Me and who else?" He looked skeptical.

"You'll have a three-hour head start."

"Okay. I can live with that. When?"

"When what?"

"When will I get the story? I don't live up here, you know."

"Midnight."

"Great. That's good planning, Chase. How about a preview? You can trust me."

"First I need a favor."

"You may always ask."

"I want you to keep Wexler's name out of it."

"So he is involved."

"A favor to me, Rob."

"Oh. And when did I accumulate this debt?"

"Rob, this story is bigger than Wexler. Believe me."

"I'll think about it."

"I made a deal to get Alex back."

"I didn't make the deal."

"Please, Rob."

"You're a hard woman, Chase."

"Only when you get to know me."

"By the way, I've another question for you."

"Go ahead."

"Do you know anything about the crazy woman who took a taxi up to Samuels a few days ago? And then disappeared? The description sounded a bit like you."

* * *

Minutes later someone knocked on the door. When we didn't immediately respond, a male voice announced he was CSS. "Here we go again," said Alex.

"Please open up." More knocking.

There wasn't really anywhere to go, so I complied. There were three of them, two men and a woman. The woman was *not* Krestoff. "Chase Kolpath?" The question came from the older of the men.

"Yes."

"The Administrator would like to speak with you." He glanced over at Alex. "And with Mr. Benedict."

"Don't you guys ever give up?" I said.

He frowned. Looked puzzled, put his official look back on. "Please come along." He stepped aside to make room.

"Before you do this, the original transmission, the one implicating Wexler, is scheduled to go out unless I stop it."

"I don't know anything about that, Ms. Kolpath," the agent said. "But I would appreciate it if you and Mr. Benedict would come with us."

I got a jacket out of the closet. A look of utter resignation crossed Alex's face. He got up and grumbled something indiscernible. We walked out into the corridor, they closed in around us, and we went up to the roof, where another white skimmer waited, identical to the one that Krestoff had used to haul us around. Moments later we lifted off. I was relieved to see that we turned in the direction of the Seawalk and not toward the gray building on the edge of the city.

Nobody said much. One of the agents asked whether I was comfortable. And the pilot spoke softly to his control. We were approaching Number 17 Parkway, the executive mansion. "It looks as if it really *is* the Administrator," said Alex.

"I guess." I was not comfortable. "Do we know whether he's involved?"

"I've no idea how high it went."

The building and the grounds were enclosed by an iron fence. We descended onto a pad off the east wing. The agents opened up, and there was a brief exchange with security people. When they were satisfied, we were escorted across a wide lawn and into the mansion. The building itself was of recent vintage, relatively small and unobtrusive, standing among the architectural giants erected by the Cleevs. "It sends the right message," Alex commented.

Once inside, we passed through an elaborate security arrangement and were given IDs. Then we were taken to a waiting room.

"He'll want us to cancel," I said, when we were alone.

"Of course. But I'd be surprised if we see him personally. He'll have somebody else lean on us. They've probably disposed of Wexler."

The room was filled with bookcases, but the volumes were all in sets and showed no sign of use. There were portraits of stern men and women who appeared to be looking off at a horizon, and a picture of a waterfall, and another of a structure with columns and porticoes set against the sea. Alex was looking through the books when an aide came in and asked us to follow her.

She led the way down a corridor lined with more pictures of still more severe people. I wondered whether anyone in power ever smiled for a portrait? A large office occupied the space at the end of the passageway. Inside, a harried-looking male staff member sat at a desk next to a closed door. "Mr. Benedict and Ms. Kolpath," our escort said.

The staff member flung a smile in our direction and spoke into a link. "They're here." He received a reply, nodded, and got up. "This way, please." He took us down another corridor. Then upstairs. And finally we confronted a large, paneled door. He opened it cautiously, looked inside, announced our presence, and stepped out of the way.

It was like walking onto a stage. The overhead was vaulted, and tinted windows filtered the light. A large carved desk, with flags behind it, anchored the place. There were maybe a dozen chairs scattered around. A long sofa was set against one wall. A fireplace crackled happily. Somehow, they'd arranged things so that it *felt* like a place where history was routinely made.

Behind the desk, rising as we entered, was Tau Kilgore. The Administrator. Himself.

He was engaged in an earnest conversation with a heavyset

guy who looked angry, and a middle-aged chestnut-haired woman who was carefully maintaining a neutral expression. "Can't be done," Kilgore was saying as he got to his feet.

The woman spotted us and raised a hand for us to stay back. "Find a way," continued Kilgore. "I don't care how you do it. But find a way." He turned in our direction and signaled us to take seats. "When we first heard of this," he said, "first heard about Greene, we immediately sent out a mission. Which confirmed the story. The thing, the ray burst, whatever, is a little more than three years away, and we are directly in the crosshairs. And somehow nobody ever thought it would be a good idea to get the word up here." He looked like a guy carrying the world on his shoulders.

"It was a rogue operation, sir," said the male. "They kept it to themselves."

"How in hell could they possibly do that, Grom?"

"We're looking into it, sir."

"I would goddam well hope so. I want everybody who was involved. Then we are going to hang their sorry asses."

"Yes, sir. I'll get back to you as soon as we have the details."

He turned toward us, still apparently seething. I wasn't sure, though. It could have been an act, carried on for our benefit. We did a round of introductions. The woman was Dr. Circe Belhower. Her eyes were intense. Not a warm woman, I suspected, under the best of circumstances. She didn't look any happier than the Administrator. She was tall and prim and humorless. The teacher for whose classes nobody ever signed up. "Dr. Belhower," he said, "is a special consultant. She's going to try to help us deal with this"—he struggled for a word—"catastrophe."

Kilgore addressed himself to Alex. "I understand you've been held a virtual prisoner, Mr. Benedict."

"Yes, Mr. Administrator. Although 'virtual' is not the way I'd describe it."

"How long?"

"Several days."

"Where?"

"They called it a custody chamber. It was on an island somewhere."

"How were you treated?"

"Fine, sir. Other than being locked in. And a pistol held to my head."

"Damn them," he said. "Well, I'm glad to hear you're okay, anyhow." He seemed barely able to contain himself. "We've just learned what's been going on. They're coming out of the woodwork now," he said. "Trying to save their asses by turning in their collaborators. I'll be honest with you, Alex—Is it okay if I call you that?"

"Yes, sir."

"I'll be honest with you, Alex—" He paused again, had second thoughts and waved away whatever he was going to say. "When you found out about this, why didn't you come directly to *me*?"

Tau Kilgore *looked* like a chief executive. He was tall and deliberate, with silver hair and gray eyes that were at once intelligent and compassionate. He was the kind of guy who inspires confidence. The word about him on the nets, though, wasn't flattering. He was described as a man who consulted only those who agreed with him, who was inflexible, who tended to confuse disagreement with disloyalty. Looking at him, I had a hard time believing it.

"We didn't really get a chance to, Mr. Administrator. As soon as we got close, they scooped us up."

"I see."

"I should add," he said, "that it was originally Vicki Greene who figured it out. And then sacrificed her life to give us reason to look into it."

"Yes. I know about her. We owe her a considerable debt. Do you mind telling me how long you've known about all this?"

"We weren't certain until a few days ago."

He digested that and leaned forward. "And *you* are about to give the story to the media. Is that correct?

"Yes, Mr. Administrator. We are."

"Have you considered the consequences of such an act?"

The guy was intimidating, but Alex went toe to toe with him. "By consequences I assume you mean the reaction of the voters."

"Of everyone on the planet, Mr. Benedict. By releasing this information, you will ensure that we will spend the next three years living in a state of chaos."

"That's more or less the reasoning the conspirators used to justify sitting on this for the last several months."

"You mean Wexler."

"You know about him?"

"Of course I know, goddammit." The color drained from his face. "Please answer the question, Alex. Don't confuse me with Wexler."

"Yes," said Alex. "We have considered the consequences. I think—"

"I don't give a good goddam *what* you think. You're about to bring the walls down. Do you realize that? How am I supposed to deal with this if you tell the general public that there was a rogue operation in their government? Don't think they won't blame me. And I know exactly what's going through your mind. It's true that I deserve a substantial chunk of the blame. But it'll create a political firestorm. We don't have time for that. These people have to have a government they can believe in. And they have to have it now."

"Maybe," said Alex, "you should have been more careful about the people you put in power."

"I'll concede the point. But that's in the past now. It's irrelevant. You're about to impose a death sentence on two billion people. And you're going to tell them, either directly or by implication, that I was hiding the truth from them. And that I am therefore responsible."

Alex's own temper began to rise. "I think there's some truth to that admission."

"Look, I made the mistake of trusting the wrong people. God knows I regret that."

"They were building shelters, Mr. Administrator. Making up bogus reports of Mute encroachments. How could you *not* have known?"

Circe broke in. "Wexler and his friends were very good at keeping the truth quiet."

"They knew," said Kilgore, "what would happen to commodity prices, to *everything*, if the word about Callistra got out. So they told nobody."

"And what did you think the shelters were for?"

"Goddammit, the reports about the Mutes took me in, too. They lied to me the way they lied to everyone else. Because they knew I wouldn't tolerate what they were doing."

I'd never seen Alex angrier. His voice shook: "Where's Wexler now?"

"We're looking for him."

"And how'd you finally find out what's going on?"

Kilgore showed us a photo. It was Bong. "Came forward yesterday," he said. "We'd always heard rumors that the reports of Mute incursions had been drummed up. And the experts were divided over the rift-in-space story. I should have looked into it. I can't believe now that I let it all go on."

"You'll be lucky if you're not forced to step down."

"If it comes to that, I won't hesitate, Alex. Meantime, I intend to do what I can for the people of this world."

"What's going to happen to Bong?" I asked.

Kilgore looked at me, startled. I got the impression he'd forgotten I was there. "Who?" he asked.

"Bong. The guy in the picture."

"We haven't decided yet." He lowered his voice. "I guess it's safe to say he'll be pretty much the last guy off the planet." He picked up a pen, scribbled himself a note, and put it in his pocket. "Well, the truth is, I'm not going to ask you to hide what you know."

"Really?"

"There's no way I can keep it quiet now. Too many people know about it. The leaks have already started. So it's best if the news comes from us. If we handle it right, we should be able to avoid widespread disruptions."

"I think you're underestimating your people, Mr. Administrator."

"I wasn't aware you were a psychologist, Alex. But I hope you're right. When are you releasing the story?"

"At midnight."

He wiped his forehead. "God."

Nobody said anything.

"All right." Kilgore took a deep breath. "This is going to sound politically motivated."

"Okay."

"It's essential that people not lose complete faith in their government at a time when they most need leadership. It will be chaotic enough as it is. What I would like, what I beg from you, is that you let me make the announcement. Hold back on what you were planning. It can do you no harm. Just until to-morrow morning."

"When did you intend to let them know?"

"Tomorrow. I've scheduled an address." His gaze shifted to me. "I need you to stay quiet until then. And it is essential that you not mention Wexler and his part in all this. If people discover there was a group within their government that knew about this in advance, that tried to use it for their own benefit, they will not trust us again. So I need you to tell the media how you found out, and I will see that you get full credit. You'll even get medals. But leave it at that. Okay?"

"Sir," said Alex, "Rob Peifer already knows part of the story."

"Peifer." The Administrator's brow wrinkled.

Alex glanced at me. "Global."

"How much does he know?"

"He knows," I said, "that Alex was held by Wexler. And I'm pretty sure he'll be able to put the rest together. But I think I've persuaded him not to say anything about that aspect."

"Okay." Kilgore's eyes slid shut.

"I can't promise anything."

"It's okay. I'll talk to his editor." He was in agony. "There's no way the Wexler business won't come out eventually. But the gamma-ray jet will be enough bad news for one day."

We sat for a long time, staring at one another.

"It's hard to believe it's really happening," said Circe.

"So what are you going to do, Mr. Administrator? Try to evacuate?"

"It's hopeless, Alex. We'll get as many people off as we can. But—" He shook his head.

"How much damage will it do?" I asked. "The gamma-ray bolt?"

Circe answered: "It'll kill anything that's exposed. It'll be possible for some people to get into shelters. But afterward we won't be able to grow our own food supply."

Alex sat motionless.

"We can't run a mass evacuation," said Kilgore. "We have about a hundred ships. They'll carry an average of fifteen people. Not quite fifteen. Chase, twenty-eight million babies will be born on Salud Afar by the end of this year. Does anyone seriously think that the entire human fleet could transport even our new arrivals?"

I called Peifer and told him the story would be delayed again. "Until tomorrow morning."

"Come on, Chase. Give me a break. I'm already starting to hear pieces of it from other sources."

I explained why we needed him to cooperate and not jump the gun. He wasn't happy, so I appealed to his patriotism. That went nowhere. I said something about being his slave for the rest of my life if he'd go along quietly. He complained that we'd caved in. He told me he'd thought Alex and I had a reasonable degree of integrity, and now we were letting a politician cover his tracks.

"Kilgore says he had nothing to do with it," I said.

"Right. And if you can't trust a politician, who can you trust?"

In the end I promised to give him the inside story and a lengthy interview.

Finally, it was time to go back to Rimway. I reserved seats on the next day's afternoon shuttle.

Neither of us was sleepy that night, so we went down to the lounge. It was called the Skylark, and it featured a woman doing dreamy stuff on a keyboard and drinks I'd never heard of, straight-ups and colbies and something that looked like liquid silver and left me feeling as if nothing mattered but the moment. We settled into a table near the keyboard and toasted Salud Afar. Long may she wave.

There were maybe twelve other people in the place, and human service rather than bots, which gave it a warm touch. A good-looking young guy came over, told us his name was Max, and said he'd be our server. He was maybe twenty-two on a Rimway calendar. I wondered whether he was married. It was hard to tell. Men on Salud Afar don't wear rings. It has something to do with their masculinity. I never quite figured out what.

But he *felt* unattached. Maybe it was the way he looked at me. Maybe it was my imagination. I thought about his chances of getting off-world when the news got out and two billion people started scrambling for the gates.

Poor Max. If he left now, tonight, that moment, he could get passage on one of the two liners that departed weekly for Rimway and Toxicon.

The lady at the keyboard was singing "Lost Hours" while she writhed. There was a young couple at a table near us, laughing and toasting the evening, and a group on the far side celebrating something. I watched a young man trying to manage a pickup with an obviously reluctant woman at the bar, and I found myself hoping he'd succeed. But she got up and moved to another place.

Our drinks came. Something called a quibble—really—for Alex. I got a Valo delight, which was the slow silver.

We whiled away what was left of the night, talking about carpe diem, how you should live for the present because you never really know what the next day will bring, what might even happen on the walk home. Except on this very unusual occasion, *we knew.*

After about an hour, Alex said he'd had enough and wandered off. I sat awhile longer, nursing my drinks. And finally I smiled at the guy who'd been trying to do the pickup at the bar. When he came over, I encouraged him, and eventually went home with him.

Not sure how Max made out. But that evening I was rooting for everybody.

THirTY-ONe

Yes, there are occasional human monsters who show up and create havoc, but the real day-to-day damage is usually done by people who mean well.

—*Midnight and Roses*

Kilgore was right. The story had leaked during the night, and in the morning the news spread around the world. By the time the media were announcing an address by the Administrator, it had already become a matter of containing a growing panic. Before Kilgore got anywhere close to his audience, there were announcements that every seat on every flight to Rimway and Toxicon had been sold out for the next year, which was as far ahead as they took reservations. Prices on the carriers spiked, allegedly because nobody would be coming *to* Salud Afar, and, therefore, the carriers had to cover their costs. In addition, a new interstellar transport company was reported to be forming. It didn't yet have a name, but it would, according to the experts, begin carrying people off-world within the next few months. The four manufacturers of interstellars were already swamped with orders. Buyers were reporting that prices had skyrocketed with the start of business. Meantime, the real-estate market crashed.

The online networks overflowed with terror. Was it really true the world would be destroyed? Why had we not been keeping watch on something so dangerous? Rumors were everywhere that the Cleevs had known for centuries that Callistra had gone nova. True believers announced that the end times had arrived. We heard stories that stars had exploded in the Confederacy as well, that the Mute worlds, filled as they were with infidels, were also going down.

Experts were everywhere, illustrating the dire effects of a gamma-ray burst with holos showing the burst itself striking Salud Afar, bathing it in radiation, soaking it, submerging it. They depicted people trying to shelter themselves, hiding in caves and basements, often escaping the radiation only to die of starvation. Or freezing to death, as weather cycles became disrupted.

Ivan got interviewed and used the term *Thunderbolt*. It immediately became official terminology.

Some experts actually seemed to be enjoying themselves. If there were skeptics anywhere, they must have bought in when Number 17 Parkway announced that the Administrator would be making an address later that morning. And as the various time zones woke up to the story, they got on board, too.

Ailos Johansen, who hosted the interview show *Imkah with Johansen*, was already calling for a vote of no confidence against the Administrator. The vote, if there were to be one, would have to be approved by the Legislature. If they agreed, the voting public would make the decision.

When Kilgore appeared, the casual, relaxed demeanor I'd seen during his other addresses was gone. He was seated in his office, clothed in the ceremonial robe of office. He looked up from a notebook.

"My friends around the world," he said, *"I have spent the last twelve hours in discussion with the chief executives of each of the Coalition states, and with other principals. You have probably already heard the news reports, so let me tell you what we know, and what action we plan to take.*

"We are faced today with a somber reality. Let me begin by putting to rest the rumors that have been circulating in recent weeks of an imminent war with the Ashiyyur. We do not wish that to happen, and we have no reason to believe it will.

"But we are *facing an emergency of dire proportions. I*

*learned yesterday that Callistra, the single star that has shone
so brightly in our heavens for centuries, that will still be visible
tonight, has nevertheless exploded in what scientists call a hypernova."* He paused. Got up. Came closer to the viewer. Managed to look like a guy who had answers. *"Callistra is a great
distance from Salud Afar. But the explosion occurred during the
time of the Third Union. The star that we still see each night in
the sky has not existed for twelve centuries.*

*"The explosion released bursts of gamma rays. These have
been sprayed in all directions, and, unfortunately, we now know
that one of them is headed our way.*

*"What does this mean for Salud Afar? The situation is not
good, but we can take action to protect ourselves. For one thing,
it is still three years away. For another, our atmosphere will act
as a shield to ward off the worst of the effects. Nevertheless,
there will be some penetration.*

*"We are working to secure assistance from the Confederacy.
We've been constructing shelters against the possibility of a
war with the Ashiyyur. These shelters will be used to protect
us when the gamma rays arrive. But in fact a simple basement
will suffice. The burst will require slightly more than three days
to pass. We have already begun storing supplies against that
time.*

*"In addition, we will evacuate many of our citizens, and we
are working to find other solutions.*

*"Now, I must be honest with you. When the burst has passed,
we will not be able simply to return to the land. It will probably
not be possible, for many years, to do any farming. To compen-
sate, we will be expanding our synthetic food capabilities. We
are taking other steps as well to protect ourselves. But our
greatest need at the moment is for everyone to remain calm. If
we see this through together, if we unite in the cause of our
common safety, we have nothing to fear."*

Kilgore continued another three or four minutes in that vein.
He announced the formation of a global executive committee to
oversee what he called global security strategy. (That sounded
as if the Thunderbolt were merely something to be gotten
through. A severe storm, perhaps, or an incursion by foreign
spies.) He promised to report regularly on what the committee

was doing, and told us that while it wasn't going to be easy, he
knew that the people of the world would rise to the occasion.
*"Let us then go forward together. Let our response in the trying
days ahead become our legacy to our sons and daughters. And
if Salud Afar endures for a million years, they will say this was
her finest hour."*

Then he was gone.

"You know," said Alex, "the guy read the book after all."

"Which book?"

He looked at me and shook his head. "Let it go, Chase."

I was due at Global to do my interview with Peifer. When I
went up to the roof to get a taxi, a small crowd had gathered,
and they were talking in hushed voices about the end of the
world. "The Administrator said it's going to happen."

"That can't be right. What the hell's he know?"

"—Never got it straight before—"

"—All going to die—"

"—Crazy—"

"—We're going to my cousin's. Voka's. He's in a safe place
away from here—"

Down in the street it sounded as if people were yelling at
one another.

Twenty minutes later I arrived at Global. It's a ground-level
pad, and the same thing was happening. Everybody was scared,
and nobody was talking about anything else.

Peifer was waiting for me in the executive offices. Staff
members were running around, peering into displays, talking
into their links.

"Looks busy," I said.

"You kidding? This is the biggest story ever. Why the hell
didn't you and Alex tell me what you were onto?"

"We didn't know. *I* didn't know until I looked up and saw
that empty sky."

"Empty sky? What empty sky?

"From the asteroid."

He escorted me to his office. Somebody came in and took
pictures. Lots of pictures. Most of them had me standing, looking up at the *Lantner* monument and the sky beyond. "You

know," he said, "when the critical information comes from looking up and seeing *nothing*, it really doesn't work well for pictures."

"I'll try to do better next time, Rob."

"You should have brought Alex along," he said.

"You didn't ask."

"I didn't know we were looking at anything like this. I thought it was about corruption. I thought the bastards knew a major downturn was coming, and they were in collusion with—" He stopped and stared at me. "Never mind. I've got a few questions for you."

"What kind of reaction is the Administrator getting?"

"Right now," he said, "they want to hang him."

"I'm sorry to hear it."

"He deserves what he gets. He stood by and let his friends run things. As long as you were loyal to the bastard, you couldn't do anything wrong. Anyhow, I wouldn't be surprised if he was privy to it from the beginning."

Somebody knocked on the door. He said, "Come in."

A middle-aged woman, looking frazzled. "Rob," she said, "check the stream."

Peifer turned on the HV. It was tuned to Global. We got pictures of a riot in a time zone on the far side of the planet. *"—And several hundred arrested."* The voice was a baritone. *"It started in midafternoon, more than an hour before the Administrator spoke. So far, there are seventeen known dead, and forty or fifty known injured, John."*

Peifer brought up the location. It was Baranda, a place I'd never heard of before. "No big deal," he said. "People there are always rioting about something."

They went back and showed a recorded clip of a man throwing a child from a rooftop ten or eleven stories high. Then jumping himself.

And there was a report that the Coalition Data Collection Agency was overwhelmed with protests.

Around the world, action committees were already forming, prayer meetings were being scheduled, and politicians in the Administrator's opposition party began to argue that either

Kilgore had been negligent or we were overreacting. "Well," Peifer said, "it looks as if you and your partner have had an impact."

When it was over, I headed for the spaceport, where Alex had said he would wait. I'd expected an angry crowd, but the place was, if anything, deserted. Alex was waiting in the departure area.

The shuttle, though, was full. A woman on the flight told me she and her family were leaving the next day for Toxicon. "We got our tickets weeks ago. It was going to be a vacation. I think we were lucky."

Two families were leaving on one of the tour ships. For Rimway.

"Thank God we have *Belle*," I told Alex. "I wouldn't want to be trying to go anywhere on public transportation."

Alex was looking out as we passed through the cloud cover. "I guess bad news is always good for somebody. Your buddy Ivan will make a fortune."

"Starlight Tours will."

We watched the newscasts during the ascent. They were filled with reports of people talking about leaving Salud Afar, of scientists disputing the government's claims, and of political commentators demanding that Kilgore be removed from office. Others maintained it was a conspiracy to drive prices down and allow some wealthy individuals to expand their holdings. Or to allow Kilgore to establish dictatorial powers. Some people said they didn't give a damn what was coming, nobody was going to chase them out of their homes.

Angry editorials were showing up: *The explosion happened 1200 years ago, and we're just finding out about it now?*

And: *Kilgore may have known.*

And: *Time to build space arks.*

Only Star in the Sky, and Nobody Noticed.

Time for New Leadership.

Celebrities and politicians were pleading for unity. This was a time to put aside our differences and work together to achieve the best outcome, whatever that might be. There were calls for worldwide prayer, and the various religions that, Peifer had told me, had always been at one another's throats, suddenly found themselves with a common cause.

Somebody was starting a Kids Off-world Campaign. They were arguing that all available space on departing vehicles be made available to children. *They are the future.* Anyone with the means to leave Salud Afar on his own was urged to volunteer help. *Take some children with you.*

Save the kids.

Number 17 Parkway announced that the Administrator would speak again that night and would outline a plan of action.

There was a sense of unreality about it all. Despite the frenzied activity, I doubted if the reality of the situation had taken hold. People seemed to be reacting as if a bad storm were coming. The question became how best to get through it. We were not yet on the *Korinbladt*, the crippled liner that had, only the year before, gotten dragged into a sun along with its more than seven hundred well-done passengers.

I looked down through drifting white clouds at a lush green landscape, filled with trees and bushes and rolling hills. And I could not believe this entire world was going to be irradiated in three years. That it would become uninhabitable for decades or more.

I couldn't help sympathizing with Kilgore, who had to face the reality that his lack of curiosity was going to cost a world full of lives. But I wondered how he could have been paying so little attention that he'd missed what was going on? But at least he seemed now to be engaged. Tonight, he'd announce a strategy.

"Good luck on that one," said Alex.

Physicists were being interviewed. Evan Carbacci of the Nakamura Institute commented that they'd always known that Callistra was unstable, and plans had been made just last month for a mission to check its status. *"If it seems a bit late,"* he said, *"you have to remember that these things tend to happen on scales of millions of years. I don't think it occurred to any of us that an explosion was imminent. In human terms. Let alone that it had already happened."*

When pressed, he got angry: *"Look, let's be honest here. The truth is that we've simply been terribly unlucky. We knew that even if the damned thing blew, the chances of our getting in the way were remote. Who'd have thought—?"*

Families were mounting pleas for anyone leaving Salud Afar to take their kids. Several watchdog organizations wanted investigations to determine who was at fault. Conspiracy theorists were arriving in force. Not only had Cleev and Kilgore known—pick one—but some maintained that a secret society had known but kept it quiet for religious purposes. (The religious purposes never became clear.) Other groups argued that in fact there was no threat from Callistra, that it was a cover-up, that the real threat was the time-space rift, which was about to descend on the planet and swallow it whole.

Despite everything, the public response was less frantic than Wexler or Kilgore had expected. It was, after all, three years away. And, as politicians always say, a lot can happen in three years.

Meantime, we got fresh reports of growing tension between the Confederacy and the Mutes, including at least two incidents in which warships had fired on each other. Someone had forgotten to turn the fabrication machine off.

I was beginning to feel guilty.

"Why, Chase?"

"We should have called that service," I said. "Gotten a group of children to take out of here with us."

Alex sighed. "I'm not anxious to spend the next four weeks with a bunch of kids, but you're right. When we get upstairs, let's check with them. But make sure we get a couple of mothers, too, okay?" He bit his lip. "I wish we had more capacity."

On the space station, we stopped for sandwiches at Sandstone's. While Alex stared at his coffee, I contacted Operations.

"You're ready to go," the watch officer said. He allowed a note of derision to creep into his voice. *"A lot of people outbound today. When do you want to leave?"*

"We thought we'd take some kids with us," I said. "The ones they're trying to evacuate."

"Yeah. Well, none of them are here yet."

"When are you expecting them?"

"Don't know. But we can have you ready for launch in ninety minutes, if that works for you."

"You have no idea at all?"

"Negative. You want to hang around, that's okay. Maybe they'll come up tomorrow. I think you're supposed to make the arrangement before you come."

"All right. We'll get back to you."

"Call them," said Alex.

I tried. The AIs were overwhelmed. When we did get through, the responses weren't helpful. Nobody knew anything. Everyone referred us to someone else. They weren't ready yet. Not online. Still setting it up. Please leave your code, and we'll get back to you.

"It's people with kids," Alex said. "They apparently didn't think to set up a separate code for people offering transport."

We left our code and waited around. Two hours later, we called again, and the situation hadn't changed. We checked into a hotel. "This could take forever," Alex said.

We eventually wound up in the hotel lobby, waiting to hear what Kilgore had to say. "Do we really want to hang around here until the bureaucracies sort it out?" Alex asked.

No. *I* didn't.

"Let's do it this way," Alex said. "Let's get out of here and go home. Once we get home, *Belle*'s yours. If you want to come back and do rescues, it's your call."

Damn.

"Okay," I said. "Let's get moving."

I called Ops again. Same officer. He looked harassed. *"I guess you haven't heard,"* he said. *"The* Belle-Marie*'s been impounded. They've all been impounded."*

"All the ships?"

"Yes."

"By whom?"

"By the government."

"For how long?"

"Indefinitely. They really didn't give us any details. But I assume they're going to use them to move people out."

"Thanks," I said.

"Sorry. Wish I could help."

Alex was wearing a tired smile. "We should have anticipated that." He spoke into his link: "Connect me with Number 17 Parkway, please." He gave a code we'd gotten from the staff.

"They can't just take *Belle*," I said.

Alex got through and a male voice answered, basso profundo. *"Executive Office."*

A few people seated around us heard. They turned in our direction and stared. Alex dialed the volume down. "This is Alex Benedict," he said softly. "I was there the other day, speaking with the Administrator." That got a reaction from our fellow patrons. Smiles, people nodding sure you did, eyes rolling skyward. "I'm calling from Samuels. We're trying to get home."

"Okay. Is there a problem?"

"Our ship has been impounded. By you folks."

"Ah." He took a breath. *"Hold a minute, please."*

Alex looked at me, shook his head, closed his eyes.

The basso profundo came back. *"Yes, sir. The directive came from the top, but compensation will be made. Instructions on how to apply are available at—"*

"I don't want compensation. I want my ship."

"I'm sorry, Mr.—Who did you say you were again, please?"

"Alex Benedict."

"I'm sorry, Mr. Benedict. The directive explicitly states 'no exceptions.'"

"May I speak with your supervisor?"

"I am sorry, sir. She's not available at the moment."

"May I speak with Dr. Belhower, please?"

"Who?"

"Dr. *Circe* Belhower."

There was another pause. *"I'm sorry, sir. There's no one with that name on the staff."*

I reminded Alex she was a consultant.

"I don't suppose," Alex said, "the Administrator is available?"

"I can put you on the list." He sounded as if he did this all the time.

"Can you get a message to him?"

"Of course."

"I need my ship back. It's the *Belle-Marie*. I'm trying to go home."

"I'll see that your message is placed in his box."

THIrTY-TWO

No garden is complete, my dear, without a snake.

—*Love You to Death*

I called Ivan, and we met in the Pilots' Club. "I guess we stirred something up," he said.

"Looks like." He sat down, smiled, looked smug. "What?" I said.

"Business is booming. They've located a world where conditions are reasonable. A place where they can start moving people. They've already got some engineers en route. It's thirteen thousand light-years from here. In toward the rim. Not exactly next door, but not like going all the way into Rimway."

"You're going there?"

"Leaving tonight. With a full load. So what can I do for you? You don't want to go back to the monument, do you?"

I couldn't tell whether he was serious. He ordered some appetizers and soft drinks for us. "They've confiscated our ship."

"They've taken everybody's."

"You know any way we can get it back?"

He shook his head. "Chase," he said, "I hate to say this, but I think you're here for the duration."

While I was sitting with Ivan, Peifer ran the interview we'd recorded and, during the wrap-up, revealed what he had on

Vicki Greene. Vicki had known months ago. Someone had tried to silence her. Who else could that be except the administration?

Hours later we heard there was a crack in the Coalition. Strictly behind the scenes, of course. The public image of world leaders working together to save a desperate situation was coming apart. Rumors had it that they believed Kilgore had known all along. Even if he hadn't, he should have. Reportedly, they wanted him to step aside.

The Administrator's second address came from the World Library in Marinox. He stood behind a rostrum and, in one of the great understatements of the age, started by commenting that he knew everybody was concerned about the gamma-ray burst. *"I want to remind you that it is three years away. That gives us time to implement several courses of action. But first I want to assure you that we are in this together. Neither I nor any of my staff will set foot off this world as long as anyone who wants to leave is still here."*

"That's pretty gutsy," I said.

Alex got that skeptical look in his eyes.

"We took several steps as soon as we became aware of what was happening. First, we have informed all the worlds of the Confederacy of our situation. We have asked their help. That message went out immediately. It will be almost three weeks before we can hope to hear from them. But I'm confident they will offer assistance.

"Second, in collaboration with all the states of the Coalition, we are moving to devote every resource we have to the manufacture of interstellars. It will take a while to get everything up and running because we need several orbital facilities. Work has already started on those.

"We have vastly increased funding for shelters. We are digging into the earth wherever conditions permit, and will be manufacturing modular units that can shield small communities. Soon, we will have shielding that can be applied to individual houses.

"Unfortunately, we cannot shield the planet, and therein lies

our greatest hazard. When the gamma-ray burst has passed, every exposed life-form will be gone. But we will survive, and when it's over, we'll plant new forests and restore its wildlife."

"That's not likely to happen," I said. "The place will have to be abandoned."

Alex shrugged. "It's good politics, though. Right now, it's what people need to hear."

"We've located a new world, Sanctum, which will serve as a place to relocate evacuees. At first, we'd been concerned we would have to haul people all the way to the Confederacy, which would have been a terribly slow process. Sanctum is less than half the distance to the nearest Confederate world. Engineers, biotechs, and farmers are already on their way. Others will be leaving within the next twenty hours. We are calling this effort Operation New World.

"At this critical time, Salud Afar needs all of us, working together. To begin, we need volunteers. Especially those with technical specialties. Consult the Coalition Bulletin Board and, please, volunteer where you can."

He came around in front of the rostrum, found a chair, and sat down. *"I will not understate the situation. We are at a crossroads, and we can only succeed with your help. We all need to start immediately conserving supplies. Store them in places where they'll be shielded from the gamma rays. Information on that can also be found at the Coalition Bulletin Board. You should be aware that we have impounded every private and commercial space vehicle that is not part of the overall relief effort. Some are being used to construct new orbiting stations. Others will carry evacuees. Compensation is available.*

"One final thing: We mean to evacuate as many people to Sanctum as we possibly can. We want to lower the population on Salud Afar. That is not because of any lack of confidence that we will come through this emergency. But the amount of supplies necessary after the event will be reduced." He leaned forward, every bit a protective uncle. *"We've had a replacement birth rate on this world for a long time now. I have to tell you that, at this historic moment, that is too many. I will not ask anyone to choose abortion. But we need everybody to take mea-*

sures to prevent conception from this day forward, until we can declare the emergency over. I understand this is a highly personal matter. But it's entirely possible that every new birth will cost an innocent person his life. And if that suggests how serious our situation is, we must take it to heart." He stopped and stared straight out at us. *"I know that you will do your part. Thank you, and good night."*

Kilgore's image had just blinked off when a group of experts appeared to discuss the situation. One, a calm guy with marquee looks spoiled by a too-neat mustache, thought the Administrator was responding with brilliant leadership to the emergency. *"We're fortunate to have the right guy in the job,"* he said. *"The people who want him out are crazy. You can't really blame him when a star explodes, but he's doing everything you could reasonably expect to counteract the effects."*

"We've known about this for decades," said another, an angry-looking academic type. *"The Greene story confirms it."*

And another, a young woman who was visibly seething: *"Greene aside, we've always known Callistra was a candidate for a supernova. Or something bigger. We should have been watching it. How we could have failed to do that, I'll never understand."*

The moderator addressed himself to her: *"Dr. Bjorg, did you ever recommend that we do a study?"*

"Not my field," she said.

"So whose is it?" demanded Alex.

"Alex," I said, "you're talking to the holograms again." He does that when he gets upset.

We'd have fought the impoundment of the *Belle-Marie*, but there was nobody to fight. Whoever we called referred us to someone else. I was proud of Alex during that period. He refused to get angry, refused to blame me for not having left when we had the chance.

We made several more efforts during the next few days to get through to Kilgore. The result was always the same: We were placed in his in-box. We checked on the compensation we'd get for the *Belle-Marie*, which, it turned out, would be considerably less than the ship was worth. That brought up another problem: The value of Coalition funds off-world would be crashing. The money we got would never buy anything for us.

We called Bentley DeepSpace, which was the transport system that ran the liners to Rimway and Toxicon. They were weekly flights, and they'd been reported filled. But we tried anyway. "I'd like passage for two to Rimway," I told them, "on the next available flight.

The voice on the other end belonged to an AI. *"I'm sorry, ma'am. The flights are full."*

"How long's the waiting list?"

"We're booked to the end of the year."

"Is that really the best you can do?"

"We've requested assistance from several transport companies in the Confederacy. So we expect we'll be able to help you shortly."

"Can we get on the waiting list?"

"Yes, ma'am. What's your name, please?"

Alex waved me off. "Let it go," he said. "If we have to, we'll get in touch with somebody at home and have them come get us."

"Who did you have in mind?"

"To be honest, I don't know any pilots other than you. But we should be able to lease somebody." He stared out at the night sky. "This trip has had its downside."

There was a confirmed report of a shoot-out between Confederate and Ashiyyurean warships. This time, a Mute vessel had broken open, and there'd been fatalities. Each side was claiming encroachment by the other, and issuing warnings. Each side was threatening war.

It was obviously an outbreak waiting to happen. Alex commented that, like so many conflicts through the ages, it would be a war neither side wanted. More like a train wreck. But both sides had politicians who were solidifying their positions by stirring up antagonism. That often secured election, but it had the effect of backing them into a corner. It struck me that Kassel hadn't been entirely honest when he claimed that Mutes couldn't deceive one another.

Meanwhile, Kilgore's optimism had to be crumbling. Mathematicians were doing most of the damage. They showed up on every conceivable talk show and blew gaping holes in the government strategy. There wouldn't be enough space in the shelters. Not nearly enough. The quantities of materials needed to protect private homes would overwhelm production facilities. Tens of millions would die during the initial blast. The survivors would quickly run out of food and other necessities. The capability to bring adequate resupplies in from the Confederacy was, at best, doubtful. And if war broke out with the Mutes, as seemed increasingly likely, that capability would probably go to zero.

"There just isn't time to do everything that needs to be done." We heard that refrain over and over.

We'd been in the hotel on Samuels for about a week when the AI announced an incoming call. Alex, gloomier than I'd ever seen him, asked sardonically whether I thought it might be Kilgore. Then he told the AI to put it through.

It was Wexler.

"Hello, Benedict," he said. *"I hope you're satisfied."* He was outside somewhere, leaning against a stone wall, dressed in a white pullover and the sort of slacks you'd wear for a walk in the woods. He ignored me, looked straight at Alex. *"I assume,"* he said, *"you understand* now *how much damage you've caused."*

Alex bristled. "At least something's being done. You were prepared to sit by and watch everybody die."

"Something's being done. You really think this government can do anything but talk? There are too many people. They'll save a few million, but we'd have saved almost as many. And given everybody else three relatively peaceful years. All you've accomplished is to create chaos."

"Kilgore doesn't think so."

"Kilgore's a politician. What else would you expect him to say? He believes what he's telling the voters, but this is exactly

the reason we didn't want him to know. The people around him understand what's coming. So does every physicist on the planet. But they won't say anything. Other than the idiots who want to see themselves on the news shows." He bit his lip and actually wiped a tear from his cheek. *"But everybody knows what's really going to happen when the tide comes in.*

"The gamma-ray burst itself will pass quickly enough. But there'll be a particle shower, and it'll go on for days. Everything green will die off. The ozone layer will be swept away. Ultraviolet light will make Salud Afar a death trap for years to come. Nothing will grow. They'll probably try to put together some shielded greenhouses, but that won't do any more than delay the inevitable." He shook his head, made a rumbling noise in his throat. *"Well done, Mr. Benedict."*

There was still no word on child evacuations. Not that it mattered anymore. Polls indicated that pessimism was growing. Eighteen percent of those surveyed described the situation as hopeless. Peifer showed up on Capital Round Table to discuss the severe inflation that had set in.

The Administrator was on every other night. He usually sat in the room with the fireplace, and he went back to dressing casually. He spoke in generalities, praising his audience for their patience and their courage, dismissing the polls, which showed confidence steadily shrinking. The message was always the same: We are working to save each other. One way or another we will get the job done. His critics kept after him. He was tightening seat belts on the *Korinbladt*. But Kilgore always managed to get the last word. *"If I took them seriously,"* he said, *"then yes, of course they'd turn out to be right. But my critics lack imagination. They want to give up. They underestimate what we, you and I together, can do. We won't let them cause us to lose hope. We will find a way forward. Together."*

Interviews with people around the globe depicted the anguish, despair, frustration. A farmer who described his earnings as "average," asked how he could be expected to get his wife and kids to a safe place. *"If you want to get to Sanctum, you have to be able to buy your way on,"* he said. *"I think the politicians who let this happen should be turned out of office and jailed. At the very least."*

A schoolteacher from, of all places, Boldinai Point, wondered what would happen to her students. *"Nobody's going to get off-world unless they know somebody. You can bet your life Kilgore and his friends won't be here when the crunch comes. Thank God for Benedict, or they never would have told us."*

And a dark-haired woman described by the interviewer as being on the list of the world's one hundred wealthiest citizens: *"I keep hearing you have to have money to get clear. I wish somebody would tell me who to pay off."*

We'd been nine days on Samuels when we got a call from Kids Off-world. They were bringing the first batch of children next day. *"You said you could take six?"*

We'd called to let them know we no longer had a ship. But the message had gotten lost somewhere. An hour later we had another call. *"Please hold for the Administrator."*

I would have sworn his hair had whitened since the last time we'd seen him. *"I'm glad to see you're still here."* Someone handed him a sheet of paper. He glanced at it, nodded, and turned back to us. *"Hello, Chase,"* he said. *"How are you?"*

"I'm fine, sir. Thank you."

"I understand we took your ship."

"That's correct," said Alex.

"I apologize. I wouldn't have wanted to let that happen. I've just had too much on my mind."

"I understand, sir."

"I never thought of it." He got interrupted again, a notebook. He frowned. Shook his head no. Came back to us again. *"Alex—?"*

"Yes, sir?"

"Actually, I'm relieved you haven't left. I'll provide transportation out if you wish. And I know this has been a severe inconvenience. But I want to ask you to stay on for a while. There might be a way you can help."

"How, sir?"

"*Let's leave that for the moment. You're staying at the Samuels Hotel?*"

"Yes, sir."

"*Very good. Make yourselves comfortable. We'll pick up the tab. But be prepared to go on short notice. I'll call you when we're ready.*"

THirTY-THree

Get out, child. Get out. Get as far from this dark place as you can.
A spirit hangs over it, infests it, drifts along its passageways,
and, ultimately, destroys all who live here.

—*Midnight and Roses*

The privately owned interstellars at Salud Afar, including the
Belle-Marie, totaled eleven. Add eight commercial vessels, fif-
teen naval and patrol, and you had the sum total available to the
Administrator for evacuating two billion people.

The station was quiet, tense, frightened. By the end of the
second week, twenty-six of the thirty-four ships were en route
to Sanctum, or on the way back. The remaining eight were either having the quantum drive installed or being retrofitted in
some way. The one-way trip would run about sixteen days. The
old Armstrong drive would have taken months.

And, finally, Kilgore announced electrifying news from the
Confederacy: *"A rescue fleet is forming,"* he told the world.
"Some are already on the way." But he warned again there
would not be enough ships for everyone. *"Most of us will have
to weather the storm on the ground. But we* can *do it. And
we will."*

He showed pictures of individual ships that were already
en route to Salud Afar, or soon would be. Passenger vessels
from Khaja Luan and Dellaconda, cargo ships being refitted off

Toxicon to carry passengers, private vehicles coming from Abonai and Salusar. *"We will survive,"* Kilgore said.

When he'd finished, Alex sat quietly for several minutes.

"What are you thinking?" I asked.

"About what's missing."

"Ummm—What's missing?"

"The navy. If the Confederacy were serious, the navy would be leading the charge. That's where their real transport capabilities lie."

"They can't come," I said. "They're virtually at war."

"I know."

"I'm not sure," I admitted, "I wouldn't do the same thing. You have to protect against the possibility of attack."

A few days later, Kilgore had more news. First he talked about a food-packaging plant he was visiting. Vitacon Nutrition was making an enormous contribution, he said, to the general effort. Then he singled out a few more people for special notice. And finally the big story: *"The first wave of private and commercial spacecraft are approaching Salud Afar. We're setting up a lottery system to ensure fairness in selecting those who will, if they wish, be evacuated. Details are posted on the Coalition Bulletin Board.*

"Also, I'm pleased to announce the first new shuttles have rolled off the line at Grimsley."

There was an explosion the next day. Helmut Orr was a physicist who was fairly well-known primarily as a media figure. He sat on panels in which scientific issues were discussed, oversaw a program explaining the latest technological advances, and insisted that breaking through to alternate universes would be possible in the near future. He loved doing shows in which he explained what would happen if ice melted at a slightly lower temperature, or if gravity was a bit stronger or the electroweak force a bit weaker. Or in which the speed of light was slower, say two thousand kilometers per hour. The situations he picked all resulted in chaos. In addition, Orr loved bad news. Anything that allowed him to point out other people's failings. He was also a regular panelist in *On the Spot*, which blended science, politics, and entertainment.

He was small, inevitably dwarfed by anyone, even the women, who appeared with him. But he was a dynamo. He got passionate about everything, about mirror matter and the interiors of stars and brown dwarfs. He was in love with the cosmos. And the day after the Administrator spoke at Vitacon Nutrition, he appeared on a panel to discuss the preparations being made to withstand the Thunderbolt. The moderator asked him if not having the assistance of the Confederate Navy would be a serious blow to the rescue effort.

He looked directly at me. *"The rescue effort,"* he said, *"is a hoax. You know what it really is? It's a distraction, nothing up this sleeve, nothing up* that *one. It's intended to keep us from realizing the truth, which is that we're all dead. Bring the navy if you want. Bring* six *navies. They'll get a few more people off the planet. But not very many. What your government isn't telling you is that in three years, we'll all be dead. All except a very small fraction. But they want us to keep cool and not make a lot of noise.*

"Well, I say we're entitled to make some noise. We've known for centuries that Callistra was unstable. And, okay, I wouldn't have expected the Bandahriate *to do anything. But they've been gone a long time now. Some of us have been pleading for a mission to Callistra, send some people out and find out what was going on, see if there's any danger.*

"But they didn't. Couldn't be bothered. Hell, you can look up there every night and see it in the sky. But you watch: When that thing starts getting close, and people are getting rattled, the same guys who told us not to worry will be the first ones out of town."

Had someone else said it, it might not have mattered. But everybody knew Helmut's name. He was perceived as the voice of reason.

The newscasts picked up the comment and went with it. Had something else happened during the following days, a scandal in the capital, or a celebrity doing something stupid, the spotlight might have gone elsewhere and the story dropped off the public's sensors. But the Callistra story was the only one in town. So it ran over and over, and it served to intensify feelings through a population becoming increasingly nervous.

One popular data site ran the headline: DEATH SENTENCE FOR THE WORLD?

The Thunderbolt—the term was in common use by then—was everywhere. Comedians worked it into their routines. ("They're offering a two-for-one special on funerals if you come early, before the rush.") The insurance industry reported that sales were off sharply. Incoming classes at colleges, medical schools, and law schools were well below normal. Deepsea, Inc., which had provided undersea rides for a generation, had sold out for an end-of-the-world special three-day submerged tour. Two manufacturers of seagoing vessels announced that they were creating modular hulls that could be purchased, hauled inland, and assembled as shelters against radiation.

Suicides were up. Weddings were taking place at an unusually high rate. Organizations that catered to kids, the Wilderness Troop, Girl Riders, Face Forward, and so on, brought in counselors to talk to their charges. Church attendance was up across the board.

Reports surfaced that older people were most affected by the situation, fearing that they would have an especially difficult time in the aftermath of the Thunderbolt.

Governments around the world encouraged volunteer groups whose task it would be to step in after the event and provide emergency supplies to those in need.

Salud Afar was rallying. People appeared every day on the HV to assure viewers that "we" would come through this. Support for the Administrator was consolidating. A week earlier it had appeared that he would be forced out of office. But his approval ratings were moving steadily up. Meantime, the shuttles continued hauling passengers to Samuels, which filled with kids and baggage. Ships from the Confederacy began to arrive, first in ones and twos, then in squadrons. It was now the shuttles that became the bottleneck. People could not be moved to the station quickly enough.

Alex suggested I recommend they use taxis.

*   *   *

We began to think that Kilgore had forgotten about us. Then one evening we got a call from the hotel lobby. A woman in business dress to see us. *"Mr. Benedict,"* she said, *"the Administrator would like to talk with you."*

"Okay."

"Your transportation has been arranged. Please report to the shuttle launch area within the hour." She was apparently trying to figure out who *I* was. *"Miss, will you be going down, too?"*

Number 17 was a beehive. Reporters overflowed the press room, shouting questions at someone I couldn't see. Staff members were everywhere, and I recognized Helmut Orr among a group of people being herded into an elevator. "It's always like this now," said one of the staff secretaries.

They were expecting only Alex. My name had been called in on the flight down. I thought I'd been cleared, but there was still a delay while they checked to make sure I wasn't going to say something disrespectful to the Administrator. Then, when everyone seemed satisfied, Alex and I were hustled inside and delivered to his secretary. "He's waiting for you," she said.

She took us back to the north wing and opened his office door. Kilgore was inside, huddled with half a dozen people. One was Circe. Heads turned our way. The Administrator looked up, gave us a strained smile, and pointed to a group of chairs against one wall. We sat down, and the conversation resumed. Have to do something about the shelters. Move faster. Get a program together that we can live with. I'm tired of the infighting. Got no time for that nonsense now. The shelters will hold a hell of a lot of people. We need to get that out to the public. Need to reassure everyone that they have a decent chance. That it's not as dark as the goddam media are saying. And there must be something more we can do. What about the gear coming in from Rimway?

It broke up after a few minutes. The participants filed out, save Circe and a tall, aristocratic-looking man with neatly combed silver hair. Kilgore waved us over and welcomed us with a smile and a handshake. "You know Circe." Turning to the aristocrat, he said, "This is Giambrey DeVrio.

"Giambrey is a member of the diplomatic staff. He was once the Bandahriate's ambassador to Rimway." He was well into his second century, about average size, clean-shaven, sharp blue eyes. He shook hands with Alex and bowed to me. "I've heard a great deal about you," he said, looking me in the eye.

The Administrator came out from behind his desk. "It's good to see you two again. Alex, would you like a job?"

"What did you have in mind, sir?"

"Mine."

We laughed for a moment, but the atmosphere quickly sobered. "I imagine it's been a difficult time," said Alex.

Kilgore smiled politely and signaled for some *imkah*. Then he plunged ahead. "The goddam world's coming apart. I assume you've seen that idiot Orr. Just when we were getting everything calmed down, he jumps in. The goddam thing's all over the media. People are desperate. Alex, they're demanding to know what I'm going to do. Most of them are behaving as if it's *my* fault." He caught himself and sighed. "It probably is. But that doesn't change where we are now. It's difficult enough figuring out a rational course without trying to deal with all these distractions. I tell you, I'm tempted to resign. Step down. Let them find somebody else if they think I'm screwing it up. But a change in leadership at this point—?" He shook his head. "If I could be sure they wouldn't put Bergen in charge, I'd probably do it—"

I had no idea who Bergen was. I learned later he was the chief executive in one of the other Coalition states.

"They think I've arranged transportation for myself and my family. They think I've known about this all along. That what's going to happen is that everybody will wake up one morning and the government will simply be gone. Son of a bitch, what have I ever done to deserve that?"

"You're a politician, sir," said DeVrio smoothly. "It happens."

Eventually he calmed down. "Well," he said, "maybe they'd like to have Cleev back."

"So what *are* you going to do?" Alex asked.

"Keep moving people off-world, as best we can. Keep building shelters. Move supplies in. We're stocking everywhere. Providing manuals for people telling them how to prepare. We're building interstellars as quickly as we can. Big ones. Liners, like the *Callistra*. Isn't that a hoot? The biggest interstellar we've got is named after the star that blew up.

"But we have to face reality. The people who are saying we can't even begin a planetary evacuation are right. We're currently turning out starships at full capacity. We've asked for help from the Confederacy. Alex, we're doing everything we can."

"But—?"

"We've done the projections. The losses will be apocalyptic."

"How many?"

The Administrator signaled DeVrio. "We estimate," DeVrio said, "with reasonable help from the Confederacy, and if we can get the anticipated production from home industry, we'll be able to evacuate about six million. As to those who stay behind, they'll survive for a while. *Some* of them will." He didn't seem to be focused on anyone. "We've asked the Confederacy to send the fleet."

"What did they say?"

Kilgore got up slowly. His eyes narrowed. "They say they can't, Alex. They say they have the goddam Mutes to deal with, and they can't leave themselves exposed." He glanced at a picture on the wall. It was a middle-aged man standing on the capitol steps. He saw me following his eyes. "It's Lowry," he said.

His predecessor. Died in office of a heart attack. Still a relatively young man. Kilgore smiled. "He was lucky."

Alex cleared his throat. "It's why you called us."

"Yes. What sort of influence have you with the Mutes?"

"With the *Mutes*? I thought you were going to ask us to try to do something on Rimway."

"No, no, no, no." Kilgore looked over at DeVrio. "We have that covered. We need someone who can deal with the Ash-iyyur." He took a deep breath. "Alex, they're so hard to stomach, there's nobody anywhere with any connections. We have no diplomatic ties. No connections whatever. The Confederacy broke relations with them a half century ago. Longer than that, really. And never restored them. We haven't done very well either.

"So there's *nobody*. At a time when we most need to talk to them, there's *no one*. Except you."

Alex grunted and shook his head. No, no. Not possible. I was shocked myself. "I have no influence with the Ashiyyur," he said.

"Alex." *No nonsense now. We have to make this work.* "We need you. We need to persuade them to declare, unequivocally, unilaterally, and immediately, a state of nonaggression. We want them to announce, publicly, that they will not attack Confederate worlds, or move into Confederate space, while the emergency lasts." He took a deep breath. "Who knows, if we can persuade them to do it, it might even lead to a lasting peace."

I'd never seen Alex look overwhelmed before. His face had gone pale, and his lips had pulled back until I was looking at his bicuspids. "Mr. Administrator, you're asking us to persuade whom—? I don't know any of their upper-tier people."

Kilgore showed that he understood. "Alex. We've had no diplomatic relations with the Mutes for a century or more. And that was the Bandahriate. Which tried to rob them. But that's another story. We've traded public insults. And yes, *we* were responsible for some of that. Most of it unfairly, I am now learning. We've launched an investigation. It appears that the reports of Mute incursions in our space over the last few months were all concocted. By Barikay and his people."

"Who's Barikay?"

"Wexler's boss. Now in custody and on his way to prison. As Wexler will be when we find him. But at the moment none of that matters. Look: I don't much like Mutes, and I don't know many people who do. But we need them. We need somebody to go in and pick up the pieces. That's you. Nobody else can do it. Nobody else would have a chance. At least nobody *I* know. So I want you to go there. Apologize to them for us. Win them over. Get the war stopped."

"That's good," said Alex. "What on earth makes you think I can do anything remotely like that?"

"All right." He looked toward me. "The truth, Alex. I doubt you *can* do it. Probably nobody can. But you're our most realistic shot. You can represent us, and at the same time you can point out that you're not part of us. You share no responsibility for what we've been doing. But our world needs their help. We only ask that they make a commitment not to wage a war that they probably don't want to wage in any case. You'll be giving them an excuse to do what they want to do anyhow."

"Mr. Administrator," said Alex, "even if we could get the pledge you want, the Confederacy would probably not be willing to take their word."

DeVrio said quietly, "We think we can persuade them to go along with a pledge."

"We hope so," said Kilgore. "To be honest, it's up in the air."

He waited for Alex to accept. Instead, Alex simply looked at him. "Why?"

"Why what?"

"Why all the animosity? Toward the Ashiyyur?"

"Hell, Alex, you know what they look like. And how they get into your brain."

"Mr. Administrator—"

"Hold it. Okay? Spare me the standard lecture on tolerance. They have the same effect on people that *bugs* do. You want to step on them. My God, Alex, they make your stomach churn. And that's without the mind reading. No. Look, we're never going to like them, and they're never going to like us. But we need to find a way around that. For now."

Alex remained silent. Kilgore got to his feet. "We're doing everything we can to save the world, Alex. We need your help. Can we count on it?

"Okay."

"You'll do it?"

"Of course."

"Good. We owe you one."

"I'm glad to help, Mr. Administrator."

"Yes. Now, as I understand it, you know one of the mayors."

"You've done your homework. But he's the mayor of a middle-sized town. He doesn't really have any influence at the top of the Assemblage."

Nobody moved for a long time. I could hear noises elsewhere in the building. Voices. A door closing. The hum of the ventilation system.

Finally, Kilgore straightened. "Well. You have a better connection than we do. And, Alex—?"

"Yes?"

"I think you're underestimating yourself."

"I hope so. Have you cleared it with the Mutes?"

"We've informed them." He became hesitant. "We've made overtures in the past. So far, they've refused to accept a diplomatic initiative. They don't like us very much."

"So how—?"

"You and Chase will be going as private visitors. Talk to the mayor. Or however it is you communicate. Explain the problem. Giambrey will be going with you. As will Circe. She'll be the science liaison. Your job is to help get access for them. If help is required."

"Okay."

"We haven't time to send a request and wait for an answer."

"I understand."

"Good." He pressed his fingertips against his forehead. "I guess that's it. That's all you need to do."

"We'll do what we can, Mr. Administrator."

"There's one more thing you'll be interested in. We'll be announcing it tonight." He looked from Alex to me, and there was a plea in those eyes. "I'll confess it's an initiative I'd keep quiet if I could, but it's not possible." He signaled Circe.

Circe's somber gaze locked on Alex. "The stakes first," she said. "If the evacuation plan goes smoothly, if the Confederates send their entire fleet, if private and corporate vehicles from the Confederacy arrive in the numbers we're anticipating, if our manufacturing capability runs without a hitch, and we are able to construct shelters and ships at predicted rates, and if the general population cooperates and does not become disruptive, if all these things happen, we will still lose almost two billion people."

My stomach felt cold. I looked out the window. It was a bright, cool day. Spring not far away. The sunlight drew a series of rectangles on the carpet.

"Consequently," she said, "we've tried to develop an alternative to evacuation and hiding out in shelters. Given adequate resources, we might be able to build a shield."

Alex's brow creased. "A shield?"

Circe nodded. "It won't be easy, but it *might* be possible."

"What kind of shield are we talking about?"

"A wall. A planetary wall that we will put between the gamma-ray burst and the world." She saw that neither of us understood what she was talking about. "Let me show you," she said.

She touched her link, said something to it, and the room went dark. A few stars appeared in the background. Then we were looking at an asteroid, tumbling gently through the night. A ship trailed behind it. It was an Akron Lance VK2, a vehicle used locally for tourists.

As we watched, the Lance closed in on the asteroid and touched down. Minutes later, ship and asteroid began to change course.

"Those are our building blocks," said Circe.

The Lance and the asteroid shrank as we drew back. There was a second ship with a second asteroid. We watched as they adjusted the vector and velocity of the rocks. Then they released them.

We followed them through deep space. Toward a long band, with tiny lights hovering around it. As the asteroids approached, it expanded across the room, stopping just short of the main door on one side and the windows on the other. We kept going, angling toward one end. The band continued to grow, and the lights became moderately brighter. It became a wall. We angled toward one end, near the windows. The lights were like so many insects. And we saw finally that they were navigation lamps. Hundreds of them. Mounted on ships. The ships were dwarfed, made minuscule, against that vast fortification. We were looking at Circe's shield.

Narrow beams, again in the hundreds, flashed everywhere along the shield's flanks. Lasers. An armada of vehicles intercepted incoming asteroids, sliced them into pieces, and delivered the pieces to other ships, which set them into the wall like pieces in a jigsaw.

"Of course," Circe told us, "none of this will happen without your assistance. And maybe not even then."

"Why?"

"Unfortunately, we don't have hordes of asteroids readily available in any one place, let alone in a strategically *correct* place. But we've been able to find an optimum site to begin construction of the barrier. And to begin moving that barrier toward its rendezvous, three years from now, with Salud Afar. And the gamma-ray burst."

"How big would it have to be?"

"The planetary diameter is twenty-eight thousand kilometers. So the shield will be roughly thirty thousand kilometers top to bottom. The gamma-ray burst will require seventy-six hours to pass through the area. Unfortunately, we can't arrange for the shield to stop in front of Salud Afar. It will keep moving."

"How fast?" I asked.

"We believe we can slow it down to about two thousand klicks per hour. That means it will have to be one hundred eighty thousand kilometers long. At a minimum."

"Is that really possible?" asked Alex.

"Oh, yes. Certainly it's possible. *Anything's* possible. If we can get enough ships. There are a sufficient number of asteroids, but some of them are remote. So we'll see. Fortunately, the shield need not be thick. A hand's width will be more than sufficient." She looked back at Kilgore, who was watching her with flickering hope. "We can do it. Given the resources."

Kilgore took over. "We're in the process now of manufacturing specialized lasers and clamps, which we'll be able to affix to whatever ships we have to work with."

"The problem," DeVrio said, "is the ships."

"How many do you need?"

The lights came back on. The Administrator got out of his chair, walked across the room, stared at the fireplace. "Lasing the shield together will be a monumental task. But collecting and herding the asteroids is even more daunting."

"How many, Mr. Administrator? Do you need the entire Confederate fleet?"

He laughed. "The fleet plus pretty much every private and

commercial vessel in the Confederacy. Plus everything we can manufacture in the next three years. *That's* what we need. Anything less than that, and this world dies." Again the room fell silent.

Kilgore came back to us and sat down on the edge of his desk. "The problem, of course, is that if we're using these ships to construct a barrier, we *can't* use them to evacuate anyone."

"So what are you going to do?"

"We're going to assume success with the Mutes. That they'll hold off. Make some sort of deal. So we'll start the planning. And start fitting the ships that have been moving people out to Sanctum. If we do not get a break with the Mutes, then we'll cancel the shield immediately and go back to hauling citizens." He sucked his lower lip. "Now, do you understand why we need you?"

Alex got up. "I'll do what I can."

"Thank you, Alex. And Chase." Kilgore sounded vastly relieved. I felt sorry for him. Weight of the world, as the old saying went. It took on new meaning that day.

THirTY-FOUR

It was not, finally, the appearance of the thing striding out of the surf toward us, but the bloodred moon that seared my soul.

—*Love You to Death*

"Make it happen." It was Kilgore's final instruction as we left his office.

When we got back to Samuels, the *Belle-Marie* was waiting. I literally collapsed into the pilot's seat, thinking how I'd not expected to see her again. "How you doing, Belle?"

"Good. I missed you."

"You've been having a big time."

"I carried a group of infants and mothers to Sanctum. Got back yesterday."

"How'd it go?"

"Sanctum is not much more than a few modular buildings on a barren plain."

"That'll change."

"I hope so."

"Has the luggage come on board?"

"Ten minutes ago."

"All right. Let's go through the checkoff."

"Before you start, we have a transmission from Number 17 Parkway. Written text. For Mr. DeVrio."

I passed it back to the cabin. Minutes later, Giambrey sent it forward:

Giambrey,
There's been another shoot-out. Ships destroyed and fa-
talities on both sides. The situation between the Confed-
eracy and the Assemblage has deteriorated to the point
that I wanted to caution you to use extreme care when
you approach them.

Circe asked if she could sit on the bridge during launch. "Sure," I said. "You enjoy spaceflight?"

She laughed. It was a pleasant sound, the laughter of a much younger woman. She seemed a different person from the one I'd met in Kilgore's office. "This is the first time I've tried it," she said.

"Really? You haven't been out before?"

"No," she said. "I've always wanted to, but somehow I never got around to it." She laughed again. "You're looking at me as if I said something funny."

"Just surprised, I guess."

"Why?"

"Because you're helping put together the most ambitious space project I've ever heard of."

The launch doors opened and a black-and-white Benson-class yacht came in, moved slowly through the docking area, and tied up at the pier opposite. It carried Dellacondan markings.

I wanted to cheer.

"Thank God for them," she said.

We watched while the pilot debarked. He was apparently alone. "So why didn't you go out on one of the tours?"

"I've always wanted to. Just never found the time."

"I understand."

"Chase," said Belle. *"Operations on the circuit."*

"Okay, Belle. Put them through."

"Belle-Marie." A woman's voice. *"You are cleared for de-parture."* They gave us a heading. It hadn't happened when I'd left with Ivan. *"More incoming traffic,"* the operator told me. *"Wouldn't want you to bump into anybody."*

"On my way, Samuels. Thank you." I released the clamps and eased away from the dock. We moved through the launch area and out into the void. Below us, Salud Afar was a golden globe, vast oceans of clouds illuminated by sunlight.

"It's a beautiful world," Circe said. "You know, you make your living out here, Chase. So you assume everybody else gets to go for a ride, too. But the reality is that hardly anyone on the surface has even been up to Samuels. Places like this"—and she indicated either the interior of the ship or the greater universe outside—"you've made into your home. And it seems natural to you that everybody lives the same sort of life. But most people down there probably couldn't even tell you how many planets there are in the system."

"But that's not you."

"No, it isn't. Chase, I've had a good life. Gone a lot further than I'd ever thought possible. But if I had it to do again, I think I'd follow the path you took. You're a very lucky young woman, but I don't think you know it yet." Through a break in the clouds, I caught a glimpse of blue ocean.

We sent a message to Selotta and Kassel to let them know we were coming. Then, approximately an hour after we'd left the station, I lined up on Borkarat, their home world, told Alex and Giambrey to buckle in, and slipped between the dimensions.

One drawback about this kind of travel is that you can't send or receive traffic en route. Should the Mutes respond by telling Kilgore to stick his diplomatic initiative in his ear, he'd have no way of contacting us to let us know.

Circe stared out at the long gray twilight of the transdimensional world and told me how she'd always wanted to do this. "Not under these circumstances, of course. But it's so strange out here."

"How was life under the Bandahriate?" I asked.

"I was a teenager when he died. A lot of people hated it, of course. Hated *him*. I'm sorry to admit this, but I didn't pay much attention to public affairs. People were out there risking themselves, trying to get rid of Cleev. And I was drifting through school. Boys and physics. It was all I cared about. And not necessarily in that order." She gave me a shy smile.

"It must have been a relief when he was gone."

"To be honest, I think things ran better under Cleev than they do now. For one thing, Kilgore's government is more corrupt.

"Don't get the wrong impression. I'm not saying I'd want Cleev back. But it isn't as black-and-white as everybody pretends."

She was a study in contrasts, upbeat and happy most of the time, but she had an existential dimension as well, deepened, no doubt, by the responsibilities she carried. Although, as I got to know her better on that long, lonely flight, I realized it wasn't merely the consequences of failure that weighed on her. She seemed, in fact, confident of success. If these creatures could really see into each other's minds, and into hers, then they would see what was at stake. And they had to possess a degree of empathy well beyond anything you found in humans. How could such a species possibly stand by and watch a catastrophe on this scale wipe out hundreds of millions when they needed to do so little to help prevent it?

No, it was something other than her mission. It was, oddly enough, the more mundane aspects of existence that sometimes broke through and affected her, the sense of passing time, of opportunities missed, of the ordinary losses one incurs in life. Young no more. Where do the years go?

While I probably spent too much time thinking about the incoming gamma-ray burst, she was quite capable of commenting that, succeed or fail, the day would come when we'd give almost anything to be able to return to such hours on the bridge, to sit with each other and munch jelly sandwiches, which we'd been doing at that moment. And I don't mean to suggest she was not concerned about the bigger picture. But she lived in the moment as much as anybody I've ever known.

Giambrey also managed not to allow the importance of the mission to weigh on his mind. "We do what we can," he said. "If the Mutes are reasonable, they'll take advantage of the opportunity to help us. This is an opening for them, as well. A chance to establish better relations and head off a war. They'd be damned fools not to cooperate."

He was originally from the City on the Crag. His physician father had visited Salud Afar as a young man, fallen in love with its wide oceans and vast forests, and maybe its sense of solitude, and eventually persuaded his wife to vacation there. She came to share his love for the place, and, after Giambrey's birth, they'd made what he described as the ultimate big move.

"Doctors were more in demand there," he said. "There was always a shortage. Not sure why. But the result was that the pay was better. Though my dad always insisted that wasn't the reason."

His smile left me feeling everything would be okay. This was a guy who'd been around a long time, and his manner suggested he knew what he was about. His presence provided a balancing point in the storm.

"I started out as a journalist," he said. "But I wasn't tough enough for the job. Couldn't ask the hard questions. Didn't like offending people. So eventually my boss suggested I should find another line of work. What I *was* good at was writing speeches. And one thing led to another."

"Tell me about the Administrator," I said.

"What do you want me to say, Chase? He's been good. He tries to do the right thing. He doesn't have the organizational skills that other chief executives have. And he's got a huge organization to run. We've only had self-government for less than thirty years. Look at where you come from, for example. Rimway. It's still a world of nation-states. But they've a long tradition of cooperating. Working together. On Salud Afar, all the nation-states are brand-new. Nobody knows what they're doing. Everybody thinks that the way to stay in power is to climb over the other guy.

"There's even a sizable portion of the population that wants the Cleevs back. You ask what I think of Kilgore? I'm amazed he's been able to hold everything together. Then, of course, to get hit with this"—the upbeat exterior faded a bit—"Thunderbolt." He sighed. "I feel sorry for him. I'll tell you, *I* wouldn't want his job."

Giambrey spent a substantial part of his time studying Ashiyyurean script. I helped by sitting quietly while he explained the intricacies to me. To be honest, I couldn't bring myself to pay much attention, but I tried. I asked questions, and listened to the answers. Circe also tried to do a cram program in the language, but she got bored, too, and gave it up.

"When we get there," Giambrey asked, "are we going to have problems getting access to what's happening? I mean, do they have HVs?"

"Yes, you'll have problems," I said. "Communications systems aren't set up for us."

"How are they different?"

"They're Mutes, Giambrey."

"I understand that. But how do they broadcast if nobody speaks? Do they transmit pictures with text?"

"If they wanted to contact *us*, yes. That's exactly what they'd do. But for themselves, it's a whole different ball game. Do you know how telepathy works?"

"No. Does anybody?"

"More or less. Signals are transmitted from one brain to another by fractal dimensional charge effects. I think that's right, but don't ask me what it means. They can only do that across a limited space. A few meters. The signal gets progressively weaker with distance. When they broadcast, say, a sports event—"

"Do they have professional sports?" asked Alex.

"I don't know. Is it okay if I go on with this?"

"Sure. I'm sorry."

"*If* they broadcast a sports event, the commentator's thoughts are, in effect, transmitted to a receiver. The receiver converts them to an electronic signal, blends the signal with the base transmission, and sends the entire package to, say, your living room. There, another converter sorts it out, gives us picture and sound. And the commentator's reactions are converted back to fractal charge effects and put out there for anybody in the room to pick up. To *read*."

"Incredible."

"Born of necessity," I said.

The most annoying part of the mission was being cut off from the world at so critical a time. We were sealed into our cocoon for almost four weeks with no idea whether, as Alex commented, full-scale war was breaking out between Mutes and Confederates.

Giambrey remained upbeat, but I could see that the man who initially had been anxious to accept the challenge grew to wish, as the days passed, that everything was over. He didn't like being out of touch either. Nothing would have helped like picking up the Nightly News. Alex suggested we cut the jump short, come up for air, as he put it, try to pick something up, then continue the flight. That sort of thing is hard on fuel. And, of course, it wouldn't have worked anyway. Anything we *did* pick up out there would have been thousands of years old.

Circe took to reading science novels and playing psychological games with Belle, in which the AI generated a random situation and they worked together to determine what the most common human response would be, according to surveys and studies conducted over the centuries. One of the situations was an attack on an ambassador arriving to conduct peace talks. How likely was such an event to lead to war? Answer: 37 percent.

She asked if I knew the odds against getting killed by a blast from a hypernova? I had no idea. She pointed out that, to date, it had happened to nobody in human history. Ever.

She also found it frustrating that we had penetrated the galaxy, were traveling through that ocean of stars, and she couldn't see anything. I tried putting visuals up for her, using the navigation display to show off planetary rings and exploding suns, but she explained she'd seen it all before, she'd sat in her living room and watched all this, and it wasn't the same as actually *seeing it*. So in the end we sat and talked and watched some shows and played loki tournaments. (Loki, for those who've never been to Salud Afar, was a card game that was very popular in the Coalition. Both our passengers were addicted to it.) Alex picked it up quickly. I dropped into last place and pretty much stayed there.

I don't think anybody slept very well. And the hypernova remained, of course, the prime topic of conversation. We went over it and over it. Circe insisted that the shield could be made to work if the resources could be made available.

Giambrey confessed that he'd never even *seen* a Mute. "I

keep reading how repulsive they are. That spending time with
one is like trying to pet a spider. And they'll know everything
I'm thinking. How's it even possible to *begin* to negotiate with
such a creature?" Kilgore's people had loaded Belle with all the
data they had on the Chief Minister and his staff. But Giambrey
said it wasn't very helpful.

The year before, I'd spent almost two weeks alone with the
Mutes. Had in fact visited Borkarat, where I'd met Selotta.
"That's the real reason you and I are here," Alex told me when
we were alone on the bridge. "You've got the experience. You're
the only real hope we have to make this mission succeed."

"So why was I the invisible woman in his office?"

"I don't know. Maybe he felt you'd be more relaxed if he
didn't put any pressure on you."

"So why are *you* putting pressure on me?"

"Listen, Beautiful. Pressure's your middle name." He grinned.
"Relax. Look, you're good at this kind of thing. So am I. Giambrey probably is, too. But he's going to be out of his depth on
Borkarat. You know it, and I know it. So does he. So he's going
to be counting on us to charm the Mutes into giving us what we
need. What they need, too, for that matter."

"Well, good luck to us," I said.

To my surprise, Giambrey took me aside and said much
the same thing. "I'm not comfortable with any part of this," he
confessed. "It's like playing loki with our cards faceup on the
table. I don't know how to begin a negotiation under these circumstances. So when we go into this thing, I want you to feel
free to advise me. Tell me what you really think. Okay?"

"Okay."

"Are they as repulsive in person as I've heard?"

"No," I said. "That's exaggerated. But you *will* have a
reaction."

"I won't throw up, will I? I've worked with Mute avatars,
and it wasn't bad."

"Okay. Good. You'll be fine, Giambrey." The reality was that
the effect didn't carry full force with an avatar. I suspect it's
because you know it's an avatar. It's more intense when a live
Mute actually walks into the room. But I kept that to myself.
"Look, what'll happen is that you'll try to smother your reac-

tion. Don't bother. Let it go, and after a while you'll become accustomed to it. The Mutes have a similar response to us. But they're pretty smart, and if you just let it happen, everybody will start laughing. It becomes a joke."

"Really?"

"Take advantage of the mission to make a few friends here. It will serve you and Salud Afar well in the future."

His jaw tightened. "If there *is* a future for Salud Afar."

So we played cards and pretended everything was going to be okay. The night before our arrival, we had a special dinner, broke out the wine, drank to the home world, and to success.

At approximately 0600 hours ship time, Belle woke me to announce we'd arrived.

THirTY-FiVe

Being truthful is okay. But it can get you just so far. If you're serious about getting things done, what you really need is public relations.

—*Etude in Black*

Borkarat was where I'd met Selotta, who still oversaw the Museum of Alien Life-forms and where Kassel enjoyed an apparently pleasant life in government unlike anything a human politician could know. Bare-knuckle politics didn't really work among the Mutes.

And that, I hoped, would prove our salvation. Maybe a quiet, reasonable approach to the issue of war and peace could be managed. The problem was that the Ashiyyur considered us an inferior species. "How is that possible?" asked Giambrey. "Our technology is on a level with theirs. And they had a head start. They were living in cities several thousand years before we got down out of the trees."

Alex was looking at an image of the Mute world, afloat in the center of the common room. "They don't measure civilization the way we do," he said. "Technology is a minor consideration. They see themselves as essentially spiritual creatures. As more philosophical, more curious, more concerned with living the right sort of life, than we are. That notion got reinforced when they actually sat down with us—with humans—and felt their skin crawl and discovered we couldn't communicate the way they can. I think they see our way of communicating the way we might see a cat's."

"We're not telepaths."

"Sure. That puts us considerably lower on the evolutionary ladder. They've had a long-standing debate over whether we'll ever achieve what they have. Some of them think we have the potential to reach their level of development, but they're in a minority."

"How about the people on the street?" asked Circe.

"When I was here," I said, "they treated me okay. That is, they left me alone, for the most part. Some actually tried to put me at ease. But you'll be made aware you're not to be taken seriously."

Less than an hour after we'd come out of jump status, we were hailed by a patrol vehicle. Alex followed me onto the bridge after Belle sounded the warning. *"Range is 1.2 million kilometers,"* she said. The weapons warning system began blinking. They were keying something on us.

"Try to look friendly," Alex said.

The patrol boat was even smaller than we were, but I could see arrays of particle-beam cannons and lasers and God knew what else on its hull. Its lights began blinking. Moments later Belle put a message on screen: INTERLOPER: STATE DESTINATION AND PURPOSE OF ARRIVAL.

"Not very friendly," said Circe.

Giambrey dictated our reply: "We are the *Belle-Marie*, a private vessel in the service of the Administrator, representing the Coalition at Salud Afar. We are on a diplomatic mission, and your government has been notified. We request permission to proceed to port."

I directed Belle to transmit it in text form. Minutes later, she put a reply on-screen. It was short: MAINTAIN COURSE. Then, after another few minutes: PLEASE FOLLOW US.

A few hours later they handed us off to another ship. Borkarat was only a bright star when we retired for the night.

We followed the escort in. And gradually, Borkarat split into two stars, which grew into a pair of *disks*, one large, one small.

We went through a second cycle of meals and sleep before it became a discernible globe, adorned with seas, continents, and clouds, attended by the inevitable moon. Watching the world grow larger, as I'd watched so many others over the years, I couldn't avoid a sense of order and disposition. Worlds floated serenely in the vast womb of the universe. They did not bang into one another, did not plunge into suns, did not get lobbed into the outer darkness. Generally.

Generally.

I guess I felt some bitterness there.

In a Darwinian universe, safety is an illusion.

Borkarat could have been Rimway, with differently shaped continents. Its gravity variance was a bit higher, but not so much that we wouldn't adjust fairly easily. When we were only a few hours from orbit, we received a live transmission. From Kassel. It was good to see him. We were going to need friends.

"Chase and Alex," he said. *"I was surprised when your message arrived. Selotta and I are delighted to see you again so soon. We welcome you and your associates. Although I wish circumstances could be better. I'll be waiting when you get in. The Planning Board has been in touch with me, and I've been appointed guest liaison. A meeting with one of the Board members has been arranged for you. We've reserved a room for you at the finest hotel in the capital. How was your trip?"*

"Uneventful," said Alex.

There was a delay of a minute or so while the signal traveled to the world, and the response came back. *"The best kind."* You don't spend much time on small talk when you have delays built into the conversation. *"Alex, I'm curious about the purpose for your visit. Not that Selotta and I aren't delighted to see you. She'll be coming in later to say hello. But it seems a dangerous time. If major hostilities break out, you could be interned here."*

That was a possibility that hadn't crossed my mind. In the past, hostilities had sometimes dragged on for decades.

"We've become diplomats," Alex said. "Nobody can touch us."

Kassel laughed. *"So I've heard. Well, that's good. In any case, we'll take charge of you as soon as you get in."*

Our escort stayed with us. When we were an hour or so out we received a text message from the operations center: PLEASE TURN CONTROL OF THE VEHICLE OVER TO US. I complied, and Giambrey sucked in some air. "Isn't that a little dangerous?"

"You want me to tell them we don't trust them?"

"No."

"It's okay. It's pretty much routine procedure at most of the bigger stations."

Just before we passed between the launch doors into the docking area, another message came in, this one for Giambrey, from Salud Afar. It was encrypted, using a system that had been downloaded into Belle before we left Samuels. It was from Kilgore: GIAMBREY, GOOD LUCK. OUR PEOPLE ARE STILL WORKING ON THE CONFEDERATES, BUT TO DATE THEY ARE IMMOVABLE. EVERYTHING DEPENDS ON YOU.

The term *Assemblage* didn't describe the reality of the Ashiyyurean universe, which consists of a loose group of worlds, outposts, orbiting cities, and scattered settlements. It's as much a social as a political entity. But a threat to one is a threat to all, and they can react with lethal efficiency. Some people think they'll eventually evolve into a group mind. A few hold the opinion it has happened already. But nobody who's had a personal relationship with an individual Ashiyyurean, as Alex and I have, would believe it.

A major part of the problem between us and them is that it's so hard for us to get to know one another. There are Ashiyyurean-human friendship societies on worlds in both systems, but progress has been limited. At best.

We docked and, for the first time in my career, I received a text message granting me permission to leave my ship. Belle wished me luck, and we climbed out through the hatch and walked down the egress tube, and there was Kassel. The robe was gone, replaced by a shirt and short breeches gathered in at the knees. They were a favorite form of casual dress among both males and females on Borkarat, but there was something absurd in seeing a seven-foot Mute, complete with fangs, looking as if he was headed out for a day in the park.

I've never been good at reading Ashiyyurean nonverbals. But it wasn't hard to pick up his mixed feelings on that occasion. He came forward and shook hands and squeezed my shoulder in a way that suggested however difficult things might get, he would support me. We did the introductions. Giambrey bowed and smiled, but all the charm was gone. He was trying hard to control his revulsion. Not to think about it. Not to look too closely at Kassel or at any of the other Mutes in the area.

I'll confess that Mutes still gave me a chill. Still knotted my stomach. Even Kassel. But it was kind of a joke between us, and he glanced my way and touched his heart twice with a fist. It was his *me, too* signal.

Circe did pretty well, as far as I could see. She shook hands with Kassel, told him she was pleased to meet him, and, I thought at the time, was amused at surprising *me*. You got any other challenges, Kolpath?

"Selotta would have liked to be here," he said, "but her duties will not permit it. She asked me to say hello."

"How is she?" I asked.

"Doing well, as always. She is kept busy watching for aliens trying to penetrate the museum." That was a reference to how we'd met, when I was trying to get a flight record out of an interstellar that was on exhibit. "She says she will make sure to see you before you leave. Incidentally, you are all welcome to visit our house. We would like very much to have you."

Mute body temperatures are about ten degrees lower than human, so their skin always feels cool. Add a bit of clamminess, and it's easy to imagine they're not delighted to see you. Toss in the fangs and the black diamond eyes located close together, predator style, and your instincts go to red alert.

A crowd was forming around us, at a discreet distance.

The reception area was absolutely silent, save for their clickety-clack music playing at a low level over the sound system. Public areas in Mute worlds are, of course, routinely quiet. One never hears a voice, and for a human that can be disconcerting.

There was nevertheless plenty of communication going on, of course. I could see it as Mute eyes turned in our direction. Their expressions changed, eyes narrowed, and fangs became more prominent. Parents moved closer to kids. I tried to think happy thoughts, but what kept running through my mind was the conviction that maybe their telepathic abilities with regard to us were overrated. I did not get the sense, for example, that they could see that I would have liked very much to be somewhere else, and that as threats went, I was nowhere on the scale.

They were disturbed at the sight of the creatures that had suddenly appeared in their midst. With the mayor, yet. Circe tried a smile and a wave. Nobody waved back.

It struck me how difficult it must have been for Kassel to come personally to meet us. I gained new respect for him. He might have stayed in his office and sent an escort in his place. Instead, here he was. That meant, in his culture as well as ours, that this was a personal rather than simply a political event.

"This way," said Kassel, speaking through his voice box. He said something about idiots as we walked through the crowd toward the shuttle launch area. Alex commented that he appreciated Kassel's presence, and Kassel remarked that "they" should all be locked up somewhere so they wouldn't be a danger to themselves or anyone else. "They" obviously picked up the thought because they all looked in his direction.

"I'm sorry they brought you all the way in from Provno," said Alex. Kassel's home was located on that island, in the southern seas.

"It's okay," he said. "They thought you would want to see me, and I wouldn't have had it any other way. Besides, it gives me a chance to educate these morons."

Giambrey asked whether Kassel had heard what was happening on Salud Afar.

"I know about the hypernova. If you mean conditions on the ground, among the people, we haven't heard a whole lot. We don't have a direct connection with the media at Salud Afar the way we do with the Confederates. And the reporting in yours is sparse. Mostly they run reconstructed images of the hypernova and ask people whether they're scared. What kind of answer would they expect? I *did* hear this morning that one of the spaceports was destroyed."

"Destroyed?" asked Alex. "How?"

"Somebody with a bomb." We walked into an elevator and everybody else got out. "There was no additional explanation." He glanced in my direction and I read it in his eyes: Dumb-ass monkeys.

Yep. That's us.

I was used to cranks and nitwits. You have large populations, you're going to have a few nutcases. The Mutes had an advantage, of course: Among their own, they could spot lunacy right away—before it could get around to making a bomb.

I stared back and made no effort to conceal what I was thinking: Two billion people were going to die even though the means to save them were probably available. But they'd die anyway because there really was no intelligent life in the cosmos. Not in the Confederacy, and not in the Assemblage. The Mutes and the Confederates would continue sniping back and forth, and the carnage would happen, and everybody would pretend it was inevitable.

He touched my shoulder. "I fear you're right, Chase. I wish I knew how to help."

Abruptly, out of nowhere, tears ran down my cheeks. Kassel wrapped me in his arms and held me.

THirTY-Six

We are each entombed within our skulls, Maria. We never really come to know each other. We do not feel the emotions of others, except superficially. Nor their fears or passions. The reality is that we are alone.

—*Midnight and Roses*

Giambrey was the only professional diplomat among us. He was accustomed to waiting upon the pleasure of whoever was in power. And of course, to him, Kassel was a representative of that power. Alex also understood the need for patience. As, I assume, did Circe. But to me, he was still simply good old Kassel. So, just as we were preparing to enter our suites, I broke protocol and asked when we'd get to see the Chief Minister. "Time is critical," I added.

The reader will have understood by now that actually speaking in the presence of an Ashiyyurean was not necessary, save to let other people follow the conversation. Nevertheless, those Mutes who understood how to communicate with us were aware that, even in a one-on-one, it was smart to let us actually give voice to our thoughts. "For humans," Selotta had told me once, "the voice is more significant than the brain. How could it be otherwise?" She'd shown her diplomatic side by observing that I was, of course, an exception.

"We are quite aware of the urgency," Kassel said, in unusually formal language. "The Chief Minister has arranged for you

to speak to the Secretary of Naval Affairs tomorrow morning."
Giambrey seemed satisfied with the answer, though he glanced
my way to signal me to stay out of it. Nothing further of consequence was discussed other than where and when we'd handle
dinner. "It would be best," Kassel added, "if I come and collect
everyone. You don't really need an escort. But it might save
confusion."

The city was a collection of spires, spheres, pyramids, and
polyhedrons laid out with artistic precision. I don't want to
imply that it was by any means symmetrical, but rather an exercise in architectural harmony. A dominant tower in the north
is set off by a pair of globes to the south. Pyramids are laid
out in sets of two and three, the whole connected by a tapestry
of illuminated polygons and skyways.

We descended through a heavy rainstorm onto a landing
pad, took an elevator down a few floors, and were ushered into
a private dining room high over the city. Back home, allowing
a delegation from a chief executive to dine with only a small-
city mayor present, would have been a major insult. And I saw
Giambrey's features harden as we sat down at the table that had
been prepared for us, and nobody else showed up.

"It's not as you think," said Kassel, softly. "We have no need
of ceremony. No use for it, in fact." He put his menu on the
table and tried to smile. "Our communication is more direct."
He kept the voice box volume low.

I caught a flicker of amusement in Circe's eyes. She leaned
over, and whispered to me, "Just as well."

"You're not big on ceremony either?"

"Chase, with these people, you're up there doing a ceremony, and you don't have any clothes."

Kassel bowed in her direction. "I believe, Doctor," he said,
"it is one of your own who described the beginning of wisdom
as knowing yourself."

"Ceremonies celebrate achievement," she said. "But they
also conceal things."

Kassel did his smile. "Exactly," he said. He'd found a soul
mate.

He did a quick translation of the menu. This dish tastes

somewhat like fried chicken. That is comparable to a steak salad. Avoid this group here, which your system will find indigestible.

On the whole, the food was edible, and some of it actually had an agreeable flavor. It wasn't anything I'd serve to house-guests, but I don't think the Ashiyyur have bread or tomatoes or most of the other delicacies that form an integral part of the human diet.

Kassel tried to apologize. "I understand they've known for two weeks that you were coming," he said. "Unfortunately, they turned it over to me at the last minute. There was no time—"

"It's okay, Kassel," said Giambrey. "It's the company that matters."

Kassel looked at me with a glint in his eyes. Giambrey had forgotten that his host knew exactly what he was thinking. It was an easy mistake to make.

Afterward, we retired to Giambrey's suite and turned on the omicron. "Let's see what's going on in the world," he said.

In some aspects, it was not unlike Interworld, carrying newscasts and people—if that term works—discussing current events, and the arts and sciences. We got pictures of panel discussions, saw and heard a hurricane pounding a Mute city, watched what appeared to be a cruise ship putting to sea. One channel carried a swimming competition. Despite their appearance, Mutes love to swim. Undoubtedly because their early ancestors came out of the oceans. The panel discussions, of course, were silent. And the nonverbals that one normally sees in a debate among humans were all but absent.

We found nothing like the comedies and dramas that had been staples of human entertainment all the way back to the classical age. I'm not sure why that is. Maybe because drama and comedy so often depend on misunderstanding or deliberate deception, or an inability to grasp someone else's intentions, the concept simply doesn't work among the Ashiyyur. How would you construct a mystery when every character is an open book?

It was an odd experience. Pictures without narration. And especially the panels, where the only sound during the course of a thirty-minute debate might be the scraping of a chair.

I tried to imagine sitting in a studio somewhere while an omicron broadcast my innermost thoughts to the world. My God, every mean, contemptible, cruel, lascivious notion I'd ever had would surface.

"I've a question," said Circe. "Why is there a picture? If this is a mental exercise, why do they need accompanying pictures? Don't the people in the discussion have a picture in their heads of the blowpipe, or the politician, or whatever it is they're discussing?"

Kassel took a moment. "If you were on a panel talking about various solar types, and you wanted to discuss, say, Rigel, do you have a firm picture of it in your mind?"

"I think so," she said.

"Bad example. How about a clear image of how the quantum drive works?"

"Nobody could manage that."

"Or of a given natural preservative. Or a specific canyon with odd features. You can't get the details right. Something would always get left out. So they do the visuals."

Ashiyyurean life provided sounds, of course. Engines starting. Waterfalls. Rivers. The banging that accompanies the assembling of a scaffold. They have a passion for music, though most of it hurts my ears. But it all served to underscore the general silence of Ashiyyurean civilization. Crowds of Mutes moved through the pristine cities, carried out assorted construction projects, wandered through malls, sat in the stands at sporting events, courted and reproduced, and did it all, save for the background noise, in utter silence.

"Not so," said Kassel, quietly, though I'd said nothing. "Noise, yes. There is relatively little of that. But if you define silence to include the absence of input, of incoming ideas and passions and hope. Of conversation with friends. Of exchange of everything in life that matters. Then no. Our lives are anything but silent."

In the morning a government skimmer arrived at the rooftop pad. Kassel joined us, and we all climbed in. The operator, a female, worked hard not to look appalled at her passengers.

Kassel glanced in her direction, and she seemed to relax slightly. "She's had training in interspecies tolerance," he said.

"Is that really what they call it?" asked Circe.

"That's the terminology." His fangs appeared briefly in that Mute smile. "We have a few problems ourselves."

All Ashiyyurean names, as used by humans, are more or less made up. They *have* names, of course. But since Mutes do not speak, we only know them in their written form, and written text, of course, does not translate into sound. Only God and the Mutes know the real name for Borkarat, though I could show you the symbolic representation for it. The Mute capital on that world, the place where we were at that moment, was New Volaria. It was, of course, a human name. At the time I had no idea where it had come from, though I've since learned the original Volaria was a barbarian capital on Regnus III during the Time of Troubles. I guess it says something about the way we perceived the Ashiyyur.

Kassel pointed down at a large, silver obelisk. "That is our capitol. The—" He searched for a word. "The *parliament* is currently in session."

"What can you tell us of the Secretary of Naval Affairs?" asked Alex.

"He's reasonable. He does not like our current stance regarding the Confederacy, and is concerned that the threat could explode into all-out war. He's also not happy with the status quo, which drains resources. Unfortunately, he considers you, humans, the Confederates, to be extremely difficult to deal with. If you pressed him, he would argue that humans have not yet attained civilization. I wish I knew an easier way to say this. But he, like most of us, thinks of you as an inferior type, with an inherent bloodlust that, over fifteen thousand years of organized culture, you have been unable to shed." He shifted his weight uncomfortably. "I'm sorry, but it's important you understand what you're dealing with."

"Well, that's encouraging," said Giambrey, trying to hide his resentment.

Kassel turned to him. "The negotiation will be unlike any you've engaged in before, Giambrey. The Secretary will know the minute you walk in the door that you wish him to stand down the fleet so that the Confederate Navy can go to the rescue of Salud Afar. If he has not already come to that conclusion."

Giambrey cleared his throat. "It's not easy being a barbarian," he said.

We drifted down onto a pad.

"Kassel." Alex was straightening his jacket. "Will you be in the meeting?"

"No. Unfortunately not. This business is far above my pay grade."

"Do you have any advice for us?"

"Keep in mind, everything is an open book. You cannot surprise him. You cannot hold anything back. Take advantage of that. Let him see your feelings for the people trapped on Salud Afar. Let him see them as I have. Let him see your desperation. And your determination, if your world survives"—his gaze turned to Giambrey and Circe—"your determination to devote yourself to calming the more barbaric impulses of your species. To working toward a lasting peace. And I see I have hurt your feelings again." He looked at each of us in turn. Yes, I thought. Damned right. You guys don't exactly have a spotless record either, and you have less excuse than we do.

"You're correct, Chase," he said. "I know. I wish it could be otherwise. Maybe one day we can all learn to be rational."

The pilot opened the hatch. Kassel glanced at her, and something passed between them. I wondered about it. *How do you manage it?* Or, maybe, *Glad that's over.*

We were at ground level, looking up at a dome that rose about six stories, supporting a tower. The tower literally soared into the sky, narrowing eventually into a needle. A small entourage of robed officials came out through a set of doors and descended from a portico to greet us. The one who seemed to be in charge, a male, was the smallest of the group. Nevertheless he dwarfed Alex and Giambrey. He wore a voice box on his sleeve. "Giambrey DeVrio?" he asked, looking from one to the other.

Giambrey stepped forward.

The Mute bowed. "Welcome to the Silver Tower. I am Tio." He swept us all up in his gaze. "If you will please come with me."

Tio took us back up across the portico and inside, into a broad passageway. I saw no guard posts. And it looked as if anyone could have walked in off the street.

He signaled for Giambrey to follow him down the passageway. One of the officials who had come out with him took charge of the rest of us. He gave us a tour of the building, but cut it short when he realized nobody really cared where the Department of the Environment was located.

"I've no way to know how long the meeting will last," he told Alex and me. "You are welcome to wait in the library, if you wish. And we have a cafeteria." He looked at us uncertainly.

Kassel suggested we stay. "It makes you look serious about the mission."

Our escort took us to a large private area, filled with portraits of robed Mutes, a few landscapes, and two or three interstellar warships. There were jacks that provided access to the vast Ashiyyurean literature. It also incorporated a substantial number of human titles, including two of Vicki Greene's novels. After about an hour, Giambrey returned.

"How'd it go?" Alex asked.

"Not sure," he said. "I made my pitch, told him how a cessation of hostilities would be to everyone's benefit. He says the Confederates can't be trusted. Big news there. But he thinks he has to keep poking them. Keep them off-balance. If they were to declare a unilateral cease-fire, he's concerned the Confederates will use the breathing space to organize their forces and launch a major strike."

"I was under the impression," I said, "that we were at peace."

Giambrey gave me a painful smile. "Not quite."

"So how'd it end?" I asked.

"There needs to be a mutual announcement. Both sides to say it's over and agree to talks."

"And you told him—?"

"We're working on it. Trying to arrange it."

"Did he say," asked Alex, "how the Chief Minister feels?"

"No. He says the Chief Minister has kept his feelings to himself."

Alex frowned. "Kassel," he said, "that's not possible, is it?"

"Sure it is. We can block others off but only for a limited time. More likely, he simply hasn't been in the same room with the Chief Minister lately."

"More likely still," said Giambrey, "he just doesn't want to say."

THirTY-SeVeN

Bureaucracies are not like people. They neither love nor hate.
They do not suffer, and they have no grasp of compassion. Most
of all, they do not make moral judgments, one way or the other.
I know that it sometimes seems they do, but believe me, Rose,
it's all politics. Or sheer neglect.

—*Midnight and Roses*

We went to a place that Kassel liked, and we tried to pretend the
meeting had gone well.

Mutes don't have alcohol. But Kassel was able to suggest a
fruit juice that tasted okay and had a mild kick. So we ordered
a round and toasted the Secretary of Naval Affairs. Then Giambrey sent encrypted messages to Kilgore and to our team in the
Confederacy.

I asked Kassel how long he thought it would take for the
Chief Minister to make his call. "No way to know, Chase," he
said. "Maybe in the morning. Maybe never. But they might
want to use this to get some leverage over the Confederacy. To
put the moral onus on the Director."

Three days later we got a message from the Secretary: *Be
advised that the Chief Minister is giving your request every
consideration, and that, furthermore, he is aware of the time
factor. Every effort is being made to arrive at a satisfactory
conclusion. I will advise you as soon as we have a decision.*

"What's he deciding?" I asked Kassel. "Whether to call a cease-fire? Or whether he'll negotiate with us?"

Kassel didn't know. "But do you want to know what I think?"

"You're skeptical that we'll get any help."

"That's correct. I'm sorry." He seemed to be staring at something in the distance. "We've spent years attacking Confederate motives. You remember how we talked about the tendency for people to fool themselves? To talk themselves into things?"

"We're not alone."

"That's right. To do as you ask, they—the administration—would have to reverse course. It would be politically unpopular. The Chief Minister would be seen as exposing Assemblage worlds to attack. Unnecessarily."

"We're talking about a *world*."

"Yes."

"And it comes down to this guy's political career."

"I didn't say that it did. I said *maybe*. Or I thought it might."

"Kassel, I'm struck that you think it might even be possible. Have you ever been close enough to get a read on this guy?"

"What do you mean?"

"To see into his mind? The way you see into mine?"

He hesitated again. "Yes."

"Do you think it's possible he might do that? Reverse course?"

"It's possible." He put that big hand on my shoulder. "I'm sorry."

"You accuse *us* of being savages."

Kassel learned unofficially that a decision was still a few days away. Circe connected with a Mute physicist and moved into quarters at a laboratory. Giambrey took to wandering around New Volaria, making as many contacts as he could. He even drew several speaking engagements, not strictly diplomatic in nature, but more scientific and cultural. It was an opportunity to win friends among influential locals.

Alex and I decided it was a good time to visit Selotta and the Museum of Alien Life-forms. So we packed up and headed out.

Humans held a prominent place as the only other known technological species, although our section was guarded by a Neanderthal avatar. He was bearded and muscular, and looked across the museum floor with a steady gaze that was simultaneously hostile and vacuous. When visitors came near him, he activated, shook his spear, growled and grunted, and made other unseemly gestures.

A substantial collection of our literature was available, and I was happy to note that the weapons section had been downsized somewhat since my earlier visit. It wasn't that the spears and guns and particle beams and disrupters weren't still there, but they were less prominently displayed than I recalled. I suspected Selotta had gotten to know us somewhat better.

Alex spent all his time in the Hall of the Humans, more or less drooling over some of the exhibits. The museum had acquired statuary, lamps, communication devices, furniture, table settings, diaries, sports equipment, religious texts, and a wide range of other artifacts, dating back as much as fourteen thousand years. "Incredible," he said. "Where did they get this stuff?" Some of it, he suspected, might have been taken from Earth during its pretechnological eras. Later, he asked Selotta, who consulted the records. "Nothing here to support that," she said. "But we're talking about a long time ago. Who knows? We can't accurately date a lot of this material."

I was interested in touring the area, but I couldn't get Alex away from the museum. Selotta couldn't leave her post, and Kassel was busy doing whatever mayors do.

On the third or fourth day, I got tired of artifacts, gathered my courage, and went to the beach. Mute females wear bathing suits that cover everything from the neck to the knees. Sleeves come halfway down the forearms. I would have complied with local standards, but nobody had a bathing suit anywhere close to my size. My outfit was pretty skimpy by their standards, so much so that I wondered whether the authorities would show up and haul me off. But Selotta assured me nobody would find me sexy. ("I mean that in the best sense," she said.) So I really had nothing to worry about.

The male suits also concealed pretty much everything from knees to neck. I wondered why a society with such easy access to the most private realities of everyday life would find it appropriate to hide their bodies so completely.

The beach was filled. As at home, there were families, and substantial numbers of young males and females in pursuit of each other. I sat for a few minutes listening to the roar of the sea. I was a few pounds heavier than I would have been at home, and I felt as if it showed. But that's an illusion. And anyhow, alone on a beach with creatures who watched me with a combination of dismay and disgust, it didn't seem as if exposure mattered a whole lot.

The sun was brighter than it would have been on Rimway. So I got up and made for the ocean. I could feel their eyes on me. But I was getting better at the game. I was able to smile amicably, say hello in my head, hope you're having a nice day, good-looking kid you have there. (That last one took some real discipline, but I think I managed it.)

Nobody was in the water. That seemed odd, but I dismissed it. Maybe this was one of those days when everybody just wanted to come down and sit on the beach. I spotted a raft about a hundred meters out. The critical thing at the moment was that it was in the water and away from the Mutes. Which made it just the place for me.

There were lots of shells on the beach. And someone had lost a ball. I strolled into the surf, felt the water tug at my ankles. Come on in. I turned and waved at one female child sitting just beyond the reach of the waves. I think, to some extent, I was enjoying the attention. Kolpath on center stage.

I got into the ocean and kept going, alternately sucked back toward the beach by the surf and dragged out by the current. The water was green and cold and could have been any ocean back home. A piece of seaweed wrapped itself around one leg. I pulled it free and tossed it away. Ahead, an aircraft was passing. A skimmer no more than a few hundred meters above the water. Otherwise, there was only the sea and that hard bright sky.

I got past the surf line and began floating over the waves. Somebody onshore, a young male, started waving at me. That seemed pretty friendly, so I waved back, put my head in the water, and made for the raft.

I'd gone maybe a dozen strokes when I noticed a group of

Mutes at the water's edge. They were waving, too. I casually returned the gesture, thinking how I was making a breakthrough. One of them, a male, abruptly charged into the water and began swimming after me. Or at least in my direction.

I'll confess that was a scary moment. I wondered whether I'd broken some social convention. In any case, I turned away and set out again for the raft.

I'd almost reached it when I became aware that my pursuer was still with me. He was splashing and kicking the water and trying to get my attention. Now, I'd had time to get accustomed to my Mute hosts, but having that thing coming after me, and better equipped to move in the water than I was, was unsettling. I tried not to turn it into a sprint for the raft, but I guess that's what I did.

He responded by hitting the water. Hitting it in my direction. Then he was coming again.

He caught me as I got to the ladder and tried to haul myself onto the raft. Grabbed my ankle and pulled me back. It wasn't a joke anymore. I looked at the beach and saw that if the Mute planned on having some fun with me, I wasn't going to get any help.

I kicked free and he stared at me. Then he jabbed one of those cold gray fingers at the shoreline.

I hauled myself up. Almost fell back in because the rungs were too far apart. Two more Mutes started into the water. One was a female.

I stood on the raft and looked back at the guy in the water. "What?" I said.

He bobbed up and down, making expressions I couldn't read. But he didn't retreat.

He showed me his fangs.

Great. I held up my hands and thought *Go away. Leave me alone.*

Then, to my horror, he grabbed hold of the ladder and started to climb it.

He stepped onto the raft, pointed at the water, and showed me a mouth full of teeth. He pointed at his bicuspids and pointed again at the water.

I got the message.

It explained why nobody was on the raft or in the ocean. He began making false starts back toward the beach. *Let's go.*

I looked around, half-expecting to see a fin. But there was nothing.

Let's go.

Well, let it never be said a Kolpath can't take a hint. I dived in and struck out for shore. He came in behind me and stayed with me.

When we got to the beach, the Mutes froze as they are inclined to do on celebratory occasions. They were all looking at us, and I knew they were talking to him.

It was an eerie experience, and it ended simultaneously for everyone. As if someone had fired a gun. They simply dispersed.

I walked over to the Mute who'd come after me and formed the words *thank you* as clearly as I could. He looked back at me and cringed. By then, I'd been around them long enough that the cringe didn't surprise me. But I wondered whether he understood the message I was trying to send.

Later that evening, when I saw Selotta, I told her about it. She said yes, there'd been a sighting of a school of *vooparoo* during the early morning. Of course, she added, I was free to translate the word any way I liked.

A *vooparoo* was a creature very much like a coelenterate, or jellyfish, with a soft gelatinous structure and long, trailing tentacles. It varied in size from near-microscopic to about ten meters. The ones seen in the vicinity of the beach had been big, and a warning had been issued. Even the very small ones, she explained, delivered a painful sting. The bigger ones were lethal to Mutes. Nobody knew how such a bite would affect a human, but I was pretty sure it wouldn't have been helpful. "I guess," she said, "the people on the beach didn't want you to be the first to find out."

Selotta's home was a white-and-gold villa at the edge of town. The walls were dark-stained to a degree that most people would have found oppressive. The furniture was large, the rooms were wide, and the ceilings were high. I found myself constantly climbing up onto armchairs. Even Alex was lost in the vastness of the rooms.

The villa had an enclosed deck, with several chairs and a table. The evening of the *vooparoo*, I was out there with Selotta while the kitchen made dinner. Alex was, as usual, buried in Mute ancient history.

Kassel hadn't come home yet. He'd been involved during the last few days in a political squabble over commercial licensing, so he'd been late getting in every evening. "Don't let him joke with you," said Selotta. "It's always like that. He pretends to be annoyed, and keeps saying he won't stand for election next term, but I've heard all that before. He likes being mayor, and the voters seem to like him. So I guess he'll be at it for a while."

She'd been preparing special meals for us. Despite her best efforts though, and those of the AI, the food tended to be much the same thing every day. But it was digestible, and that was all that mattered. She had an order in somewhere for food that she said would be more to our liking, but the delivery had been delayed. It was a long way to Khaja Luan, the nearest human world.

We were talking about Kassel when Giambrey called. *"I got some good news,"* he said. *"The Assemblage is going to issue a statement tonight, in a few hours, declaring a cease-fire. Our people in the Confederacy expect them to respond in kind."*

It called for a celebration.

Selotta had neighbors who, believe it or not, wanted to meet us. So they came over that night, six of them, plus a couple of older children. Equipped with voice boxes. Things were somewhat tense at first until we all got used to one another. Mostly we talked politics. How life would be better if we could, as one of them said, "stop the nonsense." In the end we raised glasses of fruit juice to ourselves, Mutes and people, one for all and all for one.

Mutes, by the way, do not toast happy occasions with liquid beverages the way we do. That may be because they've never discovered alcoholic drinks or anything else that distorts awareness. Maybe alcohol wouldn't work on them. I don't know. Alex thinks it's because of their telepathic dimension, that it would be bad form to introduce confusion into someone else's mind. Selotta had no idea why we would bother with such a pointless exercise. She added that she couldn't see that *I* had an explanation for it either. But they all played along.

The neighbors thought the raising of the glasses a quaint custom, and I suspected if they could laugh, they'd have been doing so. So we drank to Ilya Frederick, who was our woman in the Confederacy and who would, we all hoped, be able to talk sense to the politicians.

A female looked my way. She was young, and did not have a voice box. She and Selotta exchanged something. Then Selotta looked at me: "Kasta says it is all right for me to tell you this. She thinks it is a pity that there are not more humans like you and Alex. She thinks you are the exceptions. And that your brothers and sisters cannot be trusted."

It didn't matter. They caught on, and we toasted everybody. After we'd drunk to Salud Afar, one of them, the biggest Mute I'd ever seen, offered his hope that something could be done for that unhappy world. "As they have done something for *us.*"

"And what have they done for us?" Selotta asked, knowing the answer, I'm sure, but wanting it said aloud.

"Why," he said, "they brought us Chase and Alex."

He was a giant, and his name came out as Goolie, or something like that. He lived alone in a stone house just off the beach, Selotta explained. He'd been a teacher at one time, but now simply spent his time reading.

Kassel arrived while things were still going strong, and he happily joined the celebration. He'd heard the good news about the announcement from his own sources.

We partied into the night. Dancing was something the Mutes didn't do well. In fact, they didn't do it at all. Their music didn't encourage it, but eventually Alex invited me onto the middle of the deck and we danced under the stars while the Mutes watched with whatever reactions they might have had. Later, in private, Selotta told me they'd grown somewhat alarmed because they'd feared it might be the prelude to a sexual encounter. In plain sight. After all, she added, who knew what humans were capable of?

"But," I said, "they would have been privy to everything we were feeling. How could they think that?"

"That's the whole point," she said. "We *did* know what you were feeling."

"Oh."

"So who knew where it was going to lead? And, by the way, we have nothing against sex, even occasionally in public, but I don't think anyone would have been quite prepared for a display by two humans."

"Right."

"I'm sorry. I see I have offended you."

"No, Selotta. Not at all." The neighbors had gone home, and Alex and Kassel were outside on the deck doing man talk.

"It's good to have you here," she said.

"Thank you."

"You will forgive me, but humans are sometimes hard to understand. I know you would not willingly harm anyone."

"That's so."

"Are you a standard type?"

"Beg pardon?"

"Are your attitudes more or less typical of everybody?"

"I think so. You've visited Earth. What do you think?"

"It's too confusing to try to sort out a crowd."

I looked at her for a long time. "I think most individuals are reasonable. And have no inclination to harm others."

"Then how do you explain your history of wars? And criminal violence? I don't understand it—"

"I don't either. We tend to get together in groups, *tribes*, and we do things, and support actions, that we would never think of doing if we were alone." I looked across at her. "It's a characteristic we've never been entirely able to shake off."

Well," she said, "now that I think of it, I don't guess we're that much different."

The AI maintained a search of the news channels for word that the Confederacy had reacted. The response came just before we retired for the evening. There wasn't much of it Alex and I could make out. Just a formally dressed Ashiyyurean seated comfortably in front of a mountainscape portrait looking across

the room at us while music played in the background and
Selotta and Kassel picked up whatever message was being relayed. We knew it had become official when they turned and
looked directly at us.

"Very good," said Kassel. "The Confederates will observe
the cease-fire, and they express their hope that it will be possible to achieve a more permanent arrangement. They've even
offered reparations for the *Monsorrat* incident."

The current round of fighting had been triggered by the destruction of the Mute cruiser *Monsorrat* with its escort at Khaja
Luan. It had been carrying a diplomatic team when it was destroyed with all hands. Three of the four destroyers serving as
its escort had also been damaged or destroyed. The attack appeared to have been inadvertent, the result of a communication
breakdown, but that hadn't mattered very much.

It seemed as if everything militated against a peaceful relationship. I mentioned the tribal theory to Alex that night as we
were heading to bed, and he agreed that there was probably a
lot of truth to it. "Sometimes I think," he said, "there has to be
an *Other*, an enemy against whom the tribe can rally. Check
Haymakk Colonna," he said.

Colonna had famously remarked that peace between the
Confederacy and the Mutes would come on the day they found
a common enemy.

It was a bright hour in what had been an unrelentingly dark few
months. Alex elected to forgo his daily visit to the museum.
Maybe because Selotta was not scheduled in—or she'd *taken*
the day off, I don't remember which—but we were all seated
out on the deck in weather she described as unseasonably cool.
The windows were down, and the heating system was on. Giambrey had arrived just before breakfast, but he was consumed
with watching for more news and exchanging encrypted messages with his contacts on Rimway. They were, he said, waiting
for an announcement from the Confederates that the fleet was
being dispatched to help at Salud Afar.

That would be seriously big news.

"They've still not committed themselves formally," he
said.

Clouds drifted out of the west, the sky was growing dark, and rain was coming.

"High-level discussions are apparently under way," he continued, barely able to contain his enthusiasm. "We're hearing that Dellaconda, Seabright, and Camino are unhappy. They don't trust the Ashiyyur."

Alex admitted he understood their concerns. "It's the same story you told us," he said to Selotta. "Politicians have been telling them for decades that the Ashiyyur can't be trusted, that they're savages. Now the politicians are telling them it's okay. We were just kidding." He shook his head. "They're border worlds. If there were an attack, they'd be first to be hit."

The stakes were high. Either side was easily capable of taking out entire worlds.

Selotta turned in my direction. "You're absolutely right, Chase," she said.

I hadn't said anything, but I was thinking how irrational it all was.

The rain started and turned quickly into a downpour. A cold wind swept in off the ocean. Kassel called to ask whether we'd heard anything more. His sources wanted to know what the Confederates were going to do. There was talk the Ashiyyur might demand a summit meeting with the Executive Director of the Confederacy, Ariel Whiteside. That would allow them to determine his intentions.

The rumor had apparently reached the Confederacy. Giambrey watched the story come in and closed his eyes. "They won't permit a summit," he said. "Whiteside's given his word it won't happen."

"Why not?" I asked. "That seems like a simple solution to the problem. Let the Chief Minister see for himself what Whiteside is thinking."

"That's exactly why they won't do it, Chase. They're arguing that telepathic skills give the Ashiyyur too much of an advantage."

"That's sheer lunacy," I said.

We watched the storm beat against the windows. Alex leaned forward. "Not really," he said. "They have a point. At some stage, somebody's simply going to have to take a chance."

Giambrey reacted to something he'd just read.

"What is it?" asked Alex.

"Toxicon's rep walked out. Don't know why."

The evening wore on, and the storm showed no sign of abating. Rain got swept against the house. Kassel got home late again and came in drenched.

He arrived with a recommendation that we take a few days and do a tour. "There are all sorts of historical and natural sites within easy reach of Provno. The Kaiman Cliffs look down into the deepest known canyon on any—"

The discussion was cut short by another message to Giambrey. He read it, and smiled. Not an ordinary smile. But a wide grin with his fists in the air and his eyes blazing. "Yes!" he said. And before anyone could ask: "The Confederacy just voted to send assistance to Salud Afar."

That ignited a celebration. We hugged each other and screeched and generally carried on until the neighbors called over to ask what had happened.

I visualized the fleet setting out, a thousand ships to the rescue, cruisers and destroyers and patrol craft and support vessels of all kinds. Even then it might not be enough, but it would damn sure give Kilgore a fighting chance.

I don't know that I had ever felt more ecstatic. It was the high point of my life. It was the reason Alex and I had gone to Salud Afar. No, more than the reason: We'd gone to solve a mystery, and maybe save a few lives, if it turned out that anyone was actually in danger. I think we had both suspected that Vicki had developed a mental problem, and that in the end we would go back with only that knowledge for our trouble.

But this—We were watching while people moved to save a *world*!

Of course there's a lot to be said for waiting until the money's in the bank before you start making announcements. The neighbors showed up, and the screaming and hugging started again. There was a fresh round every time somebody new came to the door. They were all wet, most were drenched, but it didn't matter. We embraced them anyhow.

During the course of all this I asked Selotta why it was happening? "Why are your neighbors so involved?"

"Because," she said, "they'd like the constant wars to stop. But there's something more."

"And what's that?"

"They've shared everything you've seen and felt. They've been on Salud Afar, too. Through you. They've seen the children and the crowds in the streets. And they've tasted the fear."

We were still celebrating when Giambrey caught our attention. But this time he looked shocked.

One of our visitors spoke through his voice box. "What's wrong, Giambrey?"

"The Confederates are sending eleven ships. *Eleven*. Cargo and transport vessels. And that's all. The announcement was just made."

"Eleven?" I said. "What the hell do they expect Kilgore to do with eleven?"

Alex sank into a chair. Kassel simply stared out at the rain.

"A token force," Kassel said. He looked at his wife. A silent message passed between them. *Even now, they do not trust us.*

Maybe especially now.

THIrTY-EIGHT

In the end, everything is politics.

—Nightwalk

There were rumors that, despite the announcement, there was strong disagreement with the decision. That a dozen worlds, led by Toxicon, were strongly opposed. That Whiteside might even be overruled by the Confederate Council. But the following day, the Director spoke from the Hall of the People on Rimway. He sat behind the plain, battered desk that was part of his image. He looked lost in thought, his dark blue eyes peering past us into the distance. Public figures traditionally sit straight during these events, but Whiteside was supporting his jaw on one fist, his elbow planted on the desktop. His mustache, as always, was unkempt in a way that was intended to suggest a man of action, a decision-maker who could be counted on. He shook his head, as if dismayed by events, inhaled, and finally focused on us. The chair creaked as he leaned forward, reminding me that the omicron carried sound.

"Citizens and friends," he said, *"you are all aware by now of the desperate situation that has developed on Salud Afar. Administrator Kilgore is doing everything he can to alleviate the situation, but in fact there is little that* can *be done. The scale of the approaching disaster is simply too great.*

"Too great by far.

"He has appealed to the Confederate Worlds for assistance.

*I am proud to say we are responding with all the resources at
our disposal. Hundreds of ships, many operated by private corporations, and in some cases by individuals, are on their way
as I speak to you tonight. Administrator Kilgore has found a
world that is being converted into a refuge. It is not by any
means close to Salud Afar, but it is the nearest that nature has
provided.*

"We will be helping to move as many of his people there as
we possibly can. We are sending supplies, engineers, and other
specialists who will assist in the effort to erect shelters on the
new world, which they've named Sanctum.

"In addition, we will be sending the Alberta, with its escort
of destroyers and support vessels to assist in any way they can.
Finally, I'm pleased to report that the Council has voted an aid
package totaling six hundred million."

When he was finished, the imager pulled back, and we saw
that four senior Council members were in the room with him.
It was a display meant to signal unity.

He thanked us for our attention, reassured us that the Confederacy would continue to do whatever was humanly possible,
and delivered his signature "good night," looking away as he
did so, as though other decisions required his immediate attention. That quickly, it was over.

In the morning, we heard the reactions from Assemblage repre-
sentatives and other prominent Ashiyyureans:

"An opportunity has been missed. And it will not come
again."

"What else can be expected from a race of yappers?"

"The truth is that the Confederacy does not wish to help
Salud Afar. That world has, after all, remained outside the
human politique. And now they will pay the price. And their
politicians, of course, will try to blame it on us."

"The real reason for the Director's reluctance is that he
intends to move against the Assemblage and hopes this may
give him the opportunity."

The attacks gathered force. We were noisemakers, barbarians,
savages, troglodytes, and something that Kassel translated—
with an amused glitter in his eye—as Yahoos. We were not to be

trusted. We were fanatics. We were hopelessly low on the evolutionary scale. One young female, interviewed at a flight school, commented that eventually it would become necessary to exterminate us. She went on, according to Kassel, to suggest that the coming catastrophe at Salud Afar would be exactly what humans deserved. That Salud Afar had nothing to do with the Confederate decision seemed to have gotten past her.

Late in the afternoon of the third day after Whiteside's announcement, a group of Kassel's neighbors showed up outside. These were the same ones who'd celebrated with us earlier in the week. They gathered at the front door and waited patiently for Selotta to answer. (Mutes, of course, don't need to knock to signal their arrival.)

We were in the living room. Alex and Kassel were playing chess. Kassel, who could see the reason behind every move Alex made, had tried to level the playing field by wearing a blindfold. But it didn't matter. Alex was still getting hammered. Circe had rejoined us. She, Selotta, and I had been talking about what we thought would come next, when Selotta detected our visitors. I got up with her, and when I saw them at the door, my first thought was that they'd come to run us out of town. Or worse.

Selotta stopped to glance back at me. Her diamond eyes were simultaneously amused and sad. "It's all right, ladies," she said. "They're still friends."

There were six or seven of them. They came in, and they all stood looking at one another and at Selotta, exchanging something. Then, as if they were a single organism, they turned in our direction. One came forward, with a voice box prominently displayed on his collar. "Circe, and Chase, and Alex," he said, "we know what you are going through, we have listened to the slurs that are going around, and we want you to know that we are aware you're not cruel idiots." He stopped. Looked behind him at the others. Touched his lips with a forefinger. "Perhaps I didn't phrase that as I should have."

One by one they reached out and touched us. By human standards there wasn't much to it, simply pressing fingers against a forearm, or a shoulder. But it was *not* an Ashiyyurean gesture. "We want you to know," he continued, "that, if need be, we will stand with you."

There probably weren't more than two dozen human beings in that entire world. Alex said he'd seen two, a young couple, during his first day at the Museum. They'd been delighted to introduce themselves and spend a few minutes with him.

Three others showed up at different times on the omicron. They all tried to defend the Confederacy's action, arguing that surely anyone could understand their caution. They expressed their dismay that hostilities continued between the two species, but they were all certain that a peaceful future lay just over the horizon. They themselves of course found individual Ashiyyureans to be unfailingly polite and, as one said, "good people." We just have to give it time.

Give it time.

While a tsunami of gamma rays raced toward Salud Afar at light speed.

Giambrey also showed up on the omicron, doing an interview. The one dicey moment came when he was asked to comment on the decision by Whiteside to send only a handful of naval ships to Salud Afar.

"I understand why he did it," said Giambrey, seeing no advantage in criticizing the Confederate leader. *"I'm sure it doesn't reflect a lack of trust in the Ashiyyurean leadership, but is simply an act of caution. I would have preferred he send more assistance, but I think we have to admit at least that it's a start in the right direction."*

I couldn't help wondering how the fractals were playing for the Mutes. It's a lot harder to deal in nonsense when you're sitting on a nudist beach.

Alex grinned at me. "Dead on, Chase," he said.

I hadn't realized I'd said it aloud, and thought for a moment that Alex too had been poking around in my mind. "The nudist beach?" I said.

"No. Not nudist. They got you off that raft. When the, what was it, the *vacabubu*, was there. Right?"

"*Vooparoo*," I said.

"My point is, they came to your rescue."

"Of course they did. What would you expect, Alex?"

Alex looked at Kassel. "When you guys are on the omicron, your thoughts are picked up and broadcast, right?"

"That's correct," said Kassel.

"How about Giambrey? Did the system pick up *his* thoughts as well? Or did he have to be translated in some way?"

"The interviewer reads Giambrey. It's the interviewer's reading that gets broadcast rather than Giambrey directly."

"Why?"

Kassel hesitated. "Because," he said, and trailed off. "Because the system simply doesn't work with human brains."

"We're too dumb?" suggested Alex.

"I wouldn't put it that way."

Selotta broke in: "Human brains operate at a different energy level. I don't know the details, have never been good at fractals, but that's the reality."

"Tell me," said Alex, "do you read humans as easily as you do each other?"

"No." She shifted her position on the chair. Tried to get comfortable. "No. Humans are more difficult."

"How about human nonverbals? Are you able to interpret them?"

Her eyes grew luminous. "You mean like how the pitch in your voice changed when you asked whether we think you're not too bright?"

"That's what I thought." He turned back to Kassel. "Why has no one been here to interview *us*?"

Kassel took that one: "They have Giambrey. When they found out a delegation was here, they'd naturally want to talk primarily to the ambassador."

Giambrey was still talking. Selotta had lowered the volume, but I caught part of it. "*I'm sure,*" he said, "*we can find common ground to get over this difficulty. We simply need to dialogue more often.*"

"*Dialogue*'s the wrong verb," I growled. "We need to *talk*."

Alex looked far away for a moment. "Kassel," he said finally, "could an interview be arranged for us?"

"Sure. You're thinking about Chase on the beach?"

"Yes"

"Ah," he said. "It might work."

"Me on the beach? What are we talking about?"

Alex got that look in his eye that I associated with a request to run off to Backwater IV to secure an ancient cooling system. "Chase," he said, "would you be willing to do an interview?"

"Me? Not on your life, sweetheart. I'll take on sea monsters, if you want, and ride taxis into the upper altitudes, and I can even deal with ghosts in the woods. But I don't do interviews."

"All you have to do is say what you think."

"Alex, why?"

"Trust me."

"Why don't *you* do it? You do this kind of thing all the time."

"That's the problem. I might be a bit jaded. *You* are the one who was out on the raft. Nobody else *can* do it. Anyhow, you're a much more sympathetic person than I am."

Selotta squeezed my shoulder. "Chase," she said, "he knows what he's talking about."

Kassel made a call. It, too, like so much else on this world, was silent. He simply looked at his link for a minute or two, did no physical reaction of any kind, and closed the device. "We are all set," he said. "And we have exactly the right person to conduct the interview."

"Who?"

Kassel stood silently for a moment. Then: "He says we will use the name 'Ordahl.' And I should tell you he's the local equivalent of Walker Ankavo," said Kassel.

They claim they can only read conscious thoughts, but I don't believe it. Walter Ankavo was probably the most celebrated journalist on Rimway. But he hadn't crossed my mind in months.

Alex claimed he didn't get it from him either. Well, whatever. In any case, he would arrive the next day. "They're going to record it in the morning and broadcast it tomorrow night," Kassel said.

"I don't think this is a good idea," I said.

"Chase, you'll be fine. We need to get the general population past the notion we're savages. Who better to do that than you?"

"I agree," said Kassel.

"Lord," I said. "When it blows up, I want everybody to remember it wasn't my idea."

"It won't blow up."

I climbed onto a chair. Wished my feet could touch the floor. "Will we be going into a studio somewhere?"

"No. They're going to do it here. They figure you'll be more comfortable that way."

"They got that from you."

"Possibly." He tilted his head, which was meant to indicate I shouldn't worry. "You'll be fine," he said.

"What am I supposed to tell them? What's the point of all this?"

"All you have to do is talk to Ordahl," said Alex. He gave me an encouraging smile. "One of Selotta's neighbors made the comment that things would be better if they and we could socialize a bit. That we've never really had a chance to get to know one another. That's what we want to do here. We want the public to see the very best we have to offer."

"So you're hanging *me* out there? My God, Alex—"

"Just go along with it," he said. "Be yourself. And run with your instincts. You'll be fine."

"Right."

"You *will*," said Selotta. "If the thought passes through your mind that Mutes are incredibly sexy creatures and much to be sought after"—she glanced at Kassel, who let his head drift onto the back of his chair—"there's no need to be defensive. Everybody will understand.

"Keep in mind that language is a code. Ordahl, and his audience, won't be able to read the words you form in your head. Only the images. And the emotions. And whatever other drives you have going on."

They arrived in a blue-and-gold skimmer and hovered over the villa. "They're taking pictures," said Kassel. After a while they landed and brought equipment inside. Directed by a female, a team of three moved the furniture around, set up the recording gear, explained to Selotta and Kassel how, once they got started, everybody other than the principals would have to leave the building. When they'd finished, they climbed back into the skimmer, promising to return shortly, and vanished into the late-morning sky.

"How big an audience does this guy get?" I asked.

Kassel thought about it. "The latest surveys show forty million or so. It's *big*. The critical thing, though, is its composition. It includes the"—he paused, searching for a phrase—"the movers and shakers. You want to make a splash, this is the way you do it." He paused and looked in the direction the skimmer had taken. "I wish I could get them to pay this much attention to *me*."

Make a splash. That called the *vooparoo* to mind again.

It might not have been so bad had Alex not kept telling me I'd do fine. You won't screw up. After all, what could go wrong? Don't worry, Chase, you're a natural. After a while he stopped. Maybe he figured out he wasn't helping, or maybe our hosts read my state of mind and advised him to knock it off. Whatever, Selotta tried to change the subject to what a good dinner we were going to have. Kassel started talking about the Mute philosopher Tulisofala and the Kaiman Cliffs, and Alex pretended to read.

Two hours later, the skimmer came back. The female climbed out and came inside. She made some adjustments with the omicron. She was still not wearing a voice box. I think she regarded Alex and me as pet chimps. She stiffened, so I knew she had picked that up. I pictured a banana. Really like them. Yum-yum. She kept working while I munched the banana. Selotta suggested that was not the way to win them over.

Meanwhile, a second skimmer arrived, and a guy who was obviously Ordahl stepped out and looked around. He wore a bright gold robe. I watched him take a chain out of a small black package. It was his voice box, which he studied for a moment before looping it around his neck.

He strode imposingly up the walkway.

Kassel met him at the door and showed him inside. He was your standard Mute, almost two heads taller than I was. His skin was not gray, like all the others I'd seen in my limited travels, but almost gold. There was, of course, no expression to read, just the long jaws and the diamond eyes. He did an exchange with Selotta and Kassel. Then, after a few seconds, they all turned to Alex and me. Kassel did the introductions, and Ordahl responded by saying he was pleased to meet us.

One of the many problems inherent in communicating with the Ashiyyur is that whoever manufactures the voice boxes apparently makes only two types: one for each gender. Otherwise, the voices are identical. So at first, while we tried to get set up, I was seldom sure whether Kassel or Ordahl was talking. It would have been okay had either moved his lips. Kassel grasped the situation and moved well away from Ordahl so it became easier to know where the voice was coming from.

Finally, everybody filed outside. They took seats in the skimmers, or on the deck. The female closed the doors, and I was alone with Ordahl. He asked if I was ready to begin. That was purely a formality because he had to know I wasn't ready, and never would be.

"Yes," I said, trying to *be* casual.

"Relax." He let me see his fangs and pointed at the chairs. A smile or a promise of extermination? "Why don't we sit, Chase?"

The chairs had been placed facing each other in front of a lavender curtain mounted by the crew specifically as a backdrop. "Sure," I said. "I'm ready when you are."

"Good. We won't start recording for a few minutes. If that's okay with you."

"That's fine."

"May I make a comment?"

"Sure," I said.

"You look very good."

"I beg your pardon?"

"Don't misunderstand me. You are everything I'd hoped. You're quite *alien*. And you're unsettling. Not someone with whom I'd want to be alone. That's precisely what we want. I'd been concerned that you would simply look like a different life-form. But you really do have a quality that is"—he stopped, trying to think what he wanted to say—"disquieting."

"Okay. I'm glad I didn't disappoint you." I let him see my incisors, but he didn't seem to notice.

"Good." We talked for a few minutes, about my impressions of Borkarat, and how difficult it was to communicate using grunts, snarls, and aspirates. Then he asked again whether I was ready.

"Yes." Let's get it over with.

A green lamp blinked on. "Chase Kolpath, I'd like to welcome you to *Newsmaker*. The show has been running for thirty-two years, and you're the first human who's been our guest."

"It's a pleasure to be here, Ordahl."

"May I ask how long you've been on Borkarat, Chase?"

"Just a couple of weeks."

We went back and forth for several minutes. What was my connection with the mission from Salud Afar? How had I come to be on that world? Was it really true that the Administrator's staff knew of the Callistra event before we reported it to him?

Uh-oh.

"I really have no way of knowing the answer to that, Ordahl. But I'd be shocked to learn that the Administrator had been aware of the problem in advance."

We went through a series of preliminaries. Would I explain what I did for a living and why I'd come to Borkarat? What did it feel like to be isolated inside my mind? What was my reaction to living among a race that communicated so differently? Did I feel a sense of release to know that I was now open to others, and that everything I knew could be made available to them with no effort on my part?

"No," I admitted. "It scares the daylights out of me."

"Why? Why are humans so frightened of truth? So literally terrified that others will find out what they think? What they feel? Are they really that deceptive?"

"Nobody's frightened of the truth, Ordahl. But we think privacy counts for something, too."

"Yes. Thus you value your ability to conceal the truth from one another."

"Sometimes truth is painful. For example, revealing some parts of daily life is tasteless. There are details of physical reality that we all know about, but we don't want them pushed into our consciousness on a regular basis."

"Such as?"

"Such as whether my notable interviewer feels a need to go to the bathroom."

I wondered how a comedian got by on a world in which nobody ever laughed?

"What," he asked, "is a comedian?"

His tone suggested an adult trying to talk sense to a child. I resisted the impulse to fall back on my charm. My soft gray eyes and long black hair. I had good features and a killer smile. Ordinarily, they were more than enough to cow male opposition. But I had no way to charm that hulk. Whatever allure I possessed was missing in action.

"Surely," he said, "you must understand that many of the problems between your species and the Ashiyyur spring from the willingness of humans to engage in deceit."

"Some of the problems are a result of Ashiyyurean hubris."

"Ah. Could you explain, please?"

"Ashiyyureans think they are superior. I'm not sure why they would believe that, other than that they share a common consciousness. Are you more intelligent than we are? If you were, surely you'd have found a way to make peace with us. I know we can be noisy neighbors, but we don't want to be fighting incessant border wars. And neither do you. Neither side profits from them. Why are you unable to persuade us to do what is in our own self-interest?"

Eventually we got to the point. "You came hoping to enlist a promise from us that we would call a halt to hostilities so that your combat fleets could go to the rescue at Salud Afar."

"Yes. That's correct."

"And you got that promise. We have agreed to stand down during the emergency."

"Yes."

"Let me run your Director's response." Whiteside appeared, standing on a podium, surrounded by flags and symbols of the Confederacy. *"We will be sending the* Alberta, *with its escort of destroyers and support vessels to assist in any way they can."* "Eleven ships," said Ordahl. "Do humans value the lives of their own so cheaply that they cannot bring themselves to get serious about a rescue effort?"

"He doesn't speak for me," I said.

"He speaks for the Confederacy. He was elected by you, was he not?"

"Not by me. By the voters."

"Twice, in fact."

"Yes."

"Then how can you imply he does not represent you?"

"Okay, look: In this, he doesn't represent me, and I suspect he doesn't represent a majority of the people across the Confederacy. I don't really know about that, though. I can't speak for them. But they've already started voting with their resources. They're sending food and supplies. Those who have ships have, in large numbers, begun traveling to Salud Afar to lend what assistance they can.

"For God's sake, Ordahl, two billion people live out there. There's a plan to save them. If we can get sufficient ships in place. I'm sure you already know about the shield, but let me go over it anyhow for your viewers."

I did. I explained, visualized, agonized over, however you want to describe it, the effort that had every potential to succeed, to save a world. I pictured families in parks, and women with children on beaches, and people reading quietly in libraries, and crowds listening to concerts. "Unless the shield can be made to work, all these people will die. You ask me about Whiteside's decision, and you want to hold me responsible for it. That's silly. We have a leader who, for political purposes, or ideological ones—Who really knows?—will play on old animosities and old fears, and will hold the fleet back. He does not speak for me. But I understand why they don't trust the Ashiyyur. And because of that, they'll stand by while a world dies."

"Because of us?"

"They don't trust you. And you're behaving as if the attacks at Pelioz and Seachange never happened."

"Those were provoked."

"From our perspective, that is not so. And they came without warning."

"Chase—"

"Look, let's not drag this out of the closet again. All this animosity has gone on for two centuries, and both sides have a lot to answer for. So we're at a point where neither side trusts the other. And because of that, we're about to do something that we'll be answering for as long as there's a human anywhere. And maybe you will, too.

"The truth is that Whiteside's decision to keep the fleet at home is pure politics. He knows that the fleet ultimately cannot protect the Confederate worlds. It can only retaliate in the event of attack. The same is true of your force. Defense is not possible against the kind of armament we mount. So it really wouldn't matter whether the fleet was at home or not. It wouldn't save a single world. It only means that retaliation would take a bit longer. And I'd ask Director Whiteside, and the people of the Confederacy, whether that delay of a few weeks is worth the sacrifice of a world.

"We and you are the same. Where it matters, there is no essential difference. Plato ranks with Tulisofala. You stage *Hamlet*. We love our children, as you do. We enjoy the beach in summer, as you do. I was on a beach the other day and swam out to a raft. I wasn't aware that a *vooparoo* warning had been issued. What was a *vooparoo* anyway? I had no idea.

"But one of your children came out to warn me. To get me off. Even though he couldn't communicate with me. Even though he put himself at risk. Even though he was repulsed by the way I look, he came for me.

"He acted. Despite everything, despite even his instincts, he acted. It's what we need to do." I was looking at Ordahl, but I was talking, finally, to Whiteside. "You have an opportunity now to forge a bond between the two species. And you're blowing it, Mr. Director.

"I'm asking you to do what that young male did the other day. You risk nothing except political advantage. Send the fleet."

THirTY-NiNe

Sometimes life is like the sea. You are alone at the edge, trying to hold back the tide. You anchor your feet and you scream against it, but it does not matter. It surges around you. The sand sinks beneath your feet. It will have its way despite all your efforts. They are as nothing, and you are easily swept aside.

—*Love You to Death*

When it was over, I was trembling. Ordahl adjusted his robe, got up, and said thanks. "You got angry. That's good. I like those who get angry."

The female came in with the technicians. They began disassembling equipment. Then they were gone.

Alex gave me a hug and told me I'd been brilliant.

It felt good to hear that, but it was more or less what he would have said no matter what.

Circe took my hand. "Good," she said. "If you're lucky, they won't try to arrest you when you get home."

"They'll do some editing, of course," said Kassel. "But I'd say you came across like an eagle." He savored the word, and he looked at me with open admiration.

"Thank you. Nothing embarrassing got picked up, I hope?"

"I was surprised to discover," said Alex, "that you think mathematicians are sexy."

"My God, Alex. That's not true. I've never—" I turned to

Selotta. "He's making it up, right? I mean, he didn't even get the mental part."

Selotta looked down at me. "Yes, love. Nothing like that happened."

"Thank God. Alex, I'm going to shoot you."

"We did see *some* things, though," she continued. "But nothing, I think, that would have embarrassed you. For example, your regret that your father did not live to see what you've accomplished. He died before you got your pilot's license."

"That's so," I said.

"You think Alex is an especially bright man."

Alex kept his face impassive.

"That's also true," I said. "Although males provide a fairly low standard."

That brought a smile.

"And there's someone from several years ago that you are still in love with."

"Jerry Crater!" I was horrified. "That got out?"

"Afraid so. But it is nothing to be ashamed of."

Alex's smile widened. "Good old Jerry, huh?"

"Leave it alone, boss."

"In any case," he said, "I think we can call it an unqualified success."

"Good. But next time you want to volunteer me for something, I'd like to be consulted first."

We watched the show that evening. Twice. First time through I simply listened to my responses. Then we shut down the sound and Selotta translated the telepathic side. It wasn't as bad as I'd expected. In fact, it tracked the dialogue pretty closely. And yes, there were occasional blips in which I thought how my shoes hurt, and how I'd be glad when it was over, and how the interviewer had all the flexibility of a block of wood. And maybe most damning, how I wished human beings could learn to behave rationally. "I'm not sure of the correct term here," Selotta explained. "I used *human beings*, but you were thinking of all of us."

I was thinking that it sounded close to treason.

I was still trying to get my reaction calmed down when we

got word of another confrontation. A Mute cruiser damaged, a Confederate destroyer, the *Arbuckle*, lost with all hands.

"I'm tired of it," I said. "I'm ready to leave."

So was Alex. Giambrey and Circe would stay on to try to work the diplomatic side.

There was never any real question, I suppose, that we'd go back to Salud Afar. They needed the *Belle-Marie*. Alex pointed out that if the ship was going to spend the next three years hauling refugees from that world to Sanctum, he'd be of no help, and could probably just go back to Rimway.

But something drove him to return. Maybe it was a sense there was still a service he could perform for the Administrator. Or maybe he couldn't bring himself to leave me in the midst of a global disaster. In any event, he declined my offer to drop him off at home. "Let's go back," he said. "Maybe I can help build shelters or something."

In the morning, there was news that six had died on the Mute cruiser. By midday, while we were packing, the Confederacy issued a protest over the "unprovoked attack." The star drive on board the *Arbuckle*, they said, had malfunctioned, and that was why they had unexpectedly arrived in Ashiyyurean space. They demanded an apology.

Anybody who knows anything about interstellar travel knows the odds against such an event. *"Doesn't matter,"* Giambrey told us over his link. *"You get your story out there, and people will believe it."*

I was getting requests for more interviews, which I politely declined. I also got word that a couple of commentators in the Confederacy had branded me a traitor. *"In the enemy capital,"* one of them said, *"Kolpath talks as if both sides are equally at fault."* They were calling for a boycott of Rainbow Enterprises.

And finally, as we were heading out the front door, saying good-bye to our hosts and to a few of their neighbors who'd come over to see us off, there was word of another incident: An Ashiyyurean cruiser hit and disabled near Casumel. Again, there were casualties.

* * *

Kassel announced he would go back to the capital with us and would stay until we were safely on board the *Belle-Marie*. "Wouldn't want you to get lost," he said.

Circe also accompanied us on the flight to New Volaria, where we met Giambrey and had lunch. He was discouraged. "Idiots in charge on both sides," he said. "They couldn't even tell you what they're fighting about. It's reflexive."

"I'm sorry to hear it," said Alex.

"What frustrates me is that if we could pick a few halfway-rational people out of the streets on both sides, and put them in power, they could probably settle it. And it would be over."

"You may be underestimating the intensity of the problem," said Alex. But when Giambrey wanted to turn it into a debate, Alex changed the subject.

Circe would stay in New Volaria with the ambassador. We said our good-byes and went up to the rooftop pad to get a taxi. And a strange thing happened: A group of Mutes recognized me and came over to signal their support. They *applauded*. A *human* gesture.

We got into our taxi and made for the spaceport. While we were en route, Kassel took a call from somewhere. Then he twisted around in his seat to look at me. "Bon Selvan wants to meet you, Chase."

"Who's Bon Selvan?"

"She's one of the proctors." His eyes closed. And opened. "You should go."

"Kassel, what's a proctor?"

"There are seven of them. They're the advisors to the executive board. It's hard to explain. But she's a very high-level VIP."

"Okay. Is there a point to it?"

"Yes, there's a point. She doesn't approve of the way relations with the Confederates have been handled. You want to take a first step toward creating a settlement, give her something to work with."

Bon Selvan was seated in a garden, in the shade of a small tree, surrounded by clusters of bright red and yellow flowers. Birds sang, and I saw a snake slithering over the black iron fence that surrounded the enclosure. The proctor was clothed in an orange robe, with a dark brown hood draped over her shoulders. I entered through a glass door. She rose, my escort bared fangs, used his voice box to inform me who she was, and withdrew, closing the door.

Bon Selvan studied me for a long moment. "Chase Kolpath, I take it you are not impressed with our leadership."

"I don't wish to be impolite—"

"You cannot be impolite around us, child." She showed me to a seat.

And, yes: I was thinking that it was hard to understand how, after thousands of years, two species that call themselves intelligent could not manage their affairs without resorting to butchering each other.

"You are absolutely right, Chase. There are reasonable individuals, but they have not yet learned how to form groups, governments, that behave in a rational way. I must admit I do not know why that is."

While I thought about it, she told me she was pleased to meet me.

"And I am glad to meet you," I said. I was about to frame my next question: Could she help find a way to ease the rising tensions? Could she conceive of a way to head off the approaching war?

"You think war is coming, Chase?"

"Yes, I do."

"I'm not so sure. This relatively low level of combat has intensified in recent days, but I think it is an aberration. My real fear is not for a war."

"What then?"

"It is that we will go on for years as we are now, with the bloodshed and the waste of resources and, yes, the risk of all-out war."

I've said elsewhere that Mutes do not do nonverbals. That they do not have faces, in the human sense. Rather the lack of animation suggests a mask. But there was something in Bon Selvan's eyes, and in her mask, that was utterly bleak. "I see," she said, "that you wonder why I asked you to come. I wanted to have you in front of me, to know whether the passion I detected in that interview last evening was real."

"It was real."

"I have never known a human up close. I've had a lifetime of listening to those who think humans are malevolent, dishonest, savage. That they, you, operate on a lower plane. Even your good friend Selotta thinks you and your friend Benedict are aberrations."

"I know."

"I see that you are returning to Salud Afar."

"Yes."

"When you get there, please assure Administrator Kilgore that there is a faction here, not only on Borkarat, but across the Assemblage, that is not happy with our current posture. We will do what we can to create a more flexible policy toward the Confederates. He must understand, though, that we cannot be seen as encouraging the Confederacy to go to the rescue of Salud Afar. Such a tactic on our part would surely be misread by them. But let him know we will do what we can."

"I will."

"Very good. One more thing you should be aware of: Your comments, which are being distributed throughout the Assemblage will be, for the majority of our citizens, their first opportunity to experience rapport with a human. I don't know how this will play out, but I think we could not have done better." She looked around at the flowers. "Are they not lovely?"

It was good to see the *Belle-Marie* again. We got in, closed the hatch, and she said, *"Hello, Chase."* I said hello back, went up onto the bridge, and climbed into my seat. It was a marvelous feeling to sit in a chair designed for my body size.

"Chase," she said. *"I have a text message from station ops."*

I suspected we were going to get an escort out of the system. "Let's see it," I said.

She put it on the board: CAPTAIN KOLPATH, THE *BELLE-MARIE* WILL BE THE THIRD PRIVATE VESSEL TO LEAVE TODAY FOR SALUD AFAR. ONE MORE IS SCHEDULED OUT LATER THIS AFTERNOON, AND

THREE TOMORROW. I THOUGHT YOU MIGHT LIKE TO KNOW. SIRIAN
KOSLO.

"*Koslo,*" said Belle, "*is the chief of operations.*"

A few minutes later we had a text message granting clearance to depart. I acknowledged, and asked that my regards be
passed to Mr. Koslo. Then I alerted Alex and waited for him to
get into the harness. When the green lamp came on, I released
the clamps and we moved away from the dock.

Forty-six minutes later we lined up with Moria and Salud
Afar and made our jump.

I didn't enjoy the flight back. By the time we arrived, Kilgore
would know that the talks had gone nowhere. The Confederacy was sending a few warships to help, and a handful of Mutes
were coming. That was it.

I made up my mind that I'd upgrade my license when I got
to Salud Afar; it was for class-C interstellars. They were the
smallest category, usually yachts like the *Belle-Marie*, and
commercial vehicles that hauled a few VIPs around. I'd want to
be able to handle some of the larger cargo ships. So, while we
charged back through interdimensional space, I spent much of
my time studying.

Alex, as usual, pored through archeological records and artifact inventories. I've mentioned before that he was not difficult to ride with. And he hadn't changed. When things went
badly, he didn't descend into morose self-pity as I think I did. I
can recall his reminding me that we didn't yet really know
the results of the diplomatic effort, and that it hadn't been
my responsibility in any case. Not that it mattered whose responsibility it was. My part of the mission had been to handle
transportation.

In any case, the ride was interminable. The weeks dragged
by, and I felt caught within the narrow confines of the ship. I
wandered through its spaces, inspecting the cargo area every
other day and checking the supplies in the lander. I spent extra
time in the workout room. With Alex, I toured ancient pal-
aces and historic structures. We floated down the Kiev canal,
and drifted through Jovian skies, on approach to Che Jolla

Base, during the days when it housed Markum Pierce, the poet-physicist whose diaries provided a brilliant record of the early colonies.

He took to asking me regularly if I was okay, if there was anything he could do. "Don't give up," he said. "It might still work out."

Hard to see how, I thought, barring divine intervention.

Finally, on the thirty-third day of the flight, it was over.

We came out of jump about forty hours from Salud Afar. It was actually good to see the nearly empty skies again. Varesnikov and Naramitsu were both visible. And the galactic rim. And, off to port, Callistra. Blue and brilliant and happy as if nothing had happened.

Belle's comm lights came on. *"We have traffic."*

"More than one?"

"Still coming in. One from the Administrator. Other than that, no end in sight at the moment."

I called Alex up front. "Put the Administrator on," I told Belle reluctantly. "Let's see what he has to say."

A Kilgore avatar, of course. He was in his office, and I knew as soon as I saw him that something very good had happened. *"Congratulations, Chase,"* he said. *"We didn't get anywhere with the Confederacy, but it looks as if every Mute who can beg, buy, or borrow a ship, is on the way. We're in your debt."* He looked over at Alex. *"You, too, Alex."*

"What happened?" he asked.

Again, of course, there was the inevitable delay as the transmission traveled to Salud Afar, and the reply came back. In the meantime, the avatar simply froze.

"We've also been informed," he said, *"that several corporations in the Assemblage have suspended other activities and are now in the process of turning out superluminals specially designed to help us."*

"Chase's interview?" asked Alex. He was beaming.

"Who knows? It certainly didn't hurt." His features melted into a grin. It was the first time I'd seen him look happy.

"So," I asked, "will there be enough? Ships, I mean?"

"We'll be able to move a substantially larger portion of the

population than we expected. Maybe as much as five percent.
We've gotten some resistance, by the way. A lot of people don't
want to ride with Mutes."

"Mr. Administrator, I'm sure that part of the problem will
sort itself out. But I was talking about the shield. What's happening with the shield?"

"Ah. The shield. No. Unfortunately, everything we project
indicates that we will still come up short. Even if the Confeder-
ates were willing to forget about the eleven ships and send their
entire fleet instead, which they aren't, it would still be a hit-or-
miss proposition. We've had to make a decision. Waste valuable
time and resources on a project that is unlikely to come to-
gether, or use everything we can get our hands on to move
people off-world. Anyhow, I wanted to let you know we appreci-
ate your help."

We started working our way through the other transmissions.
They came from mothers, grandparents, politicians, owners of
bars, kids in classrooms, almost all saying thanks. They'd heard
the sound version of the interview and were giving me credit for
the improvised fleet from Borkarat and the Assemblage, which
was already en route. Universities wanted to bestow academic
credentials, somebody was going to name a foundation for me,
and several towns offered real estate if I would consent to move
there. There would be a Chase Kolpath Park in a place called
Dover Cliff, and a historical site on Huanko Island, provided I
agreed to visit. I was offered endorsement for lines of clothing,
perfumes, and games. And I should mention upward of two hundred messages from guys who wanted to take me to dinner.

There were also a few crank messages accusing me of treason, of consorting with the enemy, of encouraging alien lunatics who wanted nothing more than to destroy the human race
and carry off our children.

It was usually Alex who got all the attention. This time,
though, nobody mentioned him. Nobody extended him any
credit in the proceedings. Nobody proposed to him. Nobody
even threatened him.

"It's the way it is with celebrity," I said, magnanimously.
"Up one day, down the next."

He laughed. "You earned it."

There was also a newswrap from Fenn Redfield on Rimway. Some administration officials at home were saying I'd been disloyal and were calling for an investigation. "Maybe I should look at some of the local real estate after all," I said.

Alex laughed. "You're a hero. Before this is over, it's White-side who's going to have to get out of town."

It was three hours after midnight on shipboard when we docked at Samuels. We locked down, opened the hatch, walked out into the egress tube, and were greeted by a small crowd that applauded when they saw us. Among them I counted half a dozen Mutes.

It was a good feeling. Maybe we were making progress. We waved and signed a few autographs. Then, when we were walking away, one of the Ashiyyur came up beside me. A female. I stopped and looked up at her. She said, "Chase—"

It was too loud. "Yes?"

She fiddled with the voice box. "Sorry. I can't control the volume on this thing."

"It's okay. What can I do for you?"

"There was a man back there. Who wants you dead. 'You' being both of you, but especially your friend, Alex."

Behind us, the crowd was dispersing. We didn't see anybody we recognized. "Who was it?" Alex asked. "Did you get a name?"

"No. Couldn't read it." She turned and looked. "He's gone now. He had a cane. Walked with a limp."

FORTY

Praying will not help, Ormond. Someone needs to do something.

—*Nightwalk*

It had to be Wexler.

Alex and I exchanged glances. "I guess he's still upset," said Alex.

"You really think he's out to kill us?"

"I don't know. What's the best possible construction you could put on what she told us?"

We started making our way out of the area when I heard someone sobbing. The sounds came from the crowd directly ahead. They were gathered around a boarding tube. We saw a few men and women and a lot of kids, and everybody was hugging everybody else. A couple of operational people were trying to move them up the tube. Move the *kids* up the tube.

I asked a bystander what was going on. "It's part of the evacuation program," she said. "They're taking the kids to Sanctum."

"Parents stay here?" I asked.

"Pretty much. Two or three mothers go along, depending on the capacity of the ship." Some of the younger children were trying to hang on to the adults. They had to be pried loose. We listened to promises about how Mommy and Daddy will see you soon, go along with the nice lady, Jan, and everything will be fine. Some of them descended into hysterics. The struggle was still going on as we left the area.

"What do we do about Wexler?" I asked, grateful to be able to change our focus. "There's a security office down on the lower level."

"Not a good idea."

"Why not?"

"If he's watching us, and I'd be surprised if he isn't, he'll see us go in. If that happens, we'll lose our advantage."

"Which is what?"

"He doesn't know we've been warned. We should let the security office know, but do it by link."

"Okay."

"Try to look happy, Chase."

I smiled and started whistling.

"Happy," he said. "Not goofy."

"Right. What else do we do?"

"Where's the restaurant?"

"Sandstone's is just up ahead."

"Okay. Let's go in. We'll do it from there."

"Wouldn't it be a better idea just to get on the shuttle and get away from here?"

"We're going to have to deal with him at some point. Once we start running, we'll be doing it permanently."

"Okay. But I'm not sure it's a good idea to sit in Sandstone's, where he can get a clean shot at us. Why not at least get out of sight?"

"Wexler's a survivor. He'll want to take us down, then have time to take the shuttle groundside. That means he'll try to get to us in a private place."

It made sense. "You think Krestoff is with him?" I was looking around, trying to do it surreptitiously. Not easy.

"We better assume she is."

We went into Sandstone's and got a table back in the corner, away from the windows. No booth, because we might need to move quickly. "You still have the scrambler, Chase?" he asked.

It was in the utility bag slung over one shoulder.

"All right. Let's get a reservation at the hotel."

"We'll have to use our real names." The secondary account had lapsed.

"That's okay. Maybe it's just as well to make it easy for the lunatics to find us." He braced his chin on one hand while he considered the problem. I called the hotel. They had a suite available.

"No," said Alex. "Two rooms."

He ordered drinks. Then he called the security office. He identified himself and told them there were two wanted criminals running loose on the station.

"And who are these criminals?" asked a female voice. Its owner sounded skeptical.

"Mikel Wexler." He spelled it for her. "And Maria Krestoff."

"Okay. How do you know they're on the station?"

"I saw them."

"You're sure?"

"Yes."

"All right. One moment, please."

The restaurant was about half-full. But I saw no familiar faces either inside or out in the concourse.

"Ah, yes. Here's Wexler. Hmmm. Okay, Mr. Benedict. You have a personal acquaintance with these people, do you?"

"Yes."

"With both of them?"

"That's correct."

"Very good. Are you staying on the station?"

"Yes."

"You're at the hotel?"

"That's correct."

"All right, thank you. We'll keep an eye out. And we'll be in touch."

We sat looking at each other. "What do you think?" I said.

"Well, they'll arrest them if they happen to run into them."

While we tried our drinks and contemplated ordering some real food, I let the service people know that we'd changed our plans and they should route our bags to the hotel.

                              *   *   *

An hour or so later we strolled into the lobby. This was the point at which my nerves began to work on me. They'd put us on the fourth floor and I remember half-expecting to find Wexler waiting inside the elevator, or around the corner, as we headed for our rooms. I dug the scrambler out in the hallway. We checked my room. With weapon drawn. We were not going to underestimate the good doctor.

When we were satisfied, I put my bags away, turned on the HV, and left the lights on. Tried to make it look as if I was in.

Then we went through a similar procedure in Alex's room.

If it seems that we were overreacting, please keep in mind that we'd been through a lot. Anyhow, Alex said he had no doubt we'd have visitors within the next few hours.

He said hello to the AI, whose name was Aia. She had a soft female voice. "Aia," he said, "can you do an impersonation of Administrator Kilgore?"

"You mean," she said, *"can I reproduce his voice?"*

"Yes."

"Of course." She gave us a sample, claiming that liberty was a boon to all persons everywhere. She delivered it in his rich deep baritone.

"Good," said Alex. "Perfect. I'm going to want you to do something for me."

"If it is within my capacity, sir."

The rooms were smaller than those you'd get in a hotel of a similar class groundside. But they were as attractive. Everything was done in silk and lavender.

We even had a balcony overlooking the concourse. Above us, the overhead was transparent and provided a spectacular view of the outside. At the moment, we were looking out at the rim of the world, illuminated by a setting—or rising—sun. I wasn't sure which.

I walked out through a glass door and inspected it. The balconies were connected by a narrow ledge. I looked at it for a long time and decided even Krestoff would not have been able to negotiate it. I went back inside, closed the glass door, and drew the curtains.

We talked for a while. Watched a report on the evacuation. Everybody was excited by the help coming in from the Confederacy and the Assemblage. The shield barely made an appearance in the conversations, other than as an example of the desperation of world leaders. *"It was never plausible, Jay,"* said one commentator. *"They'd have had to pull the entire evacuation fleet to work on it, with next to no chance of success. I think the route they've chosen, moving as many people off-world as they can, and concentrating on building shelters, is the way to go."*

We didn't talk much, and when we did, we kept our voices down. We did not want anyone outside the door to realize there was a second person in the room. We didn't really expect to fool Wexler, but it could do no harm.

I eventually drifted off to sleep in my chair. When I woke, Alex pointed out that it was early morning on the station, but we were in dinner mode.

"Sure," I said.

He picked up the hotel guide. "Maybe we should have it sent up."

"Why? I thought we decided we were safer in public places."

"We have to go out in the corridor and take the elevator. If they're going to try anything, I want them to have to come to us."

"Okay."

"And we might try just ordering one dinner. Mine."

"Because I'm in my room."

"Good. Yes." He called down. Ordered the special, with a glass of white wine, and a cinnamon bun. We waited, heard the sound of the elevator, heard footsteps in the hall. Then a door opened somewhere, and everything was quiet again.

We went through another false alarm before finally getting a gentle tap at the door. Alex signaled me to move to the bathroom. When I was out of sight, he opened the door.

"Good evening, sir." The voice was not Wexler's.

Alex moved back out of the way. An attendant carried a tray and a small bottle of wine into the room. He left the door ajar behind him, and I angled myself to watch.

He set the tray on the coffee table, opened the wine bottle, and produced a glass, which he filled. He set down a cloth napkin and the silverware. Alex tipped him, he said thank you, and was gone, closing the door behind him.

Alex sat down in front of it. "Well," he said, "that didn't work."

"No, it didn't."

He looked down at the dinner. Steaming fish, a vegetable, and toast. "I'll split it with you."

"Or perhaps with *me*." The voice came from the far end of the room. Krestoff.

She stood just inside the balcony curtains. Holding a blaster. I'd underestimated her. "Don't make any sudden moves," she said. "Kolpath, come out here, where I can see you better. Yes, that's good. Right there.

"Benedict, get up, do it slowly, and go to the door."

Alex pushed the tray aside and got to his feet. I was still standing. "This isn't a good idea," he said. "You're just getting yourself in deeper."

"Do as I say. Just turn the knob so you release the catch. Don't try to open the door."

Alex complied.

"Now step back into the center of the room. With your little sex object." She spared me a brief smile.

Alex came back in. The door opened, and Wexler entered. He was carrying a bottle. Hard liquor of some sort. "Alex," he said. "And Chase. It's so good to see you again." He pushed the door shut and took a scrambler from his pocket. "I was afraid for a while that you might not come back."

"You're going to get caught," said Alex. "Why go through this?"

"I'll get a measure of satisfaction seeing you pay the price." He looked at the sofa and the uneaten meal. "Please, both of you, sit. Finish what you were doing."

We stood looking back at him.

"*Sit.*"

We sat. Krestoff strolled in, leaving the balcony door ajar. She was grinning at me. "Kolpath," she said. "*You're* the one I've been looking for. Mikel, I'd like this one for myself. Can we arrange it?" She kept her eyes locked on me. "How about that, honey? Just you and me?" She put the blaster down on the seat of one of the chairs. "We'll put the toys away and settle things up close."

Wexler shook his head. "Maria," he said, "don't get careless. You'll get your chance."

She recovered her weapon and took a seat on the edge of the chair. Alex paid no attention to her. "What exactly do you want?"

"You were out there when they were loading the *Quevalla*. You should have a sense by now of the pain you've caused."

"Don't be absurd, Doctor. Some of those tears expressed relief. People getting their kids out of harm's way."

"I didn't mean *them*, you imbecile. Those scenes are recorded. Broadcast all over the world. How many people do you think are watching whose kids *won't* be moved? Who are still going to be sitting in the cities when the Thunderbolt comes? They have three years of misery in front of them. All because you and your partner wanted to go hunting for glory. Damn you." His gaze now encompassed me as well. "Damn you both."

"I think you're getting a little overwrought."

"Two billion people will not get off-world no matter how big the fleet. Two *billion*, Alex. You've taken three years of normal living from each of them. Do the math."

"Keeping this kind of secret was not your call."

I could hear Wexler breathing. "Alex, are you really so stupid that you think I made that decision on my own?"

"I know there were others. That's not the point."

"It's a democratic government. Or *was*. I suspect it'll be coming apart now."

Alex tried the toast. "You're implying Kilgore knew all along."

"Am I really? Maybe you're not so slow-witted after all." He sighed. "Well, I suppose we should get on with it."

Alex lowered his gaze to the scrambler. "You're not really going to use that thing in here, are you?"

Wexler shook his head. "Of course not. Unless I'm forced to. But you're going to have an accident."

"Oh? What did you have in mind?"

"You're not aware of it at the moment, but you and the young lady here are having a party. At this very moment. Unfortunately, you're both drinking too much. And, as these things will happen, she's half out of her clothes." He turned to me. "Kolpath, take off your blouse."

I hesitated.

"*Now*, honey," said Krestoff.

I opened it. I had nothing beneath it.

Wexler picked up two water glasses from a cabinet, opened the bottle, and filled them with a cocoa-colored liquid. He set them down on the coffee table. "This is *korala*. It's rather strong. A glass of it will leave you both a bit more accommodating than you are at the moment." He looked back at me. "Please, Kolpath, get out of that terrible-looking blouse." He stood back while Alex reached for the glasses and passed one to me.

"What will happen here is that you two are enjoying yourselves, but unfortunately you will drink too much, and, regrettably, you'll both fall from the balcony." He shrugged. "It's a sad end for two who have done so much for Salud Afar, but you will have the consolation of dying in each other's arms. And, in addition, I think you will find the *korala* will ease the trauma."

"We're not lovers," I said.

"Really? Well, more's the shame. But nobody would believe that. Now, please, my dear, the blouse. I really must insist."

The blouse was tucked into my slacks. "Do you mind if I get up? I can't get it off sitting here."

He considered it. "Of course," he said. "But do please be careful."

I wanted to clear my angle on Krestoff. I didn't want to have to climb over the coffee table to get to her.

Alex also stood. Wexler signaled for him to sit back down, but Alex ignored him. "Whatever happened to the hero of the Revolution?" he said. "How did you become a cheap bureaucrat? How did you get bought off?"

"That's enough," said Wexler.

Alex crossed behind me, clearing his own angle on Wexler. "You've no compunctions about sacrificing anybody for your bosses, do you? Even Vicki Greene?"

Vicki Greene was the start button for the AI.

Kilgore's voice broke in: *"Wexler, have you no decency at all? How dare you?"*

The voice was calm, angry, disappointed. Not bad for an AI.

It distracted them both for the moment we needed. I was across the room before Krestoff could turn her attention back to me. I knocked her off the chair. She tried to bring the blaster around as she hit the floor, but I grabbed the hand and simultaneously got in a punch to the gut. She doubled up, and the weapon blew out the ceiling.

We traded punches, and I smashed the hand with the weapon against the wall. Above us, somebody yelled *hey*. And an alarm went off.

The blaster came loose. We rolled around on the floor, each of us trying to get hold of it. Finally, she kicked it away. I grabbed the wine bottle and brought it down on her head. She hit me with a lamp. "Bitch," she said. Even under those circumstances, she kept her voice level.

We got more or less to our feet and traded a few punches. Then she fell over a footstool, and I got to the blaster, scooped it up, and turned to see how Alex was doing. Not so well, it turned out. His fight had stumbled out onto the balcony. Although Wexler was the older and smaller of the two, he looked considerably more experienced in personal combat than Alex was. Meanwhile, Krestoff was getting to her feet again, making comments about my parentage. I leveled the weapon at her. "Stay put," I said.

She glared at me. "Afraid to take me on?" she asked.

"Hell," I said, "I'm tired of you." Wexler's scrambler had fallen to the floor. I kept her at a distance while I picked it up. I was trying to juggle the two weapons and change the setting on the scrambler to nonlethal. She saw her chance and jumped me. I whacked her with the blaster. She went to her knees, and I hit her again.

It was a good clean shot.

Wexler had Alex bent over the balcony rail. Beyond them I could see the dome and the sky, with Callistra just about to set behind the planet. Somewhere music was playing. The alarm was still wailing, and someone began pounding on the door. I could hear voices in the corridor.

Alex and Wexler banged against the rail, creating the possibility they might both go over. I got the setting I wanted on the scrambler and leveled it at Wexler. "Back off," I said. "Let him go."

The guy had a suicide impulse. He made an effort to throw Alex over. I didn't want to fire because I couldn't be sure which one I'd hit. So instead I went after him, reversed the weapon, and hit him in the head with it. Anybody who's used a scrambler knows it's light, and hitting somebody with it doesn't do much more than make the target angry. Wexler slammed me with an elbow and sent me reeling. Then he turned back to Alex. The guy was a nut.

But Alex got a punch in and threw him momentarily off-balance. Meantime, I guess I'd had enough. I charged full tilt into Wexler.

I'm not sure whether I intended to push him over the side. I was in a rage by then, and I remember thinking there was a chance he'd land on somebody. Whatever really caused it, he crashed back against the rail and grabbed Alex. I banged into him again and apparently caught him off-balance. Either that or I was stronger than I realized. He went over the top, flailed wildly, grabbed me, and very nearly took me with him.

He had my arm. Clung to it, the whole time screaming at me. I was hanging on to the railing, halfway over, when Alex came to my rescue. He pulled me back. Hung on while Wexler began to slip away. Ignored him when he screamed for help.

Then he was gone, one last dying shriek, suddenly cut off.

I stood there for a few seconds, not saying anything. I looked to see whether Wexler had done any damage below. A crowd was gathering, but nobody else was down.

Somebody was still banging on the door. I went back inside and opened it.

FOrTY-ONe

The house was closing in on us. Doors were slamming, windows were shutting. "Get out," she said. "While you can."

"But, Ilena," I cried, "there is no way."

"Find one. Or make one."

—*Nightwalk*

The security people came. Then the CSS. They took Krestoff away, finally subdued. They collected Wexler's body. Asked some questions. Took notes. Moved Alex to a different room. Set a guard, just in case.

An hour or so after they'd gone away, we got a call from one of Kilgore's staffers. *"We heard about what happened,"* she said. *"We wanted you to know we appreciate the strain you've been under. And we're glad the danger is past."*

"Thank you," said Alex.

"When an opportunity presents itself, we'll find an appropriate way to express our gratitude. Meantime, if there's anything we can do for you, don't hesitate to get in touch." She gave us a private code that would allow us to reach her.

We never did eat dinner that night. Alex's meal had gotten as cold as his appetite. We went down instead and sat in the Pilots' Club. It was empty. "They're all out running refugees to Sanctum," said the host.

We had a couple of drinks. Two or three people came in. Then, after about an hour, my link sounded. *"Ms. Kolpath?"*

"Yes."

"I'm with the Coalition Transport Authority. As I'm sure you're aware, we're moving people off-world. I'm sorry to say that, acting in accord with executive order 504911, we've impounded your interstellar."

"You've already done that once."

"Really? Well, however that may be, we're doing it again."

"I wish you wouldn't."

"I understand completely. In any case, we have no discretion in the matter. We'll be making some improvements in the ship, and we'd like you to remain as the captain, and help in the evacuation effort. Can we count on you to assist us?"

Alex shook his head. "I wonder what happens to people who *don't* have friends in high places."

"Sure," I said. "I'll help."

"Excellent. Can you leave tonight?"

"Tonight?"

"We've no time to waste, Ms. Kolpath."

Alex was signaling me that he'd call Kilgore's people. Get it killed.

"Sure," I said. "Can you give me an hour?"

"We can do better than that. Your passengers are already in the station. We've scheduled you out at four."

That finished the drinking, at least for me. We sat in desultory silence, contemplating a bleak future. Three years hauling refugees for me, and God knew what for Alex. While the world slowly tumbled toward oblivion.

When the time came, we said good-bye. I left him alone in the Pilots' Club, the guy who'd figured it out and warned the world, who'd made the rescue effort possible. He wouldn't be allowed back in without me to escort him.

I went back to my room and got my gear, much of which, fortunately, I hadn't unpacked. I sent it down to the loading dock and checked out of the hotel. Then I headed for the operations center. If I was going to be taking people to Sanctum, it seemed like a good idea to find out where the place was.

Fourteen thousand light-years, in the general direction of the galactic rim. It was one of eleven worlds in the system, and its sun was a yellow dwarf. Of course, at that range, it was invisible to the naked eye. I got my vectoring data and headed for the ship, which was waiting at the dock when I arrived. A technician assured me the *Belle-Marie* was all set to go, that they'd made some adjustments inside, and stored food and water for the flight.

Each boarding area was designed to service two ships. A second vehicle was also preparing for departure. It was small, smaller even than the *Belle-Marie*, but it bore Ashiyyurean markings. I stood for a minute, watching while four kids were separated from a small group of adults and led on board by a young woman. A female Mute stood off to one side. The captain, I suspected. The last of the five passengers disappeared into the tube, and the Mute hesitated. She and the remaining adults regarded one another with caution. And uncertainty. Then she raised one long arm in farewell. Or good luck. Or God bless. The humans waved back. A scene like that, a few months earlier, would have been unthinkable.

We boarded the *Belle-Marie*, and the technician showed me six additional acceleration couches, doubling *Belle*'s carrying capacity. And they'd upgraded life support. "When you get back," he said, "we'll put in an extra washroom. In the meantime, you'll have to get by as best you can. Let us know"—he didn't crack a smile—"if we can do anything else." He checked something in his notebook, said, "Okay, that's good," to no one in particular, and started for the hatch. He put one foot into the tube, stopped, and turned. "By the way, your AI will have the names of your passengers, and the time of their arrival, which I think will be just a few minutes now. It'll also have contact information for when you reach Sanctum."

He left and I sat down and said hello to Belle.

"Hi, Chase," she said.

I was expecting another load of children. I was relieved when a group of technicians and engineers showed up. I know that sounds hard-hearted, but the prospect of riding all the way to Sanctum with kids in a state of near hysteria was just more than

I wanted to deal with. I wondered how the Mute in the other ship, who'd be even more tuned in to it than I would, could handle it. It occurred to me for the first time that maybe they had an off switch.

My passengers piled in, and I introduced myself. We could all see that privacy would be at a minimum and we'd have to live with make-do accommodations. Within a few minutes we were on our way. And I discovered this flight would be as painful, in its way, as the shipload of kids I'd anticipated. My passengers were all leaving behind families, lovers, friends, for whom there was no room on the *Belle-Marie*, or probably on any other ship during the next three years. The kids, and the adults who cared for them, were getting all the priority. Nobody could argue with that, but that didn't alleviate the pain. So my passengers would go out to Sanctum and do their assignments. Afterward, they'd have a choice: They could stay, and be clear of the Thunderbolt. Or they could go back to Salud Afar with next to no hope of being evacuated later, and take their chances. They were, understandably, being encouraged to stay at Sanctum.

It was a long flight. We had to establish a sleeping schedule to provide accommodations for everyone. Despite the supplementary life-support setup, the air became oppressive. There were always two people sitting on the bridge. The rest—other than those logging sack time—were spread around the common room, a few relegated to using the deck because there wasn't enough seating. The electronic game systems didn't work too well under crowded conditions, and I made a mental note to bring some cards next time.

They took it in stride. Everybody understood that the stakes were high, but the narrow bulkheads pressed on us all. We scheduled the entertainment, one show in the afternoon, one in the evening. We ran musicals, comedies, and thrillers. Nothing heavy. Strictly lightweight stuff. We even resurrected bingo, which, Alex tells me, was invented by the Dellacondans more than two thousand years ago. And might even be older than that. (In fact, Rainbow Enterprises had recently sold a bingo set from that era for a small fortune.)

And we talked. Before we were finished, everybody's life story came out and got put on the table. One woman had been abandoned by her parents, one of the guys had lost a son in an accident at sea. One of the structural foundations techs started having breathing problems halfway across. It was a scary business, but fortunately extra oxygen tanks had been put on board, and we were able to bring him out of it. But he was a concern the rest of the way.

When, on the thirteenth day, we jumped out into Sanctum space, everybody cheered. I could have arranged to have a patrol vehicle pick up the foundations tech, but he insisted he was okay, and he wanted to stay with the *Belle-Marie*. I went along with it, and he had another spell the next day. We got him into the hands of the medics okay, but it threw a scare into everybody.

While I was in orbit around Sanctum, we picked up a transmission from Number 17 Parkway, in which Kilgore thanked his friends in the Confederacy for the support they'd been sending. He included the fleet, but he was really talking about the private citizens who had swarmed to his aid. I wondered if he'd been smart enough to send a similar message to the Assemblage.

Sanctum was, of course, a work in progress. Even the space station was still under construction. The world didn't have a moon, so it was unlikely to become a permanent habitat. But it had oceans and open plains and forests. The only look I got at groundside was from orbit, though, so I didn't see much. Lights were visible on the dark side. And they downloaded a tour of the place for me. Although I never did anything more than take a cursory glance. You've seen one forest, you've seen them all.

I'd have liked to stay a couple of days. Get out of the ship for a while. But I had become part of the official schedule, and there were passengers waiting for me back at Samuels. So they serviced *Belle* while I stretched out for a couple of hours on a real bed. Then I was on my way back to Salud Afar.

For the people hauling refugees out to Sanctum, it would be an endless stream. For three years, I expected there would be nothing else in my life, two weeks in a jammed ship, two weeks in an empty one, hauling people who were leaving behind everything, and often every*one*, they loved.

I wondered whether Wexler might not have been right.

* * *

When I got back to Samuels, there was no trace of Alex. I left a message saying hello, sorry to have missed you, catch you next time. They gave me almost *three* hours to relax, then I was back at the boarding area to pick up my next set of passengers. They were kids this time. All four years of age or under, plus two mothers. They screamed and cried their farewells, and we finally got them all on board. I took a deep breath, and we launched.

The kids cried round the clock. The mothers did what they could, and showed, I thought, endless patience. I tried to help to the extent I could. But none of us knew how to calm the ongoing hysteria.

By the third day, they both had bloodshot eyes. "Got to be a better way to do this," I told them. I decided a couple of cats might help, and I made a mental note to put in a request.

The older of the two mothers, an attractive blonde, commented that they only had to put up with it for two weeks. And the other one immediately dissolved into tears.

After I delivered them, I sent a message to the people running the evacuation, ordering my cats, and informing them that, even though I understood the reasoning behind trying to save the kids first, separating children from their mothers was cruel.

I knew that if they responded at all, which was unlikely, they'd ask me for an alternative. And of course I wouldn't have one. It didn't matter. They never asked.

I made the jump back into Salud Afar space and was beginning to wonder whether I could really continue like this for three years. I knew they were trying to train more pilots to give us a break in the routine, but it would take a while. I was about two days out, sitting feeling sorry for myself when Belle came to life: *"Chase."*

"Yes, ma'am. What've you got?"

"I'm not sure. Intruder alert, maybe."

"Intruder alert?"

"I'm scanning a lot of ships. Warships."

"Where?"

"Most are near Salud Afar."

"What kind of ships?"

"All kinds. Cruisers, escorts, destroyers—thousands *of them."*

"Hell, that's *good* news. Belle, the Confederacy has come to the rescue, after all."

"Chase, they're not *Confederates. They're Mutes."*

FOrTY-TWO

Whatever happens from this moment on, Holly, remember that I was here when you needed me.

—Nightwalk

"Belle, are they reacting to us?"

"They know we're here."

"Okay, give me manual."

"You have it."

They were all around us. None that I could see without the scopes. But the kinds of weapons these things carried made that dim consolation. "Let me know if we light up, Belle."

"Of course."

"Okay, give me a channel to the station."

"You're open."

"Samuels, this is the *Belle-Marie*. Approaching from Sanctum. What is status, please?"

"You'll have to get in line, Belle-Marie. *We see you. Hold steady on present course. I'll give you instructions in a few minutes."*

"Ops, I'm out here surrounded by Mutes."

"That's affirmative. Don't worry about it."

"Why not?"

"They're here to help."

"How do you know?"

"They said so."

"You believe them?"

"What's the alternative?" He signed off. Moments later he was back. *"You're Chase Kolpath, right?"*

"Yes."

"Okay. We're going to move you to the front of the line, Kolpath. You're being taken off assignment. We'll have a replacement waiting. When you dock, please report to the ops center."

"Samuels, can you tell me why?"

"Don't know why, ma'am. Just come on in."

The head of the line doesn't mean a whole lot when you're two days out. But I proceeded accordingly. On the way in, I picked up reports that the evacuation was going to go a lot more quickly, and that work was moving ahead on a second, larger, space station. Meanwhile, more shuttles were coming online. Spaceports were being designated around the globe, where landers could descend to pick up passengers. Ships coming in from the Assemblage had already arrived at Sanctum, carrying supplies and engineers.

I got in as quickly as I could, burning extra fuel on the way, and reported to the chief of the watch. He said he was proud to meet me, told me a private shuttle was waiting, and handed me two sealed envelopes. One contained the following: *Celebration tonight (the 20th) at the Sariyavo Hotel. Your attendance mandatory. Congratulations. Tao Kilgore.*

"You Sirian Koslo?" I asked.

He grinned "Yes."

"Thanks."

"My pleasure. Go get 'em, Chase."

The other was from Alex: *Chase, they're telling us that if you make a reasonable jump, you'll be able to get to the Sariyavo for the party. If not, the Administrator promises me they'll throw another one tomorrow. Or over the weekend. Or whatever it takes. You're the lady of the hour.*

If the situation had improved, I wouldn't have known it charging through Samuels. The children were still there, surrounded by dismayed adults, waiting for their rides to arrive. There was still only a handful of Mutes in the concourse. And, considering the way the locals steered clear of them, it was just as well.

I was halfway to the shuttle launch area when two CSS agents scooped me up. "Heard you were on the way, Ms. Kolpath," one of them said. "If you'll follow us, please."

I love playing the VIP. They opened the hatch for me, the pilot asked to shake my hand, and they provided a box of goodies to munch on on the way down. My luggage arrived, and they stowed it in cargo. Was there anything else they could do for me?

"Sure," I said. "What's it about?"

"You don't know?"

"Should I?"

"Chase, you're the woman who brought the Mutes."

There were no other passengers. As soon as I was belted down, we were on our way. We passed through some storm clouds and arrived at the Marinopolis spaceport in a driving rainstorm. They transferred me to a government skimmer, and we took off and headed east toward the center of the city. Fifteen minutes later we landed on the roof of what I assumed to be the Sariyavo, where I was handed over to two other agents. They collected my luggage, refused to allow me to touch it, took me inside, down one floor, and opened a door to a luxury suite. Lights were on, candy had been placed on the bed, music was playing softly. "Your room while you're here, ma'am," one of them said. She opened a closet to reveal an exquisite black gown. "I think you'll find it's the right size."

"It's nice," I said. And I know that was a dumb response, but I wasn't functioning at full capacity.

"They're just getting started in the main ballroom. When you're ready, call us, and we'll escort you down." She smiled. "Take your time. The party won't really start until you get there."

I could hear the noise before I got out of the elevator. Music. People laughing and cheering. The agents took me to the entrance and turned me over to one of the best-looking guys I've ever seen. Mash Kavalovski. He was the son of a treasury secretary from one of the associated states. The music stopped, and the crowd cleared a space for us. He kissed my hand, and said he was honored to meet "the hero of the hour." A cheer went up. A few Mutes were sprinkled through the crowd. Times were changing quickly.

Mash danced with me while everybody backed away. Then they all joined in. When the music stopped, Mash handed me over to Alex.

"Alex," I said, "how've you been? I missed you."

He was all smiles. "I missed you, too, love. How was life with the Transit Authority?"

Somebody brought me a purple-colored drink that left me feeling as if I owned the world. There were more introductions to people from around the globe. To more people from the Confederacy. To fleet officers. And to Mutes, some in uniform, some not. Eventually I wound up back in Mash's arms. "Chase," he said, "I don't suppose I could talk you into running off to the Golden Isles, could I?"

I wasn't very familiar with what passed for dancing in Marinopolis, but I'm fairly flexible. Mash and I were gliding around the floor when the music changed tempo, slowed, and switched to "Time of Glory." It was the cue for the Administrator to make his entrance.

And there he came, through a side door, still in conversation with someone. He broke it off quickly, mounted a rostrum, and waited for quiet. The music stopped. Everyone turned to watch. "Good evening, ladies and gentlemen," he said. "I'd like to welcome you all to this special celebration in honor of some very special people. These have been a pretty happy few weeks. And we have more good news tonight.

"The good news first: The Confederacy has announced that the bulk of its fleet is being committed—" It was as far as he got. The crowd applauded loudly, and for several minutes it would not stop. Finally, when it did, he proceeded: "—The bulk of the Confederate fleet, virtually all of it, is coming here to assist us—"

The applause started again.

Kilgore tried to continue, but his voice got drowned out. The crowd was out of control, cheering, clapping, embracing each other. I got hugged and kissed and passed around, and I didn't mind it a bit.

Eventually he got control: "—There's more—" he said. "Ladies and gentlemen, it's my happy duty to inform you that we believe we now have the resources to put a shield in front of the world. Even as we speak, work has begun."

If the other announcements had gotten everyone excited, that one blew the roof off. The Administrator took a few sheets of notepaper from his pocket, glanced at them, shrugged, and put them back. It was, I thought, not a time for details.

While the hall continued to rock, he shook hands with everyone he could reach, including several of the Mutes. Those who were not in fleet uniforms wore brilliantly colored robes. I knew enough about them now to understand bright colors reflected good times.

Eventually, the audience subsided. "There's something else," he said. "The Coalition wants to recognize some of the people who made this night possible." An aide wheeled a table out, up an incline in the side of the rostrum, and placed it beside him. There were medals on the table. With ribbons.

"The Grand Award of the Coalition is bestowed for outstanding service. It has been given to only four individuals during the entire thirty-year history of the Coalition. We will double that number tonight.

"To Alex Benedict, who was first to grasp what had happened, and whose quick action to bring it to our attention made it possible to confront the problem. Alex, would you come forward, please?"

Alex loved public recognition. Well, in all honesty, who doesn't? He strode through the crowd and up the three steps of the rostrum. The Administrator examined the medals, selected one, and placed it against his breast. He let go and took a moment to admire the award. "Thank you, Alex," he said.

Kilgore invited him to speak. Alex looked out over the crowd. "It's an honor," he said, "to have been in a position to assist the people of Salud Afar."

More applause. And the Administrator picked up a second medal. "Is Chase Kolpath in the audience, please? Chase, are you out there?"

My heart stopped.

Now, I'm not going to pretend I didn't think I'd made a major contribution to what was happening. But I didn't expect to get any recognition for it. Usually the recognition goes to Alex, Alex says something nice about me while he's accepting the award, and that's the end of it. And it struck me as I left Mash on the edge of the dance floor and walked forward that he hadn't mentioned my role. *He'd known.*

I mounted the steps. Kilgore gazed happily out at the crowd. "I'm not sure where we'd have been without Chase. She did much to bring the Ashiyyur and the Confederates here tonight. And she was largely responsible for sidestepping efforts by a rogue unit of this government to keep the Callistra event secret." He smiled at me. "We'll always think of her as the lady who rode the taxicab into orbit."

Of course I hadn't had the acceleration to achieve orbit, but that seemed picky at the moment.

He pressed my medal to my gown and gave me the floor. I tend to get stage fright, so I just said thanks and hustled back down off the podium.

"Next," said Kilgore, "the Coalition would like to recognize the lady who helped mobilize support for us in the Assemblage: Bon Selvan. Bon, would you come forward, please?"

I hadn't realized she was there. The crowd quieted as she strode across the dance floor. The three steps up to the podium didn't fit her very well, so she simply ignored them and climbed up in one stride. It broke what might have been an awkward moment. There was some laughter, then a wave of applause. Kilgore held her medal and looked up at her. The audience laughed again, as did Kilgore. He couldn't reach an appropriate place on the robe, so she bent down, and he smiled and attached the medal. Then he got serious. "I don't know what to say, Proctor Selvan, except that we will always be grateful to you and your companions. We know it wasn't easy to do what you did. And that the Ashiyyur were willing to take a risk in sending their fleet here. I hope this will be the beginning, as someone once said, of a long and beautiful friendship."

She turned to face the audience. "Thank you, Mr. Administrator. Thank you all. We share your sentiments. Unfortunately, our joint history has not been an admirable one. Let us begin today. Let us make this a first step on the long road to cooperation and harmony."

"The final award," said Kilgore, "recognizes the contribution of a young lady from Rimway, who came here seeking inspiration, and who discovered the terrible danger that was rushing toward us. She sacrificed her life and a brilliant career in an effort to warn us. This award will be placed in a special station in the Coalition Hall of Fame. Ladies and gentlemen, we all owe a great debt of thanks to Vicki Greene."

The celebration lasted well into the night. I danced with Alex and Mash and half the males in the place, including several of the Mutes. I won't try to describe how that must have looked. You'd have had to see it.

I talked with Proctor Selvan, and received an invitation to visit her whenever I could. "How did all this happen?" I asked her. "How is it possible?"

She gazed serenely down at me. "It was too good an opportunity to miss. We knew that from the moment the situation first developed. But we needed someone to help us pull the trigger. To create the political wave. You did that rather nicely when you spoke to the Chief Minister." She drew back her lips. "That's the wrong word. *Connected* is as close as I can get. When you *connected* with the Chief Minister."

"You mean the interview?"

"Of course."

"But I wasn't talking to him. I had the Director in mind. Whiteside."

I got the fangs again. "You were talking to *both*," she said. "And it appears both got the message."

Toward the end of the evening, I found myself back in Alex's arms. "Brilliant performance, Chase," he said. "From start to finish."

"Thanks."

"I guess you'll be wanting a raise."

"I could live with it."

He grinned. "We'll figure it out on the way home."

"Okay."

Kilgore must have noticed Alex was getting ready to leave. He came over and shook his hand. "Thank you, Alex," he said. "We'll never forget what you've done."

Alex looked around. And ushered us—himself, the Administrator, and me—toward a corner. Kilgore signaled his security people, and they formed a wall to keep everyone at a distance.

"What is it, Alex?"

"Mr. Administrator, I was surprised you mentioned the rogue element."

"The crisis is over, Alex. Anyway, there's really no way to keep something like that quiet. Best to get out in front with it."

"Yes, sir. Of course. You know Wexler made an attempt on our lives."

"Of course."

"But he wasn't in it alone. May I ask whether you've acted against those who were involved with him?"

"We've found some. Perhaps all. To be honest, we can't prove criminal intent against any of them because we don't think they knew why they were getting the warnings."

"Mr. Administrator, you can't really believe that."

"No, of course not, Alex. But knowing it and proving it—" He shook his head. "Those who were involved have been terminated from their positions. Sent quietly away."

"I see."

He gazed into Alex's eyes. "Was there something else?"

For a long time, Alex stared back. There was more he wanted to say. Maybe about power and responsibility. Maybe simply about paying attention. "No," he said finally. "Nothing else."

"Good. I'm glad you and Chase were there to help set things right." He shook Alex's hand and turned on his heel and walked off, but got only a dozen strides away before several of his guests approached him. One held up a drink to him as we watched, and offered a handshake. His smile returned.

FOrTY-THree

People like to say, during a journey, that only the journey matters,
and not the destination. Believe me, Lia, the destination matters.
Oh, yes, it matters.

—Dying to Know You

Even with the Salvation Fleet, as it became known, combining
the naval forces of both sides with a vast number of private and
commercial vehicles, escaping the Thunderbolt was still a near
thing. It was never clear that the shield could be assembled in
time, or, if it were, that it would be possible to synchronize its
arrival at Salud Afar at the exact hour it was needed. No task
had ever seemed more daunting.

The decision to go ahead with the shield stopped all evacuation attempts. When it became firm, it provoked worldwide
criticism. The Administrator was put under extreme pressure,
and there were even two assassination attempts. But he stayed
with it, and when the critical hour arrived, so did the wall to
block off the deadly gamma-ray burst.

Today he stands not only as a towering hero, but he has also
become a symbol of the interspecies peace movement. No one,
they will tell you, has done more to promote a reasonable rap-
prochement between the two civilizations.

We did not see him again, in person, after the awards ceremony.
When we checked out of the hotel the next morning, we found

flowers waiting for us, with a text message that he wished us
well, and informing us that we would always be welcome on
Salud Afar.

I spent a rousing weekend in Kayoga, the city of romance,
with Lance Depardeau. He'd recognized me from the news accounts and told me he would never have believed anyone would
be crazy enough to take the chances I had in the taxicab. A few
days later he showed up unexpectedly at another celebratory
luncheon, and proposed to me. "It's short notice, and I know it's
not smart to commit myself so quickly, and I'm risking losing
you. But I'm also going to lose you if I stand by and watch you
go back to Rimway."

He was right, of course. We'd be too far apart to carry on a
serious relationship. So I said thanks, but let's wait and see. I
fell in love with him, and left him. I entertained for a while a
dream of eventually going back, or maybe of his coming to
Rimway. But it never happened. And he recently let me know
he'd met somebody.

I tracked down Jara, who was assigned to the Traffic Control
station in East Quentin, outside Marinopolis. Unlike Lance, she
hadn't gotten a good look at who was riding in the taxi. She was
too busy trying to hang on to the door.

I arrived as her shift finished, and said hello. She, too, knew
me immediately as the woman who was getting all the attention
in the media. But she didn't connect me with the runaway cab.
When I told her, her face darkened. "You could have gotten us
both killed."

"I had to keep going," I said. I told her about the asteroid.

"Why didn't you just explain?"

"Because the CSS was after me. I couldn't afford to—"

"Look"—she wanted no nonsense from me—"I haven't
been following the story that close. But I don't appreciate what
you did. Next time, you might try trusting us." And she turned
away.

Reporters found the young Ashiyyurean male who'd followed
me out to the raft. The interview that followed was translated
into standard and made available all over the Confederacy. He

gallantly denied any special claim of heroism, but admitted he'd thought twice about going into the water with both me and the *vooparoo* running loose. The reporter, also a Mute, asked without a trace of humor which of us had been scarier. I'm happy to report he gave first prize to the *vooparoo*. But he had to think about it.

Rob Peifer wrote *Callistra: The Hunt for the Devil's Eye*, recounting the entire story. It's won awards and has made Peifer one of the most visible journalists on Salud Afar. At least that's what he says. He is currently working on a biography of Vicki Greene.

The book made celebrities of Orman and Shiala, who'd rescued us from the crash after our escape from the plateau. They were recognized by a local civic group as the Citizens of the Year. Alex and I attended the ceremony.

We took Ivan and his wife to dinner the night before we left for home. We owed them a major vote of thanks. Alex has since sent him a comm link that was once owned by Karis Timm, the legendary physician.

When I finally got back to Rimway, Ben told me there was no point going any further, and we became an ex-couple. It was a pity. I liked Ben.

Alex brought the Churchill book home with us. He admits that yes, it was a theft of sorts, but Kilgore didn't know what he had, had no appreciation for it, and, anyhow, he would never have made sense of what Churchill stood for. And technically, we'd found it lying loose.

It sold recently for an amount that would have covered double our expenses for the entire Salud Afar mission.

A new recreation center was recently erected in Moreska, and named for Edward Demery, who lost his life trying to warn the world. His partner in that effort, Jennifer Kelton, is also remembered. Travis University, where she once taught math and physics, has named its science lab for her.

* * *

Years after the publication of her last novel, Vicki Greene remains a major figure in the literary world. The people who decide such things maintain that it is too early to know for certain, but most seem to be betting that she will reign with Teslov, Bikai, and Gordon as the giants of the age. And, of course, on Salud Afar, she will always be remembered as the woman who put things together, who figured out why someone thought it didn't matter whether an obscure wedding ceremony had a religious dimension, and how it connected with a forgotten asteroid.

epilogue

The skimmer began its descent through the late-autumn sky. Below, the town was indistinguishable from a thousand others on the vast prairie that separates the western mountain chains from the eastern forests. It was located on a river, a tributary of the Myakonda, in an area of moderate temperatures. The climate was pleasant. Snowstorms were rare, tornadoes nonexistent.

Cory Greene looked down from the skimmer. He saw the school, two churches, and several hundred houses set along quiet streets, surrounding parks, and ball fields. Several ball games were in progress. "Nice area," he said.

Obermaier was still sitting with his eyes closed. He wasn't happy. "You understand, Mr. Greene, I do not approve of this."

"I understand, Doctor."

"Ordinarily, I would not even have considered your request. To my knowledge, this has never been done before."

"I understand."

"It's a clear ethical violation."

"I know."

"I'd much prefer we simply leave things as they are."

"That would be unfair to her."

"So is disrupting her life."

Greene was weary of the conversation. How many times were they going to go over it? "Doctor, I've signed the protocol. I won't identify myself to her. After today, I will never return to this town. I will tell no one about what we are doing here. And I will, under the most severe torture, not reveal the location."

Children were jumping rope in the streets. Kids were playing on swings and chasing one another through backyards. Several people glanced up from a bench as they passed overhead.

They started down.

Greene's heartbeat picked up.

"We've informed her we're coming," said Obermaier. "She knows we have news, but she has no idea what that might be."

"Okay."

"She'll recognize me. She thinks I'm an uncle. So please let me do the talking. If questioned, you should inform her you're here strictly as an observer."

They were descending toward a modest single-story home at the end of a tree-lined drive. It had a lawn, a picket fence, and a large flowering bush in front.

"Is that where she lives?" he asked.

"Yes. She's a music teacher now."

"That's hard to believe."

"I suppose so."

They drifted down and landed on a pad shared with the house next door. Cory opened the hatch just as church bells began to ring.

Obermaier looked at him. "You're sure now you want to do this? There'll be no going back."

"I'm sure."

"She's quite happy with her present existence. She has a family, which we've gone to quite a lot of trouble and expense to put together. You're going to disrupt all that."

"I know."

"Okay." Obermaier took a deep breath and let it out slowly. The church bells stopped and the town seemed very quiet. "You understand this won't restore her mind. It won't set everything back as it was."

"I understand." He opened the door and admitted a cool

breeze. There was a light on in the living room. He gripped the rim of the hatchway, slipped out of his seat, and stood on the pad. "Even if she can't remember, she deserves to know who she was. Who she *is*."

He led Obermaier across the front of the house. A lamp came on in the entrance, and an AI asked who was there.